Also available from

COURTNEY MILAN

and HQN Books

Proof by Seduction
Trial by Desire

And coming in October 2011

Unclaimed

COURTNEY MILAN

Unveiled

HQN™

Recycling programs
for this product may
not exist in your area.

ISBN-13: 978-0-373-77543-9

UNVEILED

Copyright © 2011 by Courtney Milan

This edition published by arrangement with Harlequin Books S.A.

For questions and comments about the quality of this book please contact us at Customer_eCare@Harlequin.ca.

www.HQNBooks.com

Printed in U.S.A.

Dear Reader,

One of my first memories is waking up very early in the morning to play with my sister. Anyone who has brothers, sisters or children can guess what my second memory is: getting into a massive screaming fight with that same sister. (She won. She always won.)

There's nobody I love quite like my family. They know all of my embarrassing secrets. They can make me laugh with a few short words that make no sense to anyone else. But anyone who knows me that well inevitably knows how to get my goat—*all* of my goats.

When I started to write about Ash Turner, I knew he was going to be the kind of man who could accomplish anything—whether that was making a fortune for himself, seducing a reluctant woman or simply solving a problem on a tenant farm. With a hero that capable, I knew that Ash needed a challenge—something so impossible that even *he* could not overcome it.

So I gave Ash brothers. His brothers can see past all that strength and still laugh at him. Deep down, when Ash thinks of his brothers, he knows he'll never be good enough for them. Family is Ash's greatest strength and his biggest weakness. He'll do anything for his brothers… and, as Margaret Dalrymple soon discovers, he's ruthless enough to do it, even if it causes other people problems.

I'm really excited for you to meet the Turners, and I hope you enjoy reading about them as much as I loved writing them.

Courtney

Acknowledgments

I had a lot of help writing this book.

The discussion about marriage I had with Tessa gave rise to the central premise of this book; Tessa, Amy and Leigh talked me through the basics one cold morning in Vail, and the Northwest Pixies brainstormed titles on a Friday night (Darcy Burke gets the credit). I couldn't do anything without Kristin Nelson, my wonderful agent, as well as the remainder of the agency staff: Sara, Anita and Lindsay. My editor, Margo Lipschultz, pushed me to make this the best book I could, and the team at Harlequin Books once again did a phenomenal job with the amazing cover and the work in producing this book.

The Vanettes, the Pixies, Destination Debut and the Loop that Must Not Be Named—without any of you, I would have gone insane.

The lovely staff at Montacute House answered numerous strange and silly questions. Darren did his best to correct my execrable Latin. Franzeca Drouin, as always, went above and beyond the call of duty. Elyssa Papa is still my favorite beta reader ever, and I rely on Kim Castillo for pretty much everything else.

Finally, I need to thank my husband for listening to me read parts aloud and not wincing, and my dog, for curling up patiently at my feet when I was too busy writing to take him to the dog park.

The cat gets no thanks. I still have scars.

Unveiled

For Mom, who always believed I could do anything despite copious evidence to the contrary.

CHAPTER ONE

Somerset, August 1837

SO THIS WAS HOW IT felt to be a conquering hero.

Ash Turner—once plain Mr. Turner; now, so long as fate stayed Parliament's hand, the future Duke of Parford—sat back on his horse as he reached the crest of the hill.

The estate he would inherit was laid out in the valley before him. Stone walls and green hedges hugged the curves of the limestone hill where his horse stood, breaking the brilliant apple-green growth of high summer into gentle, rolling squares of patchwork. A small cottage stood to the side of the road. He could hear the hushed whispers of the farm children, who had crept out to gawk at him as he passed.

Over the past few months, he'd become accustomed to being gawked at.

Behind him, his younger brother's steed stamped and came to a halt. From this high vantage point, they could see Parford Manor—an impressive four-story, five-winged affair, its brilliant windows glittering in the sunlight. Undoubtedly, someone had set a servant to watch for his arrival. In a few moments, the staff would spill out onto the front steps, arranging themselves in careful lines, ready to greet the man who would be their master.

The man who'd stolen a dukedom.

A smile played over Ash's face. Once he inherited, nobody would gainsay him.

"You don't have to do this." The words came from behind him.

Nobody, that was, except his little brother.

Ash turned in the saddle. Mark was facing forwards, looking at the manor below with an abstracted expression. That detached focus made him look simultaneously old, as if he deserved an elder's beard to go with that inexplicable wisdom, and yet still unaccountably boyish.

"It's not right." Mark's voice was barely audible above the wind that whipped at Ash's collar.

Mark was seven years younger than Ash, which made him by most estimations firmly an adult. But despite all that Mark had experienced, he had somehow managed to retain an aura of almost painful purity. He was the opposite of Ash—blond, where Ash's hair was dark; slim, where Ash's shoulders had broadened with years of labor. But most of all, Mark seemed profoundly, sacredly innocent, where Ash felt tired and profane. Perhaps that was why the last thing Ash wanted to do in his moment of victory was to hash through the ethics.

Ash shook his head. "You asked me to find you a quiet country home for these last weeks of summer, so you might work in peace." He spread his arms, palms up. "Well. Here you are."

Down in the valley, the first ranks of servants had begun to gather, jockeying for position on the wide steps leading up to the massive front doors.

Mark shrugged, as if this evidence of prosperity

meant nothing to him. "A house back in Shepton Mallet would have done."

A tight knot formed in Ash's stomach. "You're not going back to Shepton Mallet. You're never going back there. Do you suppose I would simply kick you from a carriage at Market Cross and let you disappear for the summer?"

Mark finally broke his gaze from the tableau in front of them and met Ash's eyes. "Even by your extravagant standards, Ash, you must admit this is a bit much."

"You don't think I would make a good duke? Or you don't approve of the method I used to inveigle a summer's invitation to the ducal manor?"

Mark simply shook his head. "I don't need this. *We* don't need this."

And therein lay Ash's problem. He wanted to make up for every last bit of his brothers' childhood deprivation. He wanted to repay every skipped meal with twelve-course dinners, gift a thousand pairs of gloves in exchange for every shoeless winter. He'd risked his life building a fortune to ensure their happiness. Yet both his brothers declared themselves satisfied with a few prosaic simplicities.

Simplicities wouldn't make up for Ash's failure. So maybe he had overindulged when Mark finally asked him for a favor.

"Shepton Mallet would have been quiet," Mark said, almost wistfully.

"Shepton Mallet is halfway to dead." Ash clucked to his horse. As he did so, the wind stopped. What he'd intended as a faint sound of encouragement sounded overloud. The horse started down the road towards the manor.

Mark kicked his mare into a trot and followed.

"You've never thought it through," Ash tossed over his shoulder. "With Richard and Edmund Dalrymple no longer able to inherit, you're fourth in line for the dukedom. There are a great many advantages to that. Opportunities will arise."

"Is that how you're describing your actions, this past year? 'No longer able to inherit?'"

Ash ignored this sally. "You're young. You're handsome. I'm sure there are some lovely milkmaids in Somerset who would be delighted to make the acquaintance of a man who stands an arm's length from a dukedom."

Mark stopped his horse a few yards before the gate to the grounds. Ash felt a fillip of annoyance at the delay, but he halted, too.

"Say it," Mark said. "Say what you did to the Dalrymples. You've spouted one euphemism after another ever since this started. If you can't even bring yourself to speak the words, you should never have done it."

"Christ. You're acting as if I killed them."

But Mark was looking at him, his blue eyes intense. In this mood, with the sun glancing off all that blond hair, Ash wouldn't have been surprised if his brother had pulled a flaming sword from his saddlebag and proclaimed him barred from Eden forever. "Say it," Mark repeated.

And besides, his little brother so rarely asked anything of him. Ash would have given Mark whatever he wanted, so long as he just…well, *wanted*.

"Very well." He met his brother's eyes. "I brought the evidence of the Duke of Parford's first marriage before the ecclesiastical courts, and thus had his second marriage declared void for bigamy. The children resulting from that union were declared illegitimate and unable to inherit. Which left the duke's long-hated fifth cousin, twice removed, as the presumptive heir. That would be me." Ash started his horse again. "I didn't do anything to the Dalrymples. I just told the truth of what their own father had done all those years ago."

And he wasn't about to apologize for it, either.

Mark snorted and started his horse again. "And you didn't have to do that."

But he had. Ash didn't believe in foretellings or spiritual claptrap, but from time to time, he had…premonitions, perhaps, although that word smacked of the occult. A better phrase might have been that he possessed a sheer animal instinct. As if the reactive beast buried deep inside him could recognize truths that human intelligence, dulled by years of education, could not.

When he'd found out about Parford, he'd known with a blazing certainty: *If I become Parford, I can finally break my brothers free of the prison they've built for themselves.*

With that burden weighing down one side of the scale, no moral considerations could balance the other to equipoise. The disinherited Dalrymples meant nothing. Besides, after what Richard and Edmund had done to his brothers? Really. He shed no tears for their loss.

The servants had finished gathering, and as Ash trotted up the drive, they held themselves at stiff attention. They were too well trained to gawk, too polite to let more than a little rigidity infect their manner. Likely, they were too accustomed to their wages to do more than grouse about the upstart heir the courts had forced upon them.

They'd like him soon enough. Everyone always did.

"Who knows?" he said quietly. "Maybe one of these
serving girls will catch your eye. You can have any one
you'd like."

Mark favored him with an amused look. "Satan,"
he said, shaking his head, "get thee behind me."

Ash's steed came to a stop and he dismounted slowly.
The manor looked smaller than Ash remembered, the
stone of its facade honey-gold, not bleak and imposing.
It had shrunk from the unassailable fortress that had
loomed in Ash's head all these years. Now it was just
a house. A big house, yes, but not the dark, menacing
edifice he'd brooded over in his memory.

The servants stood in painful, ordered rows. Ash
glanced over them.

There were probably more than a hundred retainers arrayed before him, all dressed in gray. He felt as
sober as they appeared. Had there been the slightest
danger of Mark accepting his cavalier offer, Ash would
never have made it. These people were his dependents
now—or they would be, once the current duke passed
on. His *duty*. Their prosperity would hang on his whim,
as his had once hung on Parford's. It was a weighty
responsibility.

I'm going to do better than that old bastard.

A vow, that, and one he meant every bit as much
as the last promise he'd sworn, looking up at this
building.

He turned to greet the majordomo, who stepped
forwards. As he did so, he saw her. She stood on the
last row of steps, a few inches apart from the rest of
the servants. She held her head high. The wind started
up again, as if the entire universe had been holding its
breath up until this moment. She was looking directly

at him, and Ash felt a cavernous hollow open deep in his chest.

He'd never seen the woman before in his life. He couldn't have; he would have remembered the *feel* of her, the sheer rightness of it. She was pretty, even with that dark hair pulled into a severe knot and pinioned beneath a white lace cap. But it wasn't her looks that caught his attention. Ash had seen enough beautiful women in his time. Maybe it was her eyes, narrowed and steely, fixed on him as if he were the source of all that was wrong in the world. Maybe it was the set of her chin, so unyielding, so fiercely determined, when every face around hers mirrored uncertainty. Whatever it was, something about her resonated deep within him.

It reminded him of the cacophony of an orchestra as it tuned its instruments: dissonance, suddenly resolving into harmony. It was the rumble, not of thunder, but its low, rolling precursor, trembling on the horizon. It was all of that. It was none of that. It was sheer animal instinct, and it reached up and grabbed him by the throat. *Her. Her.*

Ash had never ignored his instincts before—not once. He swallowed hard as the majordomo approached.

"One thing," he whispered to his brother. "The woman in the last row—on the far right? She's mine."

Before his brother could do more than frown at him, before Ash himself could swallow the lingering feeling of sparks coursing through his veins, the majordomo was upon them, bowing and introducing himself. Ash took a deep breath and focused on the man.

"Mr.— I mean, my—" The man paused, uncertain how to address Ash. With the duke still alive, Ash, a mere distant cousin, held no title. And yet he had come here as heir to the dukedom, on the strictest orders from Chancery. Ash could guess at the careful calculation in the majordomo's eyes: should he risk offending the man who might well be his next master? Or ought he adhere to the strict formalities required by etiquette?

Ash tossed his reins to the groom who crept forwards. "Plain Mr. Turner will do. There's no need to worry about how you address me. I scarcely know what to call myself."

The man nodded and the taut muscles in his face relaxed. "Mr. Turner, shall I arrange a tour, or would you and your brother care to take some refreshment first?"

Ash's eyes wandered to the woman in the back row. She met his gaze, her expression implacable, and a queer shiver ran down his spine. It was not lust itself he felt, but the premonition of desire, as if the wind that whipped around his cravat were whispering in his ears. *Her. Choose her.*

"Good luck," Mark muttered. "I don't believe she likes you all that much."

That much Ash had gleaned from the set of her jaw.

"No refreshment," Ash said aloud. "No rest. I want to know everything, and the sooner, the better. I'll need to speak with Parford, as well. I'd best start as I mean to go on." He glanced at the woman one last time, and then met his brother's eyes. "After all, I do enjoy a challenge."

FROM HER HIGH PERCH on the cold stone steps, Anna Margaret Dalrymple could make out little in the features of the two gentlemen who approached on horseback. But what she could see did not bode well for her future.

Ash Turner was both taller and younger than she had expected. Margaret had imagined him arriving in a jewel-encrusted carriage, pulled by a team of eight horses—something both ridiculously feminine and outrageously ostentatious, to match his reputation as a wealthy nabob. The man who had taken everything from her should have been some hunched creature, prematurely bald, capable of no expression except an insolent sneer.

But this man sat his horse with all the ease and grace of an accomplished rider, and she could not make out a single massive, unsightly gem anywhere on his person.

Drat.

As Mr. Turner cantered up, the servants—it was difficult to think of them as *fellow* servants, when she was used to thinking of them as *hers*—tensed, breath held. And no wonder. This man had supplanted her brother, the rightful heir, through ruthless legal machinations. If Richard failed in his bid to have the Duke of Parford's children legitimized by act of Parliament, Mr. Turner would be the new master. And when her father died, Margaret would find herself a homeless bastard.

He dismounted from his steed with ease and tossed the reins to the stable boy who dashed out to greet him. While he exchanged a few words with the majordomo, she could sense the unease about her, multiplying itself through the shuffling of feet and the uncertain rubbing of hands against sides. What sort of a man was he?

His gaze swept over them, harsh and severe. For one brief second, his eyes came to rest on Margaret. It was an illusion, of course—a wealthy merchant, come to investigate his patrimony, would care nothing for a servant clad in a shapeless gray frock, her hair secured under a severe mobcap. But it seemed as if he were looking directly inside her, as if he could see every day of these past painful months. It was as if he could see the empty echo of the lady she had been. Her heart thumped once, heavily.

She'd counted on being invisible to him in this guise.

Then, as if she'd been but a brief snag in the fluid silk of his life, he looked away, finishing his survey of the massed knot of servants. Beside her, the upstairs maids held their breath. Margaret wished he would just get it over with and say something dastardly, so they could all hate him.

But he smiled. It was an easy, casual expression, and it radiated a good cheer that left Margaret feeling perversely annoyed. He took off his black leather riding gloves and turned to address them.

"This place," he said in a voice that was quiet yet carrying, "looks marvelous. I can tell that Parford Manor is in the hands of one of the finest staffs in all of England."

Margaret could see the effect of those words travel like a wave through the servants. Backs straightened, subtly; eyes that had been narrowed relaxed. Hands un-clenched. They all leaned towards him, just the barest inch, as if the sun had peeked out from behind disap-proving clouds.

Just like that, he was stealing from her again. This time, he robbed her of the trust and support of her family retainers.

Mr. Turner, however, didn't seem to realize his cruelty.

He removed his riding coat, revealing broad, straight shoulders—shoulders that ought to have bowed under the sheer villainous weight of what he'd done. He turned back to the majordomo. He acted as if he were not stealing onto Parford lands, as if he hadn't won the grudging right to come here in Chancery a bare few weeks ago to investigate what he had called economic waste.

Smith, the traitor, was already beginning to relax in response.

Margaret had assumed that the servants were *hers*. After all those years running the house alongside her mother, she'd believed their loyalties could not be suborned.

But Mr. Smith nodded at something Mr. Turner said. Slowly, her servant—her old, faithful servant, whose family had served hers for six generations—turned and looked in Margaret's direction. He held out his hand, and Mr. Turner looked up at her. This time, his gaze fixed on her and stayed. The wind blew, whipping her skirts about her ankles, as if he'd called up a gale with the intensity of his stare.

She couldn't hear Smith's commentary, but she could imagine his words delivered in his matter-of-fact tenor. "That's Anna Margaret Dalrymple there, His Grace's daughter. She's stayed behind on Parford lands to report your comings and goings to her brothers. Oh, and she's pretending to be the old duke's nurse, because they're afraid you'll kill the man to influence the succession."

Mr. Turner put his head to the side and blinked at her, as if not believing his eyes. He knew who she was; he had to know, or he'd not be looking at her like that. He wouldn't be stalking towards her, his footfalls sure as a tiger's. Now, she could see the windswept tousle of his hair, the strong line of his jaw. As he came closer, she could even make out the little creases around his mouth, where his smile had left lines.

It seemed entirely wrong that someone so awful could be so handsome.

Mr. Turner came to stand in front of her. Margaret tilted her chin up, so that she could look him in the eyes, and wished she were just a little taller.

He was studying her with something like bemusement. "Miss?" he finally asked.

Smith came up beside Margaret. "Ah, yes. Mr. Turner, this is Miss…" He paused and glanced at her, and in that instant, the growing bubble of betrayal was pricked, and she realized he had not given her secrets away. Ash Turner didn't know who she was.

"Miss Lowell." She remembered to curtsy, too, ducking her head as a servant would. "Miss Margaret Lowell."

"You're Parford's nurse?"

Nurse; daughter. With his illness, it came to the same thing. She was the only protection her father had against this man, with her brothers scattered across England to fight for their inheritance in Parliament. She met Mr. Turner's gaze steadily. "I am."

"I should like to speak with him. Smith tells me you're very strict about his schedule. When would it least inconvenience you?"

He gave her a great big dazzling smile that felt as if he'd just opened the firebox on a kitchen range. As bitterly as she disliked him, she still felt its effect. *This* was how this man, barely older than her, had managed to make a fortune so quickly. Even *she* wanted to jump to attention, to scurry just a little faster, just so he would favor her with that smile again.

Instead, she met his eyes implacably. "I'm not strict." She drew herself up a little taller. "*Strict* implies unnecessary, but I assure you the care I take is very necessary indeed. His Grace is old. He is ill. He is weak, and I won't brook any nonsense. I won't have him disturbed just because some fool of a gentleman bids me do so."

Mr. Turner's smile grew as she spoke. "Precisely so," he said. "Tell me, Miss…" he paused there and lowered one eyelid at her in a shiver of a languid wink. "Miss Margaret Lowell, do you always speak to your new employers in this manner, or is this an exception carved out for me in particular?"

"While Parford lives, you are not my employer. And when he has—" Her throat caught at the words; her lungs burned at the memory of the last grave she'd stood beside.

Hold yourself together, Margaret chided herself, *or he'll know who you are before the day's over.*

She cleared her throat and enunciated with particular care. "And once he's passed on, you'll hardly have need of my services. Not unless you're planning on becoming bedridden yourself. Is there any chance of that?"

"Fierce and intelligent, too." He let out a little sigh. "When I'm in bed, I don't suppose I'll want your services. Leastwise, not as a nurse. So yes, you are quite correct."

His eyelashes were unconscionably thick. They shielded eyes so dark she could not distinguish pupil from cornea. It took her a moment to realize that what he'd said went well beyond idle flirtation. Smith coughed uneasily. He'd overheard the whole thing, from

that unfortunate compliment to the improper innuendo.
How horrifying. How lowering.

Still, the image came to mind unbidden—Mr. Turner,
stripped of those layers of dark blue wool and pristine
linen, his skin shining gold against white sheets, turned
over on his side, that smile glinting just for her.

How *enticing*.

Margaret pressed her lips together and imagined
herself emptying the chamber pot over his naked form.
Now *there* was a thought that would bring her some
satisfaction.

He leaned in. "Tell me, Miss Lowell. Is Parford well
enough for a little conversation? You can accompany
me to the room and make sure I don't overstep myself
or overexcite him."

"He was alert earlier." And, in point of fact, her
father had insisted that when that devil Turner arrived,
he wanted to see him straight away. "I'll see if he's still
awake and willing to speak with you."

She turned away, but he caught her wrist. She turned
reluctantly back towards him. His naked hand was
warm against her skin. She wished he hadn't removed
his gloves. His grip was not tight, but it was strong.

"One last question." His eyes found hers. "Why
did the majordomo hesitate before pronouncing your
name?"

So he'd noticed that, too. In circumstances such as
this, only the truth would do.

"Because," she said with a sigh, "I'm a bastard. It's
not precisely clear what name I should be given."

"What? No family? No one to stand for you and
protect your good name? No brothers to beat off unwanted suitors?" His fingers tightened on her wrist a
fraction; his gaze dipped downwards, briefly, to her

bosom, before returning to her face. "Well. That's a shame." He smiled at her again, as if to say that there was no shame at all—at least not for him.

And that smile, that dratted smile. After all that he'd done to her, he thought he could waltz into her family home and take her to bed?

But he gave a sigh and let go of her hand. "It's a terrible shame. I make it a point of honor not to impose upon defenseless women."

He shook his head, almost sadly, and turned to gesture behind him. The young man who had accompanied him when he'd arrived loped up the steps in response.

"Ah, yes," he said. "Miss Lowell, let me present to you my younger brother, Mr. Mark Turner. He's come into the country with me this fine summer so he can have some quiet time to finish the philosophical tract he is writing."

"It's not precisely a philosophical tract."

Mr. Mark Turner, unlike his brother, was slight—not skinny, but wiry, his muscles ropy. He was a few inches shorter than his elder brother, and in sharp contrast with his brother's tanned complexion and dark hair, he was pale and blond.

"Mark, this is Miss Lowell, Parford's nurse. Undoubtedly, she needs all her patience for that old misanthrope, so treat her kindly." Mr. Turner grinned, as if he'd said something very droll.

Mr. Mark Turner did not appear to think it odd that his brother had introduced him to a servant—worse, that he had introduced a servant to *him*. He just looked at his brother and very slowly shook his head, as if to reprove him. "Ash" was all he said.

The elder Turner reached out and ruffled his younger

brother's hair. Mr. Mark Turner did not glower under that touch like a youth pretending to be an adult; neither did he preen like a child being recognized by his elder. He could not have been more than four-and-twenty, the same age as Margaret's second-eldest brother. Yet he stood and regarded his brother, unflinching under his touch, his eyes steady and ageless.

It was as if they'd exchanged an entire conversation with those gestures. And Margaret despised Mr. Turner all the more for that obvious affection between him and his younger brother. He wasn't supposed to be handsome. He wasn't supposed to be human. He wasn't supposed to have any good qualities at all.

One thing was for certain: Ash Turner was going to be a damned nuisance.

CHAPTER TWO

MR. TURNER CONTINUED to be a nuisance as Margaret led him up the wide stairway towards her father's sickroom. At first, he said nothing. Instead, he gawked about him with a sense of casual proprietorship, taking in the stone of the stairways, and then, as they entered the upper gallery, the portraits on the wall. It wasn't greed she saw in his gaze; *that* she could have forgiven. But he was an interloper at Parford Manor, and he looked about him with the jaded eye of a purchaser— searching out the flaws, as if he didn't want to say too much by way of compliment, lest he raise the price too high in subsequent rounds of bargaining.

He glanced out the leaded windows. "Pleasantly situated," he remarked.

Pleasantly situated. Parford Manor was the center of a massive estate—fifty acres of parkland on the most beautiful rolling hills in all of England, surrounded by tenant farms. The gardens were the labor of her mother's life, a living, breathing monument to a woman who was even now fading from common memory. And he thought it was merely pleasantly situated?

He was a boor.

"Beautifully maintained," he said as they passed a tapestry in the stone stairs.

She rolled her eyes, which thankfully, as she walked ahead of him, he could not see.

"The manor needs a bit of updating, though."

Margaret stopped dead, afraid to even look in his direction. He came abreast of her and turned to look at her.

"You don't agree? All that dark wainscoting downstairs. Tear it down—get some bright papers on the wall." He gestured above to the gallery's ceiling. "New chandeliers—Lord, it must be dark in here, of a winter evening. Don't you think?"

He was absolutely intolerable. "The gallery was last renovated by the duchess herself, a decade prior. I shouldn't like to set my tastes against a sensibility as refined as hers."

His brow furrowed. "Surely you have an opinion of your own."

"I do. I believe I just expressed it."

There was a bit too much asperity in her tone, and he looked at her in surprise. Of course; a nurse wouldn't have been quite so bold in her speech. Not to a duke's heir. Not even to a wealthy tradesman who held the power of her employment in his too-large hands.

But what he said was "So. I'm a lout to think of altering her choices. I suppose I am fouling up a great lot of tradition. But only to improve, Miss Lowell. Only to improve."

Margaret's life had hardly been improved when he'd made her a bastard. That, however, she couldn't say. Instead, she sighed. "Are you always this chatty with servants?"

"Only the pretty ones." He cast her another sidelong glance, and a grin. "The pretty, intelligent ones."

A beat fluttered in her stomach and Margaret started walking again. Down the gallery, into the hall beyond. She stopped before a wide wood door. "We're about to enter a sickroom, so consider restraining your flirtations. His Grace is not well."

Mr. Turner shook his head, solemn again. "A shame. I'd prefer him in his study, hale and hearty. There's little honor in vanquishing an invalid."

Margaret gripped the brass handle of her father's door. She couldn't look back at him, for fear he'd read the truth in the rigidity of her features. Her mother's locket hung heavy on its chain, a great weight around her neck. "Is that why you did this, then? Is that why you had the duke and the duchess's marriage of thirty years voided for bigamy, their innocent children declared bastards and disinherited entirely?" Her voice was shaking. "You claim to have too much honor to importune a woman without family, but let a man have a dukedom, and you feel free to…to *vanquish* him?"

There was a long pause behind her. "Are you always this chatty with your employers? I should imagine the Dalrymples—and no, Miss Lowell, I would not describe your employer's poisonous offspring as either 'children' or 'innocent'—would have stamped that trait right out of you."

Margaret closed her eyes. Poisonous, was she? She wondered what she had done to deserve that particular epithet from a man she had met only this day. "I served the duchess when she was ill." True; she'd spent her waking hours in her mother's sickroom. "She was never well, these last years, but when you announced to the world that her husband was a bigamist—that she herself had been nothing more than an adulteress for the last thirty years, you destroyed her. She simply lost her will to continue. She was dead a few months later. To hear you talk about the circumstances that led to her death in so easy a fashion is utterly repellant."

He didn't answer her, and she turned to look at him. He was watching her seriously, his lips pressed together. He looked as if he were actually *listening* to her, as if she had something important to say. Maybe that was why she continued.

"You weren't the one who had to urge her to eat. You didn't watch the light in her eyes wink out and die. You men never see the consequences of what you do. All you care about is that in the end, you collect the title and the estates. That's not honorable."

Another longer pause. "You're perfectly right," he finally said. "It wasn't honorable. It was revenge. I doubt you understand the complexity of the family relationship. But, at least, I didn't *intend* to cause the duchess's death. Parford, on the other hand…" His fingers clenched at his side. "I doubt Parford could say the same of my sister, were you to query him on the matter. As for the worthless boys he called sons? Quite frankly, after what they did to my brothers at Eton, I'd have wished far worse upon him."

"Richard and his friends must have been quite the terror, to justify having his title stripped."

"Richard? You're calling the former Marquess of Winchester Richard?"

Rather than answer that, Margaret swung the door open and pushed it inward. "His Grace is waiting."

Mr. Turner gave her one last long, searching look. Her heart thumped as he perused her face. Surely he would know what her little slip of the tongue had meant. But he just shook his head and entered the room. She followed behind.

Over the past few months, Margaret had learned to hide how completely aghast the sight of her father left her. She knew, rationally, that he was ill. But between her visits—even if no more than an hour elapsed—this image of him, thin as a fence rail and swathed in bedclothes, never managed to lodge in her memory. She remembered him healthy and robust, larger and more incomprehensible than the sky itself. That memory had riveted itself in her imagination, unable to be dislodged by something so trivial as the passage of time. In her heart, he couldn't change. Her father was bigger than her, stronger than her, more frightening than her.

Reality had been cruel. He'd shrunk into a glazed shell of a man, holding on to life with the same tenacity that held him upright in this perfect seated posture. He ought to have been lying down.

"Parford," Mr. Turner said. He put his hands in his pockets and stood there, glowering, all his chatty conversation evaporated. He was as still as a tombstone, looking forwards. That rigid stance seemed entirely at odds with his easy manner to a servant.

Her father rolled his head lazily to regard him. "Turner."

Mr. Turner stared at him for one long instant before swiveling away. He turned to a basin on a nearby table, and when that could not hold his interest any longer, his gaze moved to a jumble of medicines in brown apothecary's bottles.

He picked up one and turned it over. "Well. My finely honed speech, saved all these years, seems too big for this room after all."

"Oh, pull up your trousers and be a man. What in God's wide world are you waiting for?" That whiplash crack of authority in her father's voice set Margaret's teeth on edge. "Just get it over with, Turner. Say your piece, and then let me sleep."

"It seems unsporting to crow about my triumph to

a linen-clad scarecrow." Mr. Turner set down the laudanum and looked over. "But I suppose you wouldn't
have it any other way, would you?"

Her father let out another exasperated sigh. "Get
on with it, Turner. I'm dying. I have no wish to spend
my last days enduring your endless hand-wringing and
shilly-shallying. We both know how this is supposed
to go—eyes for eyes, and all that. Am I supposed to
beg you, as you once begged me?"

Margaret had no idea what her father was speaking
about.

But Turner must have, because he scowled. "You're
making a mockery of this."

"That's not your line," Parford snapped. "You're
supposed to throw my own words back at me. What
did I say to that smelly, bedraggled child who visited
me? Oh, yes: 'We have as much blood in common as
the queen has with a pig farmer.' I *did* say pig farmer,
didn't I?"

"Coal miner, actually. And at the time, George was
king."

"Damn. My memory is full of holes. Still, you've de-
viated from the script. Here you are, heir to the Duchy
of Parford, despite everything I did. Aren't you going to
grind my nose in it? Will that satisfy your vengeance?
Or would you prefer to drive a dagger through my chest
and drink my blood?"

Mr. Turner set his jaw and reached sharply for a
small sack at his waist. At that sudden movement,
Margaret felt a small shock of fear go through her,
and she darted forwards, her hand reaching out to stop
him—

"Relax, girl," her father grumbled. "What do you

suppose he's secreted in that tiny little pouch? The world's smallest rapier?"

Mr. Turner merely glanced at her and pulled something from the pouch and threw it forwards. "Here. This is yours."

It landed on the Duke of Parford's lap, and for once, that harsh stream of words dried up. He stared at it and then closed his hand about it. "A sixpence? Oh, no! I'm feeling revenged upon."

The entire conversation was opaque to Margaret.

"*The* sixpence," Mr. Turner said grimly. "When I came to you and begged for your intercession, you threw it in my face and told me the only thing you wanted me to get was a bath. My sister died, my brothers—" He shook his head. "I told you I would make you sorry. And now here I am."

"Yes. Congratulations. You've stolen a dukedom. Am I supposed to care?"

"You stole it yourself. I didn't make your children bastards. I didn't steal their inheritance. It was you who did it, so certain your first wife would never come to light. And now you're reaping your own punishment."

Her father leaned back against the cushions. "Me? Punished? Hardly. I'm the duke—and I will be until I die, which hopefully will be soon." He yawned widely. "Once I have passed on to the next world, I can hardly care what becomes of my pitiful bastard offspring in this one." He leaned back.

Margaret's spine felt tight with tension. Her hands flattened against the plasterwork behind her. Her father had never been demonstrative or affectionate. Still, she'd always believed that he cared for her, even if only in his high-handed fashion. At his words, she wanted to melt into the wall and simply disappear. The hair on her head, scraped into that awful bun, pulled against her scalp.

But her father didn't glance her way. "You seem to be under the impression that I give a damn about those whelps I sired on that whey-faced chit I was forced to pretend was my bride. You're wrong."

That "whey-faced chit" was Margaret's mother— sweet and soft-spoken, warm and gentle and loving. She was barely six months in the grave. Margaret stared straight ahead, her hands clenching.

"Now, if you've finished berating me, go away. I'm bored." Her father leaned his head against the wall and closed his eyes.

Mr. Turner stared at him for a few moments, his jaw working. Finally, with one last look at Margaret, he left. Margaret closed the door behind him and turned to her father. He lay on the bed, his eyes shut as if he were sleeping. She doubted he was. She watched the ragged rise and fall of his chest, unsure what to think.

What on earth had Mr. Turner been alluding to? This was clearly not the first time her father had spoken with him. There was more to Mr. Turner than just a voided marriage and a grab for a dukedom, but if so, this was the first Margaret had heard of it. More important, had her father's unkind words been an act, put on to convince Mr. Turner her father didn't care about his children, and to thus shield them from revenge? Or had he spoken the simple truth?

As if sensing her questions, he opened his eyes. He must have seen the hurt on her face, because he expelled his breath in disgust. "Oh, Christ, Anna. You're already a girl and a bastard. Don't make yourself triply useless by crying."

Margaret was beyond tears. She'd shed them all months ago, for all the good they'd done. But shame settled against her skin like a fine burning net. Over the past months, she'd had everything stripped from her: her name, when it was discovered that Lady Anna Margaret Dalrymple was a bastard. Her dowry, when Chancery decided that as illegitimate offspring, she wasn't entitled to the funds settled upon her mother.

Margaret took a deep breath. She had been scoured clean of everything except the hard truth of herself. It coiled, deep inside her, like a spiked little ball.

"Would you like a glass of barley water?" she asked calmly.

Perhaps her father took that smooth inquiry as meekness, because his lip curled. He didn't understand. It took every ounce of strength she had not to simply turn on her heel and walk out of the room. Because Mr. Turner had been right about one thing. It had been selfishness on her father's part—pure, utter selfishness— to lie to her mother, to pretend to marry her, to beget offspring he'd known were legally unable to inherit.

"None of that tepid stuff, now," he warned her.

The water was room temperature against her wrist, but she had no desire to send down to the icehouse. In fact, in her current guise as lowly nurse, she might have to go herself. She poured the liquid as it was, a tiny act of defiance, proof that inside she was still Lady Anna Margaret. She wasn't some nameless bastard servant in a great house, to be ordered about at whim.

She leaned over the Duke of Parford and held the glass to his lips.

"Pfaw," he protested, and water dribbled down his chin.

But he drank, and she raised a handkerchief to his face and dabbed away the excess moisture.

If some unknowing artist had glanced at this tableau, he might have titled it *Father and Daughter.* He might have captured the fine weave of the linen she used to dab excess moisture away, the comforting touch of her hand on his shoulder. Every perfunctory detail he might see, and render on his emotional palette as a gesture of love.

It wasn't, not anymore. Margaret had loved her father once. Perhaps she still did. But at the moment, she could not find any trace of that emotion. What was left?

Duty. Honor. Obligation. Maybe just a perverse desire to demonstrate to her father: *See? This is how you go about not betraying your family.* She would show him. She didn't need to be received as nobility to be noble.

If everything else had been stolen away, that much of her, at least, remained.

Ash exited Parford's sickroom only to discover a procession lying in wait for him. The housekeeper, a Mrs. Benedict, introduced herself. She was accompanied by Smith, the majordomo, and a Mr. Dunridge, who was apparently the land steward. In the finest of old traditions, he was going to be Shown About and made to appreciate what he stood to inherit.

It wasn't hard to show suitable enthusiasm. Parford Manor was a beautifully maintained house. It seemed lived in without being ragged. Even the parquet floors had an understated beauty, the sort of luminous glow that came from years of beeswax and care.

The manor was even older than that long-ago split

between the Turners and the Dalrymples, he mused as he was led outside into the formal gardens. The grass was green and springy beneath his feet. No lawn a mere decade old could ever achieve that complacent health. It seemed not just a bit of turf, but an entire organism, spread before him.

His many times great-grandfather had once been lord here. The man had perhaps once walked upon this very path. He might have turned this selfsame corner, around the long, low holly, and seen the slow roll of the river beyond.

A bit daunting, that history. When he was a boy, his father had taught him about his noble relations, as if that ancient history somehow made him special, more interesting than other mill owners' children. But that happy accident, that divergence from nobility all those great-grandfathers ago, hadn't done any of the Turners much good. It hadn't fed them or clothed them. Fortunes had come, and fortunes had been given away in mindless acts of insane charity.

Now, Ash stood on the cusp of the dukedom. He'd vowed he would care for his dependents—every one of them, from Mrs. Benedict, who continually stopped to reaffix her cap with pins that kept sliding from her gray hair, down to the last maid toiling over a copper kettle in the scullery.

Parford had, of course, got the matter completely backwards.

Yes, he'd thought of revenge. But thoughts of cold vengeance had given way to stark reality. There was no use trading eyes for eyes, when he'd been able to provide for his brothers by trading rubies instead.

Ancient history, indeed. The families had split, prob-ably around the same time that the solid row of elms had been planted along the western drive. Ash's fore-bearer, a younger son, had married a manufacturer's daughter for wealth. He'd taken the name of Turner in exchange for a fortune—much to the fury of the rest of the Dalrymple family, who'd viewed the act as a mercenary betrayal. Time had passed. The elms reached halfway to the heavens now. The old Turner money had dwindled and disappeared before Ash had resurrected it. And yet the remnants of that bitter dispute still festered.

No; Ash didn't just want revenge. He also wanted to take care of his own. Until this morning, however, he'd thought only of his brothers and his business. He hadn't comprehended precisely how *many* responsibilities he was inheriting.

His responsibilities were not all unpleasant, though. There was, after all, Miss Lowell.

Miss Lowell was a surprising, delectable contradiction of a woman. She was intelligent, fierce and loyal. She looked soft in all the right places, but when it came to the ones she cared for, she was hard as flint. She seemed formidable, and Ash appreciated formidable women.

She was a mystery, and Ash was going to enjoy unraveling every delicious clue, until he'd stripped every last inch of her naked. In every sense of the word.

Their group made its way back to the manor by way of a path that hugged the river. When they reached the house once more, the steward and the majordomo took their leave. Mrs. Benedict opened the outside door to the glassed-in conservatory. It was littered with buckets of rose cuttings and potted plants, awaiting permanent placement. From there, she led him down a hall and into another parlor. Windows looked out over the gray river in the distance.

"There's one last thing," Mrs. Benedict said, coming to a halt. "I have standards for the conditions under which my girls must work."

"In my London townhouse, I grant my servants a half day every week and a pair of full days each month."

She let out a puff of air. "That's not what I meant." She squared her shoulders fiercely and then looked up. "I insist on this, Mr. Turner, as a condition of my employment. You and your brother are young, healthy males. I'll not have you imposing on my girls. They're from decent families. It's not right to put them in a position where they can't truly say no."

Ah. *Those* sorts of working conditions. Ash had a feeling he was going to like Mrs. Benedict.

"You won't have to worry about my brother," Ash said. *Unfortunately.* "As for myself, I didn't get where I was by indulging my wants indiscriminately. Besides, I had a sister, too. I couldn't use any woman so cavalierly without her memory intruding."

What he had planned for Miss Lowell could hardly be considered *cavalier.* He considered it more along the lines of a regular campaign.

But Mrs. Benedict must not have heard that unspoken caveat. She gave him a sharp nod. "You're not what I expected, sir."

"I'm not what I expected, either."

She let loose a sharp chortle and reached into the pocket of her apron. With a metallic clink, she withdrew a chatelaine, heavy with keys, and unfastened the clasp of the ring. "I believe you." She fished around and removed one. "Here."

He held out his hand.

"It's the master key." She placed it into his waiting palm. "If you misuse it, I'll have your ears, duke's heir or no."

The key she put into his hand was heavy iron, the bow fashioned into wrought curlicues. Interwoven amongst those was the stylized sword that was so prominent on the Parford coat of arms. Ash stared at it in bemusement before shoving it into a pocket. Mrs. Benedict, however, was already opening the door onto a long hallway, her interview of him concluded. She marched away as if she were the commanding general. Ash shrugged and followed after.

"Now," she said as he came abreast of her once more, "tell me of your dining arrangements. Shall I manage the menus, or do you need to be consulted?"

"I trust you. But speaking of dining, it occurs to me that my brother and I make dreadfully uneven numbers. Once the rest of my men arrive from London, there will be no remedying that, not with any influx of women. But for this evening…" He trailed off invitingly.

Mrs. Benedict frowned as she walked. "Well, there's the Misses Duprey, Amelia and Catherine, over north of Yeovil. They'd be delighted with an invitation. Further afield, we might think of Lady Harcourt's daughters—a bit on the young side, fourteen and sixteen. Though Lady Harcourt wouldn't mind in the least—she's eager to marry them off."

Ash choked. God. A fourteen-year-old child. He wouldn't know what to say to such a creature.

"No," he choked out. "Not Lady Harcourt. Definitely not her daughters." Whoever they were. When he became the duke, he would have to know who these people were. He'd have to figure out the best way to accomplish that—after all, it wasn't as if he would actually *read* a copy of Debrett's. "Nor the Misses Duprey, whoever they might be. The lack of feminine conversation, you see, will be felt in a few hours' time—and I doubt Lady Harcourt would forgive me if I sprung an invitation on her with no notice at all. No, Mrs. Benedict. I was thinking more along the lines of…you."

This last line was delivered as they stepped from the hallway into the grand entryway.

"Me!" The housekeeper's mouth dropped open. She stopped walking—right in the midst of the grand tiled hall—and clutched her skirts. She turned to him and peered into his face. Perhaps she was looking for telltale signs of madness. Finding neither rolling eyes nor froth at his lips, she shook her head.

"Me?" She managed to turn the syllable into a question. "I'm no lady to be taking my meals with the master. I'm a servant, sir, and a good one. I wouldn't know—that is, I couldn't carry on a conversation with a duke's heir."

"Nonsense," Ash said. "You've done precisely that, this past half hour. You've watched the Dalrymples, haven't you?"

At her faint nod, he smiled. She was already disposed to like him, however tentative that feeling was on her part. Now it was time to foster that delicate inclination.

He heard a noise from upstairs, as of a door closing. After a few moments, the quiet echo of footsteps in the upper gallery followed. The hairs on the back of his neck tingled.

"Can I tell you a secret? You must know the family history—that there was bad blood between the Turners and the Dalrymples, that my brothers and I grew up in near poverty."

She sniffed and looked away. "This isn't a household prone to gossip about its masters. I see to that. In fact, if you *do* hear any such talk, don't you listen to it. Come to me, straight away, and I'll set the culprit straight."

"Oh, no. I'm not accusing you of gossip. But perhaps you might, from time to time, have heard about the masters' less fortunate relations?" He gave her his most cajoling smile, and she softened.

"Perhaps," she allowed.

"The truth is, I feel more comfortable conversing with servants than I sometimes do with my peers. This transition has been most sudden for me. A person like you could do a lot of good for someone like me. The way I see it, you're barely a servant. You're essentially the mistress of this house."

"Well." Mrs. Benedict preened just a bit under this praise. Ash gave her another smile, and she glanced back, faintly encouraged.

"Your manners are lovely, your speech precise. You're not so different from a lady yourself—managing the household, seeing to it that everything is just right for the master's convenience. The only difference between you and a lady is that you're given a salary." She looked at him with wide eyes and a half smile. He could almost feel her will bowing before his—and a housekeeper in a manor this large, with this many servants, had considerable strength of character.

It had always surprised him when he heard other merchants talk about the difficulties of keeping household servants in line, or the frustration of attempting to hire diligent accounting clerks. Ash had never had any problem getting people to do as he wished.

If you gave people compliments, they tended to like you. If you confided in them, they were likely to trust you. And if you then asked for their help, they were yours forever. Of course, it helped that Ash genuinely liked almost everyone. People could sense that; it was as good as a master key on a housekeeper's ring, opening up the affections of even the most recalcitrant of individuals.

"A lady? Me?" She caught a stray curl of gray hair and twisted it around her finger. "Go on with you." Her words said, *stop this nonsense,* but she was smiling. She didn't really mean it.

The footsteps he'd heard traversing the gallery earlier began to descend the stairs. He felt her arrival, a prickle of awareness settling against his skin. He wouldn't turn. He wouldn't look at her.

"So," Ash continued, looking straight at Mrs. Benedict, "it would help me and my brother immensely if you would sit at the dinner table and eat with us. You'll rescue us from countless male arguments. By your simple presence, you'll help teach me what I need to know in order to uphold my dignity as Duke of Parford."

While he had no doubt that Mrs. Benedict would be a fine addition to the table, the woman he'd been waiting for was descending the stairs right now.

An appeal to Mrs. Benedict's pride, her sensibilities and her service to the title. Was anything left to offer? Ah, yes. One last thing.

"And I can already tell that you know this neighborhood intimately. You know its people. You know who they are and what they need. If I'm to be duke—and I intend to be a good one—I need to know what you know. Please say you'll do me the very great honor of dining with me."

She stared up at him, her cap sliding askew once more, as if she were trying to decide what to think. "For a man who claims to need someone to teach him finesse," she said dryly, "you are far too agreeable. Are you this talkative with all the servants?"

Miss Lowell came to stand behind them with that last word. He could feel the draft of air that presaged her arrival, could smell that faint, sweet scent that clung to her. He imagined her placing her hands on her hips in disapproval. He stifled a grin and pitched his voice to carry.

"No, Mrs. Benedict," Ash said. "Only the pretty ones."

"Go on with you!" Mrs. Benedict wagged her finger at him, as if he were a wayward child. "I'm fifty-five, if I'm a day, and I've watched every last hair on my head turn to gray."

Ash frowned at her and peered at the unruly curls peeking out from under her cap. "Silver," he said. "Like moonlight, I think."

She burst into laughter then, and Ash knew he'd won. It wasn't flirtation—no sense of awareness had passed between him and the housekeeper. It was something sweeter and friendlier. He'd seen her as a person, rather than as a servant, and she knew it.

"There," Ash said. "It's settled. You'll dine with me."

Mrs. Benedict acquiesced to Ash's upsetting of a social order older than William the Conqueror with a nod.

Ash turned casually. As he did, he saw Miss Lowell. He started and consciously widened his eyes, pretending he'd been unaware of her standing two feet off. Her head was turned to regard him, her eyebrows drawn down, as if she were uncertain what he and Mrs. Benedict might have to laugh about. She didn't know he'd already identified her by the faint hint of roses that trailed around her, filling the entryway with her subtle perfume. That, and he'd known no other house servant would have dared to come down the main staircase with the housekeeper watching.

"Ah," Ash said, "and this solves the other half of our dilemma, Mrs. Benedict. Our numbers are still uneven. My brother and I couldn't possibly sit down to table with just you. We'd overwhelm you with our idiotic masculinity."

"Oh?"

"Oh," Ash said, with great finality. And then he let out a great sigh. "There's only one possible solution. I suppose Miss Lowell will have to join us, as well."

CHAPTER THREE

MR. TURNER'S ILL-FATED supper invitation actually went a long way towards easing Margaret's fears. He had seemed so persuasive, so glib, that she had begun to worry he would soon lead all the servants astray. But he could, after all, make mistakes. This one would prove enlightening.

There was a reason servants did not sit with their masters at table, and it had nothing to do with pride or condescension. Margaret folded her hands primly in her lap, as the footmen served the soup course. She was in for what promised to be an evening of very awkward conversation.

What was Mr. Turner to do, after all? He couldn't very well ask Mrs. Benedict about the course of her day. What could the woman possibly say in answer? "Well, I pressed your laundry, polished your silver and then oversaw the preparation of your meals." No doubt Mr. Turner thought this meal would be a perfect opportunity to impose upon Margaret. She suppressed a grim smile.

The classes didn't mix.

At one time, she might have thought that with haughty self-assurance, content in her own superiority. Now, she understood it as a bleak truth. Every lady of her acquaintance had stopped answering her letters— even Elaine who had once clung shyly to her side.

The walls of the dining hall were decorated with the portraits of dukes from ages past. Even her own ancestors would look down their noses at her, if they could see her through their painted eyes.

But she hardly fit with the servants. She was both mistress and supplicant, nurse and daughter of the house. She was isolated from everyone. It might have been petty of her, but she was glad that Mr. Turner was about to taste some of that same bitter solitude.

There was not the slightest indication on Mr. Turner's face that he knew the tangle that awaited him. His valet had arrived in the servants' coach and had turned him out splendidly. Those broad shoulders were only emphasized by his navy blue coat. His dark hair was rumpled almost perfectly, and the crisp lines of his cravat formed the perfect contrast with his easy manner. He was far too handsome for his own good.

Handsome or not, he'd soon discover that the boundaries of rank and privilege could not be superseded by decree, no matter how warm the accompanying smile. It didn't matter where anyone ate. Servants were still servants. Bastards were still bastards.

But nobody had informed Mr. Turner of this incontrovertible fact. As the footmen placed wide bowls of celery soup before them, he turned towards Mrs. Benedict. The housekeeper was seated at his honored right. When Margaret had dined with her family, they'd used the entire expanse of their long dining room table. Mr. Turner, apparently, had asked for other arrangements. This table had been procured, and it felt small and close and uncomfortable, as if they were attending a crowded dinner party. Without the party.

"Mrs. Benedict," Mr. Turner said as the footmen whisked the covers off the green soup, "I was thinking of investing in cotton, and I wished to ask you a few things."

"Oh." Mrs. Benedict's face turned red. "Mr. Turner, I know how to dose a goose with castor oil, and I have a secret formula to get the shine back into silver. Investment—" she pronounced the word gingerly, as if holding up a dirty handkerchief "—that's not for the likes of me."

Inwardly, Margaret nodded.

"You want to talk to one of your peers, or a solicitor. I'm just a simple housekeeper."

Mr. Turner picked up a spoon. "Nonsense. It is precisely *your* opinion I want. Men of my station would simply sniff and tell me nobody of good breeding wears cotton, and not to bother with it. But there's money to be made if I ignore the gentry's prejudice. I could sell five hundred times the amount to people like you. You are important."

As Mr. Turner spoke, Margaret could see a change pass over Mrs. Benedict. She unfolded her arms. Her eyes widened. By the time Mr. Turner favored her with his final, brilliant smile, the woman had a soft, foolish grin in place.

"Well." She fiddled with the cutlery and looked up. "There's rags to start. Cotton—it absorbs water, and so I've used it for dishcloths."

Mr. Turner nodded. "Go on." He tasted his soup and looked back at Mrs. Benedict, focusing on her as if she were the only person in the universe. She continued, tentatively at first, and then with greater confidence. As she spoke, Mr. Turner leaned towards the housekeeper, his gaze riveted on her. Every aspect of his face said the same thing: *You matter. You are important. Your observations are valuable.*

It stung. Not just that Mr. Turner ignored Margaret; her pride had been beaten down enough over the past few months that such a slight would hardly even tickle. No. It stung that she was *wrong*. It stung that he could transition from a man who could court votes in Parliament, to someone who could sit down and talk to a servant and find his welcome. That he should belong everywhere with everyone, while she had no place with anyone.

Mr. Benedict and Mrs. Turner progressed from the topic of cotton to the mill in the village, and from there to tenant farmers. Margaret was so used to her father's style of autocratic demand. Every word he voiced was a command. It came out a shout, as if he had to rail to be heard above the cacophony of a wide and clamorous world. Mr. Turner spoke quietly, but everyone strained forwards to hear his words.

Even Margaret.

He was good at winning others over, she realized. It did not augur well for her future. What would happen when he brought this smiling bonhomie to bear on the members of the House of Lords who would decide the question of legitimacy? Richard might scream and protest and threaten, but it was not often the lords got to choose their own members. Had she no personal stake in the matter, she would have chosen Mr. Turner, too.

She stared grimly ahead of her. Her soup was replaced with creamed peas; peas were followed by fresh-caught fish, and fish by roast beef. She watched the plates stream by, unable to do more than take a few forkfuls of food. If her brother was not legitimized, the vast bulk of the family's entailed inheritance would fall to Mr. Turner. She had no illusions about her relative importance. Her two brothers would lay claim to whatever scraps remained.

She could feel all her hopes for the future dissolving in the wake of his damnable likeableness.

Mrs. Benedict spread her hands, continuing a conversation Margaret had ceased to follow. "There's always been land disputes, sir."

"I'll talk to them, then." Mr. Turner spoke as if any problems would simply be concluded with a bit of plain speaking. Likely, Margaret thought bitterly, with him, they would be. Life seemed to rain gifts on this man. Wealth. Station. Legitimacy.

Margaret didn't think she would have dared to dislike him, had he not taken so much from her. She looked away, feeling petty.

"Miss Lowell. You have my apologies. We're boring you."

Her eyes cut back to him. "No. Of course not."

"Yes, we are. It's either that or we're upsetting you. I won't stand for either. Come now. What is it?"

"It's just…" She searched for an answer that would satisfy him. But as she looked into his face, all thoughts of lies disappeared. "You are the most cheerfully ruthless individual I have ever met."

A big grin spread over his face, and he gave a guffaw. "Cheerfully ruthless! I like that. Should I adopt it as my motto? Would it look well on my coat of arms? Mark, how do you say 'cheerfully ruthless' in Latin?"

"Nequam quidem sumus," his brother intoned. It was the first he'd spoken all evening, and he said the words dreamily. Up until that point, she'd thought he was the fine young scholar that he appeared—a little distracted, and wiry-thin. But Margaret had spent time around her brothers when they came home from

Eton—enough to recognize a few words of impolite Latin. She choked.

Mark looked across the table at her, all blond good looks, and dropped her a wink. Margaret revised her estimate of him from "painfully serious scholar" to "mischievous schoolboy."

"Alas," the elder Mr. Turner said, "that lacks a certain panache."

"Don't you know Latin?" Margaret asked in surprise.

"Never went to school." He leaned back in his chair. "Never had the time for it. I went to India with a hundred and fifty pounds in my pocket, determined at fourteen to make my fortune. But Mark's the scholar now." He turned to his brother, and it was obvious from every line on his face, from the fierce smile that overtook him, that this was no idle boast. No matter what his brother might have said in Latin. "Did you know that he's writing a book?"

"Ash," Mark said, with all the unease of a younger brother being praised.

"His essays have been published in the *Quarterly Review;* did you know that? Three of them, now."

"*Ash.*"

"The queen herself quoted from one not two months prior. I had that from a friend."

"Ash." The younger Mr. Turner ducked his head and put his hand in front of his face. "Don't listen to him. It was frippery. Pretty language, but nothing original. Nothing to be really pleased about. Besides, she didn't even remember my name."

"She will." There was a glow in Mr. Turner's eyes. "When you're the brother of a duke? She'll know your

name, your birth date and the number of teeth you had
pulled at eleven years of age."

Mr. Turner leaned forwards, as if speaking a vow.

And, she realized, he was.

Margaret felt the bottom fall out of her stomach.
This was what he wanted—not her father's estate, nor
his title, nor even the revenge he'd spoken about. *This*
was where all that ruthless intensity concentrated: on
his brother.

And Mark, for all his teasing, accepted this as his
due. He simply took, as a matter of course, that his
brother loved him, that he might tease him in Latin and
receive this…this powerful endorsement. Mr. Turner
would never call his brother useless. Of all the things
that the Turners had and Margaret lacked, this camaraderie seemed the most unfair.

"Yes," he said, catching her look. "More of my
cheerful ruthlessness, I'm afraid. And now you know
my greatest weakness: my brothers. I want to give them
everything. I want everyone in the world to realize
how perfect they are. They are smarter than me, better
than me. And I'll do *anything*—cross anyone, steal
anything, destroy whatever I must—to give them what
they deserve."

Margaret dropped her eyes from that fervor. She felt
strangely small and intensely jealous.

She had never felt that sort of ardor about anything—or anyone—in her life. The table seemed even
tinier in that large room, a tiny craft adrift on a wide
sea of parquet. Behind her, the stares of her painted
ancestors bored into her back.

She drew in a deep breath and turned to his younger
brother. He looked a little embarrassed at that out-

burst—but not surprised or uncomfortable. Just as if his brother had ruffled his hair.

"So, Mr. Mark Turner. What is this book you're writing?"

He leaned back in his chair. "Just Mark will do. It'll be confusing enough if you have to call us both Turner."

Both the Turners were rather too casual. But as a servant, Margaret could hardly object. She inclined her head in acknowledgment.

"I'm writing about chastity."

She waited for him to guffaw. Or even to give her that mischievous grin again, signaling this was another of his schoolboy pranks.

He didn't.

"Chastity?" she repeated weakly.

"Chastity."

He hadn't said it as one would expect to hear the word—with serious overtones, in a humble, reverent voice. He said it with a sparkle in his eye and a lift to his mouth, as if chastity were the best thing in the world. Margaret had met a great many of her brother's friends. This was not an attitude that was common among young gentlemen. Quite the opposite.

"You see," he continued, "the focus in all the works on chastity to date has often been so philosophical that it fails to engage the general populace on a moral level. My goal is to start with a practical approach, and…" He trailed off, with the air of someone realizing that his enthusiasm for a subject was not matched by those around him. "It's enormously exciting."

"I can see that."

Mr. Mark Turner was the same age as Edmund, a few years younger than Richard. She couldn't imagine

her brothers—or any of their friends—writing a philosophical defense of chastity. They likely couldn't even
speak the word without laughing.

Her lip curled in memory.

"Chastity," said the elder Mr. Turner in a dry voice,
"is not one of the things I'd planned for my younger
brother to embrace."

An uncomfortable silence settled over the table. The
two men exchanged level glances. What was encoded
in those looks, Margaret could not say.

"This isn't a conversation for mixed company," Mrs.
Benedict put in.

Mark shook himself and looked away. "Too true.
Alas, my work is by necessity aimed at men. If I were
to write about chastity for women, it would no doubt
slant towards a different sort of practicality."

"Oh?" Margaret asked.

"Don't encourage him," Mr. Turner warned. "When
he has that gleam in his eye, no good can come of it."

Margaret turned to Mark. "Consider yourself encouraged."

Beside her, Mr. Turner made a noise of exas-
peration.

"I was thinking more of a compendium. 'Places to
strike a man so as to best preserve one's virtue.'"

"What?" said Mr. Turner. "There's more than the
one?"

"Gentlemen," pleaded Mrs. Benedict, but to no
avail.

"What do you say, Miss Lowell? Would ladies have
any interest in such a guide?" Mark smiled at her. "Ash
tells me you've no family to speak of. Does that mean
no brother has ever taught you to defend yourself?"

Edmund had taken her aside when she turned

fourteen and advised her that if she kept her legs and her mouth clamped shut, she might land a marquess. That had been the end of his helpful advice. She shook her head.

The lines about Mark's eyes softened. "Well, then I'll have to show you." He shot a glance at his brother across the table and smiled again—this time, more impishly. "After all, *I* have no problem if *my* brother is forced to embrace chastity." He picked up his fork, applying himself to the meat in front of him as if no further conversation were necessary.

Perhaps he'd not fully realized what he'd implied with those careless words.

By the dour look in Mr. Turner's eyes, and the slow shake of his head, his brother was not amused.

Margaret heard both the words and the meaning behind them. So much for Mr. Turner's vaunted honor, his claim that he wouldn't prey upon a woman alone. The realization turned the bite of turnip in her mouth to charcoal. They'd talked about her already, as brothers were wont to do. In the space of one day, Mr. Turner had already made plans to seduce her—plans so firm, he'd shared them with his younger brother. She'd heard Edmund speaking with his friends often enough, discussing *this* widow or *that* willing wife, when they didn't know she could hear their conversation.

No doubt Mr. Turner thought she would fall into his bed. Women probably did, for him. That relentless pull tugged her now, even when she wasn't looking at him. Women laid their hearts at the feet of men like him—a man so ruthlessly intense as to take one's breath away, and cheerful enough to make one laugh while he did it.

But then, for all his cheerful intensity, he'd aimed that ruthlessness at her before.

A year ago, she'd been the belle of the ball, the toast of the town, a diamond of the first water, engaged to a peer of the realm. She'd been the closest thing to a princess that there was.

Then Ash Turner had intruded in her life. She had been nothing but an afterthought to him, if that. Still, the toast had been charred by the fire; the diamond had turned out to be carved ice, destined to melt in the first heat of gossip.

He'd robbed her of her name, her dowry, her *everything.* If after all of that, Mr. Turner thought he would get one scrap of affection from her, he was badly mistaken.

ASH NEEDED TO HAVE a conversation with his brother about *discretion.*

After that first frozen stare, half horror, half betrayal, Miss Lowell had simply stopped looking at him. And that, Ash decided, was a very, very bad thing. The pudding came—a mercy to kill the conversation—and she sat in place at table, moving the mixed fruit and cream about with her spoon. Her lips pinched together and her complexion went from pale pink and animated to gray and closed.

There was a gold chain around her neck. The necklace disappeared into the high neck of her gown, weighted into a narrow V, as if there were some heavy locket suspended on it. He felt a hint of jealousy, wondering who had given it to her, and what she might hold inside it.

No doubt she was wondering how to fight him off. That made him feel like some sordid roué, thinking of nothing but his own pleasure. But as little as he'd been in polite company, even Ash knew better than to issue a clarification. "No, Miss Lowell," Ash could imagine himself saying, "I would never force myself on you. I mean to seduce you into willingness. That's all." That would get him a fork stabbed through his hand, by the black look she gave her pudding.

Thank God the knives had been removed along with the beef.

She finished moving the fruit around her plate. Supper was breaking apart—Mark made the customary excuses on behalf of the gentlemen—and still she'd not met his eyes. This was *wrong*. He couldn't let it continue.

When she left, he followed her. They had barely reached the landing of the stairs before she turned on him. There was a ferocious light in her eyes, and he held up his hands to show he intended her no harm.

"Miss Lowell. I'm afraid my brother has given you the wrong impression."

She let out a puff of air. "I know how gentlemen talk when they are amongst themselves," she said dismissively. "Don't imagine you can hide it."

By "gentlemen," she likely meant men like Richard and Edmund Dalrymple. Ash could just imagine what those worthless parasites would have said about a too-pretty nurse, with her too-kissable lips and that alabaster skin. No doubt there'd been other indignities visited upon her when they'd been in residence. That was likely the reason Mrs. Benedict had thought it necessary to establish rules of conduct from the beginning. Neither of those worthless boys had ever understood concepts like *honor* or *consent*. Ash felt a current of anger go through him, just imagining the importunities that might have been visited upon her. He wasn't like *them*.

"No," he said curtly. "I don't think you know what I'm like."

"You want to take a kiss. You want to take me to your bed. And you've boasted to your brother that you'll do it. Don't prevaricate, Mr. Turner. You want what every so-called gentleman wants."

"You don't know what I want." His voice sounded hoarse and he found himself looking at her. She was just the right height for him—tall enough that he might simply tip her head back and take that kiss, without even asking.

"Oh?" Her voice echoed with scorn.

He stepped towards her. For all her brave words, her eyes widened. But she didn't move when he reached out to her. She stood her ground, her expression stoic, as if his touch were just one more burden to be endured.

What had happened to her, that she didn't even flinch when he touched her shoulders? He ran his finger lightly along the line of her gold chain, tracing it back along her collarbone to the nape of her neck.

"If this is your idea of a prelude to seduction," she said haughtily, "all you've managed to do is make my skin crawl."

Ash doubted that was true, by the slow change in her breathing. He undid the hook his fingers found in the necklace and slid the chain from her neck. It was heavy; the expected locket came from between her breasts as he pulled the chain. It was a surprisingly well-made piece, ornate and with a hint of aged tarnish that suggested it was an heirloom.

She snatched for it, but he turned swiftly, holding it away from her.

He wondered whose face he might see if he were to undo the catch of the locket. He didn't want to know. If it were Richard, or worse, Edmund…

"Give it back." She grabbed again.

He fished in his waistcoat pocket with his free hand until he found the bounty he'd received earlier that day.

"This," he said holding up the prize, "is the master key to the manor. I received it from Mrs. Benedict just this afternoon. It unlocks every door here. Including, presumably, yours."

He held it up by its iron shank and slid the gold chain of her locket through the bow made by the sword. When he let go, the key slid down the necklace and clanged against her locket. She jumped. He reached for her hand and piled the whole thing in her palm—chain, locket and key.

"I don't want to take a kiss," he said. "I don't want to take you to bed." He closed her hand about the locket, pressing her fingers into it. "I don't want to take anything from you. Do you understand?"

She swallowed and shook her head.

"I want you to *give* me a kiss. I want you to forget the idiot man who gave you this and then walked away, leaving you alone." He squeezed the hand that held her locket. "I want you to know that if you don't wish to kiss me, you can rid yourself of me with this simple expedient. Look me in the eyes and say, 'Ash, I have no desire to be your sordid love slave.' And I will simply walk away. Go ahead. Try it."

She met his gaze. "Mr. Turner—"

He brought his hand to her lips, not touching her, but close enough that her breath warmed his fingers. "No good. You at least have to call me Ash."

She pulled away from him, playing with a strand of hair that had escaped the knot atop her head. Even bound together, that mass of dark hair made an impressive coil. If she brushed it loose, it might reach her waist.

"Come now," he said. "Such a little thing I'm asking for."

"What kind of a Christian name is Ash?" She shook her head. "What is wrong with Luke or John or Adam?"

This was not something he wanted to talk about. "It's not my Christian name. It's a…a use name. Of a sort." His mother had given all her children full Bible verses for names. Telling her the mouthful of a name he'd been born with would simply take too long. "I don't have a Christian name. I have…" Ash paused, frowning. "I have a *label,* recorded in a parish register. And it's of no moment. Everyone who knows me calls me Ash. If you are going to refuse to be my love slave, you should at least do me the honor of not Mr. Turnering me."

She looked up at him from behind wisps of hair that had fallen from her knot. For the first time that evening, he caught a glimpse of one hint of a dimple, an unwilling smile that quirked her lips. That amusement was a fragile, delicate thing, as insubstantial as moonlight on water. He held his breath, waiting. But she dispelled it with a shake of her head.

"It's too familiar. People will say—" She stopped, and ran one hand down the serviceable fabric of her dress. "They'll say I'm reaching above my station."

He shrugged to hide his appalled reaction. Miss Lowell had fire. She had intelligence. She had an almost haunting beauty. And yet she wouldn't reach above what she saw as her station? What a monstrous waste.

Whoever was in that locket had a lot to answer for.

"I am going to guess," he said quietly, "that you've heard about your *station* all your life. That you've been told, over and over, what you can and cannot do because of some foolish accident of your birth."

Her nostrils flared, and her fingers clenched around the key he'd given her.

Ash continued. "What do *they* know? Do they hear the secret dreams you whisper in the dark of the night? Don't let your station in life strangle you."

Her bosom held motionless, as if she didn't dare exhale.

"If I never so much as breathe against the skin of your wrist, I want you to forget what you've been told."

Her hand had gone to her wrist as he spoke, as if she felt the heat of his breath there.

"So call me Ash," he said with a smile. "Call me Ash, not for me, but as a small defiance. Call me Ash because you deserve it. Because your *station* is just so many words in a parish register, not a sentence of death."

She swallowed and swayed towards him—not even an inch, but still, she moved. Ash stood very still, willing her closer. She opened her lips a fraction and wet them. His blood stirred at the sight of the pink of her tongue.

"Ash." She breathed the word as if it were the last name on earth. He stood there, almost tipsy at the sound of it on her lips. Yes. *Yes.*

"Yes?" His own voice was hoarse.

She looked him in the eyes. And he saw there every last scrap of strength, every inch of backbone that he desired. She drew herself up straight. He could almost taste her on his tongue.

"Ash," she repeated more firmly. "I have no desire to be your sordid love slave. Now leave me *alone*."

CHAPTER FOUR

THE SUN WAS SO HOT at noon the next day that waves rose from the track in front of her, blurring the small town two miles distant into indistinct smudges of brown. Margaret's hairpins bit into her scalp like aggressive little insects.

She'd composed a letter to her brother last night. When they'd first come up with this plan, they'd imagined that Margaret would see Mr. Turner only in passing and would have just the servants' gossip to send on. But she'd filled pages with her account of that first evening. After she'd penned a factual account of the day, she'd added the following:

None of this captures the essence of the man. For all his mercenary tradesmanlike mannerisms, Ash Turner is far more dangerous than we believed, for a reason that will not sound sinister when I write it: he makes people like him. Think on what that will mean when he addresses the Members of Parliament who will vote on the question.

This letter to her brother was now tucked into the inner pocket of her mantle, the hard corners of the paper poking her ribs in tangible reminder. She had stayed behind because her family needed her. Because when Parliament resumed in mid-November, it would debate whether to pass a bill granting her family the extraordinary remedy of legitimacy.

Her role here had been simple when they'd conceived it: she was to document Mr. Turner's every failing. She would transcribe letters, dictated by her father, adding her own observations. These observations would demonstrate that Mr. Turner was unfit to manage the estate. The evidence would be collected, collated and sent to the lords in the autumn, when her brothers presented their petition.

Margaret had thought sending a letter would be as simple as asking her father to frank it and leaving it on the front table with the remainder of the post. She hadn't truly thought through her deception. Had Mr. Turner been bent on sport or drink as her brothers were, simplicity would have sufficed. But what seemed like half his office had arrived this morning—a regular cadre of sober businessmen who had taken over one of the gatehouses. They were all dedicated to serving Mr. Turner, and they were constantly coming and going. Any one of those men might see her leaving the letter in the hall. They would wonder why a simple nurse was writing to the Dalrymple brothers. She'd had little choice but to carry the letter into town, where the vicar's wife would assist her.

The walk had already proved hot and uncomfortable.

But halfway to the village, the sullen summer silence was marred by hoofbeats. Hoofbeats were not a good sign. Margaret pulled her bonnet ribbons about her chin. With her brothers gone, only the Turners would be about on horseback, riding on Parford land. And somehow, she didn't imagine that Mr. Mark Turner—gentle, sweet Mark who wrote about chastity—had sought her out. That would have been too easy.

The horse cantered into view, coming around a bend in the hedge.

Of course it had to be the elder of the two brothers. The taller one. The larger one. The *dangerous* one. Of course she had to be set upon by the man who'd destroyed her life. And of course it happened at the precise moment when the last of the starch deserted the collar of her gown. Mr. Turner looked as if he'd no notion that the sun shone overhead. No sweat beaded on his forehead; no flush of heat colored his cheeks as he rode up beside her and slowed his horse to a walk. He manufactured no polite excuse for his presence. Instead, he looked her up and down, from her dusty half-boots to the drooping bonnet on her head. And then he smiled.

"Am I intruding?" he asked.

"You're always intruding." Simple truth.

"Ah." He spoke with a faintly puzzled air, as if nothing could have left him more confused than a woman who didn't know she was supposed to kneel down and kiss his feet at the first sign of his interest. No doubt he was befuddled for good reason. Had she truly been the woman she appeared—an illegitimate servant— she would no doubt have found him very nice indeed. A lowborn nurse would not have cared that his money had been made in trade, that the title he stood to inherit had been won through legal machinations.

And, Margaret had to add, in truth he didn't strike her as the typically gauche nabob, flush with sudden wealth. He carried his wealth so confidently one almost didn't notice it was new. Margaret adjusted her bonnet again. But as she pulled it up an inch, her hairpins poked her neck once more.

"You do realize," he said, "you are allowed to speak to me."

"I can't possibly. You're kicking up dust. I can scarcely breathe, let alone carry on a conversation."

It wasn't true. There'd been a fine rain last night, which had left the ground moist and springy—not so wet as to be muddy, but not so dry as to toss up clouds of dirt.

He didn't contradict her obvious lie, however. Instead, his smile broadened. "If I take you up on my horse, no doubt you'll breathe more freely."

Just the thought of being lifted onto that beast made her lungs tighten. He would set her before him. She would feel his thighs pressing into her, his hands straying against her body... No. She'd never been one for foot kissing. She wasn't about to start now.

"Why do you persist in saying these things?" she asked. "I have been perfectly clear on the matter. A *true* gentleman wouldn't wait for a second dismissal."

"No." His voice filled with a dark humor. "A *gentleman* would have just taken you to bed to begin with, without bothering to ask for permission. Luckily for you, I was too busy making my own way in the world to learn to be a gentleman." He tossed his head back. "If you want to know why I keep pestering you, it's because you remind me of Laurette."

"Laurette?" Margaret repeated the name with distaste. It sounded tawdry, the sort of half-Frenchified affectation a mistress would adopt. "I doubt it can be quite proper for you to speak of her."

"I met her in India." His eyes sparked at her in amusement, as if he knew precisely how discomfited she was. "I kept her for a little more than a year, before I realized she needed more than I was able to give."

"Mr. Turner." She could imagine Laurette now—a beautiful Indian woman, her skin dark, her limbs entangled with his. And why, oh, why did that image fill her with heat instead of disgust? Another yank of her bonnet strings, but this adjustment served only to drive the pins harder into her scalp.

He grinned at her discomfort. "It's Ash, if you recall, not Mr. Turner. As for Laurette, at first she was wary, but as time went on, she came to sleep with me at nights."

"Mr. Turner! I won't listen to this." She put her hands over her ears, but she could not keep out the sound of his voice.

"When she was young, I had to cut her meat into very small cubes. Even then, though, her teeth were needle-sharp. My hands were perpetually in bandages."

Margaret stopped dead in the path. Her hands fell to her side. The sensual image that had persisted in her head disappeared in a swirl of impossibility, just as Laurette grew tiny fangs. An unpredictable bubble of laughter almost escaped her, before she managed to convert it into a mere disbelieving puff of air. "Mr. Turner," she said, investing his name with all the starchy scorn she could muster. Under the circumstances, it wasn't much.

Mr. Turner drew up his horse a few paces ahead. He wheeled to face her, his eyes bright. "Yes. That was very bad of me. Laurette was a tiger. I was…accompanying a man who shot her mother for sport. He took the pelt and left the cub barely able to feed herself. It took me hours of searching before I finally found her hiding in the underbrush. She was the tiniest thing—barely the size of a ship's cat. And she looked into my eyes from the bramble with the most baleful glare. What I thought was if I could win this magnificent creature's regard, it would truly mean something."

On those last words, he looked into Margaret's eyes. For just one second, Margaret wished she *were* the sort to tumble into love over a pair of handsome brown eyes and a lovely set of shoulders. That she could ignore who she was—who *he* was—and what he'd done. But she couldn't.

Maybe he could manufacture the ring of sincerity in his voice, could manipulate the warm directness of his gaze. But it didn't matter even if he meant what he said.

He might make her forget the itch of her hairpins. But when he left, they would still be there, piercing her scalp. He couldn't change reality, and she wouldn't forget.

She glanced up at him reluctantly. "What happened after you found the cub, then?"

"I reached for her. She bit me." He smiled, looking off into the distance. "It was worth it."

She had to look away, as well. More dangerous, even, than those piercing brown eyes was that implied compliment. He'd just told her that she was worth it—she and all her prickles.

And he hadn't said it because he wanted sixty thousand pounds in the five-percents. Nor because she was the key to forging an alliance with an old, noble family. No; he could have any of the other women who no doubt had signaled their willingness to kiss his feet. Instead, he'd chosen to pursue her. And no matter how impure his motives, she felt all the force of that compliment. Not going to her head, like bubbles of champagne, but sinking deep into her skin.

She tugged on her bonnet strings again. "Is that how you see me? Wild? Savage?"

"Fierce. Protective. Implacable when angered, but I believe your affection can be earned. And you've been hiding in a veritable thicket of rules made for you by society. You're cribbed about by the requirements of gentility, when genteel society has never done you any favors. Why do you even wear a bonnet, when you hate it so?"

Margaret sniffed, her hair pins itching once more. "I don't know what you could mean," she said untruthfully. How had he known?

"You've tugged on your bonnet strings five times in this conversation already. Why wear one, if it's so uncomfortable? Have you any reason for it, other than that it is what everyone else does?"

"I brown terribly in the sunlight. I'll develop freckles."

"Oh, no. That sounds awful." He spoke with exaggerated solicitude, but he leaned down from his horse until his nose was a bare foot from hers. "Freckles. And what do those dastardly spots portend? Are freckled people thrown in prison? Pilloried? Covered in tar and sprinkled with tiny little down feathers?"

"Don't be ridiculous."

He moved his hand in a lazy circle, ending with it stretched towards her, palm out. As if to say, *explain why.*

"Pale skin—a white complexion—is superior," Margaret said. "I don't know why I am defending a proposition everyone knows to be true."

"Because *I* don't know it." Mr. Turner slid his finger under her chin. "Yet another reason why I am glad I am not a gentleman. Do you know why my peers want their brides to have pale skin?"

She was all too aware of the golden glow of vitality emanating from him. She could feel the warmth in his finger. She shouldn't encourage him. Still, the word slipped out. "Why?"

"They want a woman who is a canvas, white and empty. Standing still, existing for no other purpose than to serve as a mute object onto which they can paint their own hopes and desires. They want their brides veiled. They want a demure, blank space they can fill with whatever they desire."

He tipped her chin up, and the afternoon sunlight spilled over the rim of her bonnet, touching her face with warmth.

"No." Margaret wished she could snatch that wavering syllable back. But what he said was too true to be borne, and nobody knew it better than she. Her own wants and desires had been insignificant. She'd been engaged to her brother's friend before her second season had been halfway over. She'd been a pale, insipid nothing, a collection of rites of etiquette and rules of precedent squashed into womanly form and given a dowry.

His voice was low. "Damn their bonnets. Damn their rules."

"What do you want?" Her hands were shaking. "Why are you doing this to me?"

"Miss Lowell, you magnificent creature, I want you to paint your own canvas. I want you to unveil yourself." He raised his hand to her cheek and traced the line of warm sunshine down her jaw. That faint caress was hotter and more dizzying than the relentless sun overhead. She stood straight, not letting herself respond, hoping that her cheeks wouldn't flush.

You matter. You are important. He was doing it again, but this time, he was doing it to *her*. He was subverting some deep part of her as easily as he'd won over Mrs. Benedict. What he'd whispered seemed more intimate than the touch of his glove against her cheek. It wasn't fair that this man, this one man who had utterly destroyed her, would be the one to pick her deepest desire out of the maelstrom of her wants.

"Am I asking so much, then? I only want you to think of yourself."

"That's sophistry. You know you have your sights set on a great deal more."

He smiled in wry acquiescence. "For now, Miss Lowell, I'd be happy with nothing more from you than a little defiance."

She looked up into his dark eyes. A little defiance, he called it. Just a little defiance, to believe that she mattered.

But she needed more than a *little* defiance to call upon now. She couldn't let this continue. A few more days of this, and he might begin to convince her of his sincerity. When he looked at her with that fierce light in his eyes, she could almost feel the world bending about him. She could feel herself drifting to land at his feet, ready to do his bidding. If he continued to pay her those extravagant compliments, she might actually start to believe him.

She took his hand where it touched her cheek and moved it firmly to rest against the buff fabric of his breeches.

"Mr. Turner, you fail to understand."

He lifted one eyebrow, and Margaret stood up

straight and glared at him. "I'm not a cat. I'm not a canvas. And I'm certainly not about to become an enterprise for you to cosset and charm into docility. You want a little defiance?"

His head cocked at an angle, as if he couldn't believe the words she was saying.

"Good," she said. "Then you may try this: leave me alone. For good. Don't talk to me. Don't browbeat me. And for God's sake, don't try to seduce me."

He looked at her quizzically. For a second, she thought she'd pushed him too far. She was sure that his pleasant manner would evaporate into scorn. That he *would* force that kiss on her, no matter what he'd said before.

Instead, he sat back on his horse, touched his hat and disappeared down the track.

IT HAD BEEN MORE than a week since Ash had been sent on his way, but Miss Lowell was never far from his thoughts—or indeed, from his person. Right now, in fact, she was a mere two rooms away. He could sense her presence, tantalizingly close.

"No. Keep your elbow tucked close to your side." His brother's instruction wafted down from the hall, both enticing and damnably irritating.

Ash stared at the pages in front of him, more determined than ever to concentrate on the letters before him and to block out the vision that came to mind with those words. He couldn't see Mark, but his voice carried. Ash could just imagine what was happening at that moment.

"Like this?" Miss Lowell's response.

"Yes, better. Now bring it up. Quickly, now."

Ash envisioned his brother standing in the parlor.

He could stand behind Miss Lowell, his fingers wrapping about her hand. Sometimes, he thought that Miss Lowell had accepted Mark's offer to teach her to defend against a man just to drive Ash mad. He was certain Mark had offered with that exact end in mind.

Brothers. Ash shook his head.

Ash wished he'd had the bright idea to teach Miss Lowell how to hit a man. There were so many opportunities for touching. But then, that was why she would never have accepted. Not from him. Not yet, at least. Everything worth having, he reminded himself, was worth waiting for. Every day that passed in which he did not importune her worked in his favor. She would learn that he could be trusted, that he wasn't going to harm her. That wariness would eventually leave her eyes. Patience won all battles, revealed all secrets. If he could figure out how to reach her once…

Instead, Mark was the one reaching her. Or, rather, being Mark—he was not reaching her at all.

Because Mark wouldn't take advantage of any of those delightful opportunities to fold his hands around hers. Ash had purposefully walked by the parlor during Mark's lessons several times this past week. He'd walked as if he hadn't cared one whit about what his brother was doing with Miss Lowell. Still, he'd managed to ascertain a great deal from the corner of his eye.

They'd thrown open the broad double doors, for propriety's sake. So far as Ash could tell, Mark had never laid so much as a fingernail on Miss Lowell. Instead, he stood a proper three yards distant. Two of the upstairs maids had joined them—at first, to serve as reluctant chaperones. But as the days had passed, they'd joined in earnest as giggling participants. If Ash judged the matter right, the maids were giggling, *willing* participants, who wished Mark would do more than instruct.

It was just like Mark, to be surrounded by women, and yet to take no advantage.

Ash wasn't sure if he was more annoyed at Mark, for stealing time with the woman who had riveted his attention, or jealous of Miss Lowell herself. After all, he'd planned these weeks as a way to spend time with his younger brother. A way to build common experience, to finally forge a connection that would bridge the many differences between them. But when Mark wasn't teaching Miss Lowell effective ways to bring a man down, he buried himself to his neck in books. The summer contained no horseback ambles across wide fields, no lazy trips to the river armed with fish hooks and bait. There were no evenings spent drinking port and discussing politics.

No; the only place Ash ever met his brother was here in the library. And to put it mildly, libraries had never been Ash's specialty. In point of fact, he would rather dig a well for Parford Manor using a spoon made of cheese than read about—he turned the volume over in his hands—*Practical Agriculture.* Looking at the table of contents alone made him feel exhausted. An incipient headache formed at his temples. But he stayed here with the damned book, because when Mark was finished with Miss Lowell, he would come into the library. And before his brother threw himself headlong into his work, Ash would have a narrow opportunity to speak with him.

So he sat here, pretending to make sense of subtitles on soil.

It was another fifteen minutes before he heard Mark

bidding Miss Lowell farewell. She left first, walking past. She didn't even glance into the library as she went by. It had been like that for nine days, now. Ever since he'd talked to her on the path, she had flatly ignored him. For nine days, he'd been forced to listen to the two most interesting people on the estate make friends with each other. Ash let out a small growl of frustration.

At that moment, Mark sauntered into the room. He took one look at Ash and shook his head.

"Don't be ridiculous, older brother." His voice was annoyingly cheerful. Ash was convinced he put on that bright expression on purpose, just to annoy him. He became even more sure when Mark leaned over the arm of his chair and favored him with a brilliant smile. "I've never even touched her, you know."

"It hardly matters. Neither have I."

"That was rather the point." Mark pushed away from Ash's seat and turned around. "Come now. Chastity builds character."

Ash held back a rude noise. He'd wanted to spend time with his brother, not antagonize him further.

"If you must know," Mark continued, "she reminds me of Hope."

A brief band of pain constricted about Ash's chest. "She's nothing like Hope." But his brother's words brought to mind a picture of their sister, her hair long and dark, her smile fragile. It was an image he couldn't forget, even had he wanted to. She should have been a grown woman now. She would have been, if Parford had acted when Ash begged him to do so.

"What do you remember of her, anyway?"

"Not enough. Her hands. Her laugh. I remember that after she died, everything seemed to change so quickly. It was as if she had been the gatekeeper to all that was good in the world, and with her gone…" Mark shrugged again. "But all that's over. Still, I remember enough of the nightmare that followed to know that it's a hellish thing to be alone in the world, unprotected."

"Miss Lowell doesn't need protection from *me*."

"She's employed by the Dalrymples, Ash. What do you suppose will happen to her when we leave and Richard and Edmund return? Do you fancy leaving her to their tender mercies, then?"

He hadn't fancied leaving her behind at all. But if he said that, Mark would tease him all the more. "I hadn't thought what would happen when we left," Ash said stiffly.

"No. You wouldn't." Mark spoke this piece of brazen treachery with an utterly matter-of-fact manner.

Ash flinched. He could not make himself look away from his brother's gaze. He spent half the days wishing Mark would talk to him. It was in moments like this that he wished to take it all back. He wished he could push his brother away. That he could forget what he had done to his brothers—or rather, what he *hadn't*.

"Christ, Mark."

"You don't always think about others the way you should," Mark said simply.

That criticism cut more deeply than the reference to Hope. Mark stated it so mildly, making the wound sting all the more. Mark's gaze was as piercing as only someone who had survived the precise contours of one's faults could be.

"I think about others every damned second of the day. It's because of you that I'm here, after all, because of what I wanted to give you—"

"And still you stomp about, leaving little eddies of destruction in your wake."

Hell. Guilt was bad enough, without having his brother point out his every flaw. Ash had been the one to solemnly swear that he would protect and defend the younger children. He had been the one who had nodded as his father told him that their mother was given to excess. He'd solemnly promised to temper her zeal.

He'd failed. A few years later, despite his best efforts, his sister had died. A few months after that, Ash had left for India, determined to make his fortune and thus undo everything their mother had done.

But he'd left his brothers behind. He would never be able to forget the sick sensation he'd felt when he found Mark and Smite on his return, pale and thin, alone on the streets of Bristol. It had made so much sense to leave them. But nothing he did could repair what had happened to them in his absence. They wouldn't even talk of those years, not to him.

And that hadn't been the only time he'd abandoned Mark. Just the first.

"Very well," he said stiffly. "You are quite in the right. I should never have left. I failed Hope. I failed *you*."

A puzzled look flitted across Mark's face. "How is it that we are talking about *me,* then?"

"Every time I look at you, I recall how I've failed you. There. I've admitted it. Are you happy now?"

"Happy that you look at me and see failure?" Mark's voice was tending towards scorn now, and his lip curled. "Hardly."

Christ. He was cocking it up again. "I know you're not a failure. You took a first at Oxford."

"In case you hadn't noticed," Mark said hotly, "I'm a good deal more than that. Granville himself said I was the brightest student he'd seen in the thirty-five years he'd been in philosophy. And this—" Mark gestured at the pages that lay on the table in front of him "—this will show everyone what I can do. Even you, Ash. Even you. So don't look at me and see failure. I haven't failed anything."

This had all gone horribly wrong. "Don't get so upset, Mark. I'm not questioning your intelligence. Or your capabilities."

"What *are* you questioning, then? It can't be my principles, seeing as how you have none of your own to speak of."

"Oh, it's *my* principles you object to, then?" Ash felt the whole bitter weight of his responsibilities shift restlessly. He'd done *everything* for his brothers—*everything*. Mark *was* his principle. And if Ash's hands were a little dirty, it was because he'd wanted to keep his brothers' clean. "They're a hell of a lot more honest than your own," he snapped.

He wished he could take the words back as soon as he'd said them, because Mark actually gasped in surprise.

"What do you mean by that?"

Ash didn't want to answer. He didn't want to let Mark know that there was yet another barrier between them, another one of Ash's many failures. But Mark gestured, and the words tripped out anyway.

"Maybe you're too young to remember what it was like before father died, or what happened in those years afterwards. You might not remember the day Mother decided to take to heart the Biblical command that one should sell everything one had and give it all to the poor. Nice, in principle; in practice, it leaves your own children starving, housed in rat-infested penury. We lost everything we should have had—modest comfort, education. She traded a secure competence for some stupid words she didn't even understand."

"You're the one who never understood Mother," Mark said.

"As if I could. She was mad, Mark. Plain and simple."

Mark's lip curled. "There was nothing plain or simple about her insanity."

"Maybe it doesn't seem that way to you. But I was supposed to protect you—all of you. Her principles killed Hope. They almost killed you and Smite. And throughout it all, Mother clung to dead words in a dead book, paying no attention to the living around her. Maybe you can understand why I mislike the notion of my youngest brother clinging to more dead words. Maybe you can understand why I wince, knowing that my little brother, who spent his childhood with a woman who quite literally went mad with her principles, is spending the summers of his youth practicing the same sort of abstemious insanity that he grew up with. Do you want to know why I've failed you? Because I haven't been able to save you from a woman who has been dead these past ten years. I haven't saved you from anything."

Mark stared at him, his hands curled into fists. "You don't know *anything*," he spat. "Not about me. Not about Mother. You can be such a great *oaf* sometimes."

"Oaf? Is that the best insult the brightest student in thirty-five years of philosophy can muster? Call me a damned bastard. Curse me. Consider a little blasphemy, Mark. It would make me feel a great deal better, knowing you were capable of even a little sin."

"Far be it from me to leave you unsatisfied. Ash, you can go to bloody hell. It is the height of hypocrisy for you to criticize what I choose to do with my time, when I know for a fact that you haven't even bothered to read my work. Not one word."

Despite the finality ringing in his voice, he looked at Ash with an expectant hope in his eyes. And Ash knew what his brother wanted. He wanted to be contradicted. Wanted Ash to spit out that he'd read the carefully bound essays his brother had so proudly sent to him over the years.

But Ash's best effort—"I stumbled through the introductory paragraph, before I threw up my hands in despair"—would hardly mollify his brother. The truth choked him, and if it were to come out, it would destroy Ash's last chance of forging any sort of connection with Mark.

When he remained silent, Mark shook his head. "I don't know why I bother. Some days, I think Smite has the right of it."

The final sally, and Ash had nothing to say in response. Mark swept his gaze around the room at his books, stacked in neat arrays along the table near the window. Finally, he picked the top two from the pile and walked out.

He didn't even stamp his feet as he left.

CHAPTER FIVE

MARGARET ENTERED THE room where her father stayed. His breathing, thin and reedy, echoed. He lay on the bed, his eyes closed, his skin as translucent as bone china, and looking nearly as fragile. It made her feel breakable herself, to see him so vulnerable. She closed the door behind her, and the curtains at the window fluttered weakly.

In her pelisse, she had tucked the letter that had been brought up from the vicar's wife this morning. Richard had finally written her, and until this moment she hadn't had a chance to look at the missive in private. Not that he'd been in any rush to communicate with her; it had taken him a full week and a half to send his first message.

She could hardly have broken the wax seal standing in the marble entry, after all. She might have run into Ash Turner. He might have simply plucked the pages from her hand. And then he would have known that she was one of the Dalrymples he so hated.

And then…

And then her imagination well and truly carried her away. It had been nine days since she'd so forcefully told him to leave her alone. And in that time, he'd subjected her to an ardent, soul-grinding, will-destroying campaign of…nothing. No attempted kisses. No conversation. No endearing little compliments, designed to erode her will into submission. It was almost enough to make her grant the man a grudging sort of respect.

She saw him daily. She could hardly help it; he'd taken over the suite of rooms off the gallery on the second floor, and she passed by his chambers several times each day on the way to her father's sickroom. But he was so often surrounded by the men he'd brought up from London. The estate was aswarm with them; she supposed that diligence was necessary when a man was in trade.

It was discomfiting, to say the least, to discover that he so diligently performed his responsibilities.

Margaret shook her head and broke the seal on her brother's letter. It separated into two sheets of paper. One page, covered in both sides, written in a dense hand, was labeled as information for her father. She set it to the side.

The other was addressed to her, and she felt a small thrill of pleasure at being remembered. Richard was a handful of years older than she. He'd always been kind. He, no doubt, knew how difficult it was for her to pose as a servant on the estate where she had once been in charge. He knew how irascible their father had become. And perhaps he had waited so long before writing because he remembered that tomorrow was her birthday.

The very thought brought a wash of loneliness. This year, after all, there had been no stream of birthday wishes from friends. It would be nice to know that one person in the world besides Ash Turner did not take her for granted.

She unfolded the sheet. It was depressingly void of content, except for a few short lines.

M—

Received your letter. A. Turner's presence is bad enough. But I am alarmed to hear M. Turner is present. Beware. He's a dangerous beast. Don't spend time alone with him.

He'd signed with a flourish. She stared at the words, her lip curling in dismay.

That was all he had to say? No words of encouragement, nor of thanks? No other response to the missives she'd sent his way? She could have read him quite a lecture. But it was pointless remonstrating with a man who was many miles distant. Richard was busy and no doubt just as taken over by worries as she was. He'd focused on what he thought was the most important point: her welfare. She couldn't fault him for that.

And yet…Mark Turner, dangerous? The notion seemed laughable. Richard couldn't have been talking about the Mark she knew, with his philosophical writings about chastity. He couldn't have heard Mark's quiet, careful, educated speech. Mark had been teaching her a few ways to avoid unwanted advances. He was the last man she might ever imagine as dangerous.

Or. Well.

Come to think of it, there *were* those lessons. She'd seen her brothers box together on occasion. There had been a strict code to the blows allowed—fists only, aimed at the torso and definitely no lower. She doubted very much gentlemen discussed the precise angle at which to punch a man, so as to most effectively break his nose.

How on earth had gentle, quiet *Mark* learned such ungentlemanly tricks?

She sat back, dissatisfied. At that moment, her father gave a quick snort; the tenor of his breathing changed from the even ebb and flow of sleep to the harsher arrhythmia of wakefulness. He gave a rasping cough.

Margaret stood and walked over to him. It took a few minutes to see to his physical needs—a little soup, some barley water—that was all he would take. As he ate he shut one eye and looked at her, a hint of confusion on his face.

Blink. Blink. He shook his head, and then blinked again.

"Is something the matter?"

"No. I feel delightful. I might be ten years old. I'm staying in my bed for the sheer enjoyment of laziness, don't you know." He let out a puff of breath. "Yes, something is the matter, you foolish girl. I'm dying, and it's awkward and not particularly entertaining."

There was no response to be made to that piece of impoliteness. He was still her father, but since the day he'd awakened and found himself unable to stand without assistance, he'd become more belligerent. Crueler, harsher. The same man, and yet vastly different. He'd always been so controlled; being bedridden likely didn't agree with his nature.

"Besides," he muttered, "it will pass in a few minutes. It always does."

"Is that an indication that something is amiss, aside from the usual? Shall I fetch a physician?"

"Why put yourself to the trouble? The physician can have only two things to say: either I will continue to waste away at a predictable pace, or I have begun to perish faster. Neither possibility seems of particular assistance to me at the moment. I would rather not be poked and prodded if I am about to go on to my eternal rest." He continued to blink his eyes, and then he began to wink with his left eye.

His behavior had become increasingly erratic, but there was little Margaret could do about it.

Margaret sighed. "Very well, then. I've a letter for you from Richard. Shall I read it aloud, or would you prefer to read it yourself?"

"From whom?"

"From Richard."

He stared at her blankly.

"You do recall your eldest son, Richard."

"Nonsense." He snorted and waved a hand. "I haven't got any sons."

Margaret felt her hands clench around the paper. He'd been acerbic this past year, but this was the first indication she'd seen of the forgetfulness that sometimes plagued the elderly.

"Sons," her father continued, "by definition can inherit. As Richard cannot, I must assume he's classified as a daughter." He met her eyes. "And that means he's essentially worthless."

Oh. So he was just exceptionally hurtful today, then. Not forgetful. Margaret's jaw set. He was ill. He was unhappy. He was also being particularly cruel. But if she stood up and walked away now, nobody else would take care of him.

"Well," she finally said, "let me pour some more of this worthless soup down your gullet. And then I believe I shall manufacture an answer to Richard's letter and pretend it comes from you. I shall send him your love and affection. Perhaps I shall add—for myself— that as you spoke of him, a tear of remorse trickled down your cheek."

"Remorse?" he groused. "That's the best you can manage for me? A puny, girlish emotion like remorse? None of you have an ounce of spirit. You can write whatever you wish, so long as I needn't listen to Richard's endless hand-wringing."

"I shall dot your *i*'s with flowers," she told him without mercy, "and cross your *t*'s with a line of hearts."

He stared at her a second, as if, after all this time, he had finally realized that there was a hint of rebellion behind her saccharine kindness. "That," he said, with a shake of his head, "is the thirty-eighth reason why daughters are useless."

It was going to be a long evening. And tomorrow was going to be a long birthday.

MARGARET HADN'T COMPREHENDED quite how long the night would be when she'd finally fallen, exhausted, into bed. She slept fitfully for hours. But then the clock rang downstairs, its chimes indistinct and muffled by distance. Margaret came awake counting: nine, ten, eleven, *twelve*. The stroke of midnight slipped past her with as little ceremony as the moment deserved. The end of one day, slipping into another. Nothing—and nobody—would set this day apart from any other.

It was August 22, and today was the first birthday that Margaret would spend without her mother. She breathed in air, heavy with summer heat. Still the same air as the day before. Nothing had changed in her endless, thankless service. Nothing was going to.

Her mother had not been given to elaborate ceremony. But every birthday that Margaret could remember, the duchess had spent a few hours with her daughter. When she was four, they had planted a rosebush together. Her mother had given her thick gloves just for the occasion and let her pat the dirt in place under the careful auspices of the gardener. Every year thereafter, they'd added to the gardens—a slim beech tree one year, a profusion of tulip bulbs the next. But usually it was roses. They'd planted a different variety each year, despite the oncoming winter. Her mother had always made sure that those plantings survived— even if they'd had to resort to moving the plant to the conservatory in autumn.

It suddenly seemed unbearable that Margaret was trapped in the dark on the third floor, in a servant's room where she could not even smell the late-summer roses. Now that the clock had fallen into silence, the house seemed still and empty. Parford Manor had never seemed lifeless when her mother was in residence. But tonight the air was close and stagnant, and the house seemed utterly devoid of any animating presence. In a few years, no one here would even remember the old duchess. Margaret was the only one who couldn't forget.

She stood up in the darkness and fumbled for a wrapper to pull around her shift. When she'd tied the belt around her waist, she slipped from her room.

She fumbled her way down the cramped, lightless staircase that led from the servants' quarters to the main halls. After that, the moon lit the way before her, silver light gilding black walls. In the dark velvet of night, she could pretend the house was still her mother's. She could walk through the halls as regally as if she were still the acknowledged daughter of the house. She found her way to the main staircase and started down it, spreading her arms wide in greeting. Every inch of this house echoed with her mother's memory—from the wide sweep of the banisters, polished with a formula drawn from her mother's repository of household knowledge, to the paintings lining the walls, painstakingly chosen from the family's store in the attic.

Her mother had purchased the paper for the walls of the grand entry eight years ago. She had carefully picked out every piece of furniture that stood in the rooms on each side. And now that Margaret had reached the ground floor, she could smell the deep summer scent of roses in bloom. The aroma took her back to her childhood, to the years when her mother was well enough to trim the bushes herself.

The scent drew her not outdoors but to the conservatory in the south wing. The door squeaked slightly as she opened it; the wood had swollen in the heat.

Even in summer, when the gardeners had no need to force blooms, the glassed-in walls contained a few potted orange trees, a smattering of plants still too delicate to be exposed to the elements and, in the very back, among a jumble of trowels and hand rakes, the prize she had come here to find: buckets of cuttings taken from roses and encouraged to take root. They were nothing but little sticks of wood and thorn, but when she gingerly pulled one from the dark bucket of water where it stood, white threads of new roots glinted in the moonlight that filtered through the windows.

In the darkness, it was hard to locate the tools she needed—a pot, big enough not to cramp the roots that would eventually grow, and a trough filled with a mix of soil and lime. Her mother would have wanted her to don gloves, but she couldn't find them in the cabinet without lighting a lantern. And if she did, someone might see the light shining through the windows.

The dirt in the bucket clumped in thick clods. She picked up a lump in her hands and then broke it apart into loose, dry soil in the pot before her. She could feel the dirt getting beneath her fingernails as she worked. She hadn't realized why she had come here; she'd felt as if she were chasing some ephemeral spirit. But it felt right. If nobody else could remember her birthday, she would. She would have to transplant this new life, fragile and delicate though it was, in the dark of night.

It was a mindless task she performed, squeezing dirt into the pot. She worked methodically, two handfuls at a time. Squeeze and let fall; squeeze and let fall. There was a comforting rhythm to it. She felt as if her mother herself might have stood beside her, her hands covered with dust. Her body felt too rigid, her hands too small to contain the moment.

Her chest tightened with some inexplicable emotion, one that she didn't dare name.

She crumbled dust into dust. And ashes…

The door to the conservatory squeaked open. She froze, but the dirt in her hand pattered into the pot. That rain of soil seemed immensely noisy in the silence of the night. Had someone heard it? Had someone *seen* her? Here at this little table in the back, nobody would find her, not without entering the room.

Footsteps came forwards, traversing the maze of tables and troughs and orange trees.

That tightness in her chest grew.

Please, let those footfalls belong to Mrs. Benedict— someone comforting, who would look at her, clad in this thin wool wrapper, covered in dust. Someone who would understand without her having to voice a word of explanation. Let it be someone who would know that she *needed* this moment, that on this day of all days, she needed to feel a connection with her mother. Let it be anyone but—

But *him*. He came round the little break of potted

oranges, scarcely three feet from her. The moonlight had smoothed away the fine lines on his face. In the dark, he looked younger and less dangerous. He wore a pair of trousers and a fine lawn shirt, and not much else. He'd not bothered to tuck the tails in, but he'd rolled the sleeves to show his wrists. Manly wrists, thick and strong, with a fine layer of hair scarcely visible. His feet were bare.

His eyes widened as they came to rest on her. He looked into her face for one long second before his eyes dropped down—down her dust-covered shift, the robe cinched simply at her waist. She felt naked before him.

His gaze felt as unwelcome as an invading army.

"Miss Lowell. What in God's name are you doing?"

He spoke as if it were *his* home, as if *she* were the interloper here. Of course he thought it true, under the circumstances. Still, bile gathered in her belly, and the tight knot in her chest squeezed even tighter. Who was he to question her? Who was he to interrupt her? He'd already taken her mother from her once. How dare he do it again? Her hands clutched around the heavy clods of dirt.

And then he took a step towards her.

It happened so fast that Margaret wasn't even sure where the impulse came from. But before the thought had a chance to form in her head, she acted. "Go away," she hissed fiercely. "Get out. Get out *now*." As she spoke, she pulled her hand back, swiftly, and hurled one of the clods of dirt she was holding directly at him. It flew through the air—suddenly everything seemed so slow—she wished she could grab back that violent, raging impulse, but it was already too late.

The clod smacked into his chest with a sick sound, like an axe splitting a pumpkin. In the light of the moon spilling through the glass, she could see clumps of dirt clinging to the luminous white of his shirt. His mouth opened slightly, in shocked betrayal. She felt just as stunned as he looked.

Oh, no. She hadn't really thrown it. She couldn't have done.

But she had. Ever so slowly, he raised one hand to brush particles from his eyes.

She was panting, her fist clenched around the other clod of dirt. The rage had slipped from her grasp, leaving her with only the cold certainty of what she had just done.

It wasn't his fault that her father had been a bigamist. It wasn't his fault her mother had been ill. It wasn't even his fault, really, that she was a bastard and her mother—her kind, gentle, graceful mother—had been made an adulteress. It wasn't his fault that she was so dreadfully alone, that her future seemed so dreary. It wasn't his fault.

It just *felt* as if it was.

He stood stock-still, as if she had turned him to stone when she struck him with that bit of soil.

What had she come to? How must this appear to him? She was wandering about the house—at night—in her shift and stockings, wielding a trowel and trying to find, hidden in this pot of dirt, a woman who had been buried in the churchyard months ago. He must suppose she teetered on the very brink of madness.

Not so far off, that. Deep inside her, for the first time in months, a knot dissolved and a well of emotion breached her rigid walls. It hit her with all the force of floodwaters, and it was only her determination not to cry in front of this man that kept her from being submerged by the power of the riptide. With that undercurrent of hot anger gone from her, she could understand what the feeling was that pressed against her chest.

It was grief, almost crushing. She wanted her mother back. Instead, she'd gotten…him.

He still hadn't said a word to her. He didn't criticize; he didn't bellow in protest. She couldn't make out his eyes, but she could imagine him watching her in the dark. Those eyes would be cold and calculating.

Perhaps he was trying to figure out how to best use this moment to his advantage. He'd shown her respect before. No doubt in the morning, that would disappear. She had no idea what would take its place.

Finally, he raised one finger to tap his forehead, as if miming a gentlemanly tip of the hat. And he turned and left her alone, just as he'd done on that dusty road more than a week before.

The gesture had to have been meant sarcastically.

If she knew anything about men, she knew she would eventually pay the price for her foolish, unthinking reaction. A man as ruthless as he was would find a way to use her lapse to his advantage, to turn that single instance of violence into a repeated threat which he might hold over her head. Margaret's hands were shaking in the dirt. She felt on the verge of a fever. Still, she raised her chin and went back to her work—filling the pot with soil, patting it around the cutting, carefully continuing the work she had started.

Tonight, she had a new rose to plant. Payment could wait.

PAYMENT WAITED A SCANT fifteen minutes.

Margaret finished filling the pot with dirt and

reached for the cutting. A thorn pricked her thumb as she pulled the slender branch from the water, but she had traveled beyond pain and into numbness now. She patted it into place and gently arranged the soil around the stem.

The door opened again. Soft footfalls again—his, no doubt. A little shiver went down her spine, but she straightened her back. So he wasn't going to wait for morning to show her the ruthless side of his personality. No more benevolent, tolerant employer; no more sweet words whispered about her strength, her magnificence.

Margaret had few illusions about what would happen next. A man could put on any airs he wished when he had the desire to please. But strike a man in the middle of the chest after midnight, and all his cruelest impulses would come out. All she knew was that she wasn't going to give him the satisfaction of weeping.

Now she would discover what sort of man Mr. Ash Turner really was. She could not bring herself to look up and meet his eyes. He crossed the room until he stood over her. In the night, he cast no shadows, but she could feel the darkness of him anyway, looming over her. She could feel the heat of his presence, as if he were a piece of solid iron recently removed from a blacksmith's fire. She concentrated on the dirt in the pot, patting it unnecessarily into place. Her skin prickled under his gaze; the hint of some sweet thing tickled her nose.

The gentle clop of clay set upon wood sounded. She blinked and looked up—not to his face, but to the surface of the table. He'd placed a cup on the bench before her. She stared at it, at his fingers on the handle. Fine hairs sprouted from the back of his wrist. His fingers seemed strong and capable. Fragrant steam rose from the vessel.

Of all the ways she had imagined him taking revenge, this had not appeared on any of her lists.

Her gaze traveled up his waist, his chest. He'd changed his shirt, thank God; she wouldn't have to stare at a splotch of dirt marring his linen. Finally she met his eyes. "What is that?"

He pushed the mug towards her. "A toddy of steamed milk, honey and nutmeg. A jigger of rum, for good measure."

"You woke the cook for this?"

"Mrs. Lorens? God, no. I can warm a little milk on the range myself."

His arm returned to his side. Those hands could have been overpowering. Almost frightening in their strength, as ruthless as he was. She'd never thought before how gently he used them.

She swallowed.

"It's a remedy for sleeplessness," he continued. "I used to make it for my brothers when I found them up and about at night."

He spoke casually, as if the nocturnal lobbing of soil was a regular occurrence in the Turner household, one usually met with hot drinks and a comfortable discussion. She could almost see him, puttering by the cast-iron heating plates.

"And did you often find your brothers wandering about at night?"

His eyes glinted at her. "In the first few months when I was back from India? I found them living on the streets, you know. They'd almost forgotten how to sleep."

"On the *streets?* A duke's cousins? That can't be correct."

"Sixth cousins, twice removed. And while I am *correct,* it certainly was not right. Parford didn't care." He spat those words out.

It took her a moment to realize that he wasn't angry at her. This wasn't some form of complicated revenge. She couldn't yet think what to say.

He shook his head. "Speaking of whom, I'll have someone look in on the duke in the early morning. Sleep late. You'll need it."

She looked up at him, but he was already turning away, as if dukes' heirs had nothing better to do than to deliver hot drinks to their dependents and tell them to sleep past the morning bells.

"Mr. Turner. You do realize I'm a servant, don't you?"

He cast a tolerant glance over his shoulder. "I was one, too. Before I made my fortune. If I lost it all, I'd be one again. This notion of class that we English hold to—it's an interesting delusion. You don't *have* to be a servant, Miss Lowell, just because you were born as one."

She shook her head blankly.

"I crossed three oceans in a cramped hammock hung in the bilge, utterly besieged by rats. And yet here I am now. What does that tell you?"

"That you were quite, quite lucky?"

He smiled again, this time with a little shake of his head that indicated he knew what she'd not said. She couldn't have missed that aura of confidence he radiated. The air around him was simply more invigorating. Mr. Turner wasn't *lucky.* He was strong—so strong that he had no need to be jealous of power in others.

"When I looked at myself, I never saw a servant. What do you suppose I see when I look at you?"

For months, everyone who had looked at her had seen a bastard.

What did he see? She couldn't answer. She didn't *know.* She wasn't even sure what she believed of herself, when she passed by a looking glass. These days, she tried not to look. Under his perusal, she had no response.

What he dismissed with that lazy shrug of his shoulders was more than a delusion. It had been the guiding light of her life, the true constant of the North Star. Her belief that she'd been better than others because of her birth had seemed an unshakeable foundation. But that light had snuffed out and north had disappeared in a dizzying whirl. She'd been left fumbling in the dark for some hint of direction.

She hadn't spoken yet, and he just smiled at her one last time and walked away.

Margaret had always thought a man seduced a woman by making her aware of his charms: his body, his wealth, his kisses. How naive she had been.

Ash Turner seduced her with the promise of her own self. She longed to believe him, longed to believe that the nightmare of the past month was nothing more than a delusion, that if she simply screwed her eyes tightly shut, she would be important again. And that desire was more alluring than any promise of wealth, more irresistible than any number of heated kisses pressed against her lips.

In her life, she'd met indulgent men, autocratic men, absent-minded men who forgot her existence when she was not around. But a man like him… He stood so far outside her experience that she'd not been able to recognize him. But there it was, the conclusion inescapable. He thought she was magnificent. And he meant it—*really* meant it—beyond all possibility of fabrication.

Of all the recent disasters to befall her, this one—that this man, of all men, admired her—seemed the most devastating. Could he not have been someone—*anyone*—else? For a long while, Margaret stared at the cup in front of her, the steam curling upwards and away.

She mattered. She was important. She clutched those thoughts to her heart, and they made her grief bearable. Slowly, she reached out and pulled the mug forwards.

The contents were every bit as sweet as she'd imagined.

CHAPTER SIX

ASH HAD INSTRUCTED Miss Lowell to sleep late, but he'd been up at first light himself. Work wouldn't wait. And indeed, it did not. His morning messenger arrived just after the clock struck half-ten in the morning.

The fellow was one of the new men Ash had hired just a few months before—what was his name again?—Isaac Strong; yes, that was it. The man walked stiffly, his legs no doubt learning to move properly once again after being cramped in a carriage all the long voyage from London. The whites of his eyes were shot through with red, and as he was conducted into the front sitting room of the suite Ash had taken, he rubbed the black skullcap on his head wearily. He didn't see Ash sitting on a sofa near the window. He looked as tired as Ash felt.

"Mr. Strong. It's your first visit out, yes?"

As he addressed Strong, the man jerked to attention, all signs of his weariness evaporating in a flurry of consternation.

Operating at a few days' remove from London had numerous disadvantages. Most of them, Ash had been able to alleviate by dint of having well-trained, competent men in London. A smaller number of them were needed here, though, and so his men took turns traveling out to speak with him.

Not so efficient as some of the alternatives. But then,

the alternatives were rendered problematic by other considerations.

"It is Strong, isn't it?"

Strong nodded, puffing his chest out. "Sir," he said tightly, as if he were some newly commissioned subaltern. And then, like that selfsame hapless officer, he fumbled with the brass buckles on the satchel slung about his shoulder. Before Ash had a chance to ask him whether he needed to rest or refresh himself, he pulled out a fat sheaf of papers and held it out, as if an entire war depended on whatever was in those pages.

"Sir," Strong barked out, "your report, sir."

"My report?" Ash felt a prickle of consternation along the skin of his thumbs. "That's my report?"

The words must have come out harsher than he'd intended, because Strong ducked his head farther. "The report you requested on the current inclinations of the members of the House of Lords regarding the proposed act. I—" he looked up into Ash's face and must have read the distaste Ash felt curling his lips, because he swallowed, his throat bobbing "—I h-have a detailed listing, and that, along with the alphabetical appendix, should suffice to—"

"Ah," said Ash, enlightenment dawning suddenly. "You made an alphabetical appendix, did you?"

That explained the ink-stained forefinger, the thick sheaf of papers. It certainly explained the rumpled wild-eyed look that Mr. Strong was giving him. Ash suppressed a grin. "Did you include the Latin translation in triplicate?"

"The *Latin translation?*" Strong's eyes widened in abject fear. "Jeffreys made no mention of—oh." Strong snapped his mouth shut, almost viciously.

Ash had never hired fools. Gullible geniuses, now…

Strong swallowed. "Please tell me you wanted a list of every invitation the Dalrymple brothers have accepted over the past two months, complete with an inventory of the nearest coaching-houses, and a calculation of the shortest distance from London by stagecoach."

"That," Ash said, "was an exceptionally creative addition. I'll have to talk to Jeffreys. He's not usually quite so…so aggressive with the new men. Come. Let's talk in my study." He jerked his head towards the room to the right—a former parlor that he'd converted for his use.

As Ash pushed himself to his feet, Strong let out a sigh. "Sir, how much were they having me on about, then?"

"The whole report."

If silence could blaspheme… Paper crinkled as Strong's knuckles clenched about his alphabetical appendix.

Ash shrugged. "I abhor lists. I despise reports, written on paper. If I wanted a useless stack of pages, I would just have you all send couriers out to deliver them, and never mind the expense of carting my men about England. But I don't. The last thing I want to do, ever, is to sit down and read through a tangle of letters, just so that I can get to the point. I want all my reports delivered orally—that way, I can ask you questions as I wish, and I don't have to trudge through extraneous material that will be of no use to any of us."

"Did they…" Strong rubbed his skullcap again, a grimace on his face. "That is, is this because…"

"You mean, were they trying to get you sacked?"

Ash shook his head. "Jeffreys was having me on as much as you. He knows how I feel about paper." Mostly. Even his right-hand man didn't understand the true extent of it.

"Well. That rather explains the first message I am supposed to deliver to you. Mr. Jeffreys has sent up a handful of agricultural texts for you, in answer to your last query, which he said betrayed a great deal of ignorance which could not be answered by a mere sentence or three. He told me to tell you to…to…" Strong paused and looked away.

"Out with it." Ash paused at the library door. "I know they aren't your words."

"To be a man and just read through them. Apparently, he, uh, *appreciates* your views on reports."

Ash smiled bitterly, feeling the exact opposite of appreciation. "Well, your first order of business when you get back to London is to tell him to go to hell. No—write that down. I don't want you to forget. Here, I have paper—"

He stopped, looking at the makeshift desk he'd made in the parlor. He'd left it clear last night, all the spare scraps of paper bundled away to whence they'd belonged—not that he had much use for paper as it was.

But set atop the oak surface of his desk was a solitary sheet, folded in two. It was weighted down by a clay mug. A *familiar* clay mug, he realized as he picked it up. It smelled faintly of honey and nutmeg. In that instant, his remaining fatigue dissolved in a cloud of anticipation.

"Wait a minute," Ash said softly. He felt a prickle of excitement in his fingertips—an echo of the surprise he'd experienced on finding Margaret last night in nothing but a linen shift and a thin wrapper. Her hair had been down. Unbound, it had curled, and he'd longed to sink his hands in the silk of it. She'd looked like an apparition from one of his more sensual dreams. Even now, a part of him longed to go back to the conservatory, to start that conversation over again, and this time, to give in to his lust-filled imaginings. He was getting aroused, just remembering the pattern the moonlight had made on her skin.

But he'd found something better than mere animal satisfaction last night. Just as the natural curves of her body had been revealed by the night, so, too, she had slipped beyond the starchy disdain she'd directed at him these past days. There had been something raw and honest about that late-night conversation—something that had transcended the formal boundaries she'd insisted must stand between them. With those walls destroyed, anything could happen. *Everything* could happen. Ash felt as if he stood on the precipice of some tall cliff, readying himself to jump. In a few moments, he would know if the rush of wind he felt about him meant he was flying or falling.

He picked the paper up. And here he'd already refused one report. But then, this wasn't a dry, business communication. He could hardly ask Strong to read *this* aloud.

He could imagine her slipping in here, just before dawn. She would have leaned against his desk, here, bending over the inkwell. A welcome image, that, if entirely distracting—the smooth fabric of her gown falling over the sweet swell of her buttocks, framing curves that were made to be cupped in the palm of his hand. And how had she got into this locked room? Ah, yes. The master key. With that, she might have stolen into his bedchamber. She might have come to him on silent feet, to press those beguiling curves against his chest, his groin… Hell. If he'd contemplated *that* possibility last night, he truly wouldn't have slept. Not one wink.

But now was not the time to indulge in fantasy—not with Strong looking on, not when he held a more tangible—if less physically gratifying—reality in his hands. He unfolded her note gingerly. Only two short words on that paper, and a signature. Ash took a deep breath—it would have been idiotic to be nervous, and he tried to avoid idiocy—and read.

Two short little words. He read them, one by one. *I'm. Sorry.* He read it again to be sure, and the second time it said the same thing: *I'm sorry,* plainly spelled out for anyone to see. The apology was followed by an *M* and a wavering squiggle of ink.

Margaret? Or *Miss Lowell?* He couldn't tell, and for a moment he almost considered asking Strong for his interpretation. But it didn't matter what she'd called herself. That moment when she'd lobbed that bit of dirt at him—well, he'd wanted to see her in the throes of passion. Now he had. Not the passion he'd hoped for, true, but still it had been a candid, unstudied response. There would be more of those. Many, many more. Next time she looked at him with that much emotion shimmering in her eyes, he'd have better comfort to offer than a mug of warm milk.

When he looked up at Strong, Ash felt a tight little smile on his face. Those two words had warmed him more than the thought of her bending over his desk, her skirts touching the wood paneling. Her feet had been on the floor where he now stood. She had tiptoed into his suite, in the dark of night, while he lay sleeping a scant handful of yards away.

For the past week he'd been mired in place, making no progress with his brothers, the upcoming debate in Parliament, or her.

But he felt it now, a certainty burning deep inside him. It was all going to come right, and she was the key.

"Good news, sir?"

Ash folded her note in quarters. "The best, Mr. Strong. The absolute best."

"MISS LOWELL. HAVE YOU the time for another lesson?"

Margaret stopped in the hall. She'd not been sure how to face Mr. Ash Turner again after last night—after her outburst and his too-kind response. But his younger brother posed no such difficulties. Still, she remembered her brother's letter.

He's a dangerous beast. She turned to him.

"Mr. Turner—"

"Mark." He looked as innocent and unassuming as always, and dressed in white and silver, he seemed to glow with positive innocence in the sunlight.

"Mark," she acquiesced. "I've been wondering. You aren't exactly teaching me to fight by gentleman's rules, are you?"

He shrugged. "What use would that be? You'll never need to use what I'm teaching you against a gentleman who follows the rules."

"I'm merely wondering how you learned to fight this way."

He looked at her. "My brother—my other brother, the one you've not yet met—and I spent a bit of time on the streets of Bristol. You learn a great deal when survival is foisted upon you. Served me a few good turns when I was at Eton."

Mr. Turner had made the same claim, that Mark had spent time on the streets. Perhaps that was why Richard had called him dangerous. This was yet another confirmation of the unsettling disclosure Ash had made last night.

But looking into Mark's face, she saw nothing of the street waif in him. She didn't know what to think. "From the streets of Bristol to Eton. That must have been...different."

"Not so much. I made an excellent target those first few months at school. All the bullies looked to prove themselves." His smile widened, ever so slightly. "If you have to fight off five boys at once, you can't fight fairly."

A small knot coalesced in Margaret's stomach. "By chance, did you ever have to fight off Richard Dalrymple?"

"Him? Oh, no." He smiled at her.

She took a breath in relief. Somehow, if he'd struck her brother, it would make her tentative friendship with him seem all the more disingenuous.

"Just Edmund."

Her hopes fell again. "And did you fight him fairly?"

"No." His expression shuttered. "I fought him once, and that sufficed for both of us. After that, the Dalrymples bedeviled my brother and me in other ways."

He looked so innocent—his hair so blond, his eyes so blue. He was like an archangel.

Did archangels advise women on the most efficacious way to pop a man's arm from his socket? Generally, Margaret supposed, they didn't.

"You're perturbed by that, aren't you?"

"The Dalrymples are my employers. It would be odd if I felt no loyalty to them."

He cocked his head and looked at her, his eyes narrowing. "If it makes you feel better, I haven't struck a Dalrymple in the better part of a decade. Surely, after what my brother has done to them, a little physical harm hardly signifies."

Her brother had told her to beware this man. And yet… Her brother was not always right. Richard wouldn't have understood last night either—why a clod of dirt and a hot drink had brought Margaret around to an understanding that even now, she was afraid to probe.

And then, it *was* her birthday, and Richard hadn't even remembered. She deserved defiance—a little defiance.

And so she smiled back at Mark. "You're quite right," she finally said. "It shouldn't bother me at all."

SOME HOURS AFTER STRONG had given his reports—orally—and been sent to rest, Ash heard his brother and Margaret talking. Her laughter floated down the hall, twining with Mark's tenor chuckle.

His thoughts of jealousy had leached from him overnight. All things considered, he didn't disapprove of his brother making friends with her. It was just as well, and he knew Mark would pursue nothing more than friendship.

He knew Miss Lowell less well, but he could intuit that had she been the least tempted by Mark, she'd never have agreed to the lessons. She had an unfortunate, innate sense of propriety—one that Ash was only beginning to break through himself.

But now, with her apology folded in his pocket, there was no reason for Ash to wait, banished on the outskirts. Not any longer. He stood and walked down the hall. He paused by the entry to the room and peered in. The doors to the gallery were wide open. Nothing untoward could happen. And while the exercise would have been highly improper for a lady, it was merely eccentric for a few servants.

Miss Lowell and the second upstairs maid stood in the center of the room.

"You're aiming for the nose," Mark said from his vantage point by the side. "You have to practice bringing your elbow up quickly. Anything else, and you'll not have the advantage of speed or surprise—a big man would simply brush off such a strike. You can't count on being stronger than anyone, so you must be *faster.*"

"I can't," protested the maid. "Without someone there, I just can't *see* where I should be placing my elbow."

Miss Lowell cast a sidelong glance at her companion and then looked away. There wasn't a hint of agreement in her face, not a single echo of that lament. Instead she set her jaw almost fiercely. Of course. She wasn't the sort to bemoan her fate, Ash realized, nor to make protests or excuses. Not when she could simply set things to rights. He hadn't heard a complaint from her, not the entire time he'd spent in the house. She simply did what was necessary.

Even last night, she'd not made excuses for her behavior or accusations about his in justification. Anyone else in her place might have done so, but she hadn't.

There was something straightforward about her. He liked that. He already liked far too much about her, from the curve of her snub nose to the way she nodded at Mark's criticism and squared her shoulders, as if determined to get it right.

"I agree," Ash said from the doorway, "you need to see it done. You need to see someone smaller take on someone larger, so you can have a feel for what it ought to look like."

Miss Lowell whirled to look at him. Her eyes widened and a faint flush lit her cheeks. But she didn't point her finger and demand he leave. And had she been dead set against any further interaction with Ash, he was sure she would have. Instead, she glanced at Mark, as if seeking permission.

Mark pursed his lips and looked his brother up and down. Had they grown up in each others' company, they might have grappled together sometimes, as brothers did. But Ash had left for India when Mark was barely seven years of age; when Ash had returned he'd been a man, with a man's body, and his brother had been a wiry, too-skinny child of eleven. In the more than a decade that had passed since, Ash had been busy working and Mark had been off at school. They'd never had the chance to do *this*. He'd so carefully protected his younger brother that perhaps he'd missed the opportunity to make friends with him. There'd been no scrambling; no wrestling nor boxing. Not a hint of fencing practice. None of the usual chances that an older brother had to beat his brother into benevolent harmony.

Words on a page would never bring them together, no matter what Mark believed. But this...*this* might.

"Come now, Mark," Ash said. "Why don't we show the ladies how it's done?"

As an added benefit, perhaps Ash might show Miss Lowell a few things himself.

Mark smiled enigmatically and shook his head. "What do you think, Miss Lowell? Suppose a big man—a man the size of Ash—were to come after you? What would you do?"

That was not what he'd intended. As pleasant as it might have been to grapple with her, he'd prefer not to have an audience when he did so. And besides, the last thing he wanted her to playact with him was unwillingness.

"Mark, I can hardly strike a lady."

"Of course not. Perhaps you might simply reach for her wrist. Gently, if you wish." Mark dropped an eyelid in a mysterious wink, and Ash suddenly understood his brother's ploy. It was a simple matter. He would have to steel himself for the inevitable—a slap on the cheek, perhaps even a feminine blow to the gut. She couldn't hurt him, not if he were ready for whatever puny little punch she managed to deliver. But he could let her *think* she had hurt him. Build up her confidence. Build up her trust. And, in the meantime, get close enough to touch her wrist.

No possible drawbacks to that one. There was no getting around it. His little brother was a genius.

"I don't know, Mark," Miss Lowell was saying. "I—I really shouldn't like to hurt your brother. I'm not the violent sort." She glanced uneasily in Ash's direction, as if aware that the events of last night left him more than able to contradict her. "Not usually," she amended.

Ash hid a smile. If she could hurt him, it was surely

not by laying her hands on him. "I acquiesce in a good cause," he said soberly. "I can withstand a few bruises." And then, because he couldn't help himself, he added, "Besides, I don't mind the occasional bout of violence."

She colored.

Mark nodded enthusiastically at this. "Too true. He's a man. Men *like* pain. It's how we make friends, you know."

It was as if Mark had lifted the thought from Ash's head. Ash grinned. "The measure of male familiarity is the degree of barbarism to which one reverts in the absence of female companionship. A man knows he's among friends when he feels free to hoot like a heathen and bash heads like a ram." Perhaps he was overdoing it.

"Additionally, how many nurses can say they've brought the Duke of Parford to his knees?" Mark added, a glint in his eyes.

No doubt that was intended as a subtle hint to Ash. Very well. He'd let her strike him, he'd stagger about a bit, then he'd fall to the floor. An easy victory for her, and his pride could withstand the blow. *Especially* since he would know precisely how much her victory would mean.

"You'll be able to tell your grandchildren, one day," Mark said.

"Let's start this nice and easy." Ash reached out and took hold of her wrist, pulling her to him—not harshly, but gently. She looked up into his face, her eyes wide, her lips parted, subtly. He was aware of her whole body, scant inches from his. He could feel the heat of her. If his brother hadn't been looking on, Ash might have been tempted to lean down and touch his mouth to hers. As it was, he could almost taste her, she was so close. The sweet scent of her whispered against his lips—

Bam.

Something struck his chin, and his mouth clipped shut, his teeth closing about his tongue. He tasted the tang of copper. He was blinking back the stinging pain when—

Whap.

He crumpled to the floor, his knees slamming against hard parquet before he had the chance to brace himself. It took him a second to realize she'd kicked his legs out from under him.

And then he felt a touch against his groin. Not a blow, thank God, but no soft caress, either. He opened his eyes. He was splayed on his knees. Miss Lowell stood above him, her eyes sparkling.

"This," she said, her slippered foot against the fall of his trousers, "is where I would have kicked you, had you actually meant me harm. Notwithstanding your stated preference for violence and pain, I assumed I should refrain."

"Clever girl." His throat was raspy; he had to gulp in air. Part of his shortness of breath he could attribute to the bruising fall. Part of it was that she'd revealed an inch of delicate, stockinged ankle. But mostly, it was the placement of her foot, a gentle brush against an organ that was all too pleased to be touched by her, even in so hazardous a manner.

Her smile was not wide, but her pleasure encompassed her in a full-body glow. She'd taken him well and truly by surprise with that elbow to the jaw. He almost pitied the man who tried to steal a kiss from her now.

"Oh, dear. Did I fail to mention that Miss Lowell was a quick study?" There was a too-innocent tone in his brother's voice. Mark had done it on purpose—he'd put Ash at ease, set up this whole scenario, just to have him brought to his knees.

Ash could hardly disapprove.

"Miss Lowell," Ash said, "is an entrancing little witch. As well she knows."

She raised her chin smugly and stepped back, shaking her gown out to fall over her ankles.

If Ash hadn't already been on his knees before her, he'd have gotten on them now. Her hair was slightly disheveled, little strands escaping from her pins. She seemed incandescent—a sharp contrast to the inexplicable grief she'd worn last night. Victory suited her, and all the more because it had been actually won, not handed over in pretense.

He shook his head and gestured to his brother. "Come and help me up," he said. "I'm not as young as I used to be."

"Whatever you say, *older* brother." Mark strode forwards, that delighted look in his eyes. Oh, Mark had won, all right—bamboozled Ash into underestimating Miss Lowell. It was as if Mark had wrestled him to the floor himself. Ash couldn't have been prouder. Mark reached out a hand and Ash grasped it. For a moment, it was a brotherly affirmation—hands clasped together in something akin to friendship.

Ash pulled his weight against his brother's hand, and Mark braced himself. As he scrambled to his feet, he whispered. "Did you really believe that claptrap about my not being young any longer? For a genius, you can be terribly idiotic sometimes."

And with one swift movement, he pushed his brother

off balance, grappled his legs out from underneath him and, after a gratifying scuffle, succeeded in pinning Mark to the floor. For a second, they met eyes.

Mark smiled at him. And victory was complete.

CHAPTER SEVEN

WHEN MARGARET LEFT her father's sickroom that evening, Ash Turner was waiting for her. He leaned against the wall, his bulk a muscled shadow clad in brown wool. She had known this moment was coming, ever since she'd left him that written apology on his desk. He was going to find her, talk to her. He might do substantially more.

But he didn't move to do anything. Instead, he nodded at her. "Good evening, Miss Lowell."

It was impossible for her to ignore the deep rumble of his voice, impossible not to feel the palms of her hands prickle with awareness. He had treated her with kindness. True, he hadn't given her the prim and proper respect to which she'd become accustomed. But he'd given her something solid and quite a bit more reliable.

She swallowed. Her toes curled in her slippers. But then, she had decided this morning what she had to do.

"Good evening." She wasn't finished, but she felt her throat closing about the last syllable. Before she could choke on the words, she started again. "Good evening. Ash."

He didn't smile at that, but his eyes lit. A little defiance, he had called that. But it was a bigger defiance than he could imagine, to flout her family and to address him with such familiarity.

He'd earned it. Twice over.

He straightened. As he did so, the light from the oil-lamp behind him caught his features. With his head held high, the points of his collar no longer cast his chin in shadow.

And now she could see it. She stepped forwards without thinking, her breath hissing out. "Oh, no." Her thumb found his jaw; it was harsh with a day's worth of stubble. And the skin beneath those coarse, rasping hairs was discolored. She lightly ran her fingers over that bruise. "Did I do that?"

She raised her eyes to his and only then realized how close she stood to him. Inches away. She was up on her tiptoes, caressing his face. She could smell his subtle musk—masculine and earthy, with a tang of bergamot. She could feel the heat of him against her fingertips. She should step away. Her breath was burning in her lungs, her lips tingling under his appraisal. Her whole body was coming to life, this close to his. Her breasts tightened, her thighs tensed and that bud between her legs warmed.

"Yes, Margaret." He drew out the syllables, converting her name from a mere appellation into a verbal caress. "You did."

"I'm so sorry. I didn't intend—"

"Oh, no apology needed. I've found it a most useful decoration. Would you know, it has actually driven one particularly lovely woman to touch my cheek?"

Her hand stopped on his chin, where she'd been tracing an unconscious circle. "You're putting a good face on it. But—"

"None of that, now. It's as I told you—this is how

men make friends. If you know what drives a man to anger, you know him."

She shook her head. She still hadn't moved her fingers from his skin. She wasn't sure she wanted to. "That can't be rational." Even less rational was the fact that she was still staring into his eyes.

"We are speaking of men, are we not? Most of us are base creatures, little more than bundles of animal instinct. Friendship is one of our least rational responses."

As close as he was, he'd made no move to touch her. Another man who'd shown half of Ash's interest would have closed his arms about her by now and assaulted her lips. But despite the husk in his voice, he didn't strain towards her.

Her fingers still rested against his skin.

"Friends?" Margaret said. "Is that how you think of me?" She pulled her hand away, and lowered herself down from the tips of her toes.

He followed her down that inch and a half, canting his head over hers. A light sparkled in his eyes. "I spoke only by way of analogy. When I think of you, I want nothing so pale as friendship. I want more. I want decidedly more."

He was going to kiss her. She could feel it in the greedy hunger of her lips, tilting up to his. She could feel it in the clamorous beat of her heart, yearning for that completion.

"I lied to you that first evening we spoke." His breath felt like little brushes of butterfly wings against her lips, sweet and tremulous.

"Oh?"

His voice had gone deep, so deep it seemed to reverberate in her bones. His finger reached up to trace her mouth. "I *do* want to take that kiss."

Her heart stopped. Her lips parted. She felt a flush rise through her—and still he didn't press his lips to hers. Instead, he exhaled and she drank in his scent, sweet and warm.

"Oh," she breathed.

"But—" he said, and it seemed an unfair word, that *but* "—I want you to *give* me one more."

It would have been easy to shut her eyes and let him kiss her. To have the choice taken from her in one heated, passive moment, with nothing for her to do but comply. But he was asking for more than her artless submission. Not deference, not docility, but… defiance.

"I want you to choose me," he said, "well and truly choose me of your own accord. I don't want you to wait at the crossroads in the hopes that I will force the choice upon you."

What he wanted was more perilous than a kiss, more fraught with danger even than letting him slide his hands down her aching body.

"And why must I be the one deciding?"

"Because I decided upon you more than a week ago."

At those words, she drew back. He didn't look as if he were joking. In fact, he seemed almost solemn in that declaration. Still, his words jarred her back to reality. They weren't sweethearts, exchanging promises. They were not lord and lady, agreeing to court. He believed she was a servant, and Ash Turner was a wealthy, handsome duke's heir.

"Don't," she said. "Don't tell me falsehoods. You've treated me like this since—"

"Since the first time I laid eyes on you?" His words came out on a growl. "There's not much to me but animal instinct. Don't look to me for a logical discourse on your charms. I like the set of your chin. I like the way your eyes beckon me to follow you down dark, forested paths. I like that I can't bend you to my will—that you'll send me to the devil if you think I'm in the wrong."

She *wanted* to be wrong, wanted to believe that he proposed more than a simple joining of bodies. But one didn't decide such a thing the instant one clapped eyes on another person.

"You know almost nothing about me." Not even her name.

"I don't need to line up a collection of *facts* to understand how magnificent you are. I'm not wrong. I'm never wrong. Not about this."

"Such humility, Mr. Turner." Her disappointment tinged her words with bitterness. "Everyone's wrong, eventually."

"I'm not. I've no education to speak of. I know nothing of the classics. But I have this: I can look into someone's eyes and see the truth. It's how I made my fortune, you know."

She swallowed. If he'd seen the truth in her eyes, he'd not stand so close to her now. "How do you mean?"

He must have heard the warning note in her voice, because he straightened and expelled a sigh.

"Everyone else is hampered by figures and facts, projections based on rationality. Every contract must be examined for soundness by a horde of solicitors; every word in it laid upon a coroner's table and prodded until it divulges its last secrets. It takes days for most people to reach an accord. Sometimes *months*."

"And you?"

"I make up my mind in seconds. Speed matters, these days. Prices fluctuate, rising and falling with every ship that comes into port."

"What do you do, then? Sign contracts without having them looked over?"

He bit his lip. For a long time, he pressed his lips together, his expression abstracted. Then he whispered, as if imparting a very great secret, "If I trust a man, I'll sign without reading it at all. Words on a page can't stop a true betrayal. All they can do is muddy up the aftermath in Chancery. And as I've said, I've never been wrong."

Margaret took another stunned step backwards. "Doesn't that frighten you? To judge so quickly with so little evidence?"

He shook his head slowly—not an answer to her question, but a thorough rejection of her premise.

"I don't think that is at all what you mean. I think what you really want to know is whether you are frightened to have been judged so swiftly. *You* fear you might come up wanting. You fear that when all is said, and a great deal more has been done, you'll have nothing else I want, and I'll be done with you."

He described them so precisely that she could almost believe he *had* seen her fears. But these were not just idle nightmares, to be dispelled by the coming dawn. Once he discovered her name, he *would* turn his back on her. And this—whatever it was—*would* be finished.

He tapped one finger against her lips. "Kiss me," he said, "when you're sure that foolishness is wrong."

MARGARET RETREATED TO HER room in the servants' quarters with a pounding heart. She could feel the pulse in her neck beating in confused arousal. She eased the door shut behind her and stared at the yellowing whitewash.

There were very few truths in this world. One of them, though, she understood deep in her bones. A man like Ash, with his fortune and his prospects, could have anyone. She doubted he intended anything so casual as a single night's seduction—he'd devoted far too much of his energy to wooing her to discard her so quickly.

But he couldn't want her honorably. Dukes' heirs didn't marry their mistresses.

She had no sooner to think that than realization struck. Dukes' heirs *did* marry their mistresses. She could think of one who had once done so: her father.

The sordid tale had been in all the papers when Ash had filed suit in the ecclesiastical courts. The events had been no less salacious for their being fifty years old. It was hard to imagine her father young and headstrong, but he must have been so once. When he had turned twenty-one, he'd married his mistress in a hushed-up ceremony held in a tiny town in Northumberland. He'd quietly brought his wife to meet his parents—and they had just as quietly threatened him with penury if he persisted in his foolishness.

But parents—even parents who were a duke and a duchess—could only do so much. There were no legal grounds for annulment. And so that impetuous, imprudent wedding had never been spoken about. The girl had been threatened with God only knew what— destitution, dismemberment, dyspepsia. She'd been bundled off to America, where she had wed a wealthy financier.

She'd shown neither hide nor hair in England in the decades that followed, until she made more than a minor sensation of herself, testifying on the matter at Ash's behest.

So, yes. Dukes' heirs *did* sometimes marry their mistresses. But Ash surely knew that it never turned out well. Not for the duke in question, nor for the mistress and most especially not for the family, waiting in confusion on the margins.

Thoughts of family made Margaret think of Richard's letter. She'd tucked it into her lap desk, so that she might answer it at a more fortuitous time. She was supposed to tell him what she'd discovered about Ash. She was *supposed* to be finding evidence to undermine his claim before Parliament, not yearning for his kiss.

And yet, without attempting to do so, she'd succeeded. All she would have to do was write a letter that looked something like: *Mr. Ash Turner believes the notion of class is an antiquated delusion. Additionally, he is so hasty that he doesn't read his contracts before he signs them.*

Two pieces of very valuable information. The first sentiment alone was frightfully revolutionary. Nobody would install a lord who espoused such radical sentiments. And if he hadn't meant his comments in a political way…why, that was simply the price that was sometimes paid in these fracases. A little twist of the truth, and she could end this farce right now. All she would have to do was write the words down.

A simple prospect to set pen to paper. There was only one problem.

She could still feel the heat of his presence, an unconscious echo reverberating through her. She could still feel him leaning over her, his lips so close to hers. She could hear her own protest: *You know almost nothing about me*. This time, as she went over the memory, she added the truth. *I'm Lady Anna Margaret Dalrymple, and I have been lying about my identity so that I can better ferret out your faults. You mustn't trust me.*

Still, in her mind, he gave her that enigmatic smile. *I don't need facts to understand how magnificent you are, how eminently trustworthy. I'm not wrong. I'm never wrong.*

He was this time. He was utterly mistaken. She was going to betray him, and in doing so, she would tear all his calm certainty to shreds.

Except…she didn't want to do it. If he was wrong about her trustworthiness, he would have no special insight. He might be wrong about every last thing, starting with his assertion that she mattered. Margaret wanted to matter.

More than that. She didn't want to betray Ash. She didn't want to twist his words of kindness into weapons of war. She didn't want to be the one who first introduced doubt into his eyes. She wanted to kiss him, and she couldn't do that with a conscience sullied by betrayal.

She took a deep breath and reached for a sheet of paper. She would write her letter—but she would leave out what she had learned. Nobody would understand his words, not as he had meant them. If she was going to betray him, she would have to betray him with the truth, not with some twisted version of it. And so her letter was simple—uninformative, plain and, at the end, the only lie she told was when she sent her brother their father's love.

When she was done, she snuffed the single candle flame and let darkness fall.

"Ash!" Mark's voice interrupted Ash's morning conference. His usually even tones were tinged half with despair, half with anger.

Ash turned slowly in his chair. His brother stood in the open doorway, his hands clenched into fists. He hadn't donned a coat yet, and his gray waistcoat was unbuttoned. His hair was wild, as if he'd pulled it into blond little knots, and his eyes were wide.

"What have you done with it?" he demanded.

Ash had been waiting for this moment. He'd been waiting for it ever since last night, when he'd issued the order. But instead of answering directly, he pretended puzzlement. After all, the role of an elder brother was to make a younger one pull out his hair—just a little bit—before smoothing everything over.

Mark's spine straightened and he stalked forwards, placing his hands on the table. "Is this your way of punishing me for yesterday's events?"

Two of the clerks Ash had brought up from London sat next to him. They had turned to look at Mark. At this query, they schooled their faces to careful blankness. They were, after all, in on the joke.

Ash let his look of bewilderment grow. "What sins did you commit yesterday that cried out for punishment?" he mused aloud. "Did I miss an opportunity?"

"Nothing that would justify *this!*" Fists came up before him in an unconscious fighting stance. "Where, in the name of all that is holy, is my book, Ash? I've been working on it for two full years. Do you want me to get down on my knees and beg for its safe return? I will, if only—"

"Ohhhh." Ash let the syllable slide from his lips, as if he'd had no notion of what they were talking about up until this moment. "Your *book*. Cottry, can you enlighten my brother as to the whereabouts of his book?"

Mr. Cottry slid him an unamused look but replied evenly. "I believe Farraday has it, Mr. Turner."

"Farraday has it?" Mark echoed. "Why ever would Mr. Farraday have it?"

Ash gestured at Cottry.

"Mr. Farraday," Cottry said simply, "is making a copy."

The fury on Mark's face smoothed out into gratifying confusion. He glanced from Ash to the clerk and then back again, but made out nothing other than careful blankness.

"Well, then." Mark's hands unclenched. "Why is he making a copy?"

Ash leaned back in his chair. "So I can read it. Obviously."

There was a reason he loved tweaking his younger brother. Mark's mouth dropped open in stunned bewilderment. And then his eyes lit with every ounce of the happiness that Ash had wanted to see.

"But—but—you!" Mark shook his head. "I could kill you, if I didn't want to hug you right now. You great big bullying angel."

"One day, Mark, you will doubtless discover that I am not a particularly cruel man, dedicated to frustrating your every ambition. I actually would like to help you with your chosen career. Even the parts that make me uncomfortable. You want me to read your work? Then I'll read it. You had only to ask." He wasn't sure precisely how he was going to keep that promise, but he would find some way to accomplish it.

Mark inhaled. "But—this is just draft form, Ash. I still have so many changes to make, so much work still to be done. You'll tell me if there are any parts that don't make sense, will you?" Protests finished for the mere sake of form, Mark ducked his head shyly. "When do you think Farraday will be finished with his copying?"

"Cottry?"

"He'd finished the first ten pages when I left him an hour ago. It's slow going, sir. He keeps being overcome with laughter."

"About *chastity?*"

"Apparently so."

Mark's face lit even more, but he looked down at the floor and blushed, as if he were a schoolboy unused to praise. He *couldn't* understand what Ash had just promised to do. Ash might as well have offered to send him to Jupiter for a brief visit. But then, if Mark had wanted to flap his wings and embark on a voyage to distant planets on holiday...

Well. Ash would have found a way.

CHAPTER EIGHT

THE CANDLELIGHT CAST flickering shadows in Margaret's father's room, doing little to combat the dusk. Margaret tapped her foot impatiently as she studied the man. He sat, his hands clasped together, not looking at her. As if he were unaware of her presence.

"The maids say you are making faces at them." Margaret set her hand on her hip and tried to look forbidding. Likely, it only scrunched up her face. It was rather difficult to discipline a man more than three times her age, especially when he had nothing to lose.

"Bah" was her father's less-than-articulate response. He sat staring up at the ceiling, his gaze tracing the gilded plaster.

"*Unnatural* faces. You're scaring them."

"They're too easily frightened, then. I want servants, not rabbits." He glared at her, as if it were somehow her fault that he'd upset the household.

"Must you be so difficult about everything? Don't you think you've caused enough hardship already?"

The lines on his cheeks deepened as he settled in for a protracted bout of glowering. "Oh, no," he said sullenly, folding his arms about his skinny chest. "Am I making your life difficult, Anna?"

Margaret dropped her hand in the act of reaching to smooth out his hair. Instead, she turned to the bottles on the table at the side. There were six or seven of them, all lined up. It was her task to make her father take his medicines. Today it looked as if she was to have a battle on her hands. She unstoppered the first, pulling the cork out with perhaps more vengeance than the bottle deserved. The liquid sloshed with the fury of her movement, and as it did, the fumes from the acrid mixture seemed to burn directly from her nostrils into her brain. She stifled a cough.

"Don't call me Anna," she said, once she was sure she could speak without sounding upset. She poured out a generous spoonful of dark green liquid. "Nobody calls me that."

"I named you, Anna. I can call you what I wish. If I wanted to rename you something utterly horrid—something like—"

Margaret tightened her grip on the spoon and turned slowly back to him. "Margaret. You used once to call me Margaret."

"Only because Anna was your mother's name. As she's dead now, I see no reason to—mmph!"

He glowered at her again as she popped the spoon between his lips. For a second, the nasty medicine did the trick, and he simply screwed up his nose in silent, undignified protest. She pulled the spoon away—and he spat it out. Green viscous liquid sprayed in her face.

Margaret's hands trembled as she reached for a cloth. She could not do him violence. She could not. He was old. He was frail. He was her *father.* She wiped the disgusting residue from her eyes, and then looked at him. He sat, his smile perhaps a bit broader than before, his arms folded once more in self-satisfaction.

"It is almost as if you were five years old." She spoke calmly, but inside, she was fuming. "Do you know what happens to five-year-olds who do not take their medicine?"

He gave her a cold smile. "Let me guess. They are told to behave in a very stern tone of voice by someone who has no ability to control them?"

Margaret reached for the bottle and uncorked it a second time.

"No," she said sweetly. "They have it administered again."

It took seven tries and the better part of an hour to force the medicine down his throat. A year ago, she would never have been able to grapple him into sub-mission. He would have fended her off with one hand. But now, when he brought his right hand up to push at her in annoyance, she barely noticed his efforts. The difficulty lay in forcing his lips open and getting him to swallow. On the final try, she tilted his head up, held his nose and rubbed his throat until he gagged it all down.

"There," she said briskly, closing up the bottle. "Only slightly less exasperating than dosing a cat. You should be proud of yourself."

He cast her a baleful glare when she finally stepped back. "I don't want any more medicine," he whined, his voice a thin, reedy echo of what it had once been. "I don't want *you* anymore, either. You're sacked. You're *all* sacked, this entire household."

"You can't sack me. I'm your daughter, not your servant."

"Hmm." He frowned at her again as she straightened the bedclothes about him. "Well, I refuse to acknowl-edge you, then. I don't *have* to."

"Congratulations," she offered dryly. "I'm so dis-tressed." She turned to the basin to wash her hands and her face. The last of the sticky green residue that had stuck to her eyelids disappeared in a swirl of cold water.

It was at this moment that a scratch sounded at the door. She turned in confusion, but it was already opening—Tollin, one of the footmen who was stationed outside her father's rooms in the evening, had swung it wide.

Ash stood in the doorway. He'd shed coat and cravat for the evening, and the sight of him in white linen shirtsleeves only emphasized how broad his shoulders were. Her face felt sticky and hot all over again. She *had* gotten all the green liquid off. Hadn't she?

"Miss Lowell," he said formally. Not *Margaret;* not with another servant and her father present. "I've something I need to discuss with Parford. Do you suppose now would be a good time?"

It was coming on evening. Her father was difficult—but then, he grew in difficulty with every passing day. As if to underscore that, the duke gave a sharp, negative jerk of his head. He was alert, active and irascible. There would never be a good time.

"Of course," Margaret said. "He would love to talk with you. I wish you the best of luck. If you can get him to converse in an intelligent fashion for more than five seconds altogether, you will have my greatest admiration and astonishment."

"Hmm." Ash met her eyes. "Now that would be a prize worth having, wouldn't it?"

She had no response to that. She simply gestured him in. He entered, brushing past her as he did so. As before, he looked around the room. It hadn't changed much. The chamber was still littered with basins and bottles of medicines. A table stood by her father's bedside. In preparation for the evening, he'd shed the Parford signet—a gold ring, crowned by a sapphire. The blue stone had been carved with the stylized sword that graced the Parford coat of arms. Margaret had played with it, once, as a child. It had seemed large in her hands then—massive and weighty.

When Ash picked it up and turned it over, it seemed a tiny thing. He slid it onto his finger—but it stuck at his first knuckle.

"Ha!" her father said. "Sent that off to the jeweler months ago, to have it resized to fit my hands in my illness." He spread his fingers, thin insubstantial sticks. "It won't fit you now. Not until I'm dead."

Ash pursed his lips at this morbid observation, but simply set the ring back on the table. "Oddly," he said, "I've come to speak to you about that."

"My death? How kind of you to inquire. When I expire, I should like to have two women in my bed, both naked—"

Margaret had never felt gratitude quite so intense when Ash raised his hand. That was not an image she wanted embellished upon.

"I came here to examine the books, to make sure the entailed properties were not despoiled before I took title."

"What of it?" her father asked. "Why should I care?"

"Because by my estimation, the *unentailed* properties amount to little more than a few thousand pounds."

So little? It made Margaret feel almost dizzy. Why, Richard and Edmund would not just be demoted to commoners—they would be almost *poor*. As for herself…

Ash continued, not realizing he was detailing the grim state of her possible future. "Most of the estate's excess wealth came from your second marriage, and with that dissolved, the money returns to her family. What other provision have you made for your children?"

Her father leaned back. "Welcome to your revenge, Turner. You begged me to help your family, and I did not. Now you have the satisfaction of reducing mine to penury. There's an admirable symmetry. Do you enjoy it?"

Ash looked at her father for a very long time. He seemed transformed from the warm, easy man she was beginning to know. Instead, his eyes glittered, hard and cold as jet. "Yes," he finally said. "Yes, I do. I will enjoy making your pitiful children an allowance. I will relish being the one person who stands between them and penury. Every single quarter, they will know they live at my mercy. So yes, Parford, I *am* enjoying the chance to prove that I'm your superior. And all you need to do to guarantee their future is this: ask me for it."

Margaret's stomach hurt. It was so easy to forget that Ash hated her family. Her father. That if he knew who she was, he would never speak with her again—or would ask her to beg, in that cold, calculating tone.

But her father seemed unaffected. "Ask you for what?"

"Ask me for their future. No need to grovel. No need to beg. All you need to guarantee their financial security is to deliver one sentence. Consider using the word *please*."

Her father looked up. He looked behind Ash and found Margaret standing in the shadows. She couldn't imagine what he saw in her. Her hands felt cold. The color had no doubt drained from her cheeks. She knew that Ash was as good as his word—if he said he would care for her brothers, he would.

"So all I have to do," her father mused, "is just mouth a few words, and you'll provide for my brats?"

Ash nodded.

If Ash's gaze had seemed hard stone, her father's was glass, clear and cutting. "No," he said quite distinctly. "I don't believe I will. My children are all imbeciles. I said I would sack the lot of them if I could." He looked up at Margaret as he spoke, a faint air of triumph about him. "And look at this. I can."

It took her a moment to understand what he'd said. What he'd done. And when she did—when he betrayed her so easily once more, for nothing but a fit of pique— she couldn't bear it any longer. If Ash were to turn around in that moment and see her face, he would know everything.

She couldn't stay. And so she turned and fled.

ASH TURNED AT THE SOUND of her footsteps, but he saw nothing more than the swish of Margaret's gray skirts as she slipped through the door. He wasn't sure why she was leaving. And he didn't know why the few brisk steps he saw her take made him think of some palpable hurt.

It was hardly the first time she had confused him. He knew just enough to understand that he didn't understand her. He felt as if he had walked into an opera in the midst of the second act. He was baffled by the relationships on the stage, confused as to the particulars of the plot, and unlikely to decipher what had come before, as the libretto had been written entirely in Estonian. He could only surmise that she'd been wounded—deeply wounded.

When he was around her, he felt as if he were falling. As if he had once misstepped, and now, no matter how hard he tried, he could never quite set things right again. He just didn't know *why*.

The problem with working off instinct was that he wasn't always certain what he was working *towards*. He'd known he wanted her in his bed. But he was beginning to realize that he wanted more. He wanted to rid her of those lines around her eyes. He wanted to soothe the clench of her fists. He wanted to draw her to him, as gently as he could. And once he had her there...

Ash shook his head and looked up. It had been only a moment since the door had closed behind her, but Parford was looking at him. Watching Ash watch the place where she'd been.

The duke smiled knowingly, as if he knew what Ash was only just coming to realize: he *was* falling. Harder and faster than he'd anticipated.

"Now *that*," Parford said, "is truly amusing. All that effort to set yourself above me, and what has it got you?"

Ash cast him a dirty look. "After what *you've* done to the dukedom, I could hardly sully it further."

Parford waved his hand. "No, no. Carry on." It took Ash a moment to realize that the hoarse wheeze that emanated from his chest was a guffaw. "Good luck, Turner." He shook his head. "For all the good it will do you."

Ash stared at him one moment longer. It took only that instant to crystallize what was important. Not a further attempt to bludgeon some kind of an apology from this old washed-up scarecrow of a man, but to find Margaret. She'd left because she was hurt, and a large part of that had been this man's fault.

He left the room after her. He could still hear her footsteps in the gallery; he quickened his pace, turning the corner just as she reached the staircase.

"Margaret." He called as loudly as he dared, which was not loudly at all.

She stopped and turned to him. She seemed a little dazed, unwilling to look at him. But she stopped, at least, staring at the painting nearest her on the gallery wall. He walked towards her, unsure how to proceed.

"What is it," she finally asked, "between you and Parford? That seemed as if it were the tenth such disagreement, not the first."

Ash wanted to ask her the same question. "When I was young, my mother began to go mad. She sold the family concerns and gave what little funds remained to the poor. We went from living comfortably with a few scattered servants to living in squalor."

He didn't like remembering those days. He'd been so young and helpless then. He never wanted to feel that way again.

"My sister was bitten by a rat and developed a fever. And my mother refused to have a physician in. She claimed that if God wanted Hope to live, she'd do so. So I walked to Parford Manor, laid my claim of family before the duke, and begged for his intercession. For enough to pay a doctor, some medicine…for anything, really."

"Walked to Parford Manor? How far was it?"

He shrugged. "Twenty miles. It can be done."

"And how…how young were you?"

"Fourteen."

"Parford didn't provide any assistance."

"No. He laughed at me, and told me that the fewer Turners there were in this world, the happier he would be. And then he gave me a sixpence to hire myself a bath. So I returned home. Over the course of the next weeks, I watched my sister fade away. When she was gone—when she was buried outside the churchyard, in a pauper's grave—I vowed I would never be helpless again. I would never have to beg for my brothers' well-being."

She was watching him, her lips pressed together.

"What is it," he asked her, "between *you* and Parford?" He took another step towards her.

Her eyes widened, but she didn't move away. Instead, her expression darkened. "It was the duchess," she said quickly. "I can't bear it, some days. If he had any notion what he'd done to her, any sense of grief at her loss, perhaps I might be able to stand it. But…since he fell sick, he's become so…so selfish. So different. I couldn't bear to see him, unwilling to even lift a finger to help the ones he has most sinned against." Her voice choked with emotion, and she looked up at him. "I do not want to be like him." Her words sounded harsh. "I do not want to be the sort of person who casually abandons loved ones, merely because it is convenient or amusing to do so."

Ash still didn't quite understand. But in that reckless little speech, one thing had become clearer. "Who was he?" he asked.

"Who was whom?" She seemed wary and wound up, like some clockwork toy twisted to the breaking point.

"Who was he, who sinned against you?"

She did look up at him at that, and all that wary tension relaxed into sadness. "Who *wasn't* he?"

"He wasn't me, that's for damned sure."

Her lips parted. For one second, he almost thought she was going to contradict him. Instead, she shook her head. Her chin lifted in stubborn insistence. "If you must know," she said in cool, clipped tones, "he was my fiancé."

His blood stopped in his veins. When he spoke, the words seemed to come from very far away. "You have a fiancé."

"Not any longer."

His breath started again in painful relief.

"We were betrothed when I was nineteen. The betrothal lasted several years."

"Isn't that rather long for an engagement?"

"It's a delightful length for a man who doesn't wish to marry."

He itched to touch her, to run his hand down her spine until her eyes warmed. "Is it churlish of me to admit I'm glad you cried off?"

"Not churlish. Just not…based in truth. A year ago, when he visited, I brought the matter to a head, to see if he ever really intended to marry me. It was not the first time I had asked. But it was the most forceful."

"And he admitted he had no intention of doing so."

"Wrong again, Mr. Turner. He insisted he intended to do so in his own good time. He was more than willing to give me a token of his good intentions." Bitter disdain touched her voice.

"I take it his token was not a wedding date."

"No. It wasn't. His logic went something like this:

once he deflowered me, I could trust his word as a gentleman that he'd do right by me. Eventually."

"Christ." Ash simply stared at her. He could imagine how that had transpired. It was not a true betrothal she was talking about; it was a secret one. So secret, apparently, that the man forgot to mention it to his friends or family. Nothing but an excuse to kiss her. Touch her. To *have* her, while sweeping her protestations under the rug. No doubt she'd been young and vulnerable when it had started, and as it had gone on, his lies had no doubt made her all the more vulnerable. No wonder she shied away from gentlemen who found her attractive.

"Pardon me," he said. "That has to be the most mangled logic I have ever heard. I have heard men say some damnably stupid things to get a woman in bed, but that particular line could win a prize in a tavern contest."

"And I believed him." Margaret spoke softly, but now he could hear that line of anger in her voice. "I *believed* him. And then I found out—" She stopped again, briefly, and collected herself. "I found out it was all lies."

He wanted to kiss her now. Not for pleasure. Not for the sensual joy of her. But for comfort. To tell her that not all men were untrustworthy liars. But that kiss would have been for his benefit, not hers. The last thing she needed now was more physical importunity. What she truly needed after that confession…

Ash sighed. "Was he at least any good at it?"

She choked and jerked away from him. "Ash," she said, her voice unsteady, "I just told you I was not a virgin. Half the men out there would believe that my virtue was gone. That it wouldn't be a rape if you took me, even if I protested."

What an appalling sentiment. "Well," he said after an awkward pause, "that answers my question. He was terrible."

She looked up at him, her eyes narrowed. He simply looked back at her, and waited for her breath to fall into evenness. *See? I shan't hurt you.*

"Yes," she said slowly, as if she were just realizing the truth of it. "He *was* terrible, wasn't he? In fact, he was really, really bad at it." As she spoke, a small smile touched her lips.

Perhaps it was the first time she'd discovered the power of words. No doubt the memory had been a source of torment for her. It always helped to be able to place the blame squarely where it belonged, instead of allowing it to eat you up inside.

"Was it painful?" he asked.

She looked down. "It was boring," she finally admitted. "All that fuss—and once he got started, all I could think was, my God, when is this going to be over?"

Ash tamped down a smile. She wasn't going to find it boring with him. He was going to worship her, from the smooth column of her neck to the tight rosettes of her nipples. He was going to set her aflame, coaxing every last desire from her body.

She tilted her head up to look at him. No, not just *look;* she was studying him, as if he were a painting whose import she had yet to divine. Her eyebrows drew down in puzzled slashes. And then, slowly, she lifted her hand.

He didn't dare breathe. He felt as if he'd spent weeks leaving crumbs for a bird, only to have it land on a stone wall beside him. It was hell to keep still, to *wait* for that moment. But then she brushed her fingers down the side of his face and it was sweet heaven. Her touch was wary, as if she feared a sudden movement on his part. His hands clenched at his sides. God, he wanted to touch her back. He wanted to grab her to him, to press his body against hers. He wanted that kiss against his lips.

But it was exploration, as she tentatively stroked the line of his jaw. When she traced the contours of his lips, she was asking him a question. *Am I safe with you?* And no matter that he wanted to wrap her in his arms and hold her close, he could have only one answer for her. *Yes, darling. Always.* Even more than he needed the feel of her lush body beneath his, even more than his thumbs yearned to part the slick depths of her sex, he wanted her to be sure of him. It was as if she were seeing him for the first time. As if he'd been veiled in mists all the days of their acquaintance and she was only now making out his features.

These tentative caresses were discovery on her part. Not seduction. This wasn't seduction.

But damn it, he was seduced anyway. She stepped in closer—so close her skirts brushed his trousers, so close that it would be the work of a moment to trap her in his arms. He had a vast well of patience to call upon. But beneath it all, a deeper current welled up. He wanted her. Not just this tremulous reconnaissance. He wanted more than the feel of her body clasping his, more than the certainty of her physical surrender. He wanted to possess *all* of her—from her fierce loyalty to the wary strength he sensed hidden inside her.

Her hands drifted down to his shoulders. He'd shed his jacket long before, but even through his satin waistcoat, he could feel the warmth of her fingers. They pressed down on him as she lifted up onto her toes. She leaned into him, her breasts sliding against him, her arms coming round his neck. Her lips were a light flutter against first his chin, then his cheek. He bowed his head, trading every ragged exhalation with her. If she pressed against him just a little more, she would know just how badly he wanted her. He was painfully, exquisitely erect.

And she wanted him, physically. He could not miss the signs—the flush on her cheeks, the unsteady rhythm of her breath. The sway of her body against his.

Her lips found his, and a stab of exquisite desire shot through him. Finally. Endlessly. *This* was what he had been waiting for, all this time. Not a stolen embrace, to be wrested from her in the dark of night. A gift, freely given. One that he would keep forever in some small part of his soul.

Damn. He wanted to grab her to him and show her precisely how not-boring he could be. His hands clenched at his sides.

She subsided onto her toes and looked up at him.

She'd been hurt—badly. So badly that tonight may well have been the first time she'd taken that memory out and given it a firm shake. It had made her feel helpless, vulnerable. Ash knew that feeling. He hated it. He also knew how to banish that feeling of powerlessness: promise that it would never happen again, and make good on that promise through action. She'd given him a kiss. He could give a gift in return.

He reached out and touched her nose. "You told me once I was the most cheerfully ruthless man you'd ever met. Well, sweetheart, how would you like to see what happens to men who bore you? Shall I destroy him for you?"

Her eyes widened. "I haven't even told you his name."

"Really?" He favored her with a droll look. "A years-long engagement, formed young—likely kept secret, for you not to have brought the point upon him. A *gentleman,* you claim. How many gentlemen have you met, Miss Lowell, here at Parford Manor?"

She blinked at him in confusion. Perhaps she hadn't realized how much she'd revealed. It was all of a piece. What sort of man would so cavalierly treat a woman that way? There was the secrecy. The willingness to say anything, just to get a taste of female flesh. These facts all pointed in one direction.

"Oh, I can guess the identity of your hapless fiancé easily enough. It must have been either Richard or Edmund Dalrymple."

Her lips parted, and she took a step back. "No," she said. "Oh, no."

"Oh, yes," Ash said softly. "And now that I know about it, I do believe I'll destroy them both."

CHAPTER NINE

As Margaret left her father's chambers the next evening, she could not even pretend that she'd spent the day doing anything other than thinking of Ash. He presented a confusing mix of pain and pleasure to her. Pain, because he'd taken from her everything that once she'd thought mattered—because he still opposed her brothers' attempt to win back their place in society.

She'd done her best last evening to dissuade him from taking revenge on her brothers. But he'd lured her into telling him a piece of the truth. He'd seemed so safe, so trustworthy, that she'd almost forgotten who he was. Then he'd blamed her brothers—as if they would ever do such a thing—and she'd remembered all too well why she needed to keep her distance. But despite that pain, there was pleasure, too. Everything she'd once thought had mattered—her family name, her position—had washed away. Ash had looked past her ruin and seen someone important.

She walked through the gallery, the sunset painting the walls in variegated shadows—not dark, not light, but a dizzying blend of the two, echoing the muddle in her mind.

She wanted him to be right. She needed him to be wrong. And while that sounded as if she were confused, *confusion* implied uncertainty. And Margaret was dead certain that he was both the last man on earth that she *should* kiss, and the only one she dreamed of holding.

A little defiance. That's what he offered her.

A few kisses. A handful of stolen evenings. A few nights in which she might rebuild her shattered confidence. And in the end, it wouldn't matter, because their flirtation could never outlive the truth. He liked her only so long as he was ignorant about her.

The door to his chambers was thrown open to the gallery in silent, beckoning invitation. Margaret was beckoned—first by the warm lamplight, casting shadows against the walls. But as she crept to the doorway and peered inside, she was beckoned by him, too. He sat in a chair, his back to her, so that she could see nothing but the dark curl of his hair. She yearned to feel those strands against her fingers. To touch him, as she had yesterday evening. Except this time, more.

She tiptoed forwards.

He was frowning at a book. More were stacked on the table before him. As she padded up silently behind him, she could make out what he was reading: a text on agriculture—something about soil. By the pristine condition of the binding and the uncut pages, the book was new. He rubbed at his forehead testily and frowned at the page.

It was nearly nine in the evening, and far from drinking spirits, he was learning about farming. It took Margaret a moment to understand the twinge of pain that flickered through her.

Her father's land steward had tried to impress upon him the importance of an understanding of agricultural theory. To the best of her knowledge, her father had never read any of the texts the man had offered. That, the duke had snorted, was why he *hired* keen young

fellows to manage his operation—so he wouldn't have
to do it himself and could spend his time cultivating
port instead of potatoes.

Ash shook his head, as if arguing with the words.
She padded closer behind him and glanced down at
the page. *The addition of lime to hard-used soil*—she
read, before his hand intervened, cutting off her view.
He spread the page flat and picked up the penknife.
His hands were large, broad, long-fingered.

A wisp of appreciation curled through her, as he
eased the knife into the crease of the uncut pages.
There was a gentleness to his movements. Despite his
size, despite the fact that his hand covered the bottom
half of the book, he moved carefully. Could any man
truly be as perfect as he seemed? And why had this
perfect man descended upon her family, destroying everything? Why couldn't it have been someone else?

The knife slid. But instead of parting the pages in
one smooth motion, his knife slipped, the page ripped
unevenly, and—

"Damn it," he swore, sticking his finger in his mouth
before the blood could well up. "*God* damn it."

Margaret felt herself smile, even though she knew
she shouldn't. Well. That answered the question of
whether Ash Turner was perfect. Thank God he was
not.

He pulled his finger from his mouth and searched
his pocket for a handkerchief. "Damn books. Damn
words. And libraries and cold dark rooms can go to
hell." He slammed the tome shut against the table—and
just as he did, he turned enough to catch Margaret's
eye.

He froze, his face a mask of obvious, inexplicable
guilt. His fingers splayed across the book's cover. They

lay there, still for just an instant too long, before he ran his hands down the leather that covered the front chapboards. He looked as embarrassed as a man caught beating a puppy, his fingers petting the pages in an insincere, unconvincing half caress.

Margaret's smile broadened.

He must have realized how ridiculous he appeared, because he shook his head. "No, madam," he said. "There's no problem here. We were having ourselves a friendly fight, we were—between me and this book." He drawled out those words, mirroring the accent of the local men, as if he were some common laborer caught by the tavern keeper in the act of raising a chair.

She converted the giggle that rose up into a ladylike clearing of the throat, and put her hand on her hip. "We won't stand for any trouble here, sir. Must I fetch the constable?"

He glanced at the book and then back at her. Finally, he sighed. "I can tie fifteen different sorts of knots, you know."

She wasn't sure what that had to do with the price of tea in agricultural texts, but she raised a single eyebrow at him.

"I can whittle a linked chain out of a single stick of wood."

"I'm sure you can."

"I can purchase goats in twelve different dialects of native India."

"Of course." She glanced at him. "You must have a great many goats, then."

He heaved himself to his feet and turned away from the book—and towards her. Her toes curled unconsciously in her slippers as he fixed that gaze on her. There was no trace of humor on his face.

"But you've just stabbed yourself while cutting pages in a book. Oh, dear, Mr. Turner. An imperfection. Whatever will you do?"

He didn't smile in response. Instead, he rubbed his hands together. On another man, that gesture might have betrayed nervousness. But Margaret couldn't imagine strong Ash—gentle Ash—*confident* Ash— having anything so crass as nerves.

He scrubbed his hand—his unstabbed hand, that was—through his hair. "I suppose it's just as well you find out."

"Mr. Turner," Margaret started. She stopped as his eyes narrowed at her. "Ash," she continued. "Perhaps you may not have realized this, but I have discovered that you are imperfect before. This hardly comes as a surprise."

She *had* discovered it. Over the course of their acquaintance, she'd been made aware of the many, many ways in which he failed at perfection. It was just that he kept making her forget them all.

"All things between the two of us considered," he said slowly, "there is something else you ought to know." His eyes met hers. "It's rather a secret, and so I'd prefer you not spread it about."

He could not have been considering *all* things, since he didn't know who she really was. Still, his smile made her wish that he *did* know everything. And that, having been apprised of the truth, he still thought she was worthy to hear his secrets.

She felt a sick lump form in her throat. He might be the only person in the world who believed she mattered. It would be the most extraordinary gift she could imagine, if she told him who she was, and if he still looked at her with that light in his eyes—

"After all," he said with a wry shrug of his shoulders, "if the Dalrymples ever discovered this, they'd tear me to shreds and leave my corpse to be ravaged by buzzards."

—but no. He wouldn't.

"But I'm babbling," Ash said with a sigh. "Here it is." He swallowed and blew out his breath. "I can't read."

Margaret's wistful longings evaporated in a shocked curl of smoke. Her mouth dropped open, and before she could stop herself, a gasp escaped her.

"Oh, no," he said. "Not like that. I'm capable of making out words on a page. I know my alphabet. It's just…I am not any good at making sense of all those symbols. I can pick out words, but by the time I've got the next one down, I've practically forgotten the last. They never quite manage to coalesce into sentences." His voice was whisper-quiet, but he spoke with a dire urgency.

Of all the things Margaret could have imagined Ash telling her, this…this came dead last.

"But you're so…" Margaret waved a hand, almost futilely, trying to describe what she meant. "So competent."

There were a great many people who couldn't read. But most of them were chimney sweeps and milkmaids. Not heirs to dukedoms. Not nabobs from India, who had amassed personal fortunes in the hundreds of thousands of pounds.

"How have you possibly done all this?" She spread her arms wide as she spoke, indicating the library, the desk, the *account books* in front of him.

Ash shrugged and turned one shoulder away.

Margaret followed. "You're a successful business-man. You don't speak as if you were…"

He turned to her abruptly. "Stupid?" He was suddenly standing too close, his eyes tight, his lips compressed.

Margaret shook her head, unable to respond.

"Don't ask me to explain," he said. "I don't know what it is. I just can't understand words when they're written down. They feel slippery in my mind. Now, if someone were to have a conversation with me about any subject, I could follow along, and gladly. And, for some reason, numbers have never posed a problem. I can figure. But I can never understand the back-and-forth of negotiations if I cannot look a man in the eyes. *That's* what I need."

"But how is it that you never learned? Your father was a wealthy mill owner. Surely you had tutors. Some sort of education."

Ash shrugged. "I had a tutor. He taught me my let-ters. And once he realized there was a…a problem with the rest, he was as eager to hide the truth as I was. After all, if he couldn't teach a five-year-old child to read, he'd have been sacked for gross incompetence. After my father died, there were no tutors at all. Perhaps if I'd gone to Eton, as my brothers did, I'd have learned." He sounded dubious.

As he spoke, he looked into her eyes. Margaret shivered.

"Or perhaps I wouldn't have. Paper isn't enough for me. I need to see." His voice dropped low. "To hear. To smell." His gaze wandered down her face. She could feel a flush rise on her cheeks as he stopped at her lips. "To *taste*." He raised his eyes to hers again, and a small smile played across his face. "I can understand anything, if I but look it in the eyes."

She felt her chest expand on an inhale. The air was painful in the confines of her lungs. She knew *this* about him. He didn't even know her true name. "Ash," she said, her voice trembling, "that note I left you—I didn't know."

"I understood." His fingers constricted around hers. "Even on paper, I understood." He sat down again, this time sitting directly on the surface of his desk. As he did, his arm brushed hers.

"There you are," he said. "I'm not very ducal, am I? Tell me you'll keep my secret."

It was a measure of how deeply she had fallen under his spell, that she had not realized until this moment that she could use this against him. The news that Mr. Ash Turner had difficulty reading would send a ripple of consternation through the House of Lords. After all, how many bills would pass his desk for a vote? How many papers would he be expected to keep abreast of?

The truth would sink him, in their minds. Instantly and without question. Confirming a commoner as one of their own was one thing, if they begrudgingly admitted he had the bloodlines in his distant past. Confirming a near illiterate? It would never happen. They'd legitimize her brothers in an instant. She should have been singing for joy.

So why did she feel like weeping instead?

He gestured at the table. "One of my men is copying out the book Mark is writing," he said quietly. "I keep hoping that somehow, after everything I've accomplished, this time the words will come out right. I promised Mark, after all."

A flicker of emotion crossed his face—something powerful and vulnerable at the same time. The look of a man who had been knocked down but was determined to get up as many times as necessary to march on ahead.

"Besides," he added mulishly, "I heard that until Parford's setback, he spent hours in the evening in his study."

A hint of jealousy, too. She could take this opportunity to insinuate doubt into the conversation—something to magnify the vulnerability she saw on his face. It wouldn't take much. A sentence. A few words, even, to plant seeds of uncertainty in his mind.

That seemed a shabby recompense for what he'd given her.

Instead, Margaret took his hand. The cut across his palm was a brief line of red—not even bleeding. His fingers were warm and dry, and as she touched him, he lifted his eyes to hers. For all his vulnerability, there was an unquenchable relentlessness in his eyes. He wouldn't give up, no matter how much doubt she planted. And she didn't want him to give up on *her*.

She stood and silently tugged him to his feet and led him out the door. In the gallery, she dropped his fingers, lest a passing servant spot them. She padded through the columned space, Ash's footfalls echoing behind her.

She stopped at the door before her father's bedchamber and fumbled with her necklace.

The master key was still threaded through the chain, the iron skin-warm where it had lain against her breasts. The door opened inward on silent hinges.

"The duke's study," she announced. "Not currently in use."

He stepped inside; Margaret took a lamp from a nearby side table before entering herself. The light flickered unevenly as she walked.

"This," Margaret said, gesturing at a large wingback chair settled to the side of the room, "is the seat where Parford spent many an evening." She looked Ash in the eyes. "Sit," she commanded.

He sat.

"There, to your right, in that cupboard—those are the books Parford studied of an evening."

Ash glanced at her and then at the ornate brass knob on the carved doors. He hesitated.

"Go on, then. Open it."

The door opened silently.

Inside, her father's decanter stood next to three cups of cut glass. The glasses gleamed in the light. Amber liquid reflected the rays streaming from her lamp, setting colored lights to dancing about the room as she placed that lamp on the table.

"These books," Margaret said dryly, "you, too, could study."

"Oh." He glanced at them again and then back at her.

Margaret crossed to stand before him and then leaned and took a tumbler. She poured an inch into the glass and held it out to Ash.

"Here," she said. "This is the education most gentlemen receive at Oxford."

He stared at the glass in her hands for a few moments, and then shook his head. "No. I don't believe I will. I'm no Dalrymple, to put pleasure before duty."

She'd almost become inured to those comments about her family. "A shame," she said calmly. "I am."

"Putting pleasure before duty?" he asked quizzically.

No. A Dalrymple. But the moment passed, overtaken by her hesitation. Instead, she raised the glass to her own lips and took a sip. The taste of brandy overwhelmed her—dark, tawny, heady. The alcohol volatilized in her mouth. She swallowed, and it burned on the way down. Just one taste, but it was enough to sweep away her last lingering inhibitions. She set the glass down.

Before he could say anything, she leaned over him in the chair. She set her hands on the linen of his shirt, feeling the roughness of the fabric. She could feel the whisper of his breath, and it was sweeter and more invigorating than her sip of spirits.

Last night, she'd kissed him because he'd made her smile. Tonight, she kissed him to make him laugh. Her lips found his. He exhaled as she did so; she felt it, more than heard it, felt his chest heave under her hands, his lips part beneath hers. His hands came to her side, clasping her waist.

The kiss last night hadn't lasted long—just a brief, heated exchange of air, their lips mingling for a few seconds. This was more. His lips parted for her. His tongue slipped into her mouth.

He was a heady mixture of taste and scent. She could feel the hard planes of his chest, the muscles beneath her hands. She forgot about everything that had transpired between them. She forgot that anything stood between them, besides the fabric of his shirt, separating her hand from the thud of his heart. The brandy had entered her blood, and it rose, warm and pounding, to flush her cheeks.

Another caress of his tongue on hers. His hands

drifted up her sides, awakening a deep yearning inside her. It was a want so fundamental she could not imagine how it had remained dormant in his presence until now. A need to have him close. To press herself against him.

He drew her down to straddle him in his chair. Her skirts tangled about her; her knees brushed his thighs through her petticoats. It shouldn't have been possible, but her want intensified to a primal thing, one that couldn't be satisfied by just his caress against her ribs.

As if he could taste her desire on her lips, his hand inched up, slowly, until he cupped her breast. Thumb and forefinger rolled; she felt that touch clear through the layers of fabric. A shot of pleasure went through her. It was almost too intense, too intimate for her to bear. She pulled away, just so that she could steady her hands on his shoulders.

He stared up at her, and then slowly, slowly, he gave her a brilliant grin—one that lit the darkest corners of her wary soul. He was all light, no darkness. It was Margaret herself who cast shadows.

"I take it," he murmured, "this means my secret is safe with you."

She couldn't answer. Instead, she reached out and placed her fingertips against his lips. His breath heated them with a kiss. Before he could do more than give her a gentle nibble, she took them away and curled her hand into a fist. As if she could somehow protect that newfound intimacy from the cold world out there.

"I can't read books," he whispered, "but I have other skills. An instinct, if you will—this ability to *know* things, people, in the blink of an eye. It's how I made my fortune. It's how I knew, when I first saw you…"

He trailed off, and reached out and deliberately ran a finger down her arm. "I knew I could trust you," he explained. "Instantly. Irrevocably."

But she had made no promise.

Her heart constricted. How could he make her feel so warm and so cold, all at the same time? She gazed at him, her thoughts floundering somewhere between desire and despair. And then, because she had no answer for him, no answer even for herself, she leaned down and kissed him one last time.

I TAKE IT THIS MEANS my secret is safe with you.

Even half an hour later, seated alone in the tiny garret she'd adopted, Margaret could feel his body pressed against hers, his mouth on hers.

Until that evening, she'd never quite understood his smile. She'd thought his expression arrogant, overly familiar, assuming. Against her better judgment, she'd also found it attractive. But until that evening, she hadn't understood precisely how much uncertainty he hid behind it. She'd never before realized how much vulnerability he harbored.

But with her lap desk laid atop her knees, she was about to puncture those vulnerabilities, to betray that trust. The steel nib of her pen stood poised above her paper, ready to spill his story in India ink. A drop balled on the tip and fell to splash, deep black, against the page below.

Dear Richard.

Her brother. Her own *brother.* She'd grown up beside him. When she had been still in pinafores, his friend had called her a scraggly little thing, and Richard had punched him. If anyone in the world deserved her loyalty, it was Richard. She *had* to write this letter.

The next sentence would have been so simple.

Mr. Ash Turner is essentially illiterate.

If only she could write that down, her life would right itself. The Act of Legitimation would pass. She would be Lady Anna Margaret once more, and the dowry she'd been supposed to receive from her mother would be hers again. She could rejoin society; even if she never married, she need not live as her brothers' dependent for the rest of her life. A few droplets of ink, a little sand... Such tiny things could not amount to a betrayal. Not when it was her own brother she fought for. She dipped her pen with trembling hands.

Dear Richard,

There is something you need to know about Ash Turner. He is—

She set her pen to the paper to form the next word. But the nib would not move. A dark blotch of ink formed at the tip and spread, little threads of black weaving into the paper, mocking Margaret's inability to continue.

There was a reason she couldn't finish her sentence. It was because it wasn't true. Oh, the letter would be composed of entirely true things. But the import— that Ash Turner was incapable of serving as a duke— would be entirely false. It felt disloyal for her to reveal what he'd told her. It would have been wrong to betray his trust. Not when he'd looked at her and seen... everything.

I want you to paint your own canvas.

The paper waited patiently, ready to absorb her words. Whatever she wrote next, she would be painting it over, indelibly declaring her loyalty. It seemed utterly wrong to fill this space with lies about Ash. After all, he'd told her that she mattered.

He'd trusted her.

He'd broken her into pieces, and with one smile, he'd knit her back together again. There was no path of honor for her to tread, no way to be true to both her brothers and her own burgeoning sense of self-discovery. There was nothing left for her but a little defiance. Nothing left but to tell the truth. But whom would she defy? And, if she was picking amongst truths, which one could she pick for herself?

She stared at the inkblot spreading on the page, hoping to see some secret in its tangled darkness.

And when she dipped her pen again, what she wrote was this: *Ash Turner is a more conscientious man than Father ever was.*

She hadn't intended to write that sentence until her pen moved. But there it was, in solid letters on the page. It was truer than anything else she could have written. And she wasn't going to take it back.

In his first three days here, he solved that awful land dispute between Nelson and Whitaker. The land steward reports that he has already come up with a plan to modernize planting procedures. I know you hoped I would uncover some grave deficiency on his part, but we must face the truth. A man capable of building a financial empire from nothing has little to fear from the demands of the dukedom.

In fact, Margaret was beginning to entertain the sneaking suspicion that Ash would be a better duke than her eldest brother. Richard had always assumed that the ducal mantle would one day settle upon his shoulders; Ash had worked for everything he'd achieved. Richard believed that the running of the duchy was in his blood; Ash had no such preconceptions.

One could push a pack of truths together to make one despicable falsehood. She'd seen it, when it was done to her. Society had torn her reputation to tatters, starting with the truth that she was a bastard, and ending with whispered conversations, just loud enough for her to hear, stating, "I always knew there was something wrong with her."

Margaret set her pen down and shoved her lap desk to the side. This cramped room, practically in the rafters of the manor, was the best she could expect for her future, if her brothers' suit did not prosper. Duke's daughter though she was, she would likely have to enter service. She would become a governess, a companion, a nurse in truth.

There would be no fine dresses. No house of her own. She stood and walked to the window. It was a tiny slit, cut out like all the servants' windows from atop the roofs. Up here, the pigeons woke her in the morning with their squabbling.

It was night, and from the window she could see nothing but the thick velvet of mist, blanketing the rose garden her mother had loved. It had broken her mother's heart to discover that her son would not inherit these lands.

And yet Margaret thought it would break something even more fragile inside herself to betray Ash's secret in that horrible way, to expose it—and him—to the censure of Parliament. She could live without society's blessing. She could not live with her own condemnation.

Betraying Ash's secret would be like spilling dark paint on the picture of herself that she was only now beginning to comprehend.

And so she ended her letter to her brother with another truth—and a different kind of betrayal.

I'm sorry, Richard. I can't help you as we had hoped.

CHAPTER TEN

Disclosing his secret incompetence had made Ash feel more determined, not less. More determined that this time, if he tried hard enough, he would break through that hazy barrier of symbols, that he would see words and sentences instead of a shifting mass of ink. He'd finished his affairs for the day, and now it was time for more vital business: keeping his promise to his brother.

Everything he'd ever set out to accomplish, he had done. And while he hadn't been able to muster up the will to plow through an agricultural text, today he'd received something far more important—Mark's book, the copy finally finished.

Mark was different from agriculture. His book would naturally prove different. And Ash had made a promise. If he *wanted* it, he told himself, he would simply make it happen. There was no other choice.

Thus far, the force of his will had only managed to give him a raging headache. It shifted behind his eyes, the letters sliding off the page before he could pin them down, until all he wanted was to sleep—and he'd only managed to comprehend the first three syllables.

Well. Never mind with the title page—that wouldn't matter. It would all be better once he got to the meat of the argument. He flipped to the second page, ignoring the fact that it was filled with even more dauntingly squiggled ink.

He felt as if he were trying to catch pigs in the rain using only a pair of metal tongs. He barely recalled what each symbol stood for. Piecing them together into some semblance of coherent understanding was impossible.

It took him two full minutes to get through *Chapter. One. Chastity. Is.*

Before he could find out what chastity *was,* he heard footsteps behind him.

"Ash?"

Margaret's voice. Oh, hell. Ash inhaled in mingled hope and desperation. God knew it would take a miracle for him to bull his way through even the first page of Mark's book. He'd surely never manage it if Margaret distracted him with her lithe figure and the promise of more kisses. He shut his eyes, as much to ward off the incipient headache swimming behind his vision as to try to fend off that extra frisson of vitality he felt in her presence.

Behind him, he could hear her breath, could imagine the swell of her chest, rising and falling.

Shutting his eyes didn't help. He could still remember her intimate taste from last night—her mouth warmed by brandy tempered with a floral note, her body canted over his, pressing into him. But in the here and now, her hand touched his, and he reluctantly looked at her.

Even though he'd prepared himself, the sight of her still sent a little shock down his spine. Her lips were rose-pink, and oh-so-kissably full. A handful of kisses hadn't been enough. The faint color of her cheeks was broken up here and there by a hint of freckle. Her hair was braided and bound up, tight and proper, but her mouth pursed, and that hint of impropriety made him think of unlacing her from the confines of her gown, unpinning her curling hair…

Damn. He was distracted already.

"This," she said, tapping the pages in his hand, "is your brother's book. He mentioned to me earlier today you'd gotten the copy. He seemed nervous."

Ash spread the loose pages in his hands. "As you see," he murmured, "I've managed to take in so much of it already."

She bit her lip. "I thought I might read it to you."

The blood simply stopped in Ash's veins. His whirling thoughts came to a crashing standstill. His throat dried out, and he coughed. She looked down.

When he didn't respond, she glanced at him out of the corner of her eye. "I can see I've offended you. I didn't intend to imply— I apologize—"

"No." He choked the word out, and she drew back further. "I mean, no, don't apologize." He was stunned, too stunned to form a response. But he caught her hand in his. Their fingers intertwined, his grip saying what his mouth could not manage. He squeezed all his pent-up helplessness, his secret shame into her fingers.

"I promised Mark," he explained awkwardly. His inability to read was a guilty, secret part of him, something to be hidden away from the light of day under a mass of lies and misdirection. He'd invented excuse after excuse, pleaded his schedule a thousand times, ordered employees to summarize numerous documents.

But this…this, he couldn't hide.

She'd looked into his darkest degradation and whispered that he was not alone. Maybe this was what he'd felt, that fine morning when he'd first seen her out on the steps. He'd felt an echo of this moment—as if he were somehow, finally, coming home.

He nodded at Margaret. "Very well," he said. He knew his voice sounded harsh, almost devoid of emotion. It was merely because she had no idea how long he'd carried that burden in solitude. To think he might trust someone with his secret—and that she might offer to *help,* that she might bridge the gap between Ash and his brothers… He couldn't even contemplate it. If he hid behind gruffness, it was because his throat felt scratchy, as if he were on the verge of weeping.

Not that he would.

That would have been ridiculous. Almost as ridiculous as the rush of vulnerability that overtook him, as if he were some nocturnal insect blinded by the sudden light of her regard. If it had been anyone else at this moment, he might have scuttled away. But then…it was Margaret.

Instead he simply nodded at her. She took the pages from him and shuffled them into order.

"A Gentleman's Practical Guide to Chastity," she began to read. "By Mark Turner." She cocked her head and looked at Ash. "A *practical* guide to chastity? What does that mean?"

Ash shrugged. So that was what the words on the front page had said. "I suspect we are about to discover that." He put his hands on the arms of his seat, readying himself. It may have been a dry philosophical text of intellectual import, but it was his *brother's* dry philosophical text. He was *not* going to think about the juxtaposition of her full lips and the words of chastity. He was *not* going to make some juvenile witticism.

"'Chapter One,'" Margaret read. "'Entitled: Chastity is hard.'"

Ash sniggered despite himself. So much for keeping his juvenile thoughts at bay. "Yes," he murmured. "*Hard* is usually how I find myself after an unfortunate bout with chastity."

She flicked a glance at him, her lips curving upwards in amusement, and then she shook her head and read once more. "'Too often, moralists stress the need for upright behavior. But this emphasis is often impractical in its effect. When a man fails to meet one overly rigorous standard, his usual reaction is to give up on all of them.'"

With the words spoken aloud, Mark's book wasn't hard to follow. In fact, it even made sense. Ash nodded, and Margaret went on.

"'For instance, we have all heard that if a man lusts after a woman, he has already committed adultery in his heart. This admonition is rooted in good intentions—after all, one ought to keep one's thoughts uplifted at all times. Unfortunately, the base male mind, always keen on having its own way, often inverts the principle. *Well,* a man reasons to himself, *if I am already damned for committing adultery in my heart, I might as well have the enjoyment of committing adultery in the flesh.*'"

Ash let out a surprised bark of laughter—both because what his brother said was all too true, and because he could see Mark saying those words, his face lighting with irrepressible good humor. Margaret was smiling as she read, too. Dimples had come out on her cheeks.

He liked her dimples.

"'The truth,'" she intoned, "'is that chastity is *hard*. It is particularly hard for the young, unmarried gentleman who is besieged on the one hand by admonitions that he not even so much as *consider* a woman's ankle, and on the other, by invitations to avail himself of the great multitude of opportunities available to any man with a few coins to his name. For most such young gentlemen, a choice between the impossible and the pleasant is no choice at all. That is why I have written this first *practical* guide to chastity.'"

"You know," Ash remarked, "my brother is either going to win instant accolades with this book, or he's going to be charged with blasphemy and these pages will join Thomas Paine and *Fanny Hill* on the list of forbidden titles."

"Both, in fact, are possible." Margaret stared at the pages in her hand. "For a book on chastity, he has already touched on adultery and ankles. It seems surprisingly outré, given the subject matter."

"Only because you're reading it. The word *ankle* is a thousand times more provocative when spoken by a beautiful woman."

A light flush touched her cheeks. But she gave him a dry stare. "Do stop these compliments, or I might find myself sinning in my heart instead of reading."

"Are you just starting that, then? My heart has been sinning for a very long time." The dimple on her cheek deepened, but she pursed those sensual lips in a pretense of primness and gathered up the pages again.

"Now, where were we? Ah, yes. 'I have written this first practical guide to chastity.'"

Her voice was warm and filled with humor. As she spoke, she lifted her slippered foot, pointing her toe and then flexing it in an unconscious rhythm. Every so often, the slipper would fall, and he'd catch a glimpse of her bare foot. Not so much skin to get excited about, but then, it was *her* skin. And her ankle.

Mark was right. Thoughts of ankles lead to thoughts

of pushing skirts aside, following the line of that leg...

She read on.

When she spoke of sin, he thought of her. When she mentioned chastity, breathing the word at him over lowered eyelashes, she could not help but evoke thoughts of the opposite. Her voice was low and seductive, and Ash realized that his brother was right. Chastity was hard.

He was ready to take her to his bed now.

She must have felt his eyes on her, because halfway through, she glanced up at him and stopped speaking. Her tongue darted out to touch her lips, and he could not help but imagine the softness of that caress against his aching erection. And if he had been stiff before, he was rigid now.

"Ash?" she asked uncertainly. "Shall I continue?"

He cleared his throat. "I'm listening."

It wasn't just her voice or the words that brought him to this fist-clenching arousal. It was the intimacy of what they were doing. They were separated by three feet, yes. But he'd admitted to her his most private secret, and instead of flinching from him in horror, she'd made him feel whole in a way he'd never felt before.

That intimacy made a subtle, erotic counterpoint to her reading on chastity—through page after page, punctuated by her laughter mingled with his.

He hadn't realized how funny his brother was. Oh, he'd known Mark had a sharp wit and a flair for a turn of phrase, but this was that keenness of observation, condensed. The work reminded him of his brother: chaste, moral...and yet tinged with a sense of humor that elevated the pages from sober rectitude to something almost wicked.

Margaret turned to the last page that had been copied from Mark's manuscript.

"'There is no need to belabor the reasons for chastity, of course. But as a mere reminder to my readers, I outline the most important points. Male chastity is absolutely vital for three reasons.'"

Vital was the shape of her lips, making those words. *Vital* was that flash of skin covered by silk, peeking from under the dark hem of her dress. *Vital* was the ache he felt, something deeper than the mere wants of his flesh.

"'First,'" Margaret said solemnly, "'it is commanded by God and Holy Scripture.'"

Ash waved a hand.

"'Second,'" she started, and then stopped. The amused light in her eyes faltered. She glanced over at him, suddenly wary. "'Second,'" she said, "'profligacy in such relations causes harm to the families who must endure such infidelity, and to the children who result from the union.'"

He had forgotten that *she* was illegitimate. But was that something she could overlook? Her life would have been very different, had matters been otherwise. He wanted to say something to her, to remind her how little such things mattered to him. But she set her chin stubbornly, bent her head and read on.

"'And third—and most important to a chaste, practical gentleman—'" Her eyes scanned ahead once more, but this time she burst out laughing.

"What? What is it?"

She didn't respond for a few seconds, but her shoulders shook with mirth. When she finally spoke, she could barely force the words out. "'Third, as the ladies have clearly mastered the female art of chastity, our masculine inability to control our urges rather weakens our claims to be the stronger sex.'" She looked up at Ash. "He's not serious. Truly?"

Of course Mark wasn't. It was a subtle joke, precisely the sort of sly, tongue-in-cheek suggestion his brother might drop. But a more serious-minded audience might take his words to be pure truth.

Ash shook his head. "That alone will get him banned."

"I've lost count of the number of times your brother has made me laugh. Chastity is far more amusing than I had anticipated."

"Chastity," Ash said dryly, "is far more *arousing* than I had anticipated."

Margaret flushed. She sat primly on the velvet sofa, and at his words, she rearranged her ankles underneath her. "I do believe we are straying into the improper," she said.

"Oh, no," he contradicted. "We aren't straying. I had hoped we had embarked on a deliberate voyage."

Her slipper fell off her foot once more. She didn't even seem to notice; instead, she felt about for it on the ground with her foot, her toe pointed, revealing her ankle beneath the edge of her gown. And suddenly he could think of nothing but sliding his hands up the sinuous curve of her calf.

"A voyage?" she asked, her voice shaky. "But…but we can have no mutual destination."

Clearly she'd not realized they'd left the docks behind days before. "It's not about where we go, but how we arrive." Slowly. At great length, savoring every last inch of her skin.

She bit her lip, perhaps balancing her sense of propriety with her desire. And then she leaned forwards, canting towards him. As she did so, the bodice of her gown shifted. The lamplight caught the curves of her bosom. The strangled noise he heard must have issued from his own throat.

"When you do that, I can see." He made a gesture in the direction of her cleavage. "At least, I can see more."

She drew a deep breath. Her hand raised one inch, as if to block his view, but then she let her arm fall to her thigh. And then—oh, God—she leaned another inch towards him. She crooked one finger at him, and he found himself standing, drifting towards her. She licked her lips, and then she whispered, "Come here and kiss me."

He was transfixed: by the lamplit swell of her breasts, barely visible above her neckline, by the damnably enticing rose of her lips, by the clarity of her eyes, untouched by her usual grief. She smiled at him—an expression both shy and brazen, a smile as old as woman herself.

"You should always be like this," he said roughly.

"Forward?"

"Sure of yourself. Powerful. Unshadowed."

She shook her head. "I'm not sure of *myself,* Ash. I'm just…just…"

"You're sure of me."

Her head jerked up. She looked at him in surprise, and then, slowly, she nodded. "Yes. Because you'll understand the spirit in which this is offered. You'll know what it means to me."

"And what will it mean?" His breath caught, hurting him. "What will I mean to you?"

She looked into his eyes. "Oh, you told me that the first day I met you. Do you not recall what this is about? 'A little defiance,' you said. That's what I want from you. A little defiance. I want to know what it *should* be like. What I should have had, when I lost...lost it all."

Defiance. He swallowed. It wasn't enough for him— not anymore. He wanted to be more than her defiance. He wanted to be her strength, her amusement. He wanted to be her lover. He wanted to be her every wicked desire and her safe haven, all at once.

But if what she wanted at the moment was *defiance*... Well, he could give her that, too. Until she was ready for everything else.

He reached out and took her hands in his, pulling her to her feet. Her fingers trembled in his. He didn't want to know what memories plagued her. He just wanted her to forget them. She reached up on her toes and leaned into him, her breasts brushing against his chest, her fingers intertwining with his.

He couldn't help himself.

He kissed her. Hard, too; his mouth met hers with open lips, taking her with a ravenous intensity. He'd held back from her for too long, had held back this kiss, until it broke over him with all the ferocity of a summer storm. He was the lightning striking fertile ground, the hard rain driving into a field. And if he was a bolt of energy, swift and sure, she was the thunder, a low, powerful rumble that passed through him and stood his hairs on end.

Her lips were the welcoming fields, parched for his rain. She fit him, her body molding to his, her lips latching on to his. Her hands ran up his arms to his shoulders; he enfolded her in his embrace. He was hot and rigid for her, had been ever since she'd spoken about ankles. Her body cradled his erection, even through all the layers of their clothing. He could feel the rub of the fabric, harsh friction against his member.

He kissed her and with his fingers he sketched what he wanted from her. He traced her cheeks, and willed the sadness in her eyes to be swept away in the tumultuous aftermath of passion. His hand painted a line down her spine, inch by inch, and spoke of his desire to have her naked in his arms. He wanted *her,* needed her, with a sheer animal intensity that would not be gainsaid.

It was that sheer want that led his hand to her breast, that unthinking desire that made him touch her there. It was lust, pure and simple, that guided his hand to that curve. But her response—that sweet arch of her spine— meant more to him than mere lust. It was desire, yes. But it was also a recognition, twanging through him, a poignant acknowledgement that with her, he could be vulnerable.

He could barely feel the shape of her beneath her corset, but he could imagine the peak of her nipple. He could feel her response as he circled that bud with his fingers, could feel the desire in her kiss increase in intensity. She leaned against his hand. It was a form of trust.

He'd already trusted her with far more than his bodily response. Somehow, he guided her back onto the sofa. Somehow, he straddled her, loosened the sash of her dress, and then, one by one, undid the little buttons of her bodice. It was rough work, his hands jostling with every breath she took. Somehow, he finished— and thanked the Lord for a front-lacing demi-corset, finer than he'd imagined a nurse would wear. The ivory flowers underneath her dress seemed like a feminine little secret, one known by just the two of them. He unlaced this to reveal a thin shift, beneath which he could make out the dusky pink tips of her nipples—a darker rose than her lips, but begging for his kiss just the same.

He gave it, taking that peak in his mouth, while his hands slid down to her waist.

She moaned and rolled beneath him, her hips cradling his frame, his erection pressing into her thigh. He could have tasted her forever, could have let the feel of her seep into him. She came alive beneath him, pressing up. And he needed more. He lifted his lips from the curve of her breast to kiss her lips again. It was maddening, utterly maddening, to have her so close and yet so far from him. He pulled away from her—only for a moment, only long enough to set his hands on her ankles. And then he traced the perfection of her skin up, up, up the curve of her calves, to her knees.

Her skirt slid up, and still she didn't pull away from him. She hadn't flinched. Instead, she threw her head back and parted her thighs at his invasion. Her legs—God, the feel of them, warm and round and long and slim beneath his palms. He pushed a mess of petticoats out of the way.

He could have adored her knees until dawn came. He would have, had the rest of her not been so compelling. Her thighs, trembling at his touch. And then he rearranged her drawers and discovered the damp curls between her legs, the folds of her sex, wet with desire. He parted her and ran his thumb along the seam. She was rosy-pink there, too. The scent of her feminine musk overwhelmed him.

It would take so little to make her *his*. His thumb paused on her flesh. Belatedly, he realized that he'd been tracing his own wants against her skin—a figure eight, lying on its side. Eternity. Infinity.

Sanity returned, greatly unwanted. She'd asked him for a little defiance. Ash was getting carried away by the fervor of the moment. If he were to unbutton his trousers and take her, it would be shabby recompense for the gift she'd given him. From what she'd told him, he doubted she had much experience with the sweeping feel of passion. She was too overwhelmed to deny him. But then, she hadn't precisely said *yes,* either.

Ash wanted to beat his head against brick in frustration. It would probably be the only thing that would banish his lust, and then, only if he did it hard enough.

Her eyes opened. "Ash?" she said shakily. "Why did you stop?"

"Darling, if you think about where I was about to proceed, you'll have a pretty good notion. I promised you a voyage, not a tumble." Still, he was caressing her. He couldn't take his hands off her.

She swallowed shakily and then sat up, as if only now noticing precisely where his hands lay. "Oh. *Oh.*" She looked up into his eyes. "I would have…I would have let you, you know."

"You still would let me," he said. "That's not the point. I won't take you merely because it's *allowed* of me. I want you. All of you. Not just the portion of you that I managed to overwhelm."

She stared at him. "I don't understand you."

Ash pulled his hands from her. A futile attempt to dissipate the raging want inside him. It didn't work—especially not with Margaret looking at him so sweetly. His body screamed at him to complete what he'd begun, to simply take her before her thoughts coalesced into objections.

"I want you too well to desire anything except your wholehearted participation," he ground out. "Chastity… is hard. But—damn it—it's necessary. For now." He covered her hands with his and laced up her corset. When he was finished he stood and helped her to her feet. Her legs were unsteady. His own weren't much better. Still, they worked together to arrange her clothing into a semblance of unwrinkled order. After he'd retied her sash, she turned to him.

"Thank you," she said softly.

"For calling a halt?" His body was still regretting it. He didn't want her thanks, damn it. He wanted a medal for bravery above and beyond the call of duty.

"For everything," she said solemnly and walked to the door. There was an unsteady waver in her step—a tiny compensation for the pleasure he'd given up. He'd done that to her, and that thought made him fiercely possessive. Perhaps that was why he trailed after her, why, when she turned to take her leave, he kissed her once again, hard and bruising, so that she would remember him while she lay in bed tonight.

When she pulled away, he watched her go.

God, he ached all over. He needed a cold bath. He needed a good right hand. Preferably, the one before the other.

He let out his breath. It was only then that he saw Mrs. Benedict standing, frozen, down the gallery from him. She must have ascended the stairs moments before. Her eyes were narrowed, and she looked as if she were about to do murder. Oh, hell. She'd seen Margaret leave his chamber—alone, with her dress rearranged. She'd likely seen that last kiss.

"That wasn't what you think," he said.

Her nose wrinkled in distaste. "I'm not a fool, Mr. Turner."

"At least," he amended truthfully, "it wasn't *exactly* what you believed."

"I've seen the way you look at her."

Ash shrugged helplessly. "You've seen her. You've listened to her. Can you blame me?"

Mrs. Benedict tapped her hand against her skirts. "Yes," she said shortly. "I can. That poor girl has had enough to contend with without—" She grimaced and cut herself off.

"Without what?"

"Without your taking what little she has left," Mrs. Benedict said. Her voice had dropped, almost quiet, but there was nothing in her tone of softness. Instead, she spoke with a fierce promise. "Of all the girls for which I take responsibility, *she* is the one I most wanted you to leave in peace. You have no notion what you're doing."

"I have some idea what she has suffered."

Mrs. Benedict's lip curled. "I doubt it. I'll be having my key back, then. If you please." She said those last words in a tone that left no doubt: he had no choice in the matter.

"I can't."

She drew herself up—sheer bravado, for a woman who came not even to his shoulder—and marched towards him. "There *is* no can't," she scolded, her palm outstretched. "You will, or I shall—"

"I gave it to Miss Lowell," Ash confessed.

That brought her to a standstill. "You *what?*"

"I gave the key to Miss Lowell. I thought—well, I thought she ought to have it." He shrugged helplessly.

"I don't know why. It just…seemed like something she ought to have."

She stared at him in disbelief, and then shook her head. "It isn't enough. I doubt you're the sort who needs to force your way into her room, when it comes down to it." But she sounded less sure of herself. For a second, he had thought she was going to snap his head off for giving the master key to not only a servant, but a servant beneath the housekeeper. But then, this household was filled with surprises.

Hell. The only thing Ash knew was that it would take only a few more nights like this one for Margaret to grant him that impassioned *yes* he so longed to hear. And then it *would* be a tumble, not a voyage—a glorious, wicked, unchaste tumble headlong into sin. It all sounded very well for him, but for a servant, with no prospects?

No. She deserved better than that.

"I know. That is to say…" Ash heaved a great sigh. "You're entirely right, Mrs. Benedict." He'd promised the housekeeper he wouldn't despoil the staff. He'd promised *himself* the same, because these people were his dependents. He couldn't just debauch Margaret. And yet now that she was willing, keeping his hands off her would prove nearly impossible.

He shook his spinning head, trying to find his way out of this mess. And then he knew—simply *knew,* with an intensity that rattled him—how he could set this all to rights. How he could have Margaret, and his tumble, too. Of course. *Of course.* He'd already understood it in some corner of his mind, since the day he'd seen her on the steps. He'd just needed to *realize* it.

"Of course I'm right." She set her hands on her hips and glowered at him. "But I was right the last time I

admonished you on this score, as well. The only thing
I need to know is what you'll do about it."

She wanted more than a promise.

"If I stay here…" Ash swallowed and shut his eyes.
He might pontificate about honor all he wanted, but the
next time he caught a glimpse of Margaret's ankle, he
might well lose his head again. "I'm going to London.
Tomorrow. Don't expect me back for at least another
week."

IT WAS NOT QUITE NOON the next day when Margaret
ducked out of her father's chamber. The sun was shining so brightly that its rays bounced through the gallery,
the windows almost alight. And deep inside her she felt
a fierce, almost tremulous desire.

Desire—and defiance. Even if nobody else wanted
her, Ash did. This was a space of time, carved out for
her, a defiant little story she might tell herself during
these summer weeks, one in which the scullery girl got
the prince for at least one fleeting moment.

It was a pretense—he wanted her the way all men
wanted a pretty woman—but what did that matter?
She'd had enough taken from her to realize that happiness never lasted. She'd savor these moments while
she still had them.

For now, she could feel a fierce, evanescent joy about
what had transpired the prior evening. She would pay
the price for it—eventually, when he discovered who
she was.

But until then… As Margaret was well and truly
ruined, she had little to lose. They neither of them did;
Margaret had no true reputation to think of, and even
though Ash would undoubtedly despise her the instant
he knew her true identity, affairs of this nature were

ephemeral things. They didn't last. His affection for her would waver soon enough, especially as she was the daughter of his enemy.

As she passed by the chambers that Ash had taken over, she found the doors to the suite closed and locked forbiddingly. No sounds issued forth from within, and in Margaret's experience, in the late morning, Ash always had his men in there, arguing.

Perhaps they'd gone out to meet with tenants. Or to catalog the oaks.

Margaret shook her head and descended the main staircase.

The entry was flooded with light. That, Margaret realized, was because both doors were thrown open. Out on the gravel of the drive, a pair of footmen maneuvered a trunk into the boot of a carriage. Two valises stood beside them, waiting to be loaded. And standing next to them, dressed in sober brown traveling attire, was Ash.

He should have been wearing the brown hat he carried, but instead he'd tucked it casually under one arm. He was laughing, as if he hadn't a care in the world. Standing next to him was his brother. Mark spoke with him, shook his head and then waggled a finger at him, mischievously.

Margaret stood at the foot of the stairs, hidden from view by the relative shadow of the entry. Ash clapped his brother on the shoulder and then, without a backward glance, stepped into the carriage. She stared, her chest hollow.

She'd known his affection for her would fade. She hadn't realized quite how fickle it was, that he could touch her the way he had last night and then leave the next morning without saying a word to her in farewell. Margaret swallowed, but her throat remained dry.

It seemed she was to lose this, too, before it had even been found. In that too-bright sunshine, the driver leaned forwards; the reins jiggled and the team trotted off, smartly stepping down the circled drive, the carriage swaying slightly.

Well. Perhaps she didn't matter to him as much as he'd said.

The thought should have depressed her. But it didn't. Instead, her mouth curled up in amused chagrin. She had only to listen to herself. She didn't need Ash Turner—*Ash Turner,* of all people, who had destroyed her life—to tell her she mattered. If she was important, she could be important without him.

She dry-washed her hands and turned away. "Good riddance," she muttered, wishing that she meant it more.

"Pardon? What was that?"

Margaret jerked back. Mark stood, silhouetted in the doorway. "Nothing. I said nothing."

He shrugged and stepped forwards. "Ash wanted me to convey a message to you, Miss Lowell."

Margaret's heart gave a treacherous little skip. No. She'd just decided she had no further need for him. But it wasn't merely *need* she felt now. She *wanted* to know. And so what slipped out was: "Oh? What did he say?"

"He apologized for not saying farewell in person. He'll be back. And he said he would have left you a note to that effect, but…" Mark shrugged again.

Margaret looked about to see if anyone was listening, and then dropped her voice. "Well, naturally he wouldn't leave me a note."

Mark snorted and shook his head. "It's not what you suppose," he said dryly. "Believe me. I know. Ash might be aware that it would be highly improper to send an unmarried woman correspondence, but he is unlikely to care."

Perhaps Mark didn't know his brother had revealed his secret. "I had something else in mind, actually. He told me—"

"Ah. Did he feed you the excuse he always gives me? About how *busy* he is? Don't believe it. The truth is, Ash makes an extremely poor correspondent."

"Well, of course he does. After all—"

"Don't you defend him, too. When I was at Eton, for years I used to send him lengthy letters. He'd respond—with a letter written by his secretary. At the end, he'd generally scrawl a few words in his own hand, as a poor pretense of closing. In fact, he had only two or three short phrases he used. They rarely changed. Smite and I used to make a game, guessing which phrase he would slap on to the end. 'All my love' was one. 'Be well' was another. They don't mean anything, when they're offered by rote. No. I have no illusions about my older brother. You…you shouldn't either."

No doubt Mark thought he spoke out of kindness, to spare her feelings. But his disclosure had the opposite effect. All her fantasies of impermanence went up in smoke. Mark didn't know. He didn't know that Ash couldn't read, couldn't write. Her talks with Ash had seemed such harmless flirtation—heated, of course, and filled with pretty words she wanted to believe. She'd been telling herself he whispered sweet nothings all this time.

She couldn't think it any longer. Ash adored his brother. But it was Margaret he had trusted with his

secret. That didn't smack of a temporary love affair.
She had no notion what he intended at all any longer.

Her infatuation had seemed harmless and bright,
when it couldn't last. It was just a *little* defiance, one
that would hurt nobody at the end of the day.

Now her emotions felt too large to fit in her tight
skin. This wasn't supposed to mean anything. Her relationship with Ash was supposed to draw to a close.

"I tell you this because you should know not to do
anything irrevocable. I know Ash can be overwhelming," Mark said conspiratorially. "But—really, there's
no need to be overwhelmed. He's human, just like the
rest of us."

As he spoke, Margaret realized that Mark couldn't
have known. He'd mentioned to her the other day that
Ash had begun to read his book. If he'd had any notion
of the truth, he'd have realized how impossible that
was. No; until two days ago, Ash had kept his secret
entirely to himself. He'd been alone.

Alone, and still determined to reach out to a brother
who wanted him to communicate via letter.

"He makes mistakes. He's fallible." Mark glanced
sideways at her. "I overheard the maids talking about
him, and based on their chatter, I wanted to make sure
that you understood."

So the maids were talking about Ash. She knew
Mrs. Benedict had threatened dire consequences on
any who let slip the truth of Margaret's identity. But
that charade could last only so long. She could feel her
sunlit summer drawing to a close, even now.

"It's easy to forget," Mark continued. "I do it, too.
When I'm in his company, I simply cannot remember
anything else. He's warm and kind. It's only when he's
absent that it becomes obvious from his conduct that

he's not sparing me another thought. I'm out of sight, and thus out of mind." He shrugged and glanced back at her. "I barely notice, these days."

It took Margaret a moment to realize that his last words were a lie. He didn't even try to hide the unhappy quirk of his lips.

"After all," he continued, only a trace of bitterness leaching into his voice, "a few scribbled words, in his illegible hand—well, at least he remembers I exist, some of the time. Even if all I get is a half-legible promise of his brotherly affection, attached to someone else's impersonal reply."

The truth clutched at Margaret's throat.

I've learned to pen a few phrases—if I shut my eyes, I can scrawl them out by memory. But it took so long, just to learn a handful of words. I've only bothered to memorize the ones I can't get by without. She knew how much those few scrawled words had cost Ash, even if Mark did not.

"I'm sorry," Mark said. "I've upset you. I didn't intend to. Truly, I thought it was kinder for you to learn this way."

The truth itched at her. She wanted to scream it out, to shake Mark, to make him realize just how hard it had been for Ash to etch out his love on the bottom of his secretary's letters. How could he not *know?* How could he not *realize?*

But then, she'd fooled herself, too. She wasn't sure what she was to Ash. Not his lover, at least not physically. But she was something more frighteningly intimate than she'd supposed.

He'd been telling the truth to her all along, and she had been the one spinning falsehoods. She looked at his brother, at that half-defiant smile on Mark's face, as if he were daring himself to care about his brother's desertion.

"I thought," he said, "I would be glad if Ash left, because I could simply focus on my work. Turns out, it still bothers me. He promised he'd spend this last portion of the summer with me. And here we are. I don't even mean that much to him."

Margaret shook her head, a mixture of pity and anger suffusing her. When she was finally able to speak past the lump in her throat, what she said was: "For an intelligent man, Mr. Mark Turner, you can be quite, quite stupid."

CHAPTER ELEVEN

MARK WAS NOT THE ONLY stupid one. Days passed, and then a week—and still Ash did not return. August bled into September. For Margaret, the time felt strangely isolating. With Ash no longer present, Mark secreted himself in a room and worked as if in a fever. She saw him occasionally, but only in passing—and even then, he walked by her, an abstracted expression on his face, as if he were already planning out the next chapter in his book. With the Turners either physically gone or not mentally present, it was almost as if Margaret were still an honored daughter of the house.

In the days since Ash had absented himself, she had taken to walking the upper gallery in the late mornings. The wide windows faced east; in the baking heat of late summer, the room was too warm for comfort. But from that second-floor vantage point, she could catch glimpses of the London road, winding its way down green-covered hills before it dipped into the valley where her home stood. She could stand alone, and think.

As she watched the road one morning, a spiral of dust shimmered up. Margaret had felt her heart leap several times over the past days, imagining similar plumes to be horsemen. Usually, it was nothing—an illusion born of heat and dryness, or a raven, landing on the road.

Parford Manor was situated near the bottom of the hills, and the road wound in and out of view. She scanned the hills, guessing where a horseman might appear next. If he were walking at a gentle trot, he would be right there.…

Nothing. Nothing but the wave of browning grasses, broken by stone walls and dark green hedgerows.

She wasn't sure why she bothered looking.

She watched the next stretch of road avidly, but nothing appeared. It was foolish of her to hope for him, even more foolish to believe that he would appear. But then, she'd recognized for weeks that where Ash was concerned, she was a fool—a conflicted, confused, yearning fool.

She watched the hills for ten minutes before turning away to care for her father.

She hadn't waited long enough. Moments after she entered the sickroom, a commotion rose up outside. While she measured out medicine—her father was too hot to object—her pulse pounded.

When her father waved her idly away, she scurried from the room. The initial hubbub of the arrival had died away, and the gallery upstairs seemed preternaturally silent. It was only when she reached the far end that she caught Ash's voice, echoing up the stairwell.

"And how is your book coming along?"

Oh. She'd *missed* him. She hadn't realized quite how much until she heard him once again. His voice was warm and lilting, the sound of it sending a little shiver down her spine. She stopped on the first landing, just to take it in. The palms of her hands trembled, and she pressed them against the cool stone of the stairwell.

"Swimmingly. I've only the final conclusion to write," Mark responded. "Really, you ought to leave more often—you would be shocked at my ability to produce pages when I haven't anyone to bother me."

That rude noise could only have come from Ash. "You know, interacting with others is good for you. Man cannot live by writing books on chastity alone. Speaking of which, I don't suppose you tumbled any women while I was gone?"

Margaret knew Ash well enough to understand that this was a joke.

"As I'm not married," Mark said dryly, "then, no. I haven't."

"Futile hope. Ah, well. Good thing I was pinning all my hopes on the real question—did you talk to *anyone* at all while I was gone?"

There was a long pause. "Hmm. I believe I wished Miss Lowell a good day."

Margaret took a deep breath and descended the stairs. Ash was standing in the entry next to his brother, his arms crossed, his toe tapping impatiently. "How many times?"

"Um. Once a day?" Mark scrubbed a hand through blond hair that had grown too long to be fashionable and gave his brother a helpless smile.

Ash shook his head. "This is why I don't like leaving you," he groused. "I go away, and you retreat into your shell as if you were a little crab at the seashore. You're intelligent. You're amusing. You ought to see people—no, I don't mean all the time, so you can stop curling up like a hedgehog! Once or twice a day. You *like* people, Mark. Talk to them. Tell me that you at least said more to Margaret than a passing 'good day.' I suspect that she, unlike you, actually *notices* when she fails to talk to people for an entire day."

"In more important news, just this morning, I

finished a really fantastic chapter. It's all about practical ways to rid oneself of a—" Mark turned as he heard her footsteps on the final stretch of stairs, and swallowed whatever he'd been about to say.

"Rid oneself of what?" Margaret asked.

The two men had turned to her as one. It was only with the greatest difficulty that Margaret did not miss her next step. When Ash saw her, his face lit. In the dreadful heat of the oncoming noon, any additional warmth ought to have felt disagreeable. But instead, the flush that burned her cheeks felt welcome. As if he were a cool breeze and a raging inferno all at once. He didn't say her name. He didn't reach for her. Instead, he simply watched her as she descended the staircase, his eyes following her down. He placed one hand over his waistcoat pocket.

"You know what you need, Mark?" Ash said, not taking his eyes off Margaret. "You need a wife."

She missed the last step at that, and barely caught herself from sliding to his feet by clutching at the banister.

"What?" Mark sputtered. "I'm too young to marry."

"Women manage matrimony at a far younger age. And besides, with a wife, you'd discover more practical ways to rid yourself of…of lustful thoughts than whatever it is you came up with for your book. More importantly, if you had a wife, you would be forced to have at least ten minutes of conversation, once a day."

"I haven't met anyone I wish to marry."

Ash slanted Margaret a sly look and winked at her, and she felt a stab of confusion. That early talk of tumbling women, she had understood. But this? Her brothers had never talked about other women like this. In fact, Edmund had complained bitterly when she told him to dance with her friend Elaine. He'd feared that Elaine might enlarge upon a single waltz until she believed herself about to be married.

Marriage, so far as Margaret had been given to understand, was a consummation devoutly to be avoided by men of good title and ordinary character—at least, until the passage of time and the complaints of female relatives made it inevitable.

"Is something the matter, Margaret?" Ash glanced at her. "Surely you're not opposed to the concept of matrimony. I was thinking I ought to drag my brother with me to some of the society events this upcoming Season, so he can find a woman virtuous enough to satisfy his practical needs."

"In point of fact," Mark said dryly, "a wedding would be of little practical use, if she remained virtuous after marriage."

At the thought of Ash and Mark descending upon polite society… Margaret wasn't sure whether to laugh or to cry. A duke's heir with several hundred thousand pounds, and his angelic-looking brother? Oh, the schemes that would arise. The women who would swoon. The furor that would rise up, if it were bruited about that either was actively seeking a wife.

Margaret shook her head. "Aren't you worried?"

"Worried?" Ash's eyebrows rose in confusion. "Ought I be? About what?"

"About…" Margaret spread her arms wide. "You know. *Women.* You're wealthy. You're young. You're handsome, and if…if matters go your way, the two of you will be in line to inherit one of the most respected titles in all of England. Aren't you worried that some scheming chit will trap you into matrimony?"

Ash and Mark both looked up at her, their expressions mirror reflections of concern.

Then Ash shook his head. "You have the strangest ideas in your head. In your experience, how many women are there who are intelligent enough to scheme me or my brother into matrimony, but also foolish enough to force a marriage with a man who doesn't wish to have her?"

Margaret simply stared at him. "I don't—that is to say—"

"Precisely. I'm not opposed to matrimony, should I find myself in love." His eyes met hers, and she felt her toes curl.

He couldn't mean her. He couldn't possibly mean *her*. She was a servant, a nurse, a bastard. Dukes didn't marry bastards. But then, Ash had always stood outside of her experience altogether. And she didn't know *what* he intended. Not any longer.

The concept was so foreign to her—the notion of a man marrying without being bullied into it—that she could say no more. By the way he was looking at her, he no doubt remembered their conversation on this score. Her fiancé. The dreadful shame she had felt.

"Miss Lowell." His voice was quiet. "I have no idea where you received your notions. No doubt you'll tell me it's no business of mine. But I find there is something I should—no, I must—say to you." He paused and ran his tongue over his lips. "If a man ever lets you know that he sees marriage as a trap, and women as nothing but scheming connivers, you are by no means to marry him. Any man that sees your entire sex in so harsh a light has nothing to offer you."

Put that way… Her emotions swung towards him, the needle on a compass pointing northward. Hope and despair collided within her, all twining into that word.

Marriage.

Frederick could never have thought much of her, or he'd never have used her as he did. She was better off without any of the men who had paid her court and then turned their backs on her when she was announced a bastard. There was only one man who'd looked at her and seen something worth seeing. But no. She couldn't think of marrying *him,* either. Once he discovered who she was, he would despise her.

"But—" she began to say.

He chopped his hand down, as if to end all further inquiry. "But nothing. Either it's an honor to marry a woman, or it's not to be done at all, not at any cost."

But I was born Anna Margaret Dalrymple. One sentence, one admission, and all the weight of his ruthlessness would come to bear on her. He'd stopped being her enemy, but she was still his. And suddenly, she couldn't stand the thought that the easy regard reflected in his eyes might dim.

"You're not a pair of steel jaws and a strong spring, waiting to bite through a man's boot if he steps wrongly."

And why should a ridiculous compliment make her want to burst into tears? Perhaps it was the sweetness of it. Perhaps it was because, for all of Ash's apparent traveled worldliness, there was a golden innocence about him, something clear and untainted by bitter vinegar. This was the man who laughed with the housekeeper and shrugged when his brother taught the nurse how to spar.

Instead, she looked away. Mark was watching them, his eyes narrowed. If Ash had a worldly innocence about him, Mark seemed filled with an almost impudent purity—playful when he noticed you, distracted when he was too busy thinking of his own work. But he wasn't distracted now. He focused on her, as if he were suddenly seeing something new in her face.

"By the way, Margaret," Ash said, his voice pitched too low for Mark to hear. "I thought of you while I was gone."

She couldn't help herself. She looked back at him. He smiled when she caught his eyes. His gaze seemed warm. Almost—no, she could not say it, but she couldn't avoid it either—almost *loving.*

She wanted him to look at her like that forever.

But he wouldn't. In a few days—perhaps in as little as a few hours—this would all come to an end. She would tell Ash the truth of her identity. And once he knew, he would never again tell her that she wasn't a conniving schemer, that she wasn't a trap to snap about a man's foot.

This couldn't go on.

"Did you find what you were looking for in London?" Margaret asked.

He watched her, his eyes intense. He seemed to look right through her skin, into the heart of her. And then he gave a quiet, put-upon sigh. "Almost," he said. "Almost, which is the same thing as not at all. I'll let you know when it arrives."

MARGARET CAME TO HIS OFFICE as twilight fell—an action that both heartened and frustrated Ash, all at once. He had hoped that by the time he saw her again, he would have in hand what he had set out to obtain.

But bureaucracy being what it was—and Ash being, at present, only a third-rate claimant to a dukedom—he'd managed only to extract a promise to have what he wanted sent on, once it arrived. It irked him that something so straightforward was taking so long.

He wanted to claim her now.

And so instead of waiting for her to come alone to his office that evening, where he would undoubtedly be tempted to break his word, he'd asked Mark to come sit with him.

She smiled as she entered, her eyes settling on Ash and Ash alone.

And then: "Good evening, Miss Lowell." Margaret started visibly at Mark's words, and turned to where he sat. It made Ash feel that he had somehow betrayed her by conspiring to keep her virtue.

He gestured to a chair. "Sit," he commanded.

She glanced at him—no doubt wondering why he was barking orders at her—and sat. He wasn't quite sure what it meant that she didn't take the seat he'd gestured to, an embroidered chair, but instead sat on the low-backed sofa where he'd kissed her the other night. There was room on there for him to sit, room for him to slide next to her, his thighs touching hers… He could still send Mark away.

He shook his head, but while he could banish that image from his mind, he could not dispel the faintly floral scent that had swept into the room with her.

"Ash was telling me," Mark said, "about how he got Lord Talton to agree to take his side in the upcoming battle in Parliament. You *do* know about the pending legislation, don't you?"

Her jaw set. Ash could not guess whether that was because of Mark's assumption that she might not know what must have been basic household gossip, or because even now she still held some unfortunate loyalty to the Dalrymples. She gave a jerky nod, though, and Mark continued.

"Well, Talton had refused to even see him, and—"

Ash held up his hand. "Miss Lowell doesn't want to hear about my *ruthlessness*." He emphasized that last word.

Margaret looked down, her hands clasped together in a tight grip. "I suppose you found a way to charm him," she said. There was a hint of bitterness as she spoke. Was she annoyed with him for leaving her without saying his goodbyes, or for disrupting their renewed acquaintance with Mark as a chaperone? He needed to speak with her alone to find out.

And no sooner had he thought that, than thoughts of what he would do with her when he found her alone intruded. Last time he'd had her here, he'd had her skirts to her waist, and his hand between her thighs.

God. He was a lustful idiot.

"You know," Margaret said, cutting into his reverie, "I don't think you're ruthless at all. I think it's a sham. You pretend at it quite well, but what harsh thing have you ever done?"

"You've never seen me crossed," Ash said softly.

Mark made a sour sound. "You've never seen *me* crossed," he said. "Smite said once—"

But his brother shut his mouth and glanced across the table, as if thinking better of completing that sentence. That abrupt stop felt like a fist to Ash's throat. He'd never been able to read his other brother, and Smite was closemouthed on all things.

Ash sometimes suspected that Smite held him in acute dislike. He had every reason to do so.

"What did Smite say?" Ash choked those words out past the ache in his gut.

"Smite said you were our personal avenging angel." Mark dropped his eyes guiltily.

Well. It could have been worse. It could have been a lot worse. "That's true." He met Margaret's gaze and wagged a finger at her. "Cross my brothers, and I'll salt the earth under your feet. I'll raze your defenses and reduce everything you love to rubble. There. Now you've been warned."

She smiled. There was a touch of unease to that tentative curl of her lips.

"Oh, you think he's joking?" Mark said. "You cannot have forgotten, Miss Lowell, the circumstances that brought us here. This—" he waved his hands expansively at the room around them "—this is Ash's revenge on the Dalrymples."

Margaret's face shuttered. There was no other word for the pallor that crept across her skin, the sensation that she had just slammed the storm windows shut in preparation for a great gale. Her body drew subtly in on itself. "Oh?" That single word wasn't a query, but another line of defense.

But Mark didn't understand that. Likely, Mark hadn't spent time studying the moods that crept across her face. He didn't understand her vulnerabilities. He didn't understand that she was still a wild creature, a little hesitant to eat from his hand. Ash cast Margaret an apologetic glance, but she wasn't looking his way.

Mark leaned forwards. "He can't forget some small slight, delivered years ago. One that was met with more than sufficient punishment at the time. He saw the opportunity to bring the Dalrymples down—"

She would think Ash was the most capricious fellow

ever if Mark continued to tell the story in that way. "You call that *some small slight?* Miss Lowell, judge the truth for yourself. My brother sent me a note when he was six months at Eton, begging me to take him home. Naturally—" Ash heard the scorn in his own voice "—I undertook to ride out to see him. Not to take him home—I was determined that he would have the education that I did not."

She nodded, understanding what Mark did not know.

"As I recall," Mark put in, "you read me the most astonishing lecture on my duty to my name and my person. Afterwards, I was too frightened to even so much as suggest leaving."

"You see," Ash said, "he'd suffered a thousand indignities from the older boys—shoves when nobody was looking, little cruelties and taunts delivered in lonely halls. He was small for his age, then, and quiet."

She watched him, her hands clasped in a white-knuckled grip.

"And he was a Turner," Ash continued. "It wasn't enough that Parford let my sister die. Edmund wanted everyone to know that no matter what the bloodlines proclaimed, Mark counted as no kin of his."

She cast her eyes down to the carpet. Her jaw set.

Ash smiled grimly. "My brother begged me to let him come home. I refused and told him that under no circumstances would I allow him to do so. I walked away from him."

"As you should have," Mark commented.

"A few weeks later, I had this notion I should go back." It had been another one of his *instincts,* and it had practically screamed for him to return. "When I got there… I have never been so furious in my life." He could feel his fury returning, just thinking of it. "They broke his nose. They blacked his eyes. Three fingers on his right hand—"

"But," Mark put in quietly, "you didn't see the other boys."

"Ah, yes. The other boys. Edmund Dalrymple and four of his friends had taken him on together."

Margaret looked at him in shocked dismay. She shook her head. "It couldn't have been. Together? But—"

"Don't tell me what could have been. It was, in violation of all gentlemanly conduct. Apparently, they had been trying to bully him. And apparently, he hadn't given in."

"This happened years ago," Mark put in. "I see no reason to think of it. But has Ash forgotten?"

"Have they let me forget? There've been no physical attacks since then. But tell us truly, Mark. Has Edmund ever forgotten you? And Smite—Richard was never so uncouth as to attack, but I know why Smite moved to Bristol, instead of taking articles in London as we had once discussed."

Mark shook his head earnestly. "Really, Ash. It doesn't bother me—why must you take it so seriously? I try not to spare either of them my attention. I've better things to spend my time worrying about."

Ash looked up. "They have spread rumors. Innuendo. Edmund once hired a caricaturist to portray Mark as a—"

"Ash, really."

But his brother's admonition only heightened Ash's resolve. "For years, they used their station and their place in society as a way to humiliate my brothers. So, yes. I'll take their station. I'll take their place in society.

And I'll have no mercy whatsoever for the Dalrymples. If I can make their lives miserable in response, I will. And..." Ash felt a wolfish smile play across his face. "I can."

Margaret stared at him, white-faced.

"Don't tell me you agree with Mark," he said in surprise. "Turn the other cheek, and all that nonsense. If someone threatens me and my own, I won't rest until he's been taught to leave well enough alone."

"But what..." She stopped, looking down, and then looked up at him, her eyes filled with inexplicable entreaty. "What about the innocents who are hurt by your actions?"

"What innocents?" He spat the word.

Her eyes fluttered down again. "The duchess."

"That...that was unfortunate. In truth, if it had come to it, if she'd survived... I don't want true innocents to suffer. Hell, I'd make some provision for the Dalrymples. I would certainly have done something for her."

"If you had thought about it," Mark put in gently.

Margaret's lips were almost white. "And what about Parford's daughter?"

"Parford's daughter." Ash shook his head in confusion. Then he realized she must have known the woman, conversed with her during the course of the duchess's illness. "Wasn't she married off earlier? I seem to recall hearing about an engagement, years ago. I don't keep abreast of such matters. I suppose she must have suffered some embarrassment, then. But I also suppose she was used to the feeling. Wasn't she the girl who fainted in the fountain, her first year out?"

A flush touched Margaret's cheeks. "I find it quite odd that you can be so kind to mere servants, and yet so cavalier to everyone else. Had you simply not thought of how your actions would affect everyone connected with the Dalrymples?"

"What does it matter?" he asked in bewilderment. "She married some other fellow. She's well and truly out of it."

"No. I don't believe she married."

Ash snorted. "Let me guess. She fainted before she said 'I do.'"

Margaret didn't smile. Ash had the feeling that he'd fallen into a world where down had become up and right had turned into left. "Oh, come now. That was at least a little clever. Whatever her name might be— Anna, is it?"

He should have known, but then, how was he to discover such things? Consult Debrett's?

He took a deep breath. "I'm sure she is a perfectly acceptable specimen of a lady, if you like such things. But you must admit, she must be a poor creature to topple over so easily. *If* she did not do it to draw attention to herself."

Margaret met his gaze for the first time that evening. It was then he realized what lay behind her unease—a cold, inexplicable fury. "Let me guess," she said. "You have never worn a corset and a ball gown for seven hours."

He grinned casually. "Now *there's* a daring wager. Even if I did, I shouldn't lace them so tightly as to squeeze out my breath, no matter what the occasion. If someone is such a slave to fashion—"

"It's not merely the lacing. Ball gowns aren't laced as tightly as some other dresses; you need to allow more room for movement. It's the heat. And the layers. Do you know how a ball gown is assembled?"

This was what happened when he used his brother as a shield. He ought to have met her alone and convinced her to take port with him. Now, instead of getting pleasantly drunk and snuggly, Miss Lowell was lecturing him on the construction of ball gowns. He must have lost his mind. He'd certainly lost his touch.

"Yes," he said in a dry tone of voice. "I know how ball gowns are made. They are made of fabric."

She snorted. "And?"

"Thread? Ribbons? Buttons?"

She simply looked at him, one eyebrow raised.

"Whalebone? Metal? No, wait—now I see. They are composed of lead, and are purposely made heavy, to force women to walk in a slow and elegant fashion."

She still didn't laugh. "They are sewn in place. That means there is no way to remove one once the ball has begun. Once it is on, it stays on for the entire evening. Think about what that means. One cannot simply relieve oneself at the drop of one's breeches. One cannot, in fact, use the necessary at all. So before a ball, ladies do not drink or eat anything. Not for hours. During a ball, one can only wet one's lips."

He glanced at her. "Really?"

Somehow, that tone of disbelief made her blush, too. "Indeed. I've heard the maids talk about it. Eight hours on an empty stomach, whirling about, clad in seven petticoats. You would topple over, too."

"I had no idea society ballrooms were so barbarous." He said it with a smile, but still Margaret didn't return the expression.

"No doubt," she said with a lift of her chin, "you would think *me* a poor creature, too, if you swathed me up in layers of silk and withheld all water, just to see what would happen. I daresay I wouldn't last the evening. Think, Mr. Turner, before you speak. If you rely on rumor, you will never understand."

"You wouldn't collapse."

"You can't possibly know that."

He stood up, taking a step towards her. "You don't comprehend what I mean, Margaret. You're stronger than that. You'd reach deep down into yourself—just as you're doing now—and you would look the possibility in the face and tell it to go to the devil. Yes, just as you're doing with me, at this moment. Some people crumble when they're dealt a blow. You might stagger a bit, I suppose. But you? You would never collapse."

"I wish I could hate you," she said passionately.

"Yes," he remarked. "It would be more convenient for you. Sadly, you've found it quite impossible."

She stared at him. The corner of her lip twitched—not quite a smile, but the shadow of one.

"When he's like this, Miss Lowell," Mark offered from his seat on the sofa, "I usually take it upon myself to stamp out in a rage. It's impossible to argue with him, once he starts asserting his correctness as a matter of unarguable certainty. And if you stay, he'll turn your thoughts around until you don't know right from wrong. Take it from me. Ash is both perfectly right, and horridly wrong. And he will never, ever understand what he's said to upset you."

"What *did* I say?" he inquired.

She gave him that look—that one that said, *If you don't know, I shan't be telling you.* Ash hated that look.

And then she stood. "Must I stamp? Or can I sweep out gracefully?"

"By all means, sweep." Mark stood for her, and Margaret gave him a swift curtsy. She didn't even glance at Ash on her way out. Not quite what Ash had intended for the evening—sending her from the room in a confused flurry. It wasn't precisely *bad* that they had argued—the more pleasant it would be to make it up to her later. But it wasn't what he'd hoped for.

And it just went to prove: one might think one knew a great deal about a woman. One might tell her one's darkest secrets. And she was still going to make one's head spin about, by caring about things that made absolutely no sense. He heaved a sigh. He wasn't quite sure when or where the conversation had gone wrong, or what precisely he'd said to make it veer off course with such vehemence.

"Well." The syllable echoed in the now too-empty room. "Do you suppose she'll have forgotten this episode by morning?"

Mark shook his head. "She may be as stubborn as you."

"I'm not stubborn," Ash said. "I'm *right*. There's a difference."

Mark snorted. "No. I remember when Mother used to assign us Bible verses to learn. For Smite, it proved no problem—no matter how many she gave us."

She'd given too many—dozens and dozens, it seemed. She'd locked them in the parlor to learn them.

"But you'd refuse. One of my earliest memories is her beating you, and your refusing to cry. You were smiling as she switched you. As if even then, all you wanted was to prove that you bent to nobody's will but your own."

Not quite how Ash remembered that particular event. First, there'd been the fact that he hadn't *refused* to learn anything. He'd simply been unable to read.

"I always remembered that, when things got bad. I remembered thinking, 'Well, if Ash could do it, I can.'"

Ash felt a lump in his throat. "You know, Mark..."

But then, his younger brother so seldom expressed admiration for him. He wasn't about to muck that up by disclosing a tiny fact that was now a mere side note, an irrelevancy.

"Yes?"

Ash smiled. Papering over that hollow in his chest seemed impossible. But he'd smiled through beatings as a boy. And he didn't want to lose the light of respect in Mark's eyes. If nothing else, he wanted his brothers to feel safe with him—protected. Taken care of. Cosseted, even.

How safe would they feel if they knew his secret?

"I was wondering," he said, "speaking of stubborn— what think you of Miss Lowell?"

Mark settled slowly back into his seat. "You were, were you? Do you wonder about her?"

"All the time," Ash said, sitting down with a heavy sigh. He wondered a great deal about her—about the sound she would make when he kissed the nape of her neck. Whether the skin of her thighs was as soft as he remembered. What she'd look like, waking in his bed, rumpled from sleep and pleased to see him. He glanced over at his brother. "But don't you be wondering about her that way. I thought you had no interest in anything but chastity."

Mark smiled. "I didn't intend it *that* way. Only someone as corrupt as you would take what I said in that jaded manner. I meant, have you ever wondered where she *comes* from? She didn't spring up, fully formed like

Athena, the instant we landed on this estate. There's something not quite right about the situation."

That was the problem with thinking. "There is a great deal about her that doesn't add up," he admitted reluctantly. From the way Mrs. Benedict protected her, to the way the other servants jumped at her command. For a young woman—and a nurse no less—she wielded an extraordinary influence. He'd always assumed that the duchess had favored her. But, maybe…

"Ash," Mark said almost urgently, "*think*. I can't imagine why I haven't, until I saw her face just now. She's a bastard who owes the Dalrymples some form of allegiance, who—"

"Stop," Ash said. He wasn't even sure why he spoke, until he did. "I want *her* to tell me."

"Tell you *what?*"

He didn't know. He wasn't sure. "I want her to tell me why she's so sad." He wanted all of her secrets, but like her kiss, he didn't want to wrest them from her, to poke and pry and pull, until he'd stolen them entirely. He wanted the truth of her, given as a gift. "Besides, I trust her. What do you suppose I went to London to do? You don't suppose I left you to take care of any piddling business matter?"

Nothing in response, nothing but shocked silence, as Mark sorted that out. Nothing until: "Oh…" Mark's voice came out in a whisper. "Ash. You're utterly *insane,* do you know that? You've just met her. You can't just—just—"

Ash grinned. "Yes, I can. Sometimes, I just *know* things. I can't philosophize, as you do. I won't ever be a scholar or a thinker. I *know* things. I act." He shrugged. "That's what I do well. You may need everything spelled out for you. I don't."

"And have you…informed her of this yet?"

"Not a word. My men will send everything on, once the paper's issued. Apparently, the parish is taking its sweet time sending along confirmation of the particulars."

"Oh, Ash." Mark looked up at him, the most curious expression on his face. His brother set his jaw, and that made no sense. Because what he saw was neither pity nor happiness, but instead a grim look of determination.

CHAPTER TWELVE

THE TERSE MISSIVE—the only one she'd received in
weeks from Richard—arrived the next morning. The
paper listed only the lords her brother had spoken with
in the past few weeks, with instructions to pass the list
on to their father.

But it ended with an admonition for her.

*Take care, Margaret. You speak well of Ash Turner,
and that worries me. You seem to be distracted from
our overarching goal. No need to become so neat about
matters. Tell me what's wrong with him—however
small, however trivial. I need to know.*

Margaret stared at those accusing words, then shred-
ded the letter and fed it, piece by piece, into the fire.

Richard wrote in a harsh, jagged hand, without
excess verbiage. She had never before noticed the lack
in his words, but it was obvious now.

Her brothers had never been overly demonstrative,
but they had done their duty. They'd danced with her
at her come-out and introduced her to their friends, a
great mass of titled gentlemen who had admired her—
and her dowry—immensely. She had no doubt that if
her honor had been in need of defense, Richard and
Edmund would both have taken up the call.

And when she'd fainted on one warm spring night in
her first year out, it was Richard who had fished her out
of the fountain and covered her with his coat, Richard

who had cleared the back hall and ordered everyone away. In the weeks that passed, it was Richard who had kept her by his side. He'd been too important a figure— a duke's heir, the Marquess of Winchester—for anyone to risk alienating him with overly harsh gossip. And it had been Richard who had insisted that she return to London for a second season, claiming that another, more interesting, scandal would take precedence.

Richard had been right.

Someday soon, she would have to choose between Richard and Ash. She felt that choice lying across her, like a cold hand reaching out across the grave.

But how much of a choice would she truly have?

Ash was a worldly tradesman, and Margaret knew precisely what he intended to do with her. Even if his suit in Parliament didn't prosper and he was denied the dukedom, he'd eventually turn his relentless gaze to one of the other debutantes out there. With his fortune and his smiling allure, he'd be able to do a great deal better than an illegitimate woman who brought neither land nor connections to the marriage.

The truth smarted.

And then, she wasn't just *any* bastard. She was Anna Margaret Dalrymple. She was the daughter of his enemy, and the sister of two men that he hated. And she had been lying to him throughout their entire acquaintance.

No. She had no choice to make. It was only a matter of time until she told Ash the truth of her origins. She'd braced herself to do so last night, but then they hadn't been alone. He'd mocked her to her face—not knowing that it was *she* he'd ridiculed.

Once he knew everything about her, he would recant

every one of his fine compliments. Margaret wouldn't have to make a choice. He would make it for her.

And so why not write Richard now? Why not disclose the secrets Ash had reposed in her? She could spin a tale, she realized, that would make him out to be a monster. He was a man who seduced nurses, who eschewed reading not out of choice, but by necessity. He sat at table with the upper servants, upsetting the social order. And one day, one day soon, he would become her most implacable enemy.

Perhaps she kept faith with Ash because he had not betrayed her yet. Because she wanted to be a person he could trust. Because she wanted to believe that what he'd told her was true, and that despite her fall from grace, she was still a magnificent creature.

You matter. You are important.

She had to believe that for herself, because someday soon, he would no longer believe it for her.

He would…how had he put it? He would salt the earth beneath her feet and grind her into a fine dust. He would, no doubt, tell the world that she'd masqueraded as a servant and offered him her body in exchange for information. Every one of their caresses would become gossip-fodder. If she'd been ruined before, she would be utterly cast out when he revealed the truth.

Margaret let out a little sigh. When that happened, she would fight back. She would reveal his secrets if he unveiled hers. But until then, she wanted to believe that he was right. That she was the kind of woman he could trust, that at the end of the day she would not betray him.

And so when she sent her brother another empty set of platitudes, she whispered to Ash in her mind.

See? This is how I repay you.

IT WAS ANOTHER ONE of those dreadful mornings—cloudy without rain, Ash sitting in the library pretending to make sense of an agricultural text, while his brother scribbled away at his work.

It had been two days since Margaret had stormed out of this room. Last evening, she'd not come by—even though he'd waited for her until nearly midnight. He'd been left with nothing but a pile of written words, which presumably would tell him about agriculture, if he were to sort them out.

Ash snapped his book shut.

There were rows and rows of books here. Shelves upon shelves, and his younger brother was buried behind them, entombed in a sea of understanding that Ash could never comprehend. He'd substituted cold letters for human companionship. Ash just wanted him to *live*.

God. What Ash wouldn't give for an interruption.

"Mr. Turner, sir. There's someone here to see you."

Ash almost gasped in relief at Smith's words. The majordomo stood stiffly at attention, but he held no card in his hand. Ash had already had his man come through from London. He knew of no pending matters that would necessitate a visit.

"The gentleman says he's expected," Smith continued. "Where should he be put?"

Ash's confusion only deepened. He'd certainly not invited anyone. Perhaps this was one of the duke's hangers-on—a friend of the Dalrymple boys? His hands clenched.

But Mark was already standing, his face lighting with an almost painful joy. "I'll go meet him immediately," he said. He left the room at a run.

Ash followed more slowly, his thoughts whirling. Mark hadn't shown this much enthusiasm for another person in…well, the entire summer. *Had* he invited a friend down?

Why hadn't he mentioned such a thing? Not that Ash would begrudge his brother anything he wanted. And he wasn't complaining—a little more friendly conversation would do Mark a great deal of good.

Ash pattered into the entry, trailing after his younger brother. He came out of the hall just in time to see Mark grab the fellow—dark, ebony-haired—about the arms.

"My God," Mark said, "you're here already? You must have left the *instant* you received my note. You must have traveled half the night. What were you thinking?"

"You knew I would come," the man replied cheerfully.

Ash stood in the doorway. He'd heard once that diamond was nothing but coal that had been compressed for many years. He could feel his own heart withering to blackness, slowly turning into cold cinder. He wasn't sure if he should venture forwards or stay behind.

Because he had seen in one glimpse who the visitor was. This wasn't some friend, come down from London. That had been a brotherly embrace. Literally.

"Smite." Ash tried to keep the accusation from his voice, tried to keep his tone even and devoid of the emotion he felt. "But I invited you to join us the day Chancery ruled in our favor." He cut off the rest of the whine. *And you told me you were too busy.*

His brother looked over and saw Ash standing in the doorway. He didn't quite stop smiling, but it was as if all the warmth, all the humor of his fraternal greeting had been sucked from him. As if the sight of Ash had invested him with an extra pound of starch. He looked about, half grimacing, and then walked forwards, holding out his hand.

His *hand*. As if Ash were nothing more than a chance-met business partner.

"Ash," he said. "It's good to see you."

And what was Ash to do? He shook his brother's hand, because that was all that was offered. Because he'd take anything he could get from his brother, even this bare scrap of civility. He would take it, and he wouldn't complain.

He'd left Smite behind years ago, when he'd gone to India. No matter how high he set the man's quarterly allowance, he could not make up for those bleak years. Smite never spoke of that time. But then, he didn't need to. He'd accepted the education and a few hundred pounds to further his studies afterwards. That great quarterly allowance Ash had signed over to him, though, lay untouched in the account the solicitors set up, funds piling up year after year, a silent, venomous rejection of Ash's brotherly affection.

Instead, Smite lived in a tiny, narrow house in Bristol. He didn't even employ full-time servants, and his living arrangements had always seemed to be a quiet rebuke, a disavowal of Ash and the largesse he wanted to shower upon him.

Smite pulled away from Ash before their clasped hands could communicate anything like affection. He turned quickly away, his gaze darting about the room as if to take in the new surroundings.

"Just look at this." He let out a low whistle as he turned in place—as if he were truly interested in the painted plasterwork overhead. As if he weren't avoiding Ash's gaze.

"Yes," Ash said, playing along. "It's a thing of beauty." He looked at his brothers as he spoke—one fair, the other dark, both palpably incandescent. His entire family had come together, and however this miracle had come about, he was not one to discard such a fine chance in a fit of pique.

Smite crossed the room to peer at a wall. "Is that a Caravaggio? My God."

He and Mark drifted over to a picture of several cherubic-looking boys and began babbling about lighting and strokes and God knew what else—things they had learned at university, no doubt. Ash would have understood them better if they'd started chattering at him in Bengali. Just like that, Ash was left outside of the conversation, with nothing to do but notice that Smite had put on a few welcome pounds. He'd finally lost that thinnish cast he'd had about him all through Oxford.

In the brotherly lottery, Smite was both the biggest loser and the greatest winner. Winner, because if women admired Mark, they adored Smite: his shining black hair, in contrast with the snapping blue of his eyes. His features were sharp enough to be manly, but not so brutish as to rob him of an almost haunting beauty. And unlike Mark, Smite wasn't averse to taking occasional advantage of all that feminine adoration.

On the other hand, there was the matter of his name. The Bible verse their mother had given him—too unwieldy to be used in regular speech—had been shortened to *Smite* years ago. *Mark* was a common name. *Ash* was a strange one. But *Smite?* That was downright awful.

Back on the credit side of Smite's personal ledger, he had a prodigious memory. He could recite word for word any book he had read, no matter how long ago it had been. It was as if everything Ash lacked, Smite had received a thousandfold.

But then, there was the little matter of what had happened to him all those years back. When Ash had returned from India, he had found his brothers living on the streets of Bristol. Neither had ever explained why they'd left their mother. Squalid as it had become, her home should have been preferable to city streets in early spring. For any other man, those few months of horror would have faded into blissful forgetfulness, fogged over by the blanket of passing time. But there was that prodigious memory. And while Mark had stopped waking in the middle of the night after a few months, Smite never had. Not in the years he'd lived with Ash. Smite didn't forget: not whatever it was that had happened, nor, apparently, that it was Ash's fault it had transpired in the first place.

Perhaps that was why, when Ash had invited his brother to Parford Manor, the man had fobbed him off with excuses. But when Mark asked, he had dropped everything and come running.

His brothers had passed from discussion of art to some new philosophical text that had recently been released to great acclaim. Naturally, Ash hadn't read it. In fact, he hadn't even heard of it. Next to them, Ash felt profoundly empty and wistfully ignorant. He'd been trying to scrape together a fortune at fourteen, so that his younger brothers could study Latin declensions. He'd succeeded.

But he hadn't known that in so doing, he was guaranteeing that he would never again have the privilege of engaging either of them in meaningful conversation. Mark and Smite were bound together with the threads of a thousand common experiences, everything from the hidden truth of those years when Ash had been gone, to their time at university. And Ash would never, ever be able to share any of that with them.

"Do you want some refreshment?" he asked. "The cook here serves the most amazing cream teas. I can ring for some."

His brothers turned in unison, as if surprised that Ash was still present.

"I've been sitting in the coach for hours," Smite said. "The last thing I want to do is sit again. Besides, I'm not hungry."

Ash tried again. "Well, then. There's a lovely promenade that follows the banks of the river. If you would care to join me…?"

Smite turned his head to look at Mark, his eyes widening.

"No," Mark said gently. "I don't think we'll be walking along the river right now."

It was that same rebuke he always got from his brother. Smite had never spoken his accusations aloud. He just rejected every gift Ash laid at his feet, every suggestion for camaraderie, one by one. Even the gentlest slap on the face came to sting, after it had been repeated often enough. And this particular slap was none too gentle.

They were trying to get rid of him. Ash felt that hollow lump in his chest, that *distance* between him and his brothers.

I'm sorry I ever left. I'm sorry for whatever happened to you out there. I'm sorry there's nothing between us to stitch together into even a pretense of friendship. I'm sorry, Smite. But he couldn't get the words out of his throat.

"Well," he finally said. "I'll leave you two alone, then. I have work to do."

He turned his back on them. Right now, even the books waiting for him in the library seemed preferable to another rejection.

CHAPTER THIRTEEN

UNSURPRISINGLY, THE mess of ink that faced him on the pages offered Ash scant comfort. The wide glass doors in the library looked out on the garden where his brothers stood. It was hot enough that the windows had been, by necessity, thrown open. The breeze that wafted in should have been cool and comforting. Instead, it carried to him the dim rumble of their laughter—an amusement he could not share, couched in words he could not make out.

He drifted to look out the window, with the sick sensation of a man scratching at a scab—knowing that the wound was best left alone, lest it fester, but unable to keep his hands away.

Mark was pointing out various features in the garden while Smite watched. Ash felt as if he were their geriatric father, stooped by age and bearded in white, rather than the sibling who was a mere handful of years their elder. His hands clenched on the frame of the window.

"Ash?"

At that quiet query, he turned around. Margaret was standing in the doorway, her brows knit in an expression of concern. He hadn't seen her in days. He'd thought she was avoiding him.

She was dressed as she always was—in a loose frock

of dark gray muslin, the only definition being the sash that pulled the dress about her waist. Her hair was pulled back into a tight knot at the nape of her neck and pinned into place. The picture would have made another woman seem severe. But the warm, interested light in her eyes softened the effect, and suddenly he no longer felt quite so isolated.

"Is something wrong?" she asked.

His gaze strayed out the window once more, to Mark and Smite. They were happy, chattering back and forth between themselves. He wasn't so selfish as to wish them miserable.

"No." He swallowed the accompanying sigh. It sat like a lump of indigestible gristle, deep in his belly. "Nothing's wrong. Everything is precisely as it should be."

It must not have been an especially convincing denial, because she raised one eyebrow and placed her hand on her hip. "Usually," she said, "when one speaks the truth, *one* answer suffices. You just answered me three times."

He held up his hands in surrender. "Well, then. Come see what has me in such a state."

She came to stand by him. From this vantage point, they could see the shrubs of the formal gardens, trimmed into precise low squares. Rosebushes waved pink heads in the wind. And beyond that...

Smite's hair was a shade darker than the bark of the walnut tree just beyond him. It gleamed in the sunlight. He was slightly taller than Mark, and he bent his head towards his brother as they talked.

"You see?" Ash said in his cheeriest tone. "My

brothers are both here. What could I possibly have to grieve over?"

"You're not grieving," Margaret said. "I know that look on your face."

"Do you, then?" He asked the question out of genuine interest. He'd not been faced with both his brothers before this moment. How could she possibly have seen it?

"Intimately." Her voice was low. "I know what it's like to stand on the outside and look in, believing I will never be accepted. I know what it's like to yearn to be a part of something, and yet to know that it will never come. Trust me, Ash. I know."

Of course she would know. Ash put little faith in labels; in his experience, a title had never made a man worthwhile. You judged a man—or a woman—by what he did, how he spoke, the way he met your eyes…or failed to do so. But too many others eschewed actual observation in lieu of proxies. Who your father was. Whether your parents had been married. How much wealth you had, and how long it had been in your family.

"I understand," he said softly. "Your life would have been very different if you'd been Parford's daughter, instead of his servant."

She looked up at him, a sad tilt to her eyes. He had a sudden urge to burn every one of those dull, severe frocks. He wanted to replace them with vibrant silks—something to draw attention to her, to bring out the intelligent light in her eyes. Anything to chase away the haunting sadness that touched her features. It felt as if his own grief echoed through her.

She reached out and set her hand atop his. It was,

perhaps, the first time she had deliberately touched him since he'd returned from London. He sucked in his breath, hoping. He could feel the warmth of her against him. He turned his hand to press hers. He hadn't meant to grip so hard, but she did not pull away.

"I know precisely how you feel," she said. "What I do not know is why you are in here, watching them, instead of out there forcing your way in. I can attest to the efficacy of your charm."

She turned her face up to his, her dark eyes glinting.

"Can you, then? Attest to my charm?"

He had not let go of her hand. He ought to have, but he didn't dare—and she was gripping him back so hard, her fingernails cutting into his palm with the best kind of pain.

"Intimately," she said again.

He wasn't displaying any of that vaunted charm now. He dropped her hand and looked away. "I wish to God," he said passionately, "that I had never gone to India. I wish I had never left them. But I did, little knowing that the gulf my actions would open would be wider than a handful of years and a few thousand miles of ocean. I wish I had not gone."

"No, you don't."

"Pardon?" She'd spoken so matter-of-factly that he could scarcely believe what he had heard.

"You heard me. You don't wish any of this undone—not your time in India, not your stupendous fortune, nor even the suit in the ecclesiastical courts. Certainly not your place as a duke's heir. I know you, Ash. Had you stayed in England with your brothers—had you merely accepted your lot in life and sunk into poverty, you wouldn't be happy. You *enjoy* your wealth. You live to shower your brothers with presents. You would *despise* being a poor man."

He let out a sigh. "It's a hard woman who won't even let a man indulge in a little unreasonableness. That seems most unfair."

"What is unfair is that you want to have the benefits of your voyage to India without paying the price. That's what makes this world so damnably awful—the choices you must make that cost you what you most desire."

"It's more than that, though. When I went to India… it was as if I chose to be an entirely different person. I gave up the chance to be a person like my father. He was a mill owner and a tradesman—but he loved to read. He would be gone on business for weeks, and when he returned, he'd bring back all sorts of books. I used to believe he knew everything. And now, my brothers take after him. I can't. I've tried to figure it out. I've tried to become that person. But what you do when you're young has a way of sticking with you. At fourteen, my brothers were reading. I was making my first five thousand pounds." He shrugged. "I would trade every penny I had, if it would mean that I could walk down that path with them and talk like that."

"You left because your sister died, Ash." Margaret looked at him, tapping her lips with one finger. "Would you really risk your brothers' lives for the sake of their friendship?"

"No." Damn it. "Never."

She inclined her head, and he accepted that as a simple judgment. *You made your choice. Now stop whining about it.*

Too true. There had been enough of this indulgent

claptrap. "Younger brothers make me mawkish," he said by way of halfhearted apology. "They're like little repositories of sentiment. One looks at them and remembers how helpless they once were."

But Margaret was shaking her head. "I think you give yourself too little credit. Maybe you cannot speak to your brothers about books. But you can talk to them. I doubt they despise you."

"But they're educated."

She turned her head to one side and looked at him.

"*I* can talk to Mark, and *I* never went to Oxford."

"But that's different. You at least—"

She looked at him.

"You," he said quietly, "can read." And then he glanced away, so that he would not have to see his own shame reflected in her eyes.

She didn't say anything. He'd wanted her to protest, to tell him it wasn't true, that he could bridge that gap. But then, she wouldn't lie to him. He *was* uneducated. And illiterate. And while it made not a bit of difference in the world of business, she must see how impassable a barrier it posed with his brothers. He squeezed her hand, where it was still trapped in his. He wasn't letting her go—not even now, when she must see what he truly was.

She ran her thumb down his fingers. A tiny caress, but a caress nonetheless.

"When I met you," she said quietly, "I'd lost the ability to glance in a looking glass and believe I was worth something."

She repeated that touch a second time, and his eyes fluttered shut.

"And then you looked at me and you told me I mattered. You didn't need theories or arguments to make me believe it. You just…looked. And you believed."

They'd touched before—in affection, in lust, even in comfort. But her hand, stroking his, returning the strong grip he gave her—*this* was something different.

"There is…there is something I came here to tell you, Ash. There's a great deal you *don't* know about me. But right now, I want you to know one thing."

Her hand whispered up behind him, finding the nape of his neck. She drew his head down to rest against hers.

"You matter," she whispered to him. "You are important. And you are the single most magnificent man I have ever had the honor of meeting."

His breath shivered out and he put his free arm around her, pulling her close. He could feel her chest rise and fall. Her breath mingled with his.

"I don't ever want you to think otherwise. Not for an instant."

There was a fierce note in her voice as she spoke. So it hadn't been the premonition of mere lust he'd sensed, that day he'd first seen her. It had been a tiny taste of this—this intimacy that went so far beyond mere desire. It had wound itself between them, interlacing his own emotions. He could untangle their intertwined fingers, but he couldn't unravel this.

He inhaled her breath, and he believed. He leaned down and tasted her lips. There was no prelude to the kiss—no light tentative touches, to be sure of his reception. It was a full, hot-blooded exchange the instant their mouths touched, carnal and wanting. Desperate. His body reacted to the feel of her in his arms—her soft roundedness, the slim curve of her waist. But it wasn't just lust that made him pull her close.

He kissed her because she made him feel strong where he'd felt vulnerable and weak. Because she saw him—*all* of him—and didn't wince and glance away. Because she knew what he was like when he was stripped of defenses, and she reached for him anyway.

This was what he wanted—her. Margaret. No. *Them.*

When he lifted his head to draw breath, she looked at him.

"Remember," she said softly. "When—when you know everything. Remember. You are important. And…and I mean that."

And then, before he could ask her what she meant, she pulled away from him and left.

Margaret had seen Ash cheerfully powerful, as talkative as a jaybird. She'd seen him silently powerful while he was listening to those around her. She didn't like seeing him vulnerable. It made her feel odd inside—hotly angry on his behalf, and enraged that someone had made him feel that way.

Rather hypocritical; in a short space of time, when the truth came out, she would be the one to introduce doubt into his life.

She shook her head and walked down the gallery towards her father's room. The duke's chambers lay past the end of the wide hall, down another long hallway. For months, the length of that hall had been enshrouded in silence as she traversed it. The servants tasked with airing the rooms that abutted his sickroom had walked on tiptoe, for fear the slightest noise would bring on the duke's ire.

But as she walked down the hall today, she heard the deep rumble of masculine laughter. A door was ajar; as she passed by, a thin slit of daylight made a jaunty angle across the dark carpet.

Mrs. Benedict must have put Ash's brothers in the upper parlor. Margaret stopped, and another ring of laughter traveled out to greet her. Mark's chuckle she already knew. His brother, the middle Mr. Turner with the dreadful name—he must have been the one with the baritone.

Margaret set her hand against the door and pushed it open another few inches.

The brothers stood on the far side of the room, leaning towards one another as if in each other's confidences. They had thrown a window open, and they were looking out, the curtains fluttering about them. They did not see her enter, as they were both engaged in gazing into the distance, their shoulders forming one uniform wall. She would have guessed they were brothers from that unity. If that hadn't betrayed their relationship she could see some similarity in their figures. They were both lean without being skinny, tall without towering over her.

Her mother had used this parlor as a dry, stuffy place to take tea; it had the most formal arrangement of all the rooms in Parford Manor. Margaret could not recall a time when the gilded walls had ever felt a breeze. For as long as she remembered, the curtains had been tightly drawn to protect the lush carpet underfoot from the sun.

But daylight played across the window sash now,

spilling carelessly from there onto the priceless carpet.

It wasn't the sunlight Margaret minded. It wasn't the laughter that set her stomach to a slow boil. It was the way these two men stood in such close friendship, never caring that not so far from this room their eldest brother was feeling *vulnerable*. Alone.

The taller gentleman—Mr. Smite Turner—appeared to be in the midst of telling his brother a story. He had shed his coat and had draped it over one arm—a trick that reminded her of Ash. He gesticulated with the other hand. His face was turned in profile. His visage was a quiet echo of Ash's. But where Ash had dark, curling hair, this man's was cropped close to his skull, and it was almost ebony. Where Ash's skin was tinged in color from the sun, this man was pale.

One thing they had in common was that air of charisma. He said something, and Mark let out a cackle of laughter. At the same moment, the new fellow turned his head slightly and met her eyes. The friendly smile froze in place. His face stiffened; his chin lifted. His eyes grew harder, and he scanned her from head to toe.

Margaret was used to men looking her over. But this perusal didn't feel like masculine admiration. It felt as if he were cataloguing her, from the half-boots still on her feet from the gardens, to the starched white collar of her gown. He nodded once, as if he'd fit her into some mental taxonomy.

"Mark," he said quietly, "this is she, is it not?"

She? Etiquette demanded that Margaret curtsy, that she smile at this man in greeting. But he hadn't even addressed her. He'd been rude to Ash. And he was standing here, laughing with Mark, while his brother felt unwelcome. She stared back at him and straightened her spine.

"At least she's pretty," he finally said.

"That went without saying," Mark said simply. "You can always count on Ash for that."

So the brothers had spoken not only of her, but about their elder brother. Behind his back. Margaret's anger boiled over. She strode across the room to stand before the two men.

"You," she said accusingly, jabbing her finger towards Mr. Smite Turner's chest. "You may talk about *me* as if I am not in the room, but don't you *dare* do it to your brother. He risked his life for your sakes in India, and now you two leave him alone, isolated? You speak of him as if he were nothing more than a choice bit of gossip? You make him feel as if he's not a welcome part of your family? How dare *you?*" She turned to Mark. "How dare you? I thought better of you than this."

Mr. Smite Turner held his hands up, palms out, as if to stem this onslaught. A bemused expression lit his face. That gesture was so very like Ash—and the similarity only enraged Margaret further.

"Have you any notion how much you're hurting him with your carelessness?" He'd talked about his brothers with her, and every aspect of those conversations returned to her now. "He paid for your education. He funded your apprenticeship. He sends you a quarterly allowance, even if you choose not to accept it. And you repay him by excluding him from your tight little circle of friendship? By refusing *his* invitations, and then accepting one from Mark? You make this house the grounds for your own private party, and you fail to issue him an invitation. Shame on you. Shame on you *both*."

That bemused smile grew. "My God, Mark. She has a tongue on her." Mr. Smite Turner rubbed his chin with his hand. "Lady Anna Margaret, this is not what you suppose. I did not come because I wished to exclude Ash. But circumstances—"

"Circumstances? Truly? If you didn't wish to exclude him, then where is your brother now?"

The man drew back and folded his arms, and a small smile twitched his lips. "I don't know, my lady. Shall I fetch him and perform the requisite introductions?"

"Introductions? Why—" She choked on the rest of her sentence. Through the thick haze of her rage, she heard what he'd said—really heard. He'd called her *my lady*. And before that, he'd called her… Oh, God. His words seemed to echo, and her hands felt suddenly cold. He'd called her Lady Anna Margaret. *Lady Anna Margaret.* He knew. He knew.

She'd thought to have a few more days. A week, even.

"What did you call me?" A futile attempt. Her protest was too late in coming. "I'm not—I'm not—" A more ineffectual denial Margaret had never heard.

And naturally, he didn't believe it. He shook his dark head, the motion quick and precise. "No point dissembling, my lady. I saw you two years prior at the theater. You were attending with your brother, and I remember everything I see. The line of your nose. Your chin. If you would like, I could recite precisely what you wore that night, down to the pearls around your neck."

"Pearls?"

"South Sea pearls, round, with a light golden sheen. A quarter of an inch in diameter each." He shut his eyes and moved his lips, as if counting. "A strand of likely thirty such. Perhaps as many as thirty-two. I could not see the entire string from where I stood."

He opened his eyes again. He was not guessing. He was *sure*. And he was describing her mother's strand of pearls—a necklace she'd borrowed on occasion.

"I see I made quite the impression."

Mark came to stand by her. "Smite remembers everything. Precisely."

Margaret drew a shaky breath. Denial wasn't working. Defense was no longer an option. That left only attack. "That's very well," she started again smoothly, "but we are not here to talk about me, interesting as I might be. I came to ask—no, *demand,* that you talk with him."

The two brothers exchanged glances.

"Let me strike a bargain," the elder Mr. Turner said. "You stop browbeating me like a shrew for my treatment of my brother, and I'll keep your little secret. How is that for a trade?" He smiled at her negligently.

If Ash knew the truth about her, he would never look at her the same way again. He would never smile at her, would never believe that she was something special. She would become just another Dalrymple to him—and a deceitful, lying one at that. That was the inevitable end to their relationship—recrimination and anger. There was no future between them.

Margaret had no desire to rush headlong into that nonexistent future.

All she would have to do was walk away. And do so, knowing that he was sitting in his office, hurting, because these two men were too selfish to understand what they had done to him. After all that Ash had given her, he didn't deserve to have her desert him as well.

"No deal." Her voice shook. "What sort of man are you, to offer to bargain with your brother's happiness, in exchange for a moment's comfort?"

Mark and Smite exchanged glances again.

"I *told* you so," Mark said, an impish smile lighting his face. "I told you she wouldn't take the bait. And I was right."

"You did. Brat." There was no accusation in that last word though, only affection. Smite shook his head and glanced over at Margaret. "You see, when I heard that my brother—my eldest brother, who rescued me from the streets, who stayed up to three in the morning laboring over the accounts from the previous night so that he might pay for my education—when I heard that he had taken an extraordinary interest in a woman who might have been the daughter of his worst enemy—yes, Lady Anna Margaret, I *did* come running to his side. That is precisely how I repay him. I don't let my brothers come to harm."

"*You* knew?" Margaret glanced at Mark.

"I guessed."

"And still you were kind to me." Had it been an attempt to win her confidences, to use her?

"It was a recent guess." Mark shrugged. "Unlike my other brothers, I've never much believed in this foolish dispute. I knew you would keep Ash on his toes long before I believed you were a Dalrymple."

His elder brother snorted in disbelief.

Mark grinned across at her. "I would take care,

Smite. I've been teaching her how to disable a man. Her lessons continue apace."

"I'm so worried." He rolled his eyes.

"Don't let her sweet appearance fool you. She hit hard enough to take Ash down."

Margaret tapped her foot angrily. "*She* is standing right in front of you."

Smite glanced at her. "I suppose if *she* truly intended him harm, she wouldn't have cut into a rage at me. My God. Has she put him in his place like that?"

"More than once," Mark answered. "It was magnificent. You should have been there."

"You can address me in the following ways: 'Lady Anna Margaret;' or 'ahoy, you there!' or, if you should wish, just Margaret—that is, after all, what my friends and family call me. You may not call me *she*. Not under any circumstances, not when speaking to my face."

Mr. Smite Turner smiled again. There was little amusement in the expression. "I apologize for my rudeness. Mark and I…we've experienced a great deal together. When we're together, we sometimes lapse into familiarity. We love Ash. But you must understand that as dedicated as Ash is, he is also overpoweringly annoying."

He spoke those words using the same solemn certainty with which he'd pronounced her name, as if this were a simple fact. Margaret felt the bottom drop out of her stomach.

"Annoying? I hadn't noticed," she said a little hotly—and rather untruthfully, because as she spoke, she remembered the master key hanging from her neck—and his tiger-cub Laurette—and his damned insistence the other night that Lady Anna Margaret was a pitiful creature. He was easily the most annoying man she had ever met. She looked away.

The two brothers simply looked at each other, and finally Mark nodded, and Smite let out a sigh.

"If I believed you intended him harm—but you don't, do you? I suppose he charmed you out of any such thoughts in the first hour he knew you." Mr. Smite Turner shook his head. "Everything is always so simple for him."

"In point of fact," Margaret said, "it took him more than a week."

He truly smiled at that. "Good. Then he'll not trample all over you—he's wont to do that, you know. Ash just *wants* things, and generally, reality leaps to make them happen. After you've spent more time with him, you'll see."

"But I won't spend time with him," Margaret said, "not after you divulge my identity tonight." She had known this moment was coming. But it had always seemed a distant possibility on the horizon—an eventual discovery, not an imminent threat. She was about to lose him. And it should not have felt so much like a *loss*. She had, after all, known he was never hers. Not truly.

"I was ready to do so," Smite said slowly. "I came here, convinced I'd have to wrestle him into facing the truth. But Mark has dissuaded me. No, you'll have to tell him yourself."

Margaret stared at him. "Why…why would you allow me to do that?"

It was Mark who finally spoke. "Because it will cause him less pain to hear it freely offered from *you* than to have the truth come from us."

"You'll tell him by tomorrow morning," Smite said firmly. "Because according to Mark, he cares for you. And my brother *deserves* to have the truth from the woman he cares about." He stared at her, his gaze as implacable as hers had been earlier. Mark, next to him, looked no less sober. Together, they formed a solid wall of grim male intention. It almost warmed her heart, to know that they cared for him this much.

Still, she put one hand on her hip. "If you don't want him hurt," she said to the elder Turner, "perhaps once—just once—you might let him do something for you. He hates that you take nothing from him."

His chin rose. His nostrils flared. But if he'd heard what she said, he did not show it. Instead, he fixed his unblinking gaze on her. "Tell him. I'll give you one day."

CHAPTER FOURTEEN

THE HOURS BEFORE dinner dragged. Ash attempted to focus during a series of meetings with his men. The words they spoke, however, barely intruded into his consciousness. He wasn't even sure he heard his responses to their queries. His mind was elsewhere—on his brothers.

When one of his men slid a stack of papers towards him, he simply stared at it.

"What is this?" he asked quietly.

Across the table from him, Strong grimaced. Cottry, who had handed him the papers, looked up uneasily. "An accounting of the expenses estimated for refurbishing the *Lily*." Ash glanced down. The pages were mostly numbers—and numbers, unlike words, had always made sense to him. But still, there was enough text that following it would be difficult. And besides, it was the principle of the thing.

"Sir," Strong continued, "I know you don't like reports, but there are so many little details, all of which you must be conversant with, if you are to make an informed decision. So if you'll just turn to page two—"

Ash shook his head.

Books had worked for his brothers. They could have simply read what Strong presented to them and been able to engage him in a discussion of endless minutiae. For them, there was no difference between actual

knowledge and this written facsimile thereof. But Ash
had never had the trick of learning from words. He
lacked whatever magic happened behind most people's
eyes, the miracle that transmuted ink into understanding. Words were just words. He couldn't read about
agriculture and have it come to life in his mind. Until
he felt the soil between his fingers, until he watched
plants poke green spears through rich mulch, he would
never understand farming.

He sighed and pushed the papers back across the
desk. "No, Cottry."

"But, sir—"

"No buts. No excuses. My mind simply doesn't work
on paper." It was as close as he'd come to ever admit-
ting the truth to anyone, besides Margaret. "It works
on *things*—people, ships, jewels. Tangible items. I want
to be able to put my hands on something, look it in the
eye."

Cottry exhaled in frustration. "Sir. *Lily* is a ship.
She doesn't have eyes."

Ash stood up and beckoned the man closer. Cottry
swallowed and leaned in his direction. Ash looked at
him. He was an intelligent fellow. This wasn't about
Ash's supposed refusal to read documents. No—this
was something he went through with all his men at
some point. They huddled in the nest like little fledg-
lings, beaks open wide to receive what scant nourish-
ment he might deliver.

"Cottry," Ash said, with a weary shake of his head,
"I own an entire fleet of vessels. I have holdings in four
countries and warehouses in seven ports. I haven't the
time to sort through maintenance records, even if I had
the inclination." Or the ability.

Cottry swallowed.

"You're afraid," Ash said. It didn't require much intelligence to make that out. He'd seen it too many times before to miss the telltale signs. "You're afraid you've made a mistake, and that if it goes unchecked, something will go dreadfully wrong. And so you want me to look everything over. Well. I am not a balustrade, erected at the edge of a cliff to keep you from tumbling over. I am not your governess, tasked to keep you safe. I am your employer."

Cottry nodded.

"I hired you," Ash said, "because I knew you could make these decisions on your own."

Cottry inhaled. He looked a faint plea at Ash.

"The first time's the worst," Ash said cheerily. "Make the decision on your own—tell me about it—and afterwards, if you need to vomit, please try to make your way to the chamberpot first."

"Sir." Cottry sounded strangled.

"It's a ship, man, not a battle plan. If you are in error, I'll only lose money. Use your best judgment." He leaned forwards and looked the man in the eyes. "I know it's good."

Cottry nodded weakly. It was weak assent—but it was assent.

Ash gave him one last nod. "I know you can do it," he said quietly. Cottry met his eyes, and a ripple of panic passed over his face. Ash had seen that look a hundred times at this stage, and he knew precisely what it meant: *Dear God, please don't let me fail.*

As his men left, Ash realized that Margaret was right. His method of doing business had started out as a way for him to hide his weakness. But since then, he'd met too many other tradesmen who became trapped by their own myopia. They'd been too bogged down by details to successfully handle an empire.

Ash hadn't been able to comprehend all the details, and so instead, he had learned to comprehend other people. People wanted to believe they were capable, and when you told them they were, they leaped to prove it.

Ash was never going to be a scholar. But then…he didn't have to be one. He was good enough, as himself. Ash stood and brushed off his coat. It was time to give it one last try.

His brothers had been set up, along with a tray of sandwiches, in a parlor decorated in stuffy pinkness. He wondered if Mrs. Benedict had put them here out of some perverse sense of humor—the femininity of the room, with its embroidered roses and gold-scrolled wallpaper, along with a bewildering array of lace-edged pillows, was almost overwhelming.

He swung the door in. Smite was sitting alone. Of course he was reading a book.

A decanter of port sat on a nearby table, and glasses were ready beside it. Likely that was Mrs. Benedict's doing, too—although this had substantially less to do with humor and more to do with a certain practicality that understood the typical gentleman of Ash's station all too well.

Smite had not drunk the port. Instead, he sat reading his book. He turned a page and glanced down. He almost seemed to be simply staring at it for a few seconds, before he transferred his gaze to the next one and then turned again.

Ash had never really been scared. Not even in India, where on one memorable occasion, he'd found himself alone and surrounded by natives who brandished spears. He'd always had a sense of things, a knowledge of what to say—or, as was the case in that instance, how to gesture. He'd been able to look at people and intuit what they wanted, what they feared and how to provide them with the former in a way that profited everyone. But with his brothers…he had no notion of how to proceed. It was as if they were an extension of him, so close to his heart that he could not guess at the topography of their emotions. He could see no secret way into their hearts.

Smite looked up at Ash's footsteps. He simply stared at him for a second, and then, slowly, a smile crawled over his face. Ash's stomach lurched.

God, he loved his brother so much.

"I've met your Miss Lowell," Smite said.

His younger brother deployed words precisely. He'd done so even before he took articles in Bristol, but legal training had accelerated the tendency. Smite's use of the possessive was not happenstance.

His Miss Lowell. Ash liked that thought very well.

"I see," Smite said dryly, "that you don't bother to disclaim her. I do wonder if she is possibly good enough for you."

Good enough for *him?* Ash held his breath. He wasn't sure if this was a conscious slur on his brother's part, denigrating her station, or a shocking compliment to himself. "And your conclusion?"

Smite simply shook his head. "No. She is not." He turned away. Nothing more to bolster Ash's hopes. That bare dismissal felt like a slap in the face.

"Don't make hasty judgments," Ash said. "Look, stay a few nights. A week, if you dare. Talk with her some more."

Smite let out a long sigh.

It was cowardly, but Ash added, "I know Mark would enjoy your company."

"I'm leaving in the next hour."

"For God's sake, it's barely September. The courts are closed. I'd be willing to wager that the man you work under isn't even in town at the moment. Could you not stay even one night? You won't make it to Bristol by nightfall, and we're due for a storm any moment now."

Smite's lips pressed together, but he said nothing. Compliment or insult, there was no way to interpret his hasty departure as anything other than another rejection. Ash let out a pained breath. It had always been like this between them, ever since Ash had come back from India. Mark at least *tried* to talk with Ash.

"What must I do?" He strode forwards. "What must I do, that I offend you no longer, Smite? Do you want me to beg? I'll grovel. Do you want me laid low? I'll cast myself at your feet."

Smite interlaced his fingers precisely in front of him. "You have nothing to atone for. And no matter how hard you try, it cannot be made up in any event. But, Ash—" his brother raised his eyes "—you don't offend me. You never have."

His actions spoke louder than words. "You'll appear the instant Mark dashes off a request, but you won't even stay another twenty-four hours when I ask it of you? Don't tell me you would talk to *Mark* this way."

"Of course not," Smite said in disdain. "*Mark* would know better than to ask me to stay."

"But—"

"Mark asked me to come here to…meet Miss Lowell. For you, you barbarian, as it appears that when it comes to her, you are intent on diving off a cliff, headfirst. I came for *you*. Not for him."

His brother spoke those words as he always did, clean and crisp, with just a hint of wry humor. Ash stared at him, not quite able to comprehend what he'd just said. He wanted to hug him. Or, more like, to barrel him over and pin him to the ground. But so much exuberance would make him uneasy.

Instead Ash reached out his hand and lightly tapped him on the shoulder. It would have to do, as embraces went. "Thank you," he said. It seemed inadequate to the moment.

Smite looked up at him, his features held very, very still. "You know, Ash," he said quietly, "you cannot buy me back my childhood. It's not your fault I lost it, nor is it something you could purchase in any event."

They never talked of those years. Never. For Smite to bring it up on his own… Ash held his breath. Whatever had transpired in his absence, Ash *knew* he could not make up for it. It didn't stop him from wanting to try. From wanting to throw everything he had in his brother's direction, just to try to win a smile from him.

"You can't purchase my childhood," Smite repeated. His hands spread, and he flattened them on the table in front of him. He seemed distinctly uneasy. "But perhaps there is something you can do for me as an adult. Some two things."

A peace offering. After all these years of spurning Ash's attempted gifts, there was a peace offering. "Name them," he said hoarsely.

"I'd like to be a magistrate."

"Done. Hell, when I'm the Duke of Parford, I'll see

you appointed to the Queen's Bench. Do you fancy being Lord Chief Justice?"

Smite smiled and shook his head. "Stop embellishing on my dreams, Ash. A magistrate. I have no desire to sit in the assizes. I'd be satisfied to be a small dispensary of justice—someone who sees little people, and who, from time to time, might make a difference in someone's life. I know that *small* is not your style. But it is mine."

Ash nodded. "Why?"

His brother smiled faintly once more. "Because what happened to us… I want to make certain it won't happen again. Not on my watch."

"And the second thing?"

Smite's gaze slipped away. "I'm sure Mark has shared his feelings on this point. But we both know how Mark is." His fingers drummed against wood. "It's about Richard Dalrymple. I want you to take away everything he has ever cared for. Turnabout, after all, is only fair."

MARGARET KNEW SHE NEEDED to talk with Ash, but he'd been busy up until dinner, in anticipation of his brother's departure. It was almost ten in the evening when Margaret stood in her father's room, her hands on her hips, listening to him complain.

"Why," he demanded, "is it still so warm? It's September. Autumn should be coming on."

The weather over the past few days had not cooled. Instead the heat had built, a furnace stoked by each passing day. The air had grown still and stagnant. Even if Margaret had opened the windows, no breeze would have ruffled the curtains. Instead, the air hung thick and humid, like some bloated creature hunkered sullenly in one corner of its lair.

Her father continued. "It's time for fires in the fireplace, and autumn chills and the like."

"Would you like me to build you a fire?" she asked dryly.

"Don't be a ninny. I would like you to alter the weather." He looked at her implacably, as if a strong enough ducal command might cause storm clouds to gather.

"Well, then. I'll just snap my fingers and make it so. I hope that will satisfy you, Your Grace." As she spoke, she dabbed gently at his face with a towel. Since she had been left alone at Parford Manor, his incessant demands had become worse, even less reasonable. Had he ever loved her at all?

Had *she* ever loved *him?* Perhaps there had never been anything between them but duty and obligation.

"Worthless girl," he muttered, rubbing the side of his cheek.

Margaret's hands closed around the towel. She wasn't performing tasks for pay. She wasn't a bear, to dance at the end of a rope.

If she'd been confused about Ash, she was utterly discombobulated when it came to her father. If she was worthless, it was because *he* had made her so— because he'd engaged in bigamy, and because he had simply ceased to play the charade of father, once the truth was revealed to the world.

"What was that you said? I couldn't make it out." Her voice was low and fierce in her ears.

Her father's hand came to a standstill. But if he had ever had the capacity to hear the dangerous note that touched Margaret's voice, he'd lost it with age and illness. Or maybe he'd always had that irritable lift to his chin, and she'd not noticed.

"I said you were worthless, girl."

He was ill. He was old. She turned away from him, her hands shaking on the laudanum bottle with the sheer effort of restraint. She was not going to abandon him. Damn him, she would not do to him what he'd done to her. If she did, she'd be almost as worthless as he called her. She set the cloth down on the table.

"Can't even hold your own against an old man, confined to bed." His voice came from behind her, taunting. "What must I do to get a response from you? Or are you so tainted with your mother's weak blood that you can do nothing about an insult except lie down and die in response?"

At those words, her control broke. A fist seemed to clench around her heart, so tight it felt like to burst with rage.

Margaret whirled around. She was across the room in half a pace. "Don't you dare." Her voice was a low tremble; her chest was about to explode. "Don't you *dare* talk about my mother in that manner. You killed her, you and your foolish unconcern. Don't you dare tell me it's an insult that I have her blood in my veins. I'll not have it." She clenched her trembling hands on the edge of his coverlet, twisting it, while some violent part of her wished she could shake him instead.

"Ha." He smiled at her—not a friendly expression, but an almost ferocious grin. But his smile lasted too long—stretching from fierce triumphant growl into something harder, more painful. His lips drew back in a thin, painful rictus. And then, he let himself fall to the bed, simply crumpling into a heap before her eyes. "Fetch horde benedictive," he snapped.

"Pardon?" In her rage, she must have misheard him.

He was looking up at her, his eyes as fierce as ever, piercing into her. "Cord defiant misled to pivot the gunnery. Fidelity lost fortune under witness putter delight wiggle detritus with the obsequious toll for who bunting pole over the witches to view like sea."

"What does that mean? Is this some new and unfortunate way to mock me?" How many had there been over the last weeks? How much resistance and malingering had she suffered? "It won't work."

He continued to gaze at her, trembling. He almost looked helpless. "Homonym! Homonym!"

Helpless? He was terror-stricken. And with the chill of that knowledge penetrating Margaret's fury, she could see now what she'd missed earlier. He hadn't let himself fall; he'd fallen, his muscles useless. His limbs trembled now, little vibrations passing through his hands. He wasn't speaking nonsense to mock her. This was not mere recalcitrance on his part. Something was wrong. Something was dreadfully wrong. He kept talking, a string of gibberish issuing from his mouth, nonsense words strung together as if by a madman.

It had been only a few seconds since he had begun to babble, but she felt as if she had been staring at him for an eternity. She broke her gaze away and ran for the door. When she wrenched it open, the footmen bracketing each side turned to her. They must have seen the dismay that lit her eyes, because their shoulders tensed.

"Josephs. Fetch a physician. Fetch a physician *instantly.*"

The man on the left started down the hall without waiting for further instruction. Thirty minutes to go to the village on horseback. Thirty to return. And in the interim, she was going to have to keep him alive. How was she to do that, when she didn't even know what was transpiring? Worse yet: was this her fault? She'd finally lost her temper and turned on him.

A clap of thunder sounded overhead, breaking through the oppressive heat, and Margaret shivered.

Behind her, her father's voice continued. "Liquor to the fires offput less…"

"Tollin," she commanded, "come with me." The other footman followed.

Her father was shouting now, words thrown into a maelstrom of syllables, devoid of sense. He lay in bed, looking upwards, and Margaret felt cold steal over her hands.

"Should we dose him with laudanum?" the footman asked.

"I don't know." It would keep him quiet, but laudanum was tricky—too much at the wrong time, and he might lose hold of his grasp on life instead.

And what if this was the beginning of the end? What if, after all this time, the words he spouted were an apology, and she just couldn't understand it? Could she simply cut them off? What if he still loved her and would not be able to say it at the end because she'd drugged him?

"I don't know anything. He's not thrashing about. If he had gone mad, wouldn't he be thrashing?"

Tollin looked at her, frozen in horror. And that much recalled her to her position. It didn't matter that she wasn't really a nurse. It certainly didn't matter that she wasn't Lady Anna Margaret any longer. She had to *act* like her today. An untrained, inefficient girl would be of no use here, and so she couldn't be an untrained girl. There was no room for her anxiety.

She took a deep breath.

Miss Lowell, you magnificent creature, I want you to paint your own canvas. I want you to unveil yourself before the world.

Margaret straightened her spine and walked briskly forwards.

She took his wrist and felt for his pulse. His hand trembled in hers, but she found the beat, steady despite the tumultuous flow of his words. "No," she pronounced, with more sureness than she felt. "He's not mad." She laid her hand against his forehead. "The only thing he's doing is talking, and there's no harm in that."

"But—"

Margaret looked behind her to discover that Tollin was no longer alone. Several other servants had joined him—two of the upstairs maids, their hands clasped together, and behind them, Mrs. Benedict. Word would spread. This was how panic started. The last thing she needed was a household in chaos. She had to hold them together, to make sure that her father lived until the physician could come and see what was wrong. The physician would fix everything.

Until then, she needed to keep the servants orderly. They all needed something to do.

Margaret pulled her hand from her father's forehead. "He's overly warm. Tollin, I am going to need you to fetch some ice water. And extra ice from the icehouse, while you are down there."

A few seconds of faint patter at the windows, and then came the sound of rain, pelting from the sky. Margaret shut her eyes and thought of Josephs, who was no doubt riding for the physician on horseback through the breaking storm. She felt that thread of fear pulling at her, and tamped it down. He would arrive safely. He had to.

Tollin nodded, his muscles relaxing slightly. He seemed grateful to be given something to do. She would have to assign them all tasks until the physician arrived. Yet another wave of people crowded through the door. If Margaret didn't act, her father would be smothered by well-meaning servants.

"Mrs. Benedict," Margaret said, "we'll need a posset. Something sustaining—the duke will need to keep up his strength. I'm sure that Mrs. Lorens can arrange something suitable. Please send someone to the kitchens." Mrs. Benedict met her eyes and then nodded.

Margaret leaned over her father. He was still speaking, but he was no longer shouting. Now his words came out on a whisper, a wistful stream of babble flowing over her with as much meaning as the passing water of a brook.

"I believe," she announced with as much conviction as she could muster, "that his chest has taken an ill humor, which has caused his lungs to react in this unfavorable manner."

Nobody contradicted this blatant idiocy; instead, heads nodded, pleased to be able to put words to his condition. Even *she* felt better, and she knew that she'd just invented the mysterious problem herself. Not madness, nor failure; just a lung condition, like a cough or a cold.

"We're going to need to prepare something to draw the inflammation from his chest." Something harmless. Something with a great many ingredients, which would keep everyone occupied until the physician arrived. "I'm going to need a brazier for the fire and some heated water. Willow water," she said, because that would take longer to fetch. "Then cloves. A handful of crushed calendula flowers…"

She rattled off every innocuous ingredient that came to mind. So long as they kept him cool and comfortable, it was unlikely to hurt.

Outside, thunder rumbled again, and rain continued to splash down.

As an afterthought, Margaret tasked two of the maids with standing outside the room and barring entry to anyone else.

As the servants streamed out to fetch their respective items, one more person ducked his head in. It was Ash.

He frowned at Margaret and leaned against the door frame. "Miss Lowell. What's happened?"

For the first time, a thread of fear crept through her. She'd stayed behind in part to watch over her father. The notion that Ash might do the duke harm seemed ludicrous now that she knew him. And so she didn't fear Ash himself. But she did fear *for* him. She pointed her finger at him. "Don't come any farther into the room than that chair, Mr. Turner. I mean it. Stop moving."

"Good God, Margaret."

"The duke is in serious condition. If anything happens while you're present, they will say you killed him. If he dies before Parliament votes on the Dalrymples' Act of Legitimation, you'll inherit everything. You have a reason to harm him. I'll not let anyone say you took the opportunity."

Ash's jaw set. "You don't think I would actually do him harm."

Margaret put her hands on her hips. "No. Of course not. But if you imagine I'll let anyone say you did, you've gone mad. And so not another step. If you don't come into the room, I can attest that you didn't come within ten yards."

"What difference could your testimony make? You and I—" he glanced urgently at the other servants in the room "—we're friends." His voice was low. "The Dalrymples will never believe you, not when they learn the truth of our relationship."

"They'll believe me." Her jaw set. "Trust me. They'll believe. Stay there, Ash." Her father stopped babbling, his voice trailing off into nothing. The duke didn't move—which frightened her even more than his non-sense words had done. She reached for his wrist again, and was gratified when she still found a steady pulse. The fingers of his hand contracted.

And then: "Anna?" he said. His voice was quiet. "Anna, where are you?"

"I'm here." Margaret took his hand and held it. There was nothing else for her to do, nothing but to offer this scant comfort.

From his vantage point against the wall, Ash spoke. "Why is he calling you Anna?"

Tell him. Tell him now. But this wasn't the time for it, not now, not when all of her strength needed to be concentrated on her father.

"He thinks I'm his daughter." Margaret held her father's hand in hers. "Or, perhaps his wife."

"Anna," her father said. "Don't leave me."

Perhaps this was what she'd waited for, all these weeks. Margaret bowed her head and sank into the chair beside the bed. Somewhere, somewhere inside this demanding stranger who had taken her father's place, there was someone who still remembered her. Someone who still took comfort from her presence. The man he'd once been hadn't disappeared entirely.

She held on to his hand, afraid to squeeze for fear that her father would disappear before she had a chance to greet him again. She wasn't sure how long she sat there, with the rain beating against the window pane. Long enough that the servants came and went; long enough that his forehead grew hotter, that she soaked a towel in ice water, over and over, in an attempt to cool him. Long enough that the useless herbs she'd ordered steeped in the brazier and released their wild scent into the air.

Through it all, Ash stayed in the room, leaning against the entryway, watching her. He'd made no effort to come any closer. But then, he hadn't gone away, either. No doubt he had things to do—far more important things than watching her pray for his bitterest enemy.

From behind him, Josephs pushed past him in the doorway, dripping water. He'd obviously just returned from his errand.

"Thank God, Josephs. Where is the physician?"

She saw the despair in the man's eyes before he shook his head briefly. "He's off in Witcombe, my lady, twelve miles distant. Attending a birth, his housekeeper says. No doubt with the storm, he'll spend the night. No point risking his horse returning in this weather."

Behind Josephs, Ash pushed off from the wall. "Lower Odcombe has a physician."

"Yes, sir, but Lower Odcombe is seven miles away. And with the rain and it being night and all…" Joseph trailed off, eyeing Ash uncertainly.

But Ash wasn't even looking at the man. He was watching Margaret.

"You care." His words had the ring of steel. "For whatever reason."

She had to tell him. "Ash, I—"

He cut her off with a jerk of his head. "Then I'm going." He sketched her a little bow, and before she could do more than gaze after him in confused wonder, he slipped out the door.

The duke stayed silent as the candles flickered in darkness. His spirit seemed to withdraw into his body, and the silence grew. He seemed almost corpse-like beside her. He was pale and thin, lying in the bedclothes.

She'd wondered what she thought of her father before. Now she knew. She hated what he'd done, wished he'd not retreated into arrogant incivility in his illness. She didn't understand who he'd become these past months. But as confusing and heartrending as the present was, she loved the man he'd once been. And she didn't want to believe he wasn't coming back.

THE PHYSICIAN ARRIVED a few hours later. He entered the room alone. Even though his collar was still damp from the journey, he set down his medical bag, removed his dark gloves and set to work.

Without glancing at Margaret, he came forwards. He checked her father's eyes, prodded his wrist and his abdomen. Then he placed one end of a wooden cylinder against her father's chest and set his ear against the other.

Margaret waited patiently until he straightened.

"He's not in a coma," the physician said. "That's good. I'm Dr. Ardmore."

Margaret felt suddenly weak. The hours of waiting washed over her, leaving only exhaustion behind.

"From Mr. Turner's description, he's had an apoplectic fit. The effects are varied. They might last a day. They might never be alleviated." The man shook his head. "Nonetheless, you've done well to cool his head. It's one of the first steps in treatment. You must be Miss Lowell."

"Actually, I—"

"No matter. There are things to be done. He'll need to be purged of the ill humor. If you'll assist, I've brought a preparation of croton oil. You've experience, I assume, with introduction of such into the stomach. You'll find what you need in my bag. In the meantime, I must bleed him."

The man turned away, leaving Margaret to stare blankly at his black bag. She opened it and peered inside. A profusion of clamps and awls and saws stared back at her.

"Um."

"The gum tube," the doctor called impatiently from the bedside. "And mucilage—or gruel. Good God. I know you're young, but haven't you any training at all?"

There was no space left to dissemble. "I'm not a nurse. I'm His Grace's daughter."

His eyebrows drew down and he scrubbed his balding head. "How odd. I was led to believe—well." He shook his head, too tired to engage in the requisite social niceties. "Damn."

"I can still help," she said. "If you tell me what to do."

He didn't protest. "You'll have to, then."

It had been the first time in a long while that she'd

identified herself as Lady Anna Margaret. It was almost soothing to have the truth brushed callously to one side, to be treated instead as another set of hands—*competent* hands, not soft, incapable ones. It was too late at night for etiquette and formality.

He gave her more specific instructions, and after they'd fed her father the mixture, he sent her off to rest. But when she'd left the room for the dark of the gallery, rest seemed impossible. Tired as she was, she could not sleep. Not yet.

Surely if Mark knew what had happened to her father, he would grant her a reprieve. He would let her wait a little while longer to tell Ash the truth. But his brothers had been right about one thing. Whatever she was to Ash, after what he'd done for her—setting off into a storm, traveling miles and miles so that she might have a little peace—he didn't deserve her silence. Not for one moment longer.

She had one last task for the evening, and at this point, she was too weary to dread it any longer.

CHAPTER FIFTEEN

THE NIGHT WAS VERY DARK. Ash should have been in bed, but instead, he was awake in his chambers, staring at the embers of a fire. He'd shucked off his wet clothes, and wore nothing but a loose pair of trousers.

If, two months ago, someone had told Ash he would have spent hours in the frigid rain, fetching a physician to save Parford's measly hide…

He'd have believed it, but only because kindness made a revenge of its own. But he had only to remember the bleak expression in Margaret's eyes when she had looked at him to understand why he had gone. Not as proof that he was the better man; not as some stilted vengeance wrought upon a long-ago foe. He'd gone so he could vanquish the darkness from her eyes.

There had been something about her that evening—something harsh and strong. She'd assumed command perfectly, without even faltering at the notion of issuing orders to Mrs. Benedict. She'd even ordered about Ash himself. She'd been as strong and as capable as a queen.

That was the woman he wanted. He wanted that fierce loyalty for his own. He wanted to possess the commanding set of her brow, to smooth the worry from her face. He also wanted her relieved of her weary burdens, but that would come soon. He could taste that future, sweet on his tongue.

He almost wished he'd retained that master key. He'd wished, weeks ago, that he hadn't made Mrs. Benedict that promise. He certainly wished that his damned courier would arrive from London, with the requisite paperwork in hand. He was tired of holding back.

As if that wish had somehow been granted by a blessedly benevolent world, he heard the lock scrape behind him. He sat up straight in his chair, his breath catching in his throat. There was only one person who had a key to this room besides Ash himself. She fumbled with the lock—no doubt it was dark—and then swung the door open. He'd dreamed of this for so many nights, but he'd never believed it would actually happen. Margaret padded into his room.

In the pale moonlight, he could barely make out her clothing. She wore nothing but her shift. The fabric was thick, the darkness thicker. She might have been swathed in a thousand petticoats, for all the erotic detail he could make out in the dark of night. But his imagination didn't need light to see her. The sound of fabric whispering against skin fired his fantasies. He could envision the length of her limbs as she walked towards him, could almost feel the rounding of her hips, fitting against his palms.

He stood up. She stopped, three feet distant, her eyes dropping to his bare chest and then widening.

"Ash. There's something I have to tell you. It won't wait for morning."

"The duke," Ash said. "He's—"

"He'll survive," she said shortly.

"My brother." A stab of pain. "He left this evening, and in the storm—"

"The storm broke hours after he left. I'm sure

he found cover. It's not about anyone else. Or—that is—not directly."

He took a step towards her. He could see her shift ripple in the night air, forming itself briefly to her breasts before dropping away again. The palms of his hands burned. He wanted to lay them against her. Another step. She was close enough that he could make out the faint smattering of freckles across her nose. In the dark, they almost blended into the color of her skin. She was close enough for him to touch and so he reached out, winding a strand of her hair about his finger, feeling the silk of it brush over him. A tiny prelude for what was certainly to come.

Her chin rose, and she tossed her head, sliding that curl from his grasp.

"Ash, *listen* before you touch me."

"I can listen and touch at the same time." He set his hand on her hip, drawing her close. Her body fit against his, curved and soft where he was hard and flat. He ducked his head and breathed in her scent—that faint hint of roses. And she relaxed against him, laying her hands against his naked chest in a gesture of possession. His skin tingled where her palms touched him. He tipped her chin up—not to kiss, not yet, but to steal her breath from her lips, to draw the vital stuff of her exhalation into his own lungs. To feel the simple luxury of her presence.

She pushed away. "Ash. This is insane, the two of us. You don't know who my family is."

"I know enough." He exhaled, wanting to breathe away her uncertainty. "Do you suppose I would learn you the way a scholar learns a book? That you are nothing to me but a collection of suppositions, to be stored in my memory and written down for verification? No, Margaret. I know you."

He let his hand slip to her waist, to the curve of her hip, slim and smooth, and he drew her back to him. He was half-naked already, but she made no protest. The feel of her body against his was as invigorating as slipping into a hot bath. His blood took up an insistent pounding in his ears. Lower down, he felt a persistent ache, sharp and sweet, a keen wanting.

"I know you the way I've learned everything." His lips brushed her collarbone. "I know your taste. I know your scent. I know the shape of you in my hands. I know the flash of your eyes when you're angry, and the melody of your laughter. Don't tell me I don't know you. You're a woman." His voice dropped. "And you're mine."

She swallowed. "But I—"

He cut her off, pressing his lips to hers. Her hands clamped around his arms. He kissed her as if he could excise her doubts, as if he could sweep them away with tongue and teeth. If only he kissed her thoroughly enough…

She pulled away. "You don't even know my full name."

Before she could speak, he caught her face in his hands. "As it happens, I've never told you my real first name. Do you think that a little thing like an appellation matters between us? You are not some creature to be placed in a little box and labeled for a museum. I don't fret, just because I haven't acquired the proper label for you."

"But my mother—"

"My mother was insane. That doesn't change who I am."

"But—"

He looked at her. "Margaret, did you come here in the middle of the night, wearing nothing but a scrap of fabric, hoping that I would cast you aside because I didn't know you? Truly?"

She paused, her lips pressing together. Her eyes seemed to glisten in the moonlight. And then she looked up at him, her gaze heated. "No," she said. She took a deep breath and then nodded. "I suppose…I suppose I came here hoping for you. For *all* of you. But, Ash—"

"No more excuses." His lips found hers. She was his, all his. And if she thought that he might shrink from anything she might tell him, nothing remained but to convince her that he would never leave. He leaned forwards, pulling her into his embrace. He could smell her skin against him, could taste her against his lips. He flicked out his tongue, to brush against her neck.

She let out a shaky exhale, and then her hands rose to clasp his shoulders in agreement.

"I know you," he whispered against her. "Sweet as summer, and every bit as welcome." He kissed her again and felt her body relax into his. This, they had done before. It should have been familiar. And yet the knowledge of what could yet come kept Ash on edge. It made even this simple embrace mysterious, and her kiss new all over again. He ran his finger, gently, down the smocked front of her shift. He could feel the fine needlework against his fingertips. Idly, he wondered if she had done that herself—those precise stitches.

It didn't matter. Beneath those stitches lay the naked curve of her—her breast lay full in his hand, the taut nipple brushing against his palm. She shivered at that hint of a touch. And he could hold back no longer.

He leaned down and took that tip in his mouth. He tasted her through the fabric of her garment. He swirled his tongue around that tight bud. Her hands clutched him tighter. He heard himself growl in his throat, a happy sound of possession. It seemed a pale echo of the resonant thrum of his blood, pumping through him in insistent want.

"Ash," she was panting, *"Ash."* He could feel her breath against his scalp, her hands brushing down his bare back to find the waist of his loose trousers.

Oh, God. She fumbled with buttons—he couldn't breathe—and then she pushed the fabric down. Her fingers brushed his bare hips. He felt the low scrape of her nails against his thighs. He drew breath in as her exploration continued. That first delicate touch of her fingers against his groin, the sensitive flesh of his member, nearly unmanned him. She drew breath in, and then her hands clasped around him, touching him, warming the hard length of him.

She was the one to lift her head. To raise one hand and push him towards the bed.

And as much as he wanted to sink inside her, he'd not intended to take matters quite that far. "I promised Mrs. Benedict I wouldn't debauch you."

"I made a promise, too." Her voice shook. "But if this is how you must know me—then I want you to understand. Before I tell you. If you can't debauch me, let *me* debauch *you*."

Something was terribly wrong with that logic, something that would occur to him, if he gave it but a moment's thought. Good thing Ash wasn't a philosopher.

He needed no further encouragement; no sooner did he feel her hand on his chest, urging him backward, than he scooped her up and whirled her around in his arms, turning her about until they were both dizzy, and there was nothing to do but let her fall crazily on the feather tick of the mattress. She laughed up at him, her limbs splayed out, her breath wild. The moon caught the curve of her bare ankle.

Before he could move forwards, she pushed herself to sit up and reached for the hem of her shift. His erection pulsed insistently in response. His lungs burned. In one slow, deliberate motion, she peeled off that scrap of linen, revealing hips, high and curved; the dark triangle between her legs; navel, up past smooth ribs, to the perfect swell of her breast and the dark rose of her nipples. His mouth dried.

She crooked her finger at him and he drifted forwards to kneel on the floor in front of her.

"Ash, what are you doing?"

He grinned at her wickedly. "Making sure you aren't bored." He hooked his hands under her knees and pulled her forwards, settling between her legs. Then he leaned to kiss her calves, up her inner thighs. The folds of her sex parted under his exploration. He kissed her *there,* the inner center of her.

"Ash?"

He took the ripple of her muscles as encouragement. Another kiss, this time with tongue, exploring the folds of her sex.

She was wet for him; he could taste her desire, sweet and reminiscent of some fine, complicated wine. He took her with his mouth, tasting her.

"This is what I want to know about you," he whispered.

He tasted her there, and her hands squeezed his arms; *there,* and her hips thrust towards him. He circled his tongue, found the nub at the center of her pleasure, and she let out a helpless mewl.

"This is what I need. To understand the map of your body. To explore your every last secret."

Biblically, the word for making love was to *know*. It had always seemed a hopelessly effete euphemism to Ash until now. Her taste on his lips was knowledge. He took her harder, pushing her, coaxing her with his tongue. The curve of her body around his, the tension in her muscles, the grip of her fingers—they were all knowledge, deeper and harder than anything he had ever understood before. Her body stiffened. He felt heat well up around her, felt the strength of her release against his lips.

And he *knew* her.

"Oh, God," she said, her voice indistinct above him. "Oh, Ash. Ash. Ash." Her hands clutched his shoulders, hard. He felt as if he were on a boat, rocked by an enormous swell of the ocean. He felt a little dazed. He could hear her breath, hard and thready.

He pushed himself up and leaned over her.

"Ash," she said, looking into his eyes, "you are a magnificent creature."

His blood rang in his ears. She sounded languid, satisfied, and he felt a fierce sense of possessive pride. "You should enjoy this," he growled out, "this and many others like it. I'm not done."

He spread her knees wider. He felt, rather than heard, her exhale as he placed the head of his penis against her opening. Hot. Liquid. Everything real and desirable. His hands shook where they clenched the coverlet, with the effort of his restraint. He could almost taste her surprised gasp as he rubbed the head in her juices. Her body welcomed his; he could feel it from head to toe, from the way her breasts brushed against his chest to the small thrust of her hips. That tiny movement was enough to slip the very tip of him inside her.

God, it felt good when her flesh closed about him—better than anything he'd ever known. Fantastic. Excruciating.

He pulled back only to push forwards, farther. More. Better. She was tight around him, but not too tight. She opened her eyes and watched him, as if she were memorizing this moment. As if he might imprint on her bones.

And then she said the most ridiculous thing. "Don't forget me, Ash. Not ever." Her voice was a whisper against his skin.

He shut his eyes, letting the pure pleasure of their joining wash over him. "As if I could. You know I can't. You know I won't. You know me."

She didn't answer, not in words. But she drew him down.

He pushed all the way in, until he felt her pelvis against his, her legs coming to wrap around his. It was all he could do to hold back, to refrain from pounding the rising tide of want into her. She pulsed around him, quietly, rhythmically. He might have spent himself then.

He gritted his teeth and didn't.

Instead, he began to stroke into her—slowly, gently, at first; then, as she met him, harder, faster, until he couldn't tell where his pleasure left off and hers began. Until she gasped again, and he felt her clench about him, squeezing his cock as she came.

Then he, too, was following her over the edge, the wild, ragged pleasure overtaking him entirely.

Afterwards, it was better than ever—fiercer and

stronger and more tender. He had her beneath him, after all, to kiss, to lightly run his hands along her sides. He disengaged from her but pulled her close, holding her body against his, stroking her skin until his lids drooped, until his thoughts drifted from satisfaction into the near incoherence of sleep.

"Ash?" Her voice was a whisper. "Ash, we have to talk."

"Very well," he murmured on a yawn. "Talk."

"You see, there's something you need to know about me."

"Hmm," he said. Sleep beckoned. He could feel himself drifting away, finally sated, completely warm, his body tired from the night's exertions.

"Ash?" She spoke from some warm cloud, somewhere very far away. "Ash, are you *asleep?*"

He wasn't, not quite, but he wasn't awake enough to respond. He was vaguely aware of her tapping his shoulder—once, twice—before sighing.

"Oh, very well," she said. "It's not as if I was eager to tell you anyway."

The last thing he remembered was the feel of her relaxing against him in surrender.

CHAPTER SIXTEEN

MARGARET AWOKE THE next morning with a shiver running down her spine.

There was certainly no reason to feel cold. She was snuggled up against Ash, his body a warm, comforting mass against her side. If she could stay here in his arms forever, she would never feel cold again.

Last night had been a thing of magic, something that would transmute the memory of him into gold. After her unfortunate encounter with Frederick, she'd believed that intercourse with a man would be about his *taking* from her: taking his pleasure, taking her body. But when Ash had made love to her, he'd *given*: affection, certainty and, most of all, that quiet strength that made her feel she could accomplish anything.

She had only to tiptoe into his presence and he drew her into his spell.

But the morning light gave a cold, rational cast to the room about her. It was very much *his* bedchamber—from the ivory-handled razor tossed carelessly by the basin in the corner, to the sharp corners of the mahogany chest of drawers. No matter how she turned her head, the angles of the room seemed precise and masculine. Demanding, even, as if his chambers were requiring more of her than he had himself.

The magic had dissipated. She needed to return to

her father's side. If he'd worsened in the night, she'd have heard the commotion. But he was gravely ill—and she was his daughter.

Ash hadn't given her a gift last night. She'd stolen one from him.

She'd gone to his bed without telling him her true name, her birth. And *that* had been a betrayal in and of itself. It was that wrongness that made the warmth enfolding her feel so inadequate. No matter how much of his heat she took in, she had still lied, and when he found out the truth, he was going to despise her for it. He slept still, looking innocent, young in a way she'd never seen him look before.

It was a look of absolute trust, and she was about to shatter that.

She gently moved his arm and pulled out from under the covers. She shrugged into her discarded shift, wishing that she had a wrapper—or better yet, a fresh change of clothing. She hadn't expected to *sleep* with him. Anyone who caught a glimpse of her in the hall would know what had happened. If she'd thought this through, she would have made sure to bring a change of clothing. A comb.

If she had thought this through, she would never have done it.

Out the window, she saw the last gray mists of the summer morning clinging to the wet grass below. The storm had passed; in another half hour, the sun would scour the fog away, and there would be no place for her to hide.

Behind her, Ash stirred and made a sleepy noise deep in his throat. That sound caught at her, and she stared at his sleeping form. *I have to tell him.*

As if she'd spoken those words aloud, his eyes fluttered open. He blinked several times and then his vision fixed on her. A warm smile crept over his face.

"Margaret." He held out a hand. "What are you doing all the way over there? Come back to bed."

"I have to tell you something." She took a deep breath. Her heart pounded so loudly she could almost hear it in her ears, a relentless, rhythmic canter... But no. She glanced out the window again. That wasn't her heart pounding. Those were hoofbeats. A man was approaching on horseback. His form cut through the mist like a dark rock in water. And she froze on the inhale. She knew that man. She knew that *horse*.

She was barely ready to tell Ash. She couldn't face *this*—not now, not here.

She whirled around. "I have to get out of here. I have to get out of here now." She scrambled across the room.

Ash leaped from bed with a grace that belied the sleep-rumpled look of his hair. His arms found her, wrapping around her, supporting her.

"What is it?" he asked. The concern in his voice fed her panic. Her world was collapsing. Her little rebellion had reached its natural conclusion. The troops had arrived, and if she were caught in his arms, Margaret's little bit of defiance would take on a cast that rather resembled treason.

"Let me go."

Ash kept his hands on her shoulders. "You're upset. You're trembling. You must know I won't let anything happen to you."

She looked into his eyes—so sincere, so clear—and

felt a twinge of shame, twining with regret. "Oh, Ash. You can't stop it. It's already happened."

She could no longer see the horseman; she could only imagine the door below swinging open for him in silent greeting, as it had done for so many years.

"Tell me," Ash insisted. "Just tell me. If I can steal a dukedom, I can do anything."

"Please. Get me something to wear. And quickly."

He gave her a measured look and then pulled his own robe off the chest of drawers and set it around her shoulders. The warmth enveloped her once again, and with it, his scent, a complex mix of bergamot and bay rum. As she hugged it around her, he donned a pair of trousers. She could hear footfalls ascending the stairs now. If she was quick, she could make it up the servants' stairs before he arrived. He wouldn't need to know. She turned the handle.

Ash turned his head to the side, no doubt hearing those same footsteps. He set his hand against the door, open one scant inch. Margaret pulled, but he held it in place.

"Someone arrived. Someone who was granted unquestioned entrance." His eyes narrowed. "That's Richard Dalrymple, isn't it?" His voice darkened. "Or Edmund. I can guess what he did to you. Don't let him worry you. He can't hurt you. I won't let him."

She wrenched the door back another inch, and got her foot through before he caught her wrist. "You don't understand. I have to leave. I have to leave *now.*"

"I'll protect you."

"You can't protect me from this." Margaret wrenched the door open.

He set his hands on her waist. "We can face this together."

But there was no together. There could be no together. Because at that moment, Richard came up the stairs, taking them two at a time. He froze at the sight before him. Margaret knew precisely how this tableau must appear to him. Ash was bare to the waist, his hands on Margaret. They were framed in the doorway, with an obviously rumpled bed behind them. It was only a moment that Richard stood there, his mouth open. And then he charged forwards almost blindly.

"Richard!" Margaret shouted. "You mustn't—"

"You fiend!" Richard screamed as he barreled into Ash. The two men slammed into the doorway at an awkward angle. Before Ash could react, Richard beat his fists into Ash's chest again and again. Those ineffectual slaps punctuated the morning.

Ash reached out and grabbed Richard's wrist as he threw the next punch and wrenched his arm hard to his side. Richard let out a hiss of pain, thrashed and subsided.

"Listen to me," Ash said, his voice whisper-quiet in its intensity, "and listen well. You relinquished all claim to her when you left her here alone. She's *mine* now, and there's nothing you can do about it." He shoved the man hard and Richard staggered into the room, hitting the wardrobe behind him. He slouched there as if dazed, raising a hand to his head.

"Stop it! Both of you!" Margaret screamed.

Ash flicked a glance at her and moved to stand between them. "Curb your sentimentality, my dear. This beating has been a long time coming."

"You son of a bitch." Richard struggled to his feet. "Get your bloody hands off my sister."

Ash froze. Margaret could see his mouth go slack. He turned to her—and just as he did, Richard threw a punch, smashing his fist into Ash's eye.

Ash staggered back, raising his hand to his face. "Your sister?"

She could see all of the easy affection draining from his expression. She could almost taste the loss. His breath sucked in. He shook his hand out, and then he raised his eyes to Margaret's, as if asking her if it were true. As if begging her to deny it.

"Your sister," he repeated dully.

Margaret bowed her head. "I was once Lady Anna Margaret Dalrymple." Her voice choked. "I was trying to tell you, but…"

"Ah." He rubbed his eye where Richard had struck him. The skin had already begun to pinken; in a few hours, he'd sport purple. He blew out his breath, deflating.

Here it came. Here was where he denounced her. But instead, he cut his eyes toward Richard. "I suppose, then, that I deserved that."

Richard drew himself up taller and took a step forwards. "That," he said crisply, "and more. Why, I ought to—"

In one smooth motion, Ash pulled back and punched Richard, harder.

Margaret let out a muffled scream. Her brother shrieked louder, and crumpled to the floor. And Ash said nothing; he just advanced on Richard, huddled in a ball on the carpet.

"Ash! Stop it. What are you doing?"

Ash didn't turn towards her. Instead, he towered over her brother. The contrast between them could not have been more striking. Ash was wide and dark and tall; her brother seemed a pallid, frail thing, scuttling backwards until he cowered against the wall.

"I deserved your blow," Ash said harshly, "but you deserve more. You left your sister here, alone, with nobody to stand for her. What kind of man sends his sister into danger, while he himself cowers in safety?"

He *would* think of that first.

"What danger?" Richard said. "She was safe. Mrs. Benedict promised to watch over her."

Ash's hands clenched at his side, and an almost murderous silence settled in. "If *I* still had a sister…" he said slowly. But he did not complete that thought. He didn't need to; Margaret could fill in the unspoken words for him. Of course Ash wouldn't put his family in danger. Finally, he looked at Margaret. "Why did you stay behind?"

Margaret squared her shoulders. "We didn't know what to expect of you. Someone had to watch Father. Someone had to make sure you didn't despoil the estate. And…and when I agreed to do it, I didn't know you. Not then."

Ash took a step towards her. "That's not what I'm talking about, and you know it. You've been staying under a roof with two bachelors, and Mrs. Benedict or no, there's not been an appropriate chaperone in sight. You're a duke's daughter. When the news gets out, your reputation—"

"I have no reputation worth speaking of, Ash."

"Balderdash. Perhaps your brothers might have

rammed the issue of your legitimacy through Parliament after all. Even as a bastard daughter, you might have made a perfectly respectable match one day, so long as your reputation had been safeguarded. Why would you sacrifice the chance to have your own life, your own home? You must have agreed to this, knowing that the end result was that you would spend the rest of your life living in some tiny room on your brother's estate, accepting whatever scraps this cad decided to toss your way."

Richard had been watching this interchange with an increasingly horrified look on his face. Clearly, he hadn't understood what she'd agreed to do. She *had* risked her reputation. And her brother hadn't even noticed.

"Here now," Richard said on a sputter. "I sure as hell wouldn't toss my own sister *scraps*. And as for the rest, I only came back because her letters suggested she was in some danger." He cast Ash a dangerous look. "And I see I was right."

"Shut up, you. Margaret, you're worth ten of him. Why would you sacrifice so much for this rat?"

Margaret pulled the silk robe Ash had given her about her like a shield and faced him. "First, he's my brother, not a rat, and I'll thank you not to speak of him that way."

"Christ."

"Second, you cannot be thinking. I have no reputation—or at least, nothing that a reputation can buy me."

"Why? Because you're a bastard? I'm telling you, that won't matter—"

She could feel Richard's eyes on her. Still, she

met Ash's glower. "No, you idiot. Because I wasn't a virgin."

Richard gasped.

"There has never been anything for me in the future except that attic room on my brother's estate. Not since you had me declared a bastard. No man would have had me, had he known the truth, no matter what Parliament declared. And when Frederick walked away from me when I needed him most… You must understand—I would rather have scraps in the attic than accept *him*. No matter what might happen."

"I still say it was a stupid risk." Ash shook his head. "It's a damned good thing I'm marrying you."

The bottom dropped out of Margaret's stomach. This was another impossible thing, on a morning already riddled with impossibilities. She stared at Ash, blankly. "What?"

Richard pushed himself up off the floor. "I beg your pardon!"

"I'm marrying you." He was still facing her, but he brought his hand up to shove Richard back a pace. "In case you hadn't noticed, after what happened last night. What do you suppose I've been about in any event, Margaret? Don't give me that look, Dalrymple. Your sister is the only reason I haven't broken your nose into pieces, and she can't intercede on your behalf forever."

"I hadn't noticed." Margaret's voice sounded flat in her own ears. Not because of a lack of emotion—her hands shook with it—but because there was too much feeling, no room for everything she felt to fit in her voice. "And no, I hadn't supposed you were thinking about marriage. Somehow, you failed to ask."

But she was deluding herself. If he'd just wanted her body, he could have had it long before last night.

"Don't be so naive, Margaret." Her brother slammed his fist into the wall beside him. The plaster shook. "Of course he didn't ask before he knew who you were. The only reason he wants to marry you is that he knows it will help his chances in Parliament. Those who've made up their minds on the matter are split almost precisely down the middle. There are only a select handful of lords who have yet to decide. If he marries you, the eighth duke of Parford's bloodline will continue. Unconventional, yes—but it might be enough to shift the handful of votes he needs his way. He knows it, that calculating bastard."

For a second, her brother's words echoed all the fears that she had carried, in a tiny ball buried deep in her belly. She wasn't good enough. Nobody cared about anything except her station in life. Nobody would ever want her.

But Ash slowly raised his head. Those untamed nightmares didn't last longer than the bare instant it took for her to look at him, to trace that little curl that had fallen down his forehead with her eyes. He looked at her, not saying a single word.

Margaret raised her chin. "Ash wouldn't do that."

The corner of Ash's mouth quirked up. He regarded her with the same steadfast certainty he always had. Richard couldn't understand it. He couldn't know what Ash had said to her. What Ash had *done* for her. He looked at her, and he made her believe.

You matter. You are important.

And even now, knowing she had lied to him, knowing she was the daughter of his worst enemy, he gave her his support.

Richard, however, couldn't see that in the exchange of glances. "You can't know that. Did he ask you to marry him when he thought you a lowly nurse? No. It was only once he knew what he had to gain that he proposed."

"Ash wouldn't do that," Margaret repeated, calmly. "I know him. And I know he wouldn't do that."

Richard put his head in his hands. "God spare me from women who think they understand men. Mother thought she knew Father, too, for all the good that did her."

"Ash isn't Father."

"So you're marrying Turner. You're damning me and Edmund to a lifetime of bastardy, just so you can have every last luxury. It figures."

Margaret shut her eyes. "Richard, I spent last evening saving Father's life, just so you *would* have a chance to win your dukedom. After everything I've done for you, everything I've given up for you, you owe me one morning. Go visit Father. Look in on him. And let me talk to my—" Her what? Her lover? Her friend? Not her fiancé.

Richard shook his head, but when he started towards her, Ash stepped in his way. He didn't say anything; he just raised one hand, setting it against Richard's chest. Her brother backed away.

Margaret heard the door shut behind him.

"God," Ash said. "I even hate that the cad left you alone with me, because he feared a tiny thing like more pain. If he were any sort of a brother, he wouldn't care what I said or how I threatened. He wouldn't leave your side, not if he was threatened by a phalanx of soldiers."

Margaret rubbed her temples. Ash had walked forty miles, barefoot, when he was fourteen years old for his sister's sake. He *would* feel that way. But not everyone could be as strong as he. Yes, her brother was consumed by a hundred tiny selfishnesses. But most people were. It was only natural to think first of yourself. And Richard had lost so much—he'd had his entire inheritance ripped away. Of course he would jealously defend what little remained. Only a saint would think of someone else when his world was crumbling about him. It didn't make her brother a bad person. It just made him a little preoccupied.

"Don't you hate me for lying to you? I've been sorry for it for weeks. You can't know—"

"I can imagine." He set his hand on her shoulder behind her. "Easily. I'm remembering every word I said to you, every last unkind, unwarranted comment I made about Lady Anna. You must have thought me the cruelest man imaginable. These past months…your mother, the ecclesiastical suit. Your fiancé. Of course, your fiancé. Your dowry. Your place in society. My God. I had you declared a bastard. Margaret, what have I done to you?"

She buried her face in her hands, her eyes burning. She'd imagined this moment a thousand ways. In her mind, he'd scorned her. He'd cursed her. He'd walked away in a huff. She should have known that Ash would always find a way to outdo her imagination. "Ash. Please don't."

"Is Anna your name, then?"

"Anna Margaret. But Anna is my mother's name. Everyone has always called me Margaret."

"You were standing in the room when Parford said he didn't give a damn about his children. My God, Margaret. How can you bear it?"

"I bear it just fine, thank you, so long as I don't need to think of it." Her chin wobbled.

Ash accepted this in relative silence. He strode to the window and looked away. "Have you any doubt in your mind that I wish to marry you because I want you, not for any more mercenary reason?"

She looked at him, her mind jumbled. "Even you, Ash, could not be so ruthless. No. I don't believe it of you."

He paced to his chest of drawers. "But I *am* that ruthless, Margaret." He let out a breath. "I know that of me, even if you have not yet come to the realization. And your brother will try to steal that certainty from you. He'll tell you I'm lying. I want you to know in a way that your brother cannot steal from you."

"I'm certain." But she wasn't. Certainty had been a thing for last night. The more time passed, the more doubts encroached.

He didn't answer. Instead, he sifted through a pile of garments on his chest of drawers, until he found his waistcoat. Then he strode back to her. Silently he held it out, an arm's length between them. "Look in the right pocket."

Margaret took it gingerly. The fabric was rough against her hands. Her fingers slipped into the pocket and found a crinkling piece of paper. She pulled it out. For a second, she wondered if she, too, had somehow lost the ability to decode symbols. Then she realized she was looking at the reverse side, where ink had seeped through the foolscap. She flipped the paper over, and stared at the characters written in a crabbed hand on the other side. But even reading those words, she could not truly comprehend them. It was almost as if her mind had forgotten how to function, as if the symbols on it were written in an alphabet so foreign and distinct from her world that she could not understand its import.

"What is this? Why…why does it say *Margaret Lowell* on its face?"

"It's why I went to London last week. It's why I've been in a terrible dudgeon these last days, waiting for an express that never arrived. It's a receipt from the Archbishop of Canterbury's office in Doctor's Commons, where I applied for a special license."

"It's dated nine days ago."

"I know. And that is how you know that no matter what your brother tells you, no matter how he tries to make you doubt me, what I say is true. I wanted to marry you weeks ago. The great benefit I see to marrying you is that I would be married to you. I told you it didn't matter who your parents were. I meant it. I want you. Nothing else matters."

But everything else was pressing against her now. "Ash." Margaret's voice threatened to dissolve. She swallowed the lump in her throat, the incipient tears. "You are breaking my heart."

That phrase had never made sense to her before, except in metaphor. But she was being pulled in two. Making love to Ash had been a little defiance—a statement that her body was *hers,* that her life and her virtue belonged to her. That she belonged to herself and nobody could ever take that away.

But he wasn't asking for a little defiance any longer. He was asking for her allegiance. Her brother was right about one thing: if she married him, it would be a complete betrayal. Not of some unfortunate rules that society insisted upon, but of her brothers, her *mother.* If she married him, her brothers could lose their bid for legitimacy. They would be outcasts, sustained only by the tiny unentailed portions of the estate.

She had promised herself that she would be noble, even if she was no longer considered nobility. He was asking her to be selfish, to think only of her own future happiness. If she did that, she would be no better than her father.

He was asking for more than she could possibly deliver.

"I understand now," he said, "why the license took so long to issue. The archbishop's office wouldn't send it out until they could verify that you were eligible to marry, and the parish here has no records of a Miss Margaret Lowell."

"No. They wouldn't."

"Well, I'll apply again."

It wasn't supposed to be like this, when he uncovered the truth. It was supposed to be easy. Her revelation was supposed to have been the death knell of his desire. There shouldn't have been any need for her to choose between a future with him and her brothers' survival. Who was she, if she abandoned them?

Who was she, if she walked away from him?

She had learned to withstand her father's abuse. But this gentleness left her undone. There was no word in her lexicon for this sort of kindness, no space in her understanding to encompass it.

She simply shook her head. "No, Ash. I don't know. I—I just don't know."

He let out a sigh and pulled her to him. She felt his arms around her. "I'm sorry," he whispered.

She had once thought she wanted to see him sorry. She'd wanted to punish him, to rip his heart out and stomp on it, so that he would know how it felt to have his world inverted about him.

She had been wrong. It killed her. Because he wasn't hurting for himself. He was hurting for *her*.

His kindness robbed her of the cold outrage that had fueled her all this time. But for one last moment, she could pretend that they could be together. That his arms around her were solid and real, and it was the reality of her waiting life that was the evanescent, impossible dream.

CHAPTER SEVENTEEN

IF IT HAD BEEN embarrassing for Ash to greet Richard Dalrymple that morning, half-clothed, with his sister in his arms, it was even more awkward when the man appeared at breakfast. Dalrymple paused at the corner of the room and glanced in, a half sneer on his face. The expression of distaste was rather ruined by his eye, which had already begun to turn a dull red where Ash had struck him.

"I see," he said, in an accent so rarified that it made Ash want to smack him again, "that this room is infested." He sniffed at Ash, and then glanced at Mark and stiffened.

"With all of us vermin," Ash said. "Your sister—the only interesting one among us—is off tending to your father." Ash picked up his butter knife, and Dalrymple paled and flinched.

"Good God. What do you suppose I'm going to do? Eviscerate you with this thing? Look. It's quite dull." Ash shook his head, scooped a lump of butter from the crock, and applied it to his bread. "And apparently, it's not alone. You might as well eat, Dalrymple. You need to keep up your strength, especially if you imagine you're going to take on the Herculean task of bending Parliament to your will."

Mark met Ash's eye, and then bit his lip, as if holding something back. A suspicion intruded on Ash's mind—a half-remembered statement his brother had made.

"By the way, Mark, did you realize that Margaret is actually Margaret Dalrymple?"

"Ah. So she told you, then."

Ash's fingers drummed against the table, a harsh beat that took the place of actual thought. He stared at his brother. "You knew." His voice was low.

"I had my suspicions." Mark glanced at him, and then with a sigh, he added, "and then Smite came down here and confirmed them. He saw her a few years ago."

Dalrymple glanced up at this but said nothing. Instead, he sidled against the wall until he reached the sideboard, where he removed a plate. Ash ignored him.

"You knew, and you didn't tell me."

Mark gave him a half shrug. "Honestly, Ash. She said she would tell you. And I didn't believe the small delay between my discovery and her divulgence would harm you in the long run. Besides, she was half in love with you already, and I know how you are."

Ash felt a low burn of rage begin. "Perhaps you might have thought how it could hurt *her.*"

"You wouldn't hurt her." Mark sighed. "You might not…go about courting her in the manner I would prefer, but you don't hurt women. Come, now, Ash. I know you better than that. Quite frankly, it's refreshing to know you can be wrong."

Dalrymple was piling kippers onto his plate with movements made awkward, because he was still flattened against the wall. He clearly wanted to keep as far from the brothers as he possibly could. He only managed to make himself look completely ridiculous.

How had a family that produced such a fainthearted coward also come up with Margaret?

"I wasn't wrong," Ash said quietly.

"She did lie to you, Ash. Granted, she has other sterling qualities."

Ash hadn't realized how much he must have already hurt her. When he'd met her, he'd known she was sad. This morning, he'd been too dazed to truly understand what her parentage *meant*. But with a little time to sort things out, and food in his belly, he'd begun to comprehend. Now he was no longer surprised that she'd thrown a clod of dirt at him on that long-ago night. Daggers would have been rather more appropriate.

"I stormed into her life, destroyed her parents' marriage and made her a bastard. And you think that when I faced her down, holding the remainder of her life in my hands, that she should have blithely spouted out the truth? For all she knew, I would have stolen away the little that remained. I was an utter beast to her. I just didn't realize it."

From his vantage point against the wall, Dalrymple raised one finger, almost hesitantly. "As a point of order, you did the same to me, and I've yet to hear your apology."

"Oh, shut up," Ash snapped. "You're different. You deserved it. You still do."

Dalrymple's mouth snapped shut.

Mark's eyes blazed at this. "Oh, yes. Still set on *revenge,* are you, after all of this? Wishing now that perhaps when I told you to *think* about what you were doing to the Dalrymples, you'd listened? I *said* you didn't have to do this. I *said* you were wrong. But no—the great Ash Turner doesn't need to listen to logic. Or ethics."

"Oh, God," Dalrymple moaned from the side of the room. "Ethics. At ten in the morning. And you wonder why you were so constantly set upon at Eton?"

Mark and Ash turned to Dalrymple as one. "He's championing you, you dolt," Ash remarked.

"I don't truck with what's happened to you," Mark added. "But if you ever wondered why Smite outdid you so consistently at Oxford, here is one explanation. It's because you are an idiot. And perhaps because you feel free to suspend your ethics before breakfast."

Dalrymple flushed.

"If you must know," Ash said, turning back to Mark, "I don't regret what I did to the Dalrymples one bit—this incomparable ass over here deserved it. And while no doubt it hurt Margaret temporarily, once I've married her it shall all be resolved."

Dalrymple stepped forwards. "Like hell you'll marry her."

"As if you have anything to say on the matter. She's of age. She's chosen me—or at least," Ash added with a grimace, "she will."

"She won't choose you over her own brothers, you uncivilized brute. And once word gets out that you're the sort of man who ruins a lady—"

Ash wasn't quite sure how he got across the room. But he did—slamming Dalrymple against a wall for the second time that day. Eggs and pickled fish went flying.

"How," he growled, his arm at the man's throat, "do you imagine word will leak out?"

Dalrymple, held against the wall, up on tiptoes, squeezed his eyes shut. "I don't know?" His voice was very high.

"Because if you were suggesting that you would

sacrifice your sister's reputation to serve your own purposes, think again. If you do, I won't just steal your title and your lands. I will run any bank that holds your funds into the ground. I will bribe your servants to slip nettles into your bed. I will hire trumpets to stand outside your home every evening, where they will sound notes at irregular intervals. You will never have a solid night's sleep again."

"You're mad." Dalrymple licked his lips.

"Perhaps. But as the putative head of the family, I can have *you* declared mentally incompetent and committed to an asylum, if you choose to say one word against Margaret."

"I wouldn't. I wouldn't hurt my own sister."

"Ash," Mark said from behind him. "Give over. You don't have to do this."

It was either the threats, or he'd bodily pull the man to pieces. Margaret probably wouldn't approve of either. Ash lowered his arm, and Dalrymple's heels thumped to the floor.

He let out a sigh. And then he cast his brother a reproachful look.

"I'll send you *both* to asylums," he growled.

Richard bit his lip and stepped back in fear. But Mark knew him rather better. He rolled his eyes in unconcern. "Choose a quiet one for me. I should like to get some writing done."

ASH HAD NEVER ENTERED the north wing of the house before. The chambers there had been shut off during his visit. He had understood they belonged to the Dalrymple offspring; he had just never realized that one of them still resided in the household.

With Margaret's charade at an end, she'd moved

back to the room that was rightfully hers. The maid had guided him to her chamber—and then stayed.

So they were to have a chaperone. It seemed rather late for that.

Margaret sat at a table in her parlor, writing a letter. She was dressed in dark silk—not quite black, but a gray sufficiently dark to pass as storm clouds. A two-inch fall of dark lace touched her elbows. Her hair was no longer pinned up in a serviceable knot; instead, it had been braided and curled and arranged in an intricate pattern.

She wore the same gold necklace. He still wondered about that locket.

When he cleared his throat, she looked up at him. She held her pen, her eyes wary. She looked *different*— tidy and coiffed and sleek. But her eyes were still the same.

"My God, Margaret," he said.

"It is a bit much to comprehend, I am sure." Her voice seemed smooth and unruffled. It had taken him weeks to understand that this was just her way of hiding deep emotion. "This is the first time you've seen me as Lady Anna Margaret. Well." She shrugged, and spread her arms. She'd looped a knit shawl over her shoulders, and it slipped as she did so. "Here I am."

Lady Margaret's gown fit rather better than those loose gray frocks. The fringe of her shawl shaped itself to her bodice, outlining curves he'd held early this morning.

"There are a great many things I don't understand," he said.

"I suppose you should like to know why I lied to you."

He just looked at her. Now that he knew who she

was, that secret sadness she always carried with her made sense. She'd told him in the very first hour why she disliked him. She'd never given him lies. Just truths that he hadn't truly heard.

"If you must know," she began, "and given what has transpired between us, I suppose you deserve the full story, the plan started weeks ago, when—"

"Hang the plan, Margaret. I don't care about any of that. I want to know—she was your *mother*. Not the duchess. Not your employer. Your mother died. And you…you blame me. For good reason."

Her mouth stopped, midword. Her lips worked, but no sound came out. Finally she set her pen down and put her fingers to her temples. "That night I threw dirt at you—the conservatory was her favorite place. I had wanted to feel close to her. And then you came along and disrupted everything."

"You are in mourning."

Margaret glanced at her dark silk. "I've worn gray the entire time I've known you, Ash."

"I'm not referring to your clothing, Margaret. I'm referring to your spirit."

She let out a tired sigh. "Ash, you've understood a great many things. But really—what would you know about mourning a mother?"

He glanced behind them to make sure that the arm of the sofa would hide the extent of what he was about to do from the maid's watchful eyes. Then, he sat next to her and placed his hand on her knee. The gesture was casual, friendly—and yet intimate in a way that transcended mere physicality.

He leaned in and spoke in a near whisper. "My mother was complicated. Painful. At the end of it all, she was quite, quite mad. But I remember gentle moments, before she started to change. I remember when she was my safe haven. That's what made her descent into madness so frightening. Not the beatings, nor even the illness. I could remember what she had once been, and I kept waiting for her to return. Instead, she slipped further away, every time I saw her."

Margaret's eyes rounded.

"Maybe," he said, "that is part of what drove me in those early days of business. I kept thinking that if I accomplished more, maybe *this* time she would be proud of me. If I recovered the family fortune, she would value me. If my brothers went to Eton, she would honor what I had done. I kept waiting for her maternal instincts to overcome her madness."

Margaret reached out and took his hand.

"But no," he said. "It never worked."

"I am certain," Margaret told him, "that somewhere, somehow, she was aware of what you had accomplished. And that even if she couldn't acknowledge it in her lifetime, she was—*is*—proud of you."

Her fingers constricted around his hand.

"When she passed away, I cried. Don't tell my brothers—I shouldn't like to admit to weakness. But I remember what animated her, before. And I mourned the fact that everything I loved about her had died long before. I always wanted to believe that my mother— my *real* mother—was hidden somewhere in that shell of a body. But if she was, I never saw it. I had years to mourn her loss, before she was taken away for good. I still wake up nights, feeling as if something is gone. You…you've scarcely had time to believe it's happened."

"Do you always do this?" she asked, her voice husky. "Go to those who have used you poorly and explain away their sins? I lied to you, Ash. You're supposed to despise me."

"You may have noticed this," Ash said, "but I rarely do as I ought. It's a failing—and one I hope you will forgive in me." He reached out and traced a line down her cheek. "And then there's what I said about you. Did I really…did I really call you a poor specimen, to your face?"

She nodded.

"So. With all of that, why did you come to me last night?"

Her eyes widened. She looked up at him, her expression fierce. "Because you make me feel that if I were to disappear tomorrow, I would be mourned. And because…I'm hard pressed to stay away from you."

"So." He held his breath. "You'll marry me?"

She did not answer, not right away. But her sudden inability to meet his gaze told him everything he needed to know. His hands balled into fists.

"My brother talked to the physician. They've agreed that my father will not be hurt if he is moved—and that he should be taken to an expert outside of London, a man who specializes in treating apoplexy. I am going with them."

"Don't. Stay with me. I'll send for the proper license tomorrow."

She simply looked at him. "Ash, my father left his children bastards because he selfishly placed his own wishes and pleasures before their well-being. If I marry you—if that affects the outcome of my brothers' bid for legitimacy—I'll have bastardized them a second time. I will *not* do the same thing. I will not."

He shut his eyes and breathed in her breath. He

needed another chance. More time to erode her objections. To make her choose *him*.

"Well. May I say my farewells to you properly, then?" He glanced pointedly at the servant who sat at the edge of the room, pretending not to hear. "Without company?"

She nodded, and dropped her voice. "You know where, don't you? Not your office. Not any longer. They're watching that."

No. Not there.

"I know where," he said quietly.

CHAPTER EIGHTEEN

SHE HAD KNOWN HE WOULD meet her in the conservatory.

Perhaps that's why she'd twirled the knob on the oil lamp all the way up, until it radiated heat. She had hoped the light would drive away the darkness of the night.

It hadn't; instead, the lamp's yellow illumination had driven long shadows into every corner of the room. Margaret turned around, looking for him. But the only movement she saw was the flap of her wrapper. The fine silk and painstaking embroidery seemed too smooth against her skin, after weeks of staid wool and linen. Not at all proper attire, but then, etiquette had little advice to give on the apparel a well-bred lady wore to greet a man at midnight.

As she completed her turn, he stepped from the shadows, his footfalls making almost no noise at all. Margaret met his eyes. She was unsure what to say, uncertain how to start and entirely unable to speak the words she knew he had to hear. Instead she gestured at the cutting she'd planted several weeks before, the night she'd pelted him with clods of earth. "I think it will take."

He came forwards, still silent, and placed his thumb against the cane of wood. There was not much to show for those weeks—just two little nubs of growth, hints of green glinting in the lamplight.

"It might take some time, though. Perhaps it might be best to keep it indoors through the winter. The groundskeeper has a formula he uses, to manage new growth—"

Ash set his fingers against her lips, capturing the rest of her sentence. "You sound as if you are delivering instructions."

"Come this winter, only one of us will be here. It might not be me."

As she spoke, her lips brushed his thumb, a whisper of a kiss.

He took her head in his hands, gently tipping her chin up. "When I first met you, I thought there was something…almost sad about you. You hid it well—you're too strong not to. But your mother passed away not so long ago. Mrs. Benedict once told me that the old duchess loved roses."

That wound was still too tender to be probed. Margaret turned away.

But he didn't stop. "Your father seems to have no care for anything any longer. Your brothers have been too busy, scrambling to save their own hides. When have you had a chance to mourn, Margaret?"

She stepped away to examine the pots that stood on a window ledge. "She's still *here*," Margaret said. "She loved this house. The gardens. And the roses especially. Sometimes I can almost hear her footsteps around the corner. I can see her nodding in approval when the house runs smoothly. So long as—"

She caught her breath as the end of the sentence slammed into her.

Pick a house, her mother had once advised her on

love, *not a husband. Husbandly interest will fade. But a house will always be yours—yours to arrange and command, yours to gift over to your sons, warmer and more welcoming than you found it, when the time comes. A house will hold all your affection and shower love back upon you.*

That philosophy hadn't worked so well for her mother. At the end of her life, even the house hadn't truly been hers any longer. And whatever fiction Margaret maintained about this place, once Ash took the reins...

"So long as what?" Ash asked quietly.

"She'll be here," Margaret said, her throat closing, "so long as nothing changes."

But everything was changing. Over the course of the next few months, her brothers would present their case to Parliament. Her father's remaining health might slip away. She couldn't bear to stay here, to see the last vestiges of her mother's care disappear. And that meant that this was goodbye.

To the house. To her mother. And to Ash, as well.

She'd known it the instant her brother had spelled out precisely what marriage to Ash would mean. She'd always known that whatever time they had was transient and fleeting. She'd just assumed that *he* would be the one to end it.

She walked back to him and set her hands on his shoulders. He acquiesced when she pushed him to the bench. But when she leaned over him and straddled him, he pulled back from her kiss.

"There's something I must tell you," he began.

She put her fingers over his lips as she settled her thighs against his.

"Be quiet, Ash. I am trying to remember you."

In the lamplight, shadows collected on his face as his eyebrows drew down. He must have taken her meaning, because he shook his head. "Well. I am trying to *have* you." His voice was fiercely possessive. "Not for one night, nor even two. I want you every evening—mine outright, not a few hours stolen here or there. I want you during the day, on my arm. I want to know that when we're apart you're missing me; I want to know when we're together, I'm the one who puts the smile on your face." He punctuated each phrase with a kiss—against her chin, the line of her jaw, the hollow of her neck. As he spoke, his hands drifted down her sides. The light silk of her wrapper rendered his touch diffuse.

"Not that. I can't." But she didn't push his hands away.

"You will." His fingers cupped her breasts lightly, sending little shivers through her. She'd wanted one last night with him for physical comfort. She hadn't wanted this intimate courtship.

"I'm leaving on the morrow."

"So you have claimed," he said, his breath hot against her neckline.

"This is the last time we can speak— *Oh*."

He had slid her robe aside and taken her nipple in his mouth, almost roughly. His tongue circled the tip, and she could feel it draw up into a tight bud, could feel the corresponding pulse of desire between her legs. As if he, too, felt that need, he reached between them and undid his breeches. The rough fumblings of cloth rasped against her legs.

But he continued to taste her, almost leisurely. As if he were sure of her physical surrender—as sure as he was of everything else. There was no urgency in his caress, just languid pleasure. He was firmly in command, in control. His other hand freed his erection from its confines. She could feel it, straight and rigid and hot, against her thighs. With his free hand he steadied her against it, moved it into position between her legs. She felt her wetness rub against him.

"Hear this," he growled in her ear. "I didn't withdraw last night. I'll be damned if I do it now. And if I get you with child—and Margaret, I hope I have already done so—you *will* marry me."

She'd known it, deep inside her. She just hadn't let herself think it.

"I will never do to you what your father did to your mother. I will *always* be here for you." He sat on the table, and pulled her down to him.

He would. She knew it. Loyalty was in his nature, as surely as patience, understanding and the steady offer of support.

His hand stroked her back. She could not think, could not gather up enough logic to ascertain how to go forwards. Every path she could take seemed to double back into dishonor for her family. There *was* no forwards. The only direction she could imagine was *down*. And so she let gravity think for her. She slid down him an inch. His breath caught. His hands settled on her hips, and he guided her on top until she clasped him tight, her thighs resting against his.

Yes. This was what she wanted—risk and all. She wanted him. She wanted his body, the feel of him against her, inside her. Some dishonorable part of her even wanted his child, wanted an excuse to escape the dilemma that stretched before her.

She sank lower, her passage stretching to accommodate him.

"God, Margaret," he whispered in her ear. "You're so tight. So damned hot."

And now that she'd encompassed him, a more pressing matter emerged. "What should I do?"

His fingers clenched her side. "Whatever feels best for you."

"But I want to know what feels good for *you*."

His eyelids shivered shut, and his member twitched inside her. "It *all* feels good for me. Trust me. At this point, it's all exquisite. You're exquisite." His hands cupped her hips.

Tentatively Margaret rose up on her knees. Pleasure drifted through her. Through *them*. She sank down on him once more, and his hand drifted to her breast. A delicious heat engulfed her.

"Ah, yes. I really love that."

She did it again.

"Talk to me," he whispered. "Tell me what you feel. What you want."

"Touch me," Margaret whispered. "I want you to touch my back."

His hands fluttered up her back in slow, gentle caresses. She rose up on him again, finding a rhythm. Her hands found the curve of his biceps; her legs clasped the steel of his thighs. "You feel hard."

"Hard is good." His voice was husky. He thrust inside her.

"And big."

"Big is better."

His hands slipped to her hips and helped the rhythm along. She could feel her tension build, a slow fire stoking deep inside her, growing hotter and hotter with every stroke. His teeth gritted; the night air could no longer cool her skin, and her temperature rose. He insinuated his hand between their bodies, and as he pressed his fingers to her sex, ecstasy overtook her. It crashed over her in wave after glorious wave. When he'd wrung every bit of satisfaction from her body— when the fire that filled her had flared up into a bright pillar and burned everything from her—then he pressed his head into her neck.

"You feel like Margaret," he whispered. "And Margaret is best of all."

As she slumped bonelessly against him, he lifted her again, thrusting inside her. She hadn't imagined there was any pleasure left in her, but it came. It came in little sparks at first. Then it caught fire in her soul. He gasped once, and then, just as she was cresting into her own orgasm, he came, too.

For long moments after, he said nothing. Instead he put his arms around her, holding her close. He was warm. And hard. And big. She didn't want to think beyond those moments, didn't want to admit that there was anything else to say. But as their clean sweat began to grow chilled, he spoke once more. "I'll be damned, my dear, if this is the last time I have you."

He was wrong. Utterly wrong on both counts. He wouldn't have her again, and they were *both* already damned.

For the first time in months, Margaret felt the full weight of loss settle on her shoulders.

But she'd shouldered heftier burdens on her own. Her eyes stung, but this time she didn't lean on him. She didn't weep. Instead she moved his hands off her shoulders and disentangled their bodies. Disentangled his life from hers.

BY THE NEXT AFTERNOON, Margaret had left her family home and her lover.

She sat on the squabs opposite her brother. From the road, she could hear the creak of the carriage, the clop of horse hooves. They made a regular procession: this conveyance, another for the servants and luggage and yet another carefully converted to transport her father to London. They had been traveling for some hours already, and given the leisurely pace of their travel, days of their journey still waited. Those days were going to be very long, if she and Richard spent the entire time not conversing with each other. They would seem even longer if he chose to lecture her.

But so far, he hadn't said a word. He'd simply looked out his window at the passing landscape, watching hill after hill disappear into oblivion. And she'd waited, her fists clenched together, for the coming explosion.

She could already predict what he would say. It was nothing she hadn't told herself before. A lady's virtue was her most precious possession, and she'd squandered hers not once, but twice—the second time on the man who sought to destroy her family. No doubt her brother was wondering if he could trust her. Or any of the reports she'd sent.

Richard sighed heavily, and turned away from the landscape that flitted by the carriage window.

"Are you going to rip up at me?" Her voice sounded stilted and formal. After their hours of silence, it also seemed unexpectedly loud. "Because if you are, I should prefer that you get it over with."

Richard cocked his head and squinted at her. Margaret held her spine straight and met his gaze. She wasn't going to let him cow her. If she was in the wrong, it was only because there was no right choice to be had.

It took her a few moments to realize that he was squinting not in an attempt to intimidate her, but because his eyes had been dazzled by the sunlight reflecting off the lake outside.

"Do you see me as such a monster, then?" he finally asked.

She had no response. Had he been Edmund, he would have heaped aspersions on her head. But Richard was quieter than their middle brother—quieter and, she'd always thought, kinder. More understanding.

He sighed. "No, Margaret. I'm not going to remonstrate with you. I should think you've had enough of that." He shook his head. "Tell me—was Father as horrid the entire time I was away as he was this morning?"

"At least he's speaking now." Margaret shook her head. It had almost been a relief, when the first words out of his mouth had been to call Richard a girlish idiot. "He's been worse. Far worse."

"Egad." Richard sounded tired. "Well. Edmund and I got ourselves as far away from him as we dared. And we gave not the first thought to what it meant for you to be left behind. It destroys me to say it, but that Turner fellow was right. We haven't done well by you." He turned his head to look at her thoughtfully.

That Turner fellow had another name, and Margaret could not but think it—*Ash*—without conjuring up his face in her mind. That cleft chin, those solid cheekbones. And best of all, that hint of a lazy smile that took over his face as he looked at her and called her a magnificent creature…

Her brother mistook her silence. "Did he hurt you badly, then?"

Margaret shook her head. "He didn't hurt me. He didn't hurt me at all."

"He's such a big, uncivilized brute of a man. And you've looked pale and wan these past hours. You're a lady, Margaret—or, at least, a gentlewoman. And Turner always struck me as crude and…and earthy."

"Earthy?"

Richard gestured uncomfortably. "Not used to speaking with ladies, or making accommodations for their more genteel requirements."

"Ah. Yes. I suppose at first he seemed a little uncouth to me." Her brother didn't need to know precisely how uncouth. Had Ash really propositioned her within minutes of meeting her? At the time, she'd been outraged. Now, it just sounded like…like something Ash would do. Once he knew what he wanted, he was not apt to delay sharing his conclusion with others.

"You're not happy, that's for damned sure. I do wonder."

"Richard…" She paused and looked across to her brother. He was still the same man who had fished her out of the fountain all those years ago. A little abstracted, yes, but kind. Quiet. He was listening to her. He didn't want her hurt. And if sometimes her welfare failed to appear first on his list of concerns, it was natural absent-mindedness.

"Richard," she finally confessed, "he told me I mattered."

"That you *what?*"

"That I mattered. That I was important. After I was declared a bastard, nobody paid me any mind. But Ash Turner told me I mattered."

Richard's eyebrows drew down in confusion. "I understand," he said, in direct contradiction to the puzzled quirk of his lips. "These past few months must have been difficult. But Margaret, after Parliament approves our Act of Legitimation, his opinion will be immaterial. That is why it is important—no, *vital*—that you and Edmund and I present a united front. I have no fear that the House of Commons will pass the bill when it's presented to them. But the Lords, now…" He trailed off, tapping his lips. "It's anyone's guess what they will decide, and so far they are split down the middle, between those who want me legitimized, because I am innocent in this affair, and those who want me to remain a bastard, because our father so thoroughly scandalized them. The question of my legitimacy truly will come down to the votes of a bare handful."

Margaret stared at him. "The question of *our* legitimacy, you mean."

"Yes. Of course that's what I mean." He smiled at her and reached across the carriage to pat her hand. "You'll see. Once *we* have been legitimized, everyone will know you matter once more. You won't need Turner at all."

Richard simply didn't understand. Her own father had called her useless. Before she'd met Ash, she'd begun to feel flattened to the point of nonexistence.

But the sort of honor Richard was talking about was flattery, not truth. It wasn't real. Honor that was given to you because of how you were born—that was just a delusion. She wasn't going to rely on Parliament—or the people around her—to provide an assessment of herself. They were fickle and untrustworthy.

She shook her head mutely and looked out the window. *Ash will not be the only one to value me for myself,* she vowed. *There will be others—Parliament or no Parliament.*

"Why didn't you tell me about the trick Frederick played on you?" Richard continued. "The wedding had been delayed so many times, I thought you didn't wish to marry. And that I understood all too well. You should have spoken to me."

"Truly? You would have wanted to hear that your sister let herself be despoiled?"

"No, of course I don't wish to hear any such thing. But when such things are true, I ought to know them. So that I can bludgeon the fellow in question into coming up to scratch."

"Under the circumstances, I'm rather glad you didn't. I thought I loved him when I was nineteen. Now I'm aware of precisely how pitiful he is. I'm glad I'm not tied to him." She cast her brother a look. "Thank you for not lecturing me."

Richard shrugged. "Besides, I can understand what you mean. We left you here by yourself. No doubt you were lonely. And Ash Turner *is* such a brute of a man." He glanced away uneasily, running a finger along the edge of the window. "I've heard some women appreciate that sort of thing. I wouldn't know anything about that. In any event, I'm hardly the one to lecture you on chastity."

Chastity. Margaret smiled and bit back a wave of bittersweet nostalgia. "I've heard Edmund gibe you about it from time to time about it, when he thought I wasn't listening. No mistress? You could practically contribute a chapter to Mr. Mark Turner's book on chastity."

Richard looked up at her. "Mark Turner is writing a book on chastity? How strange. I wouldn't have expected it of him. Do you recall the summer that Edmund returned home from Eton, his arm broken in three places?"

Margaret nodded. "He spent the entire first two months complaining bitterly about not being able to ride, not being able to swim. In truth, I think he enjoyed the opportunity to order the staff about."

"Mark Turner broke Edmund's arm—popped it right out of the socket, in fact, and cracked his elbow. He blacked his eye and sprained his ankle. Fights break out at school. But there's a gentleman's code that governs such affairs. One doesn't break limbs. From what Edmund told me, it was done quite deliberately. So you'll imagine my surprise when you tell me that such a fellow thinks about chastity. Both our father and I tried to have him tossed out of school. I can only imagine how much money Ash Turner had to lay out to stave off that eventuality."

Margaret shut her eyes. If she had known only the Turners, she'd have said her brother was exaggerating, even lying. She couldn't imagine Mark intentionally breaking anyone's arm. He was *physically* capable of it. But mentally? Morally?

"I don't blame you," her brother said softly. "After all, I've been taken in by the Turners before, too. Once, I thought Mark was quiet and sweet." He shook his head. "As for Smite…" Richard's gloved fingers curled around the leather strap hanging from the carriage roof. "If you ever wish to hate someone," he finally said, "befriend him first. I've found it works wonders."

"But I've met him," Margaret said.

Richard sat up. "You've met him? What did you think?"

"Harsh," Margaret said. "Harsh, but fair."

Richard shook his head. "Just wait until he sits in judgment over you. There's not an ounce of mercy in him. Coupled with his eldest brother's unholy talent for turning the world on its head…" Richard sighed. "After that fight, I talked with the headmaster and convinced him to toss Mark out, as soon as the boy was capable of walking again. But somehow, Turner walked in not twenty-four hours after the incident and performed his magic. I still don't know how he could have arrived so quickly. There hadn't been time for the news to travel. The whole thing must have been deliberate. And somehow, when he left, the headmaster was smiling, and the youngest Turner stayed on the rolls." Richard shook his head. "Even then, everything he touched seemed to magically align. At the time, he seemed ancient. But now that I think of it, he wasn't even an adult."

Ash wouldn't have let a little thing like age stop him. The only part of the story that rang true with Margaret was that Ash had come to his brother's aid. But how could everything else be false? She couldn't imagine Richard trying to have Mark ejected from school for a triviality. Richard rarely paid attention, but when he did, he was remarkably fair-minded.

"Maybe," she said, "it was all a misunderstanding."

Richard glanced at her, and let out a sigh. "Margaret, misunderstandings don't break arms. Misunderstandings don't file suit in ecclesiastical courts to bastardize the issue of a duke. Misunderstandings don't get orders from courts of equity, allowing them to catalog the worth of an estate, so that the so-called untrustworthy offspring deliver his ill-gotten inheritance intact. I know that Ash Turner has got you all tangled about. But you are being used as a pawn on the board. The sooner you come to grips with that, the more likely we are to prevail. This is not a misunderstanding, Margaret. It's a war."

CHAPTER NINETEEN

London. November, 1837

LONDON LOOKED DIFFERENT to Margaret than it had the last she'd been here.

Then, the news had come at her all in a rush, too fast for Margaret to comprehend. The suit in the courts. Her illegitimacy. The dissolution of her betrothal, her mother's death and the sudden, inexplicable onset of her father's illness. She'd felt barely able to keep her knees from buckling beneath her. And so when the women she had called her friends her entire life had simply turned their collective backs on her, she had given up. She'd fled back to Parford Manor and buried her own bewildered hurt in caring for her ailing father.

The change of the seasons had exerted some little effect on the scenery. Now, instead of being dark gray, foggy, drizzly and clouded over with coal dust, the city appeared to be light gray, foggy, drizzly and clouded over with coal dust. The flowers sold by the vendors had altered; fruit sellers walking the streets had a few baskets of late berries, instead of sacks of wizened apples.

But the biggest difference was not in the weather or the wares. It was something Margaret held deep inside her. London looked different when you came back looking for a fight. Over the past week, all of the best people had returned to town once again. Parliament prepared to sit once again. As a result, knockers had been hung on doors and invitations had begun to flourish, scattering on the wind like seeds from some great plant of etiquette.

This time, Margaret wasn't going to retreat to the countryside to let her wounds fester.

Which was why for the fourth time in twelve days she stood on the threshold of the townhouse where Lady Elaine Warren lived. Margaret's maid waited on the pavement behind her. When Margaret had first begun tilting at this particular windmill, her maid had been wary and uneasy. After over a week of battle, the woman had become inured to the prospect of rejection. Now she sported only a dour expression, shifting from foot to foot. From the slouch in her chaperone's shoulders, Margaret could guess her thoughts: *Can't she hurry up and get tossed out on her ear again, so that we may finally return home?*

Not, Margaret thought grimly, until they'd made their rounds. She'd visited twelve houses today. Twelve doors had remained closed to her; doors that would have sprung wide open for her a year ago.

Margaret's dove-gray silk morning gown, trimmed with yards of fine-knit black lace, was a far cry from the sensible nurse's frocks she'd worn back at Parford Manor. Her cloak was soft and warm. Her hair had been curled and arranged, and ringlets bounced about her shoulders in gentle sways as she lifted her hand and rapped the knocker. The sound echoed against the wood: firm, but polite. Margaret was *always* polite when she went out to do battle.

A jaunty little bonnet stood atop her head, tied in place. As she stood on the stoop, waiting for a response, she could feel the long, navy ribbons slithering down her shoulders. She shifted slightly, and the silk tickled her skin.

The door opened—one battle won. The dark-clad butler took one glance at Margaret and compressed his lips. He held a silver salver, which he normally would have extended at this point. Over the many years when Margaret had visited Lady Elaine, he'd often done so—if he hadn't ushered her in immediately.

But everything had changed. This time, when the butler looked at her, he no longer saw a lady.

Margaret raised her chin. He would. He *would*.

It seemed as if she had been knocking at doors, and being turned away, for far more than two weeks. It seemed as if it had been years since she had last seen Ash, when in truth, scarcely two months had passed. The dreadful thick fog that blanketed London in the mornings had crawled over more than just the streets. It had swallowed up her memories of his features, dimmed them in cotton until he seemed an impossibility: a fairy-tale hero, too large for the life she had to live.

No, here in the clammy fog, there was only a dour-faced butler. He stood, wordlessly barring Margaret's entry into her erstwhile friend's home.

But there was one thing that Margaret carried with her from those enchanted weeks. They were words she held in her heart, words she repeated to herself every night, and again on waking. *I matter. I am important. And I am not giving up.*

Perhaps that was why, the fourth time she was faced with Lady Elaine's butler, she reached forwards and placed a card on the salver the butler had not yet proffered.

"Newton," Margaret said in her most commanding voice, "do tell Lady Elaine that Lady Anna Margaret Dalrymple has come to call."

It was both a gamble and a brazen lie. She wasn't Lady Anna Margaret any longer, even though her card proclaimed her as such in raised letters on thick, creamy stock.

From behind Newton, Margaret could hear scraps of conversation wafting to her. They came from inside the house—murmurs, and then a peal of feminine laughter. Margaret recognized that high-pitched nervous giggle, ending on a snort. Her friend's laughs were legendary. Margaret could imagine everything about the conversation Lady Elaine must be engaged in now—everything from the length of the visit (always long) to the number of times she would poke her head out of the room and call for more biscuits (often).

The butler cleared his throat, forcibly reminding Margaret that she wasn't in the front parlor, partaking of tea.

"Lady Elaine," he stated inflexibly, "is not at home to visitors."

From the sound of things, Lady Elaine was in fact at home. With visitors.

Margaret looked the man in the eye and shook her head in disappointment. He didn't blush—a man as well-trained as he would never show so much emotion—but after a few seconds, his gaze cut away.

"Newton," Margaret said quietly, "you will at least deliver my card, and allow Lady Elaine to refuse me entry personally."

Newton didn't blink. He didn't sigh. And most important, he didn't move from his post, blocking the door. But his shoulders shifted—a tiny amount, not so much as to hunch. For him, it was a clear declaration of regret.

"How many times have you escorted me to Lady Elaine's parlor? How many years have you known me?"

"Ma'am," he replied, "you'll have to take your card back."

"No, Newton. It's *my lady*," Margaret corrected softly. "If you are going to refuse me entry, you will at least do me the honor of calling me by the title I was born with."

Newton let out a pained breath. "My lady. I am not sure if I mean this as a compliment. You are the most politely relentless individual I have ever turned away from my mistress's doorstep. Refusal does not deter you. Embarrassment does not stop you. What will work?"

"I'll tell you what might work," Margaret mused. "Perhaps you might refuse me entry. And perhaps we might converse about it, politely, with me out here, standing harmlessly on the step. You can continue to valiantly refuse. I shan't raise a fuss, but because we are both polite, I might simply stand here and discuss the terms of my potential entry."

Newton's lips tugged down, in a hint of a scowl. "Terms of your entry? But your entry has no terms. You aren't entering."

She had only to wait just long enough. "Of course not," Margaret sued. "But how am I not entering? Might I come in through the servants' entrance?"

"Naturally not!"

"I don't suppose I could crawl in through a window, left obligingly open."

"Never."

The tenor of that half-heard feminine conversation shifted in front of her, from murmurs to rustles.

"I suppose I am also not entering through the back garden, then."

"N—" Newton started, but as he spoke, the parlor door behind him opened, and Lady Elaine poked her head out.

"Newton," said the woman, "could you be a dear and—oooh." As she spoke, Lady Elaine's pale eyes fell on Margaret. For days, the woman had refused to see her. Margaret had wagered that it was because her friend lacked the personal fortitude to cut her to her face. Lady Elaine was, after all, a good sort of person. A bit silly, yes, and more than a bit frivolous. But she was sweet by nature. That she was unmarried at the age of twenty-five had more to do with her lack of dowry— and her very unfortunate laugh—than anything else. She was pretty enough, in a plump, soft way, and her lips rounded at the sight of Margaret.

Confronted with the sight of her friend for the first time in months, Elaine's hand flew to her pale ringlets. "Oooh," she repeated. "Margaret. My father has *ordered* me not to say another word on your brother's behalf. He has *quite literally* ordered it."

Margaret could almost see her friend's italics, hanging in the air.

"It's lucky, then, that I don't wish to speak to you on my brother's behalf. I wish to speak to you on mine. May I come in?"

Newton didn't budge, and Elaine shook her head.

"I cannot allow it—although I wish I could. Newton has the *strictest instructions*. None of you are to pass through our doorway. I fear my father intends to side with that *simply awful* Mr. Turner, and he's afraid that

Turner, uncivilized brute that he is, will become *horribly angry* if he shows you any favor."

"Mr. Ash Turner?" Margaret frowned. "Uncivilized? Are we speaking of the same man?"

He was not the one who kept her standing on the cold threshold, in this dank, unhealthy weather. He was, perhaps, not always conversant in the rules of etiquette. Nothing he ever said was quite within the bounds of propriety. But he'd not even blinked an eye when she hurled a ball of dirt at him.

But then, when he'd thought that Richard had harmed her, he had tossed her brother across the room. Perhaps there was a bit of the barbarian in him, after all.

Lady Elaine simply stared at her. "Really, Margaret. You're the last person I would expect to be protesting the designation. He's practically a commoner. He knows *nothing* of genteel behavior. Gentlemen, of course, would never do anything outré, but commoners have not been taught to control their emotions. They are simply *incapable* of tamping down their base urges. It's bred into them."

Margaret glanced at Newton, who absorbed this news without a flicker of an eyelash. She forbore from mentioning that the commonest one among them was the only one who was not reacting emotionally.

"Let me set your mind at ease," she finally said. "I haven't come to ask you to cross your father. We're women, Elaine. We don't vote in Parliament. We don't enter into successions. We know our place. I would never expect you to intervene on my behalf. I don't believe I could have any effect on the outcome, in any event."

Lady Elaine stared at her. "I suppose…well. You make a good bit of sense. What is it you want, then?"

"Why, the pleasure of your company."

Lady Elaine laughed—that long string of wheezy chuckles, terminating in an indelicate snort. "Oh, Margaret. Even *I* am not such a goose as to swallow *that* tale."

"I mean it, Elaine. I've missed you—silly goose that you are—all these months. I've missed your histrionics. Your gossip. Your friendship. I've even missed your ridiculous laugh. I miss all my friends, and I will *not* be banished to the country. Not now. Not any longer."

"Oh, Margaret." Lady Elaine raised the tips of her fingers to her lips. She gave her head a bit of a shake.

"I am a duke's daughter. A duke's *bastard* daughter, yes." Margaret's voice trembled, but she raised her chin high. "But I am his daughter nonetheless. No matter how the suit is resolved—no matter whether Mr. Turner prevails or is defeated—I want to be accepted again. I don't expect to go everywhere. But I want more than I have now."

As she spoke, Margaret knew the obstacle was insurmountable. She could as soon beat down the Tower of London with a feather duster as foist herself on to society. That didn't mean she would give up, though.

But Elaine pursed her lips. "What do you want?"

"I want," Margaret said slowly, "an invitation."

And instead of breaking into nervous laughter again, Elaine nodded slowly.

"Perhaps," she said quietly, "I might help after all."

"You don't have to do this."

Ash didn't answer his brother's bare statement. He couldn't so much as look in his direction, as his valet was carefully knotting his cravat in a style that the man assured him was the latest fashion—sure to impress the lords he'd scheduled a meeting with this afternoon. Instead, Ash glowered in front of him, pretending he had not just had news that Margaret was in town.

"Really, Ash. You don't have to do this. Richard and Edmund Dalrymple—they're not worth doing this to yourself."

His valet stepped away to contemplate his work. Ash stared in front of him. "There is what they did to you. There is what Parford did to Hope. Hell, there's what they did to Margaret herself. You tell me—would *you* trust either Dalrymple with the responsibility of a dukedom?"

"*I've* forgiven them."

"*You,*" Ash enunciated carefully, "don't really understand what happened to Hope."

Behind him, he heard his brother move to one side. "Revenge isn't meant for us mortals, Ash."

The valet reached to adjust Ash's collar. Just as well, because he could feel it shift. "Don't you preach at me." Ash's voice was low. "I should think that we have had quite enough of that for one lifetime."

There was a longer pause, and then Mark walked round to look him in the eyes. There was no avoiding the soft censure on his brother's face. "Enough?" he asked. "What do you mean, *enough?*"

"You almost died because of our mother's absolutist adherence to dead words. I can't stand to see you imprisoned by them."

"Imprisoned?" Mark's voice was growing dangerous. But Ash was tired of tiptoeing about his brother's sensibilities.

"Yes. Imprisoned. You and Smite both. Living in abstemious denial, when you could have the entire world laid out before you. Turning down every advantage, even before it's offered. Our mother imprisoned you all those years ago, and even if you escaped her *then,* neither of you can free yourselves enough to accept what might be yours today."

Mark moved again, out of Ash's sight, and he was left to stare at the blank wall in front of him.

"Do you really suppose Smite and I are alone in that imprisonment?" Mark said from his side.

"Oh, any number of fools are as afflicted, I'm sure."

"Listen to you and your talk of *revenge.* 'Ye shall tread down the wicked, for they shall be ashes under the soles of your feet.' You're doing an excellent job of living up to your name."

"Don't call me that," Ash said.

"Don't call you *what?*"

"That."

But Mark simply snorted. "Oh, you mean this? 'And ye shall tread down the wicked, for they shall be ashes under the soles of your feet.' That is your name, no matter how much you wish to forget it. And how do you feel, playing the avenging angel, Ash?"

Ash's fists tightened, and his valet murmured in protest as his shoulders drew together. It took an enormous effort to keep from drawing in on himself, from curling up into a tight little ball, no matter what such a thing would do to the line of his coat.

Those words brought back childhood memories, none of them good. The smell of a fire, burning cheap and pungent coal; the feel of his mother's hand, almost all bone, on his wrist. And the flat despair in her voice as she regaled him with his name, chapter and verse.

It made him think of those last days with Hope, of that sure, certain knowledge of his failure.

"Stop," Ash said, feeling ill.

"You always were so stubborn. One of my earliest memories is—"

"*Stop,*" Ash begged. He didn't want to remember that sick pit of despair in his own stomach, that feeling that if he stepped out of line, if he made the slightest mistake, the thing that had taken her place might actually hurt her own children.

"She was wrong," Mark said gently. "Later, she went completely mad. She saw demons and believed that angels whispered violence in her ears. She named you for vengeance, Ash. Are you really going to pursue it?"

"What about you?" Ash croaked. "If you knew she was mad—and wrong—why do you cling to her beliefs?"

Mark glanced at him dryly. But he didn't respond to that needling. Instead, he was relentless. "Is that who you are, Ash? Are *you* the man she made you?"

Ash shook his head. "I'm—I'm just me."

"So am I." Mark looked up at him, speaking softly. "I am who I am despite Mother, not because of her. I *choose* to do what I believe to be right, despite the fact that my mother's madness ought to have poisoned the thought of all goodness. I *choose* to keep to chastity, for all that Mother's ranting made me want to go out and do just the opposite in rebellion. I choose to be the man I am, Ash. You should, too."

"But I did. I did choose."

Mark simply glanced at him and then looked away. It was disquieting, that look—as if he'd evaluated all of Ash's work and dismissed it. As if he had calculated its ethics, summed up its philosophies, dissected its morality, done whatever those things were that Mark had learned to do while at Oxford. Subjected to that searching analysis, Ash would never win.

"No," he said roughly. "Don't you dare look down on me. I haven't your education. God knows I haven't your intellect. But I'll be damned if you look at me as if all my experience means nothing. It may have been *instinct* instead of intellect that made me understand what I had to do, but don't you belittle that. My instinct purchased the clothing on your back, the education that lets you sneer at me in such learned precision. My instinct brought me back to Eton when the headmaster was on the verge of tossing you out on your ear. And now, my instinct tells me that you and Smite are desperately unhappy, for all that I've tried to remedy it."

"Ash, I—"

"And now," Ash said, overriding whatever it is Mark had been about to offer up, "my instinct says that I should pursue Parford. Tell me, Mark. Tell me my instinct is wrong."

His brother didn't respond, and the valet stepped away from Ash. Ash turned in place and glanced at his brother, who stood, watching him with a stricken look in his wide eyes.

"Ash," Mark said finally. "You don't think—you don't suppose that I *sneer* at you, do you? Just because you didn't attend school with me and Smite? Truly— our differences aside, I've never thought you less intelligent. Quite the opposite. You can do everything, without even trying. It's almost maddening. Had you gone to Oxford and taken your inevitable first beside Smite and me, you would be just as maddening. All I want is for you to explain your reasons. I can't try to convince you, if you won't keep yourself open to convincing. Once—just once—can we please talk about something beyond *instinct?*"

It killed him, that sureness in his brother's voice. No, Mark didn't understand.

Mark hadn't truly sneered at him—but only because he didn't know. Mark thought he would have excelled at school. It was the most laughable thought ever. Instinct was all he had, all he would *ever* have.

I can't read.

In his mind, he'd told his brother a thousand times. Sometimes, he imagined Mark would look on him with pity. Sometimes, he conjured up scorn. But there was one thing Ash could not imagine, no matter how many times he envisioned the scenario. He could not imagine respect.

And so he shook his head and turned away.

THE PLAN THAT MARGARET and Elaine had cobbled together had been quite simple. Margaret could not enter Elaine's house, on her father's orders, and so they had made an appointment to walk together in Hyde Park instead.

"Lord Rawlings is holding a select ball, three days hence." Elaine said, as she and Margaret strolled arm in arm on the banks of the Serpentine.

The weather was unseasonably warm for November in London. The incessant fog had been washed away in a hard rain the night before, and the sun was warm on Margaret's back. Only a breath of wind, whipping her skirts at the ankles, suggested that winter was almost here.

"I know precisely what you are thinking," Elaine continued. "Rawlings is Turner's creature. How could he not be? The man *purchased* his title, only three years before." Elaine shook her head mournfully, as if nothing were more horrific than a man who had not been born to his title.

Margaret suppressed a grin. A year ago, she would have shared that horror—the dread that the Crown was so desperate for an influx of money that minor titles were bestowed on someone whose primary worthiness was their willingness to share their wealth.

"The express purpose of the ball is to introduce Mr. Turner to some of the lords who will decide the suit, before Parliament sits. But if Rawlings would offer you an invitation, other doors would *certainly* be opened to you. Not a great many of them, true, but a few. Enough."

"And we are actually to meet Lord Rawlings here in Hyde Park? How are we to extract an invitation from him?"

"He and his friends often walk here on fine Saturday afternoons." Elaine sniffed. "He has been badgering me to attend one of his gatherings for the past year. I may not be the most *desirable* spinster in town, but I come from an old family. I suppose he thinks I will lend his silly little party some measure of *gravitas*. He cannot very well invite me without extending *you* an invitation, as well. And who knows? He is new to the *ton*. Perhaps he won't even know who you are."

"If he is a friend of A— Mr. Turner's, and furthering his case before Parliament, I don't see how it is possible that he would be ignorant of my family."

Elaine dismissed this unassailable logic with a shrug.

"Do be careful, Elaine. If word gets out that you're

championing me, you could be ostracized. I don't want you hurt on my behalf."

Elaine gave her an amused look. Then she laughed— entirely indelicately. "Margaret," she said, "I am invited everywhere and wanted nowhere. I could *hardly* lose anything of value. I'm not delicate. I'm not wealthy. I am just from a very, very good family."

Margaret bit her lip. It was one thing to know that others thought of Elaine that way. It was another to hear her laugh herself off, with so little thought. "You are also loyal and kind, and more clever than you credit. You are important in your own right."

Elaine looked at her. "What a very curious thing for you to say."

Yes. She'd changed. Before, Margaret had been a quiet, pitiful creature—passive, waiting for her life to come to her. But then all the trappings of politeness had been swept away. And she'd discovered she wasn't empty inside. She was magnificent. Even if nobody yet recognized it.

She inhaled and threw her head back. The pale sun touched her face; the wind caught at the ribbons on her bonnet and they flapped noisily.

But at that moment, Elaine reached over and grasped her wrist. "Margaret! Is that him?"

"Who? Lord Rawlings? You know perfectly well what Lord Rawlings looks— Oh."

Margaret followed Elaine's gaze, and her heart stopped. Two long months without seeing Ash suddenly disappeared.

Her hands actually fluttered, as if she were a debutante seeing her first duke. Her stomach trembled. Nothing had changed between them—nothing except that she'd learned precisely what it meant to wake up day after day without him near.

The space he'd once filled seemed an empty chasm. But seeing him didn't fill her cavernous yearning. It deepened it.

"Yes," she said softly. "That's him."

He was walking along the path in conversation with Lord Rawlings. He was dressed in black, his attire relieved from sobriety by a velvet waistcoat shot through with gold. It glittered in the sun. On another man, those colors might have seemed garish. On Ash, they illuminated. His hands were clasped behind his back; he walked slowly, as if he were marching to a funeral dirge. He looked vaguely weary.

"Oh." Elaine let the word escape in a wistful puff of air. "A shame he won't inherit the dukedom. He's rather a fine-looking man, isn't he?"

"Rather." He was wearing a top hat, trimmed with a ribbon to match his waistcoat.

"He'd almost be worth it *without the dukedom.* With those shoulders."

Margaret smiled ruefully. Coming from snobbish Elaine, that was the highest of compliments.

"Of course," Elaine added loyally, "I should *never* do such a thing to you. I could never marry such a man."

As if aware that he was the focus of their conversation, Ash looked up. He saw Margaret across the way. For one moment, he froze, just as she had. Then, he raised one hand, touching the brim of his hat in silent acknowledgement.

Elaine's grip on Margaret's wrist tightened. "He's *looking at us,* Margaret. Oh, dear. What are we going to do?"

Maybe he'd forgotten her. Maybe he'd already discarded his vow to have her again.

Maybe Elaine's anxiety had infected her with foolish doubts that meant nothing to her. She watched him across the lawn. He looked at her, as if waiting for her to make some move towards him.

If she simply picked up her skirts and ran, he would catch her.

But she'd made her choice, and no matter how it ate at her, she had to abide by it. But…doing nothing seemed too bare, too unkind. Not after everything he meant to her.

Margaret reached up and unlaced the ribbon holding her straw bonnet in place. She needed only tip her chin up to feel the sunlight against her lips—a warm kiss, laden with a mere hint of chill. Rare weather, for November. Then the wind did the rest—grabbing the straw brim and pulling it off, to go skirling away behind her.

Margaret smiled. It was a small act of defiance.

"Oh, Margaret!" Elaine said. "Your bonnet. And with that dreadful Mr. Turner looking on, too. Whatever are we to do?" She glanced behind her. "Must we chase after it?"

"We'll let it go." Margaret spoke, not even looking at her friend. Instead, she met Ash's eyes across all that distance. She could not make out their color, their expression. But she could not possibly have imagined the smile that spread across his face. He turned to her and started forwards across the lawn, his long legs eating up the distance between them. Lord Rawlings scampered after him.

Elaine turned from contemplation of the absconding

bonnet. "Margaret, he's *coming over here*. My God. Must we cut him for your brothers' sake?"

"No," said Margaret, simply, and Elaine let out a sigh of relief.

He came to a stop before her. Rawlings trailed after him uselessly, and glanced at Margaret, uncertain of the etiquette of such a situation. Nobody knew. Everyone likely imagined that they hated each other. Rawlings shrugged, as if to say, *I had nothing to do with this. Don't blame me.*

"Lord Rawlings." Ash spoke the words, but his eyes were on Margaret, warm and filled with greeting.

"Y—yes?"

"Your party Thursday next."

Rawlings swallowed and glanced at Margaret. He didn't quite meet Margaret's eyes; his gaze rose only as far as her breastbone and then slid away to contemplate a group of ducks. "There will be no…no unpleasant-ness, I assure you. None. You'll have nothing to fear." Rawlings looked away.

Ash raised his chin. "Invite her."

That brought Rawlings's head whipping around. "But you must know this is Margaret Dalrymple. *Miss* Margaret Dalrymple. If I invite her—"

"Invite *Lady* Margaret, and her brothers, too, if you must, to make it proper."

"But the purpose of the event—"

Ash held up one hand and flicked Margaret a glance. "Shall I fetch your hat for you, my lady?"

Margaret turned to track the course of her tumbling mass of straw. It bounced once on the ground, rolling. Then the wind lifted it again, and it sailed another few yards, landing in a pond behind her; to get it, Ash would have to tramp through a selection of weeds and

mud. Ducks charted courses around the dangerous profusion of silk flowers about the brim. She hadn't turned
towards her bonnet, so much as turned Ashwards. She
had ended up standing rather closer to him than she
intended.

If she asked him to get it, he'd have to shed coat
and boots. He would get that linen shirt all wet. She
let out a sigh of heartfelt appreciation at the thought,
and then, just as he was reaching for the cuffs of his
jacket, shook her head sadly. "No, Mr. Turner. Alas. I
find I like the feel of the wind through my hair."

The corners of Ash's mouth turned up just the
same.

"Invite her," he repeated.

Rawlings glanced from one to the other. "I see," he
said, his tone puzzled. Ash touched the brim of his own
hat and then the gentlemen walked on.

Beside her, Elaine stood stock-still. In her world,
there were not so many possibilities. Gentlemen either
ignored one, or…

"Margaret." She let the syllables of the name out
carefully, as if she were unsure of the damage they
could do. "Is—is Mr. Turner enamored of you?"

No matter how Margaret answered, this story would
be bruited about town. And so she settled on the simple
truth. "Yes. I rather think he is."

"Well. That's a bit of a…complication. Isn't it?"

Margaret sighed. "No doubt."

CHAPTER TWENTY

As Margaret had suspected, by the time she was announced at the Rawlings' ball, the story of the encounter in Hyde Park had made the rounds twice over, embellished at every turn. Polite society had not only been informed that the Dalrymples would be arriving en masse, but that Ash Turner, the man who'd had them bastardized, had taken one look at Margaret in the park and had ordered Rawlings to invite them. The stories Elaine related had Ash kissing her hand—this was the most forward—or gazing bashfully at her in love-struck wonder. Those who believed the latter, Margaret thought, had clearly never met Ash.

As she entered the ballroom on Richard's arm, everyone's gaze followed her. The murmurs of speculation grew to a tumultuous buzz around her.

Once, Margaret would have been one of the ones speculating as to the whys and wherefores. She would have wondered whether Turner had extended the invitation out of some dark motive, in order to settle the dispute in some wicked way once and for all. She might have asserted that he'd taken one look at Parford's daughter and tumbled headlong into love. Once, she'd have been the one sitting with her friends in the corner and guessing.

But today, she arrived with her brothers. And while everyone was interested in what would happen *to* her, and what delicious events might make fodder for the evening's conversation—nobody was interested *in* her. Not as herself.

After all, the evening's company had been made up of those members of society who took Ash's side in things. She and her brothers stood alone, a determined clump on the edge of the ballroom.

It was a relief when Diana, Lady Cosgrove, came flitting through the crowds. She was the first of Margaret's old friends to greet her here. Her door had been barred to Margaret for months, but maybe, with this invitation, all could be forgotten.

Lady Cosgrove wore blue silk with white roses in her hair, and as she approached, Margaret thought that she was one of the most beautiful women in the room. She wanted to embrace her.

"Margaret, you dear!" she exclaimed. "How have you *been* this past six-month?"

Lady Cosgrove could have discovered the state of Margaret's well-being at any point during the past half year, by the simple expedient of taking one of her calls—or, if she'd not wanted to exert herself that much, by reading one of the letters Margaret sent. But then, if Margaret was to retake her place in society, she would have to nod complacently through a great many lies, told for politeness's sake.

And so she simply smiled at Lady Cosgrove.

"And to think," the lady was saying, "you spent the summer rusticating in the country. Such a shame, when there were so many house parties to be attended. But then, you couldn't have come."

And here Margaret had thought they would make do by simply not referring to that period. Her friend's smile brightened incongruously, and for the first time,

Margaret considered the possibility that perhaps Lady Cosgrove had not come to renew their acquaintance.

"No," Margaret replied. "I could not. I was, after all, in mourning."

"In mourning!" Lady Cosgrove stepped back in surprise. "But of course—no wonder you've worn gray tonight when the color simply doesn't suit you. It's still half-mourning for you, isn't it?" And then she raised her fan to her mouth and tittered, just in case Margaret had missed her attempt at a set-down.

Margaret supposed she was intended to be hurt by that remark. Really. Did Lady Cosgrove think that after Margaret had been declared illegitimate, a little aspersion cast on the color of her gown would set her back?

It is all a sort of delusion, Margaret could remember Ash saying indulgently, *this notion of class.* Apparently, in the months since she had last seen her friend, Margaret had stopped being deluded.

Lady Cosgrove had never shown this side to Margaret before. But then, Margaret had been a duke's daughter, engaged to an earl. Back then she'd been placed too highly in society for Lady Cosgrove, a mere viscount's wife, to sharpen her claws upon.

And so rather than tearing up, as her once-friend no doubt hoped, Margaret laid her fan across Lady Cosgrove's wrist. It might have seemed a friendly gesture to anyone who watched. "You may find this curious to contemplate," Margaret said languidly, "but would you imagine, after I buried my mother, the absolute last thing on my mind was the color of my gown."

"You don't say!" The other woman smiled impudently. But before she could find another way to insult Margaret's toilette, a distinct laugh sounded in the crowd behind them. Lady Cosgrove pushed Margaret's fan away. It was at that moment that Margaret realized that she *had* seen this side of the woman before. Her jabs had merely been directed at someone else.

"Oh, dear. It's that dreadful Lady Elaine coming again." Lady Cosgrove caught sight of her and made a face. "Do not tell me she is wearing feathers in her hair. Feathers were *last* season. Everyone knows that this year it's flowers. Quickly, dearest—let's go and find Eva. I know she's about."

Had Margaret ever been so sly, so unthinking? Had she assumed that because she was a duke's daughter, she deserved only the most scintillating company?

"Come now," Lady Cosgrove was saying. "Quickly, quickly! Oh, no. Don't tell me you plan to be kind to the unfortunate little spinster again? You know I absolutely hate when you do that. How could you be so cruel to me, your dearest friend?"

No. Margaret had never been as bad as this woman. But she had not thought about what she had done. She'd enjoyed talking with Lady Cosgrove, enjoyed her fawning attentions, back when the woman believed Margaret above her in station. And when she said those horrid things about others, Margaret hadn't interfered. She felt that inaction now, with a keen sense of shame.

"Actually," Margaret said, "I was thinking of having a dinner party, with Elaine as the guest of honor. Shall I seat you across the table from her?"

"Cruel!" Lady Cosgrove said. "So cruel, Margaret, and I your oldest friend. You shouldn't jest with me in such a way. But come, we must talk. After all, I am dying to hear what you have to say about— Oh!"

"Ouch!" Margaret tried to wrest her arm from the talon of Lady Cosgrove's grip. To no avail. Her

erstwhile friend paid no notice to Margaret's attempt
to escape.

"Oh," she breathed again. "It's *he*. Did he really
walk up to you in a park? Did he really simply point
at you and tell Lord Rawlings to invite you? Just like
that? What a dreadful waste. As an unmarried woman,
you could not even take proper advantage."

It was only when Ash turned in their direction that
she finally let go, so she could smooth her blue dress
over her form. Strange; Margaret had thought Lady
Cosgrove quite pretty when she approached, but now
she noticed there were unattractive little lines gathered
at her eyes.

Margaret didn't bother to answer. Instead, she
rubbed her wrist and watched him. Ash stood half a
head higher than the men who surrounded him, dressed
in unrelieved black—black coat, black trousers and
a black cravat tied in a complicated pattern. He was
talking, politely, with those around him. But even as
he conversed, he scanned the crowd.

When his eyes rested on her, he stopped. He'd been
smiling before, in a friendly fashion. But what lit his
face when he saw her was more than a smile, more
than a grin. It was as if someone had thrown aside the
curtains of a sickroom on a glorious morning, to let
sunlight spill into every darkened corner.

What was he *doing?* Everyone would know how he
felt. He simply made no effort to hide it. She could feel
the heat of his expression, even from halfway across
the room.

The whispers began to swirl up around them.

He strode towards her, step by step, the crowd seem-
ing to part before him. He didn't stop. He just looked
in her direction and wanted her. And lo, she waited.

"Oh, God. He did. He *did* simply walk up to you in a park. He's doing it again." Lady Cosgrove poked at her ringlets. "Margaret, darling, you *must* introduce me. He is a doll of a man. And my husband has not yet returned from France."

Margaret glanced at her incredulously, but Lady Cosgrove seemed to have no sense of irony at all. She really *did* imagine that Ash might become her personal plaything and that Margaret would be willing to facilitate it.

Ash skirted around another cluster of men and women and stopped before Margaret. "Lady Anna Margaret," he said, giving her a correct little bow.

"Mr. Turner."

"May I have your first waltz?"

Oh, no. No, he could not. They couldn't. They could not do this, and certainly not in the open. Her face would reflect the turmoil she felt. And if she danced with him, his incandescent response to her would be displayed to the world.

But before she could muster up an answer, he gently took the card dangling from a ribbon on her wrist and pulled it to him. She perforce followed, the short length of ribbon pulling her towards him. He glanced at the heavy stock in his hands once—her heart held still, as she wondered if he could make out the difference between the waltzes and the simple country dances that were listed on the card—and then before she could subtly direct him, he scrawled his name on the correct line.

His thumb brushed the skin of her wrist, just beyond the edge of her glove. To anyone else, it would appear to be an accident. Margaret knew it was a caress. A promise.

"Margaret," Lady Cosgrove was saying softly at her side. "I say, Margaret."

Ash glanced at her. "And who is your friend?"

"Diana, Lady Cosgrove, may I present to you Mr. Ash Turner. Heir presumptive to the duchy of Parford. Mr. Turner, Lady Cosgrove."

The woman tittered softly.

"Hmm." Ash's voice was a trifle wary. "Should I be dancing with Lady Cosgrove?" He met Margaret's eyes as he spoke.

"Oh, please," Lady Cosgrove breathed.

Well. If they were going to occasion gossip, it was best that they did it properly.

"No," Margaret said distinctly. "You should not. Her husband would certainly not approve."

A gasp sounded beside her.

"I should love, however, to introduce you to Lady Elaine."

Lady Cosgrove gasped louder but recovered quickly. "Mr. Turner," she said, reaching out for Ash's cuff. "Do listen to me. I know that you may believe that Lady Margaret has your best interests at heart, as she is some kind of a relation, if only a distant one. But if you intend to be a duke, you must not let yourself be guided so easily, not by one such as her. Take my warning to heart: she's using you to punish me, because I kept my distance from her these past months. You know that any woman of good sense and decency would have done the same."

No, Margaret had never been like Lady Cosgrove. For one thing, she had never been so stupid. Ash's smile grew darker, and he looked at the woman. "I knew the instant Margaret spoke that she intended to use me as a weapon. What you fail to understand is this: I am her weapon to use."

Margaret's lungs burned. So much for not occasioning gossip. But she couldn't fault him. She couldn't reprimand him. She couldn't even stop her own smile from spilling out, stupidly, over her face, the truth writ large for anyone to see.

"And I asked her to direct me for that reason." Ash looked back at Margaret. "I'll be by to collect my waltz."

ASH FINALLY HAD HER in his arms again, even if it was for something as innocuous as a waltz. His hand was on her waist; her fingers rested lightly on his shoulder. And even though they were surrounded by dozens of others, at least for the moment he could pretend they were alone.

Even though he'd been able to conjure up Margaret's image in his mind these past months, the real thing was a thousand times better. He had one of her hands in his. Even through gloves, it was wonderful to hold her. He could smell the scent of roses on her. And when he leaned in, on a gliding turn, he could almost taste the sweetness of her breath.

Memory could not hold a candle to the reality of her. She set him ablaze. Her gaze flickered down demurely, and then she looked up at him, under the curtain of those lashes. Her lips curved, and his heart contracted. And then she spoke, so quietly that he leaned in to better make out her words.

"You mustn't hold me quite so close," Margaret said.

Hmph. Hardly a romantic sentiment. In fact, he'd

thought that foot of distance between their bodies rather too much as it was.

He whirled her about and smiled at her. "And why must I not?"

"Because everyone is watching, and it's not proper."

Truly? He thought they'd discarded such trivial considerations long ago. Ash looked down into her eyes and shook his head. "Must we go through this again? I'm aware it's not proper. It was highly improper for me to demand that Rawlings issue you an invitation. I'm sure that those who are overly interested in propriety would disapprove of the method I used to ask you to dance. Why should I care now? We can write our own rules."

She turned her head, and the stones dangling from her ears swayed back and forth. "Actions have consequences." Her voice was tremulous. "And maybe you don't see them—maybe *you* are unaware of them. But just because you do not pay the price, does not mean I can ignore the cost."

"Cost?" Ash looked over her shoulder at the crowds. "What cost? At the end of the day, we shall triumph."

"The last time your day ended, Ash, and you triumphed, I was declared a bastard. I was stripped of my dowry by the court of Chancery. When you triumph, my brothers suffer. So don't talk so cavalierly of what *we* shall do. There is no we. People will talk."

"Let them talk," Ash said dismissively. "What does it matter what they say?"

She let out a faint huff. "They'll imagine that we fancy one another."

He felt a smile curl his lip, and he let his hand slip down her waist, to rest against the base of her spine.

"Then they'll imagine the truth, won't they? I fail to see the problem."

She looked up at him. "But they'll use it against my brothers. If popular sentiment has us caught up in romantic trysts, minds will immediately jump to matrimony. Those who wish to see my father's bloodline continue in the dukedom might accept a continuation through the female line. This could materially harm my brothers' chances."

Margaret solemnly looked up at him as she spoke. Ash weighed his next words carefully. He didn't want to offend her, and yet he could hardly countenance lying. "I still fail to see the problem. You may recall that I oppose your brothers' suit in Parliament. I am *trying* to materially harm their prospects."

She merely looked puzzled.

"Truly, Ash," she said, "I— You can't mean what you just said. I know you wouldn't use my affection for you as a tool to achieve your own ends."

She sounded so certain. But he'd had two months— two *damned* empty months—to think of this. To contemplate what he was missing. To imagine what he would say when he saw her again.

"I know you," she was saying. "You would never use me this way. You wouldn't."

"You've forgotten. If I'm Duke of Parford, I'll be able to do *anything* for my brothers. If I pursue you openly, it raises the chances I'll become duke. I want you. I want the dukedom. It turns out, my interests coincide and I can have both." He looked her in the eyes. "I intend to do so."

She didn't look away. Instead, her eyes sparked and her lips compressed. "How efficient of you." Her hand pressed into his shoulder, cutting more deeply than it ought in a polite waltz.

He merely smiled at the epithet. In the months since he'd last seen her, he'd thought far worse things. He hadn't enjoyed the separation. Particularly as it was altogether unnecessary. He had only managed patience because his instinct had whispered that she would still be his.

He could wait. He could wait a little while longer for her.

"You told me once I was cheerfully ruthless." He looked down into her eyes. "After two months without you, I'm not feeling quite so bloody cheerful, myself. If it takes ruthlessness, I'll be ruthless. But yes, Margaret, I will have you."

She swallowed and looked away. "You told me once I had only to ask. Ash, I've made my choice. I'm asking you now: if you care for me at all, don't make overtures to me. This is tearing me to pieces. Leave me be, because I request it of you."

He was calm. He was patient. So why did his left hand, holding her, cramp with the effort of not squeezing her to him? He let out a sigh. "Your request is denied," he replied.

Her breath hissed in.

"I'll apologize a thousand times, but leave you be? No. If I thought you truly indifferent, I would surely step away. But you are not indifferent. You are not even unwilling. You are just—temporarily—unavailable. And I'll be damned if I give you up."

"Don't." She looked away. "Don't do this to me. Not when I can't stamp away without occasioning even more talk. What you're doing—it's not sporting. I have never used anything you told me as fodder for my brothers' suit in Parliament. Not even when I thought that all you wanted was to seduce me into your bed." She looked up at him. "I could have used you, Ash. I could have. So don't you do this to me."

Ash bit his lip. It turned out he was just not a well of patience. He'd won her affections. After two months spent without her—after two months when she'd walked away from him—he was actually a little angry.

"Tell me," he said as he spun her about, "tell me I am not the best thing that has ever happened to you. Tell me you don't wish to have me in your life. Tell me I don't belong."

She didn't look at him. But she was silent. He felt an almost grim satisfaction, even though winning an argument under those circumstances was all victory, no triumph.

Still, as the musicians brought the piece to a close, he leaned in and whispered into her ear. "That is what I thought, Margaret. Don't *you* do this to yourself."

THE SILENCE IN THE CARRIAGE after the ball was almost unbearable. Margaret sat, the dark enfolding her, silently glad that she could not see her brothers' faces.

"The good news," Richard said, "is that we have been positively inundated with invitations."

Margaret bit her lip.

Edmund responded. "The bad news is, it is because everyone wishes to see you and Turner again. Margaret, what could you have been thinking? Talking with him. Introducing him to your friends. Dancing with him."

"What was I supposed to do? It would have been dreadfully impolite to refuse. It would have created a scene."

"And it wasn't a spectacle when he practically kissed

you in front of everyone?" Edmund snapped. "At a minimum, you ought not to have appeared so eager to comply. Everyone is talking—absolutely *everyone*. Have you any idea what could happen if the gossips start marrying you to Ash Turner in their minds?"

"It was a waltz, not a wedding!"

Edmund sighed. "It's never just a waltz, Margaret. Matters are already touch and go, even without this latest complication. For one, we had thought Forsyth would support our suit."

The current Lord Forsyth was their mother's brother. He'd always seemed an indulgent, loving uncle. Indeed, he had doted on his sister, and by extension, his sister's offspring. He was the last person Margaret could imagine supporting Ash Turner.

"But no," Edmund continued. "He's furious at Father for what he did, and he's all too aware that with the marriage between Mother and Father dissolved as if it had never happened, the sixty thousand pounds that had been set aside for Mama's lawful female offspring reverts to him. He has convinced a group of five others to vote down the bill. *Your* sixty thousand pounds means that we need every last one of the undecided votes. We can't have you squandering a single one out of misguided romanticism."

"Edmund," Richard said gently, "she can't be held to account for the money, at least."

Margaret shook her head, but in the dark, nobody could see her denial. She shut her eyes, but it didn't help. Darkness was darkness, and there was no guidance either way. "I don't want to choose between you and Ash."

Edmund made an exasperated noise. "Don't be a naive little goose, Margaret. This is not about what you *want. Everyone* is choosing between us. That's what this act in Parliament is about—it's about the lords choosing either Turner or Richard. And this, now, is about choosing your future. Do you want to be a bastard all your life? Do you want to be ostracized from society for the remainder of your years? Choose out of selfishness, for God's sake. You know that until you've been legitimized, unthinking people will forever be giving you the cut."

Lady Cosgrove sprang to mind. "Small hardship," Margaret said with asperity. "If unthinking people won't talk with me, then I shall make friends with people who think. Which, oddly enough, seems like a good idea to begin with."

"La-di-da," Edmund said, his tone reminding her of their father. "Would you listen to that show of logic? If you won't think of yourself, then think of us."

Richard sat next to her. At those words, he reached over and gave her hand a squeeze. "He doesn't mean it," he whispered. "He is only so rude because he is so very, very worried."

If it had just been Edmund, she might have been tempted to give in to Ash. Even though he was her brother. Even though she loved him. Even though she knew she would regret such a hasty dismissal later.

But Richard… He didn't always think about what he did, but when he actually took notice, he stood by her. He had never deserted her. And if she ruined this for him, he would be a bastard. He would have a little money—a few thousand pounds, enough to scrape by, but by no means what he deserved. And while Ash had once offered her father more, she was not sure the offer was still open—or that Richard would accept it if it were made.

But both Ash and Edmund had urged her to think of herself. When she thought of *herself,* it wasn't legitimacy or money that came to mind. It wasn't even Ash himself. It was, instead, the gift that Ash had given her back at Parford Manor: the solid, sure certainty that she was someone worth having. That she was better than her father.

If she did to her brothers what their father had done to them, she could not be so certain any longer. Family didn't betray family.

She swallowed and shut her eyes. Edmund was right. It was foolish to imagine that she could avoid a choice. "What must I do?" she asked weakly. But she already knew the answer.

"People are talking already. You need to give them something substantially less romantic to discuss. We've been invited to the Rutledges' rout," Edmund said. "Turner will be there. And the instant he sets eyes on you, you are to give him the cut direct."

CHAPTER TWENTY-ONE

MARGARET ENTERED THE Rutledges' town house filled with dread. She'd had days to consider what she needed to do. She just didn't want to do it.

She could feel all of society's eyes on her, could feel the lascivious interest that rose around them. She was swept away by a flood of colored evening gowns and dark suits. All she had to do was turn away from Ash when she saw him and pointedly show her lack of interest.

So simple—and yet so impossible.

She hadn't realized quite how impossible it was until she finally saw him in the crowd. He caught sight of her. And all of her worst fears came true as he looked up at her and gently, oh, so gently, smiled.

He *smiled* when he saw her. That should not have felt like such a death knell. But it made what she had to do so much more of a betrayal—a betrayal of not just her own desires, not merely his inclinations, but of something precious between them.

She didn't smile back. She looked away. Those two things sent a rush of murmurs through the watching crowd—as if she had just been merely impolite, instead of utterly false. But not looking at Ash was as impossible as not inhaling. No matter how hard she tried to hold back her next breath, the best she could hope was to delay it for a while. All the while, her lungs burned. She ached all over. And Ash…

Oh, Ash. Through the corner of her eye, she could see him advancing on her.

Of course. Her brothers' plan was sheer idiocy, and she should have known it. Strict rules of propriety governed the interactions between men and women. There were books devoted to the art of turning away men one didn't wish to address. A complicated dance that everyone adhered to. But Ash had never read those books.

Trying not to love him was improbable. Keeping him from loving her? Now that was downright impossible. Why, oh, why, of all the men in the world, did Ash have to be *this* one? He was trying to destroy her brothers. He'd broken her heart twice over and had mended it again, better than new.

He was only a few yards away from her now. "Lady Margaret?" There was a calm, cool confidence in his voice. He knew she would turn. He knew she would look at him. He had no doubts. He never did.

And he would never stop trying, just because she looked in another direction.

There was only one way Margaret could respond. She turned and ran.

A crescendo of babble rose about her in full-voiced speculation as she darted through the crowd. She ducked through a side door, almost invisible in the ornate carving of the ballroom. She found herself in the servants' quarters. As soon as she went through the door, she knew it wasn't enough. He would follow her. He would find her here. She couldn't face him, couldn't talk to him.

She grabbed a nearby door handle and wrenched

it open. A tiny storeroom stood behind the door, little more than a closet where the household kept decorations and table linens. She stepped inside and pulled the door shut behind her.

Darkness enveloped her. Darkness and blessed silence.

Only then did she put her head in her hands. Rubbing her eyes did nothing to obliterate his image in her mind. She could still feel his smile against her skin, as if it were a tangible thing. That wicked, horrible, inescapable smile. Oh, who was she fooling? That lovely, insane, undeniably attractive smile. Pulling her arms about herself could not erase the feel of his hands, big and strong, on her shoulders.

She felt both utterly humiliated and sick at what she had done to him.

How long was she going to have to stay in this darkened storeroom? Long enough for the gossip to die down. Minutes, certainly. Hours, perhaps. She rubbed her temples. She should have just jumped in a fountain and had done with it.

Half an hour later, the humiliation hadn't subsided. Instead, her legs were cramped; there was not even enough room to sit, not with all her skirts. She had just about convinced herself she could safely show her face, when a polite knock sounded on the door. It was so ridiculously incongruous—that knock, on a storeroom. It could be only one person.

She shut her eyes and waited, but of course Ash didn't go away. Instead, he knocked again.

"Margaret," he said gently. And then, even more quietly: "Please. I know you'd like me to keep my distance—but I don't believe it's possible."

She opened the door. He slouched against the

doorjamb. His cravat was crooked. She wanted to bury her head against his chest and hold him close. She wanted to run away again. She'd have done the latter, except he was standing in her way.

"Ash, are you trying to destroy my reputation? If we're seen together alone, it won't be marriage they'll imagine we're after. And the gossip would not help either of us—not you, for using me so, nor my brothers, for their scandal of a sister."

He nodded gravely. "You make an important point," he said. "I must respect your wishes." But instead of leaving, he stepped into the close confines of the room with her, pulling the door shut behind him. Her skirts squished against him.

Oh, God. She could feel the heat wafting off him. He couldn't have kept his distance, not in the tiny space allotted for storage. His limbs brushed hers. His hands covered hers in the dark.

"Forgive me for my social ineptitude. What are the rules of etiquette," he asked conversationally, "for conversations in a closet?"

"One ought never have them."

He nodded once. "Sensible enough. I agree."

He stepped closer to her. His eyes, rendered mahogany by the dimness, sought hers.

"You agree? Then why aren't you leaving?"

"Hush," he said. "You just told me: closets are not for conversing."

He put his hands on her shoulders. He lifted one hand and brushed a wisp of hair from her face. She could barely see him, but in the close confines of the closet, she could feel her skirts bunch as he leaned into her. She had every chance to move away, every chance to shove him six inches and have him land atop the pile of rags on the floor.

She didn't do it.

When his lips touched hers, they were soft and sweet. When his arms wrapped around her, she rested against him. She drank him in, like water after a long thirst. He didn't say a word, just kissed her. Tongue touched tongue. Hands entwined with hands. His body was so familiar, and she needed him, desperately. He pulled back from her briefly.

"Ash." Margaret knew her voice was trembling. "Why are you doing this?"

"Because I adore you. Because you looked so stricken when I saw you and I couldn't bear not to comfort you." His voice was warm breath against her skin. "Did you know, when you left that room, you took all the light with you?"

"Stop," she said. "Stop trying to seduce me."

He smoothed back her hair against her forehead. "If I were trying to seduce you, Margaret, I'd have done it by now."

"In here? But—there's no room to actually do that."

His breath hissed out. "I should have done it sooner," he said. "I should have done it more, and Mrs. Benedict be damned. No room to seduce you?"

His hands came down on her hips, hard, but not painfully. And then he was lifting her up and holding her against the wall. He pulled her bodice down as far as it would go, exposing the tip of one nipple. "No room? Margaret, we don't have to lie down for me to do this." And then his mouth was on her breast, his tongue swirling around it. She gasped and shivered. But he did not relent. Instead, he brought his hand up to cup her bottom, pulling her into him, grinding her against the hard ridge of his erection. She wrapped her legs around his, bringing herself that much closer, and his hand crept beneath her skirts, sliding aside her drawers to dip into the warmth between her legs.

"Tell me we need to be lying down for me to do this," he said, his finger sliding inside her passage. "I can still feel you, can I not?" And then he adjusted her weight against the wall behind her and undid his breeches. She could feel the hard tip of him against her, blunt and powerful.

He sucked on her nipple again, and sensation swirled through her.

"And you already know we need not lie down for this."

She said nothing, throwing her head back.

"Tell me you don't want this."

"I want it." The words jerked from her, unwillingly. But she couldn't lie to him.

He entered her. Slowly. Surely. Her body adjusted to his thickness. Then his hand slipped between her legs, touching, rubbing. And finally, he began to thrust, pushing her against the wall as he did so. Her senses danced. She felt pleasure build and burn, build and burn, until it overtook her, and she was caught up in flames, aware of nothing but his touch, his slow heated slides. Their joining now, when she needed to tear them asunder.

It was both beautiful and ugly, the pleasure that rose up. White-hot radiance filled her, melding them into one indivisible being. Her hands clenched and the entire world washed away.

Just as she was gasping against his chest, he slammed inside her, hard. She clutched him tight.

For one moment, they stood, entwined in motionless wonder.

But as her breath stilled, all her doubts crept back. They weren't one. They were, indisputably, two.

But he didn't seem to notice. "There," he whispered in her ear in satisfaction. "That is what we had room to do."

"Ash." Her voice trembled.

"Don't tell me you can't. Don't tell me you mustn't."

"But—"

"No, Margaret. If you won't look at me in public, at least hold me in private."

Nobody could see them. Nobody even knew she was here, that they were together. This wasn't a betrayal of her brothers—just a physical expression of something she did not dare say aloud.

And perhaps he finally recognized how delicate that balance was, because he held her tightly and did not say a word.

AFTER ASH LEFT MARGARET, it did not take long for Richard Dalrymple to hunt him down. The man caught Ash's eye. His face was unreadable, cold as marble and twice as hard. But he raised his chin and jerked his head towards the veranda. There was something harsh and final in that movement, as if he had said, *Let's skip this Parliamentary rubbish and settle this like men.*

A wonderful notion. Ash's fists itched to satisfy him. Dalrymple stepped out into the dark, and without glancing behind him to see if Ash followed, he disappeared. Ash didn't have to think long. It took him a few minutes to extricate himself from polite conversation, another few minutes to amble across the room without drawing untoward attention.

And then he slipped outside.

The veranda was not as dark as it had appeared from the ballroom. The flagstones were surrounded by a stone wall, on which lanterns had been placed. The lamps cast a hazy warmth in the winter chill, obscuring the gardens into black, plant-shaped silhouettes. Dalrymple slouched against the stones to his right, his arms folded. Ash could feel the heat of his glower before he made out the expression on his face. But if Dalrymple imagined he could do anything to intimidate a man six inches taller than he was, he was mad.

But what Dalrymple said, jerking his thumb into the darkness of the garden, was, "Fred is out there."

"Fred? Who is Fred?"

"Frederick Talhuis, Earl of Indiver."

The name sounded familiar, but Ash shook his head impatiently.

Dalrymple let out an exasperated sigh. "The one man in all of London who is a greater ass than you. Margaret's former fiancé. My former friend. You heard what she said. You know what he did."

His temper, not quiescent to start, stirred at that. "And what do you propose we do?"

Dalrymple smiled. "Simple. We smash him to bits."

"Two on one? One to hold him down, the other to beat his face in, I presume." Ash shook his head. "I suppose that you're forgoing the Dalrymple five just to give him a sporting chance."

"The Dalrymple five? I have no idea what you're talking about."

"That is your typical mode of operation, isn't it? Five on one?"

"Still no notion, Turner. And very well. Have it your

way. I'll take care of the matter myself." Richard turned to leave.

Ash grabbed his arm. "You don't stand a chance—I would say that you hit like a girl, but I wouldn't insult your sister."

Dalrymple shook his head. "You don't want to fight him with me. You don't want me to fight him separately. Are all the Turners tangled up in such convoluted logic?"

"You misunderstand. I am going after him myself." Ash shook his head. "And you can stay here. I don't care to deliver my justice in a pack." He set off down the path.

Dalrymple scrambled after him. "Wait! You don't even know what he looks like!"

Ash didn't answer. He strode into the garden, until he caught the scent of cheroot smoke. The silhouette he made out against the oleander bush was shorter than Ash—shorter, skinnier and doubtless stupider.

There was an easy way to find out if this was the fellow he sought. "Indiver?" he asked.

"Ah. Turner. I was wondering when you would come, currying my favor. You've convinced a great many lords to take your part. You're almost to the halfway point, aren't you?"

Ash even disliked his voice. It had an oily, mellifluous sound to it.

He liked him even less when the man sighed. "You *are* quite wealthy, are you not?"

Ash stopped in front of the man. The tip of Indiver's cheroot glowed red, and Ash smelled acrid smoke.

"And," Indiver continued, having no idea of the danger he was in, "you *do* need every vote you can muster. Do you not?"

Ash set his hand on the man's shoulder. "No," he said, in as friendly a tone as he could manage. "I don't need *every* vote. I can spare this one." Before Indiver could make sense of that, he drove his fist into the man's stomach. He barely had time to let out a gurgling cry before Ash followed his strike with a blow to the kidneys. Another—and then Indiver collapsed at his feet.

How satisfying. He only wished it had lasted longer.

Dalrymple came scampering up behind him.

"That," Ash said quietly, "is what you should have done to me when you found me with your sister. You are the most ineffectual flailer."

"Sometimes," Dalrymple responded in a murmur, "I almost think I could like you."

Ash snorted. "Why bother?"

At their feet, the earl moaned slightly. Ash wasn't sure whether to be pleased that the man had survived, or annoyed that he was still twitching.

"Is that your plan?" he continued. "You attempt to befriend me? To convince me that we should reach some sort of agreement? I don't make agreements with you, Dalrymple—not of any sort. I know your type."

"After this—" Dalrymple prodded Indiver's prone form with a foot "—there's little enough we can agree on. I suppose we have reached the end of the matter. I should be grateful it took us a ten full minutes."

Ash glanced askance at the man. "I once told your father I'd make you an allowance, should I win. The offer is still open. All you have to do is *ask* for it. Politely."

"What, so I could dangle on your string, subject to

your every whim? No, thank you, Turner. I hardly want to be beholden to you."

He'd not imagined the man would take kindly to his offer. "Perhaps," Ash said in a low growl, "you thought we might split the honors. I take the dukedom. You take one of the lesser titles attached to Parford."

That seemed to take Dalrymple aback. In the darkness, his head skewed to one side. "How would you propose to do that?" He sounded almost shocked. "Is that…possible?"

"I don't know. I suppose we could petition the queen to strip off one of the lesser titles. Not," he added with a wary glance to his side, "that I would support any such thing." But perhaps that might satisfy Margaret—if not Ash's own need for vengeance.

"The queen?" Dalrymple's eyes narrowed.

"While you were out, ruining your constitution studying in Oxford, you might have heard of her once or twice. Lovely lady. Recently ascended to the throne."

"The queen can't simply strip a lord of a title on a whim. What sort of ignoramus are you?"

"She's the queen. She can do anything."

Dalrymple rolled his eyes again. "No, she can't. It's called Magna Carta, you dolt. You might have heard of it—if you'd any education to speak of. But you didn't, did you? How can you think you can run a dukedom when you're ignorant of even the most basic tenets of government?"

If Ash had been able to think, he wouldn't have done it. But thought fled before a red, furious miasma, and before he could consider, he punched. His knuckles bruised with the blow, and he heard rather than saw Richard stumble back against a tree.

"Maybe," Ash snarled, "if you'd spent a little less

time memorizing Latin and a little more actually trying to accomplish something of merit, you wouldn't find yourself in this situation."

"What, waste my life pursuing trade like you? You're mad if you think anyone would want a stinking businessman in the House of Lords, when—"

"When they could have you?" Ash said with a sneer. "Let me spell it out for you, Dalrymple. For a man in *trade,* I've garnered a shocking percentage of the lords to my side. You're going to lose. And it's because nobody likes you. Nobody has *ever* liked you—don't fool yourself. I heard the stories from Eton."

Ash had only a moment to register that Dalrymple was rushing towards him with a wordless roar, before the man careened into him, flailing wildly in his rage. Ash punched him once, and once again, but there was a fierce desperation to his opponent. When Ash took a step back, his boot caught a flagstone beneath him and he fell.

Dalrymple was on top of him, pummeling him ineffectually—really, someone needed to teach the man to use his fists—and Ash had just reached up to take hold of the man's neck when the sound of another man, clearing his throat, echoed.

"Gentlemen," said a dry voice. A pause.

Ash's hands were tangled in Dalrymple's cravat.

"I assume," the man continued, "that contrary to all available evidence, the two of you are still gentlemen?"

Damn. Hell and damn. That censorious tone could only belong to Lord Lacy-Follett, one of the few lords whose vote was not yet decided—and one of the most influential. He'd told Ash a few days ago that he could not quite decide between the strength of the son's claim and his desire to see Parford punished for his bigamy.

This was not the way to win him over.

"Lord Lacy-Follett," Ash said from the pavement. "A pleasant evening we're having, isn't it?"

"Full marks for temerity, Turner."

Ash's chin was beginning to throb. "He called—" He stopped, before he gave voice to the unbecoming whine. *He called me ignorant.* If he were going to be strictly truthful, he'd have to add one last point. *And I hit him because he was right.* Ash let go of Dalrymple and scrambled away.

"That is to say," Ash said, "Dalrymple called on me this evening so that we might settle our differences."

"I see," Lacy-Follett said in a tight voice. It would have been hard for him not to, with the pair of them rolling on the ground like schoolboys. He continued. "Gentlemen." Oh, yes, there was definitely an ironic tinge to that word. "Parliament exists for reasons other than pursuing personal gain and vengeance. It has other matters to see to than the all-consuming question of who will become the next Duke of Parford. Matters such as governing the country. Learning to act in concert with our new sovereign. Solidifying our place in the world."

Dalrymple had moved away from him. Ash slowly gathered himself into a crouch on the pavement. "As you say, Your Lordship."

"I, for one, have had enough of these antics. But everywhere you…you *gentlemen* go, people can talk of nothing else. When Parliament resumes, I have no wish to experience months of this insanity. Particularly not if the differences are settled in this juvenile form."

Ash swallowed, but his throat was still dry. "What, precisely, are you proposing?"

A click; the sudden scent of tobacco. Lord Lacy-Follett was taking snuff. When he'd finished, he answered. "Come and see me at Saxton House in two days' time. Both of you."

"And what," Dalrymple asked tentatively, "will be the purpose of this visit?"

"Why, for you to present your case to those of us who are undecided. To have the decision made. To end this foolish game, once and for all."

The night was thick, and an insect grated a harsh complaint into the heavy air. Slowly, Ash clambered to his feet.

"I trust," Lacy-Follett said into the darkness, "that you will both be present."

They would. They would.

CHAPTER TWENTY-TWO

A LADY NEVER VISITED a gentleman's house alone. And Margaret—arriving in a hired hack, dressed in a heavy cloak—had most definitely come alone. But given her destination, her brothers would never have accompanied her, and the maids would never have kept silent.

Still, the butler showed Margaret inside without a word, not questioning the assumed name she'd given him.

Ash's house was beautiful. Beautiful and new—Portland stone without, honey-wood floors within, the walls painted and papered in vibrant, warm colors. The ceiling was cunningly wrought plasterwork, gilded all over. It was rich without being ostentatious.

That understated elegance reminded Margaret of Ash.

She was conducted into a parlor, where Ash sat. His fingers drummed on his desk, and he looked up at her with a smile on his face. But he betrayed nothing else to the manservant who conducted her in.

"Ah," he said. "Miss Laurette. How good of you to come see me."

A flick of his hand dismissed the servant. Ash waited until the door shut before he stood and strode towards her.

"Margaret." Her skin prickled—his hands found her

waist, and then he was drawing her close in a rough, possessive embrace.

"Margaret," he repeated, his breath warming the top of her head. His hand made seductive little circles against her back, caresses that she felt all the way through the fabric of her gown. And then he was tipping her chin up, lowering his head to hers. Not asking, not waiting, just slipping into intimacy as easily as he might put on a pair of old, comfortable slippers.

"No. Wait. You need to hear me out first."

He raised his head. His hands tightened around her waist. "What is it?"

Last evening, after they had all come home, her brother had told her what awaited them at the gathering Lord Lacy-Follett had organized. And her wants had crystallized.

She'd held a piece of meat to Richard's blackened eye as he spoke to her. And right now, she could see the faint echo of a bruise on Ash's jaw, a discoloration of skin under stubble. She wanted the people she loved to stop hurting one another. She'd thought of nothing but this impossible tangle all night long.

"Oh, Ash." Her fingers ran along his face, and she wished she could make him well once more. "I do want to marry you."

"Now that is an easy request to grant." His lips touched her forehead. "Do you wish a large wedding or a small one? Shall we hold it soon?" He kissed her nose. "Or sooner?"

"You're speaking with Lord Lacy-Follett tomorrow."

He froze, pulled away from her an inch. "Yes. And you've realized that after that decision is made, there's no reason to hold back any longer. Either Dalrymple will prevail or…" He drew out the pause, and she could feel his lips curve into a warm smile against her cheek. "Or," he continued, "he won't. Either way, it won't matter."

Margaret drew a deep breath for courage. "But it could matter."

"You *want* to help me defeat your brothers?"

"No. I want you to step down."

His arms remained about her, but he drew away to look her in the eyes. His jaw locked. His nostrils flared.

"You don't need to be duke," she continued in a rush. "You're wealthy. More than that—when you walk in a room, people turn to look at you. You have this…this palpable presence. Even just as plain Mr. Turner, people would listen to you. Look at you."

He didn't move, didn't say anything.

"But my brothers—Ash, they don't have any of that. They'll get a few thousand pounds. Without a family name behind them, without *titles* behind them, they'll be nothing but bastards, with no place in society."

Still he did not respond, except to lower his hands from her waist.

"Please," she begged. "My father—when I found out that he was a bigamist, that I was a bastard, it almost undid me. You've told me all this time that I can accomplish things. That I mean something. Let me prove this to them."

Ash let out a sigh. "And here I'd hoped you would ask for a new carriage. No. I know. This is hardly the time for levity. But Margaret, my dear, if this were about mere revenge, I'd give it up for you. But it isn't. I have these…these feelings. These instincts. And I simply know that if I'm Parford, I'll finally be able to make matters come right for my brothers. I can't abandon them. Not again."

"*Abandon* them! You're talking about abandoning them to a life of wealth and advantage."

He shook his head. "You've met them. They're trapped. Have been in some inescapable way ever since I found them on the streets all those years ago. I can't put it right without this."

"You don't know that," Margaret began.

"But I do. I do."

"You *can't*."

"I can." His voice grew harsh. "I *must*."

"And what if you're wrong? What if you ruin my brothers' future, what if you tear me in two with worrying, and you are *wrong?* Have you never thought of that?"

His eyes glittered, and his hands drew into fists. But he did not move towards her again. "If I am wrong," he said quietly, "then I truly have nothing to offer my brothers. No intelligence. No advantage. I certainly lack their wit. If I am wrong—if my instinct is all imagination—then I am nothing but an illiterate ignoramus. Believe me. I think of that all the time."

"You're—you're a great deal more, Ash." But so much of who he was was bound up in that confidence he had, that unshakable certainty. She'd seen him uncertain and vulnerable a few times. She couldn't imagine him that way all the time.

He passed his hand over his face. "Marry me anyway, Margaret. Marry me not for your brothers, but simply because you love me. And I love you."

She hadn't realized how she wanted to hear those words until he said them. For one blissful second, everything else fell away—her endless obligations, her needs, her brothers. The thrill lasted longer than it should have, an electric tingle that coursed through her. But looking into his eyes was a window to a different sort of reality.

"You don't love me," she said slowly. "You've looked at me the same way from the instant we met."

His grip tightened on her waist. He leaned into her on a hiss. "Don't tell me I don't love you. Don't you dare tell me that, Margaret. I have loved you since the moment you read my brother's book to me. I love that you are the one woman I can trust with my weakness, that you know all the dark parts of me and do not turn away. I love the fierceness with which you protect the ones you love, even when they don't deserve it. I love every last inch of you, and I want you for my own." His words were hot, fiercely possessive, and yet he leaned his forehead against hers gently. "Although God knows, I don't deserve you."

She felt almost dizzy under this onslaught. Still, there was one truth she could not relinquish. "You love your brothers, and so you stole them a dukedom. When Mark needed you at Eton, you were there before he could even speak the words. But you are destroying my family, destroying my *life,* and you ask me to simply accept it."

His hands tightened around hers, but she did not stop.

"On any other man, I could believe this casual selfishness could be equated with love. But, Ash, I know what love looks like on you. It doesn't look like this."

"And how should *you* know what love looks like?" he demanded. He slipped a finger under the chain around her neck and pulled her locket from between her breasts. "Is it Richard in here? Or Edmund? Your father? Which unworthy man do you carry next to your heart, never to be supplanted in your affections no matter how poor-spirited he proves himself to be?"

"That's not it. It's not about choosing my brothers over you."

Her hand closed about the chain, but he held her locket firmly. With his other hand, he flicked open the catch. His breath stopped.

"My mother." Margaret's voice caught. "Gentle. Loving. Patient. Clever and funny, when my father wasn't around. She taught me everything. And she died when you revealed she was an adulteress."

He let go, and the heavy locket swung back to strike Margaret in the chest.

"Every time I look at you," she said, "I see an echo of her. Looking at you is both bitter and sweet, painful and so wonderful at the same time. It was my mother's dearest wish that her son would have her house— that her labor of love would pass on to her children. I thought that if I found a way to make her dream come true, that I might find some peace. This isn't about choosing my brothers over you. It is about trying to find a way to look at you without feeling any of that pain any longer."

"Oh," he said lamely. "Margaret."

"I didn't come here to beg you to give up the dukedom simply because I wished to hand you an ultimatum. I came because no matter how much I love you—and I *do* love you, Ash—I simply could not bear knowing that I married the man who destroyed my mother's dreams. I don't know how I could look at myself again if I did."

"Oh. *Margaret*." He did come forwards then, did take

her in his arms. And he leaned forwards, just enough to press his lips against her forehead one last time.

"God," he said. "I can't give my brothers up. I can't."

"I know," she said softly. "Neither can I."

Her words fell between them—so quiet, and yet so suffocating. There was nothing further to say, no way around this impasse. He held her. But when she gently removed his hands from her waist, he didn't stop her. When she turned and left him, he did not follow after.

Now, with everything said, even Ash could no longer come up with a reason to pursue her.

THE AFTERNOON SEEMED almost unreal to Ash. The pale light of a clammy autumn day cast ghosts of shadows across the carpet of Lord Lacy-Follett's receiving room. Ash stood shoulder to shoulder with Richard Dalrymple.

An outside observer might have thought them joined in a common purpose. Dalrymple's jaw was set, his shoulders drawn rigidly together. If the aching clench of Ash's own muscles was any indication, he looked about as comfortable.

But despite that apparent solidarity, the only solid feeling between them was a mutual desire to defeat each other—at any price. Even, Ash thought, the cost that he could never forget: the sight of Margaret leaving him, and he left with nothing to offer that would make it better. He'd lain awake all night, twisting and turning, trying to upend everything Margaret had said. But she seemed impossible. Distant.

The nine lords Lacy-Follett had assembled sat in

high-backed chairs, arranged in a half moon. Only a thin table separated Ash from them.

"Gentlemen." Lord Lacy-Follett spoke from his seat at the very center. "There must be some sort of amicable agreement that we can come to."

Ash glanced over at Richard Dalrymple. With Margaret gone, all hope of amity had fled. Dalrymple's hands were clenched around a fat sheaf of papers, which he'd rolled up. His lips were pursed; his eye had purpled. And for the first time, Ash noticed a similarity between his profile and Margaret's—a curve of the lips, a jut of the chin. He'd tried not to think what it meant, that Dalrymple was her brother. He'd tried to separate it out. It was damned unnerving.

"My lords," Dalrymple spoke with a palpable unease. He cast a tight look at Ash, and then snapped his gaze forwards to concentrate on the nine men in front of him. "If I can convince but one of you to support my suit, I'll have all the support I need to pass the Act of Legitimation through Parliament. And I am wagering that I can convince one of you to support me."

Lord Lacy-Follett glanced at Ash, as if measuring the effect of his words. He conferred, behind cupped hand, with the man sitting to his right, and then looked up at Dalrymple. "That is not our current estimate of the votes," he said.

"The votes have changed." A tight smile crept over Dalrymple's face—one that seemed at odds with his clutched fingers. "Lord Forsyth, and five others, have come to support my suit."

Ash felt a muscle in his jaw twitch, but he kept silent. Forsyth had teetered on the brink of a decision for weeks, before tentatively declaring himself for Ash.

There was another exchange of glances. And then

a man behind Lacy-Follett—Lord Dallington—spoke up. "I spoke with Forsyth just three days ago. Given… ah, given his financial situation, I find this news very unlikely."

That smile expanded across Dalrymple's face—not a pleased one; almost a grimace. "The earlier version of the Act of Legitimation, which you might have seen circulated before this? It's changed." He unrolled the papers he'd been gripping and spread the sheets in his hand. "This is the current act, which will be put to the vote."

He slid the papers across the table to the men who sat in front of him. After a pause, and with some hesitation, he handed Ash a sheet, as well.

Ash took it and glanced down at the meaningless letters. In front of him, the men were silent. Reading. Ash felt a slow beat of fear inside him. He tamped it down; he'd bluffed his way through similar situations before. He could do it again.

"My God," Lacy-Follett said. "I suppose that would take care of Forsyth. And his financial problems."

Beside him, Lord Dallington licked his lips and set the paper down. "Mr. Turner. What think you of the proposed act?"

Ash ran a hand down the paper. "I don't quite understand how this would mollify Forsyth's concerns."

"You *do* know what Forsyth's objection was, don't you?"

Ash did, but the more he could make Dallington explain, the less he had to pretend. "Humor me with an explanation."

"The Duchess of Parford's marriage settlements—or at least, sixty thousand pounds of them—had been set in trust for her lawful female issue. If the Act of

Legitimation fails to pass, his sister the duchess has no lawful female issue, and the trust reverts to him."

"I see," Ash said slowly. Even though he didn't.

"Now that the suit no longer names Lady Anna Margaret," Dallington continued, "there is no danger of Forsyth losing the money."

It was all Ash could do to keep from gasping. As it was, he felt as if he had been punched in the kidneys. He bent slightly, his hands striking the table in front of him, before raising his eyes to Dalrymple. "You—" He bit back the epithet he'd been about to hurl. "You left your own sister off. You'll leave her illegitimate, just so you can have your dukedom back."

Well. At least that explained why the man's expression of triumph seemed so unvictorious. At least he had the grace not to be proud of what he was doing. Margaret had gone to Ash and begged on her brothers' behalf. She might have had Ash. She might have been the Duchess of Parford herself. But she'd refused to abandon her brothers to illegitimacy.

"I didn't hit you nearly hard enough the other night," Ash growled. "Is that what you Dalrymple men do? You abandon your women to bear the brunt of society's hurt, just so that you can have an easy life?"

"You think this was an *easy* decision?" Dalrymple demanded.

Ash took a step closer—swiftly enough that Dalrymple flinched from him.

"Gentlemen!" Lacy-Follett said. "The point of this meeting is to avoid further violence, not to foment it."

Hitting Dalrymple had done little good so far. Violence would only convince more men to support the man's suit. Dalrymple's faithless, ugly suit.

Ash turned away, his hands fisting at his sides. What was it going to do to Margaret when she discovered that her brother had betrayed her into illegitimacy, as her father had? What would she say? How would she feel?

He could imagine her pain with a startling intensity.

And for just one second, Ash could see how to use this. Dalrymple still needed *one* of these men for his suit to go forwards. Instinct clamored inside him. A man who would betray a sister was no candidate for the dukedom. He could make the case. He could win all these men over to his side, settle the dispute once and for all.

But…but what if he did?

He had always thought of the suit in Parliament as pertaining to her brothers. Ever since Ash had met her, he'd been assiduously courting votes in Parliament to defeat the act that Dalrymple proposed. But until this afternoon, that act had included *all* the duke's children. Including Margaret.

That little detail had seemed unimportant—so unimportant, in fact, that he'd never considered it, and she had never mentioned it. But if Ash won, *he* would be the one to betray her. He would make her a bastard, twice over. He'd been trying to keep her a bastard all this time.

He had not only destroyed her life unwittingly, before he'd met her; he had continued to destroy it, even after he knew who she was. Even after he loved her.

Ash opened his eyes and glanced at his foe. The man stood, his shoulders drawn together. For all of Dalrymple's flinching cowardice, Ash felt a shameful sense of kinship with him. They'd both been too foolish to realize what they were doing to Margaret—or, perhaps, too selfish to care.

The other lords were looking at Dalrymple in barely concealed distaste.

"I do love my sister, you know," Dalrymple said defensively. "It was either this, or have nothing."

Ash's stomach burned. Inside him, irrepressible instinct clamored out.

Fight. Win. He could still have the dukedom. He could have his vengeance. He could raise his brothers high—give them every last thing they'd ever dared to want. He would never fear again that he had nothing to offer. And all he would have to do was to betray the woman he loved. Ash swallowed, but his throat remained dry. He could look back over his shoulder and finally understand the devastation he'd wrought.

So. *This* was how it felt to be a conquering hero.

There was no way to repair the damage, no way to heal what he'd done to her.

"Let me see if I understand this," Ash said to the lords in front of him. "If the lot of you support Dalrymple, he won't need Forsyth and the votes he carries any longer."

"That is correct."

When it came down to it, he had no choice at all.

Ash strode over to Dalrymple and yanked the last paper from his hand. "You sicken me," he said. He ripped it into quarters and threw the pieces to the ground.

"My lords," he said. "Here is your amicable solution. You vote for Dalrymple's bill. But only—and I do mean *only*—on condition that he rewrite it to include his sister."

Dalrymple's jaw went slack.

Lord Lacy-Follett stared at Ash. "So there is some truth to those rumors after all. Mr. Turner, if you want a different solution, something else might be arranged." He cast a glance at Richard, and sniffed. "I, for one, am not best pleased with the first scenario that was proffered to us. There are some things gentlemen ought not do, and sacrificing women for personal gain stands high on my list."

Dalrymple flinched. But Ash simply shook his head, too weary to fight any longer. Not now. Not when he'd finally understood what he was doing to her.

Lord Lacy-Follett tapped his lips. "We shall be here all afternoon discussing the matter. But gentlemen, unless you have anything further to add, you *are* excused."

Dalrymple took one shaky step towards the doors. As he did so, Ash grabbed his lapels. Not hard, not violently, but Ash twisted them just enough to let the man know that, had he wished, he could have sent him flying across the room. He leaned in. And then, as Dalrymple's eyes widened in terror, Ash whispered, "If you don't take care of her, I shall truly hunt you down. You won't be duke long enough to enjoy it."

CHAPTER TWENTY-THREE

"IT'S OVER."

Margaret stood from the seat by the side of her father's bed as Richard stepped into the room. The afternoon light fell on a lavender bruise on his face. The decoration made him look tired. Tired and almost limp. "That is, my part in this is finished." He was looking down at the carpet, and so she could not see his eyes. She couldn't tell whether he was weary in victory or weary in defeat.

The towel cut into her hands. She wasn't even sure which outcome she should pray for. For Ash? For Richard? Either one would tear her in half. Her tongue felt too thick to actually use for anything so mundane as speech. Instead, she stared at him.

He sighed and shook his head.

"What happened?" she managed to croak.

Richard shook his head. "Turner, damn his eyes, abdicated."

Her head seemed light, very light. She might have floated away in dazed, uncomprehending wonder. "Pardon?"

Richard came to stand near her. "He told them to support my suit, on condition that you be included in the bid for legitimacy."

Those words returned her to earth swiftly, painfully. Her ears rang. Her knees threatened to wobble, and she locked them, grabbing hold of one of the oak posters on her father's bed.

"What do you mean, on condition that I be included in the suit? I thought I *was* included."

Richard picked up her father's signet ring from where it lay on the table. Idly, he turned it about, and the sword carved in the stone reflected afternoon light at Margaret. As Ash had done long ago, he tried to slip the band around his finger.

It didn't fit him either, and he set it once more on the table. Finally, he looked up. It wasn't victory she saw in his eyes. It was something deeper, and just a little more shameful. "No," he said softly. "I had you taken out of the bill to win Forsyth over."

He couldn't be saying this. It couldn't be true. Margaret's hands clenched. "Tell me it was Edmund's idea." It had to have been—Edmund was a little more hasty, a little less thoughtful. Only Edmund would have—

"No, Margaret." Richard shook his head slowly. "It was mine. I knew when I suggested it that if I did, I would regret it the rest of my days. I just supposed that I would rather regret being a duke than regret being a bastard. I didn't expect Turner to give it all up," he added bitterly. "Just like that. And then what do you suppose that idiot did?"

She shook her head. Anything was possible—anything other than Ash giving up his claim on the duchy of Parford.

"He pulled me aside and ordered me to take care of you. As if I would do any differently."

Margaret simply looked back at him. "No, Richard. I think you've demonstrated precisely how well you would look after me."

He looked away, and it was as if that set her emotions free at last. Pain came first, scalding hot. And then the realization of what Richard had done really hit her. He'd been about to make her a bastard again. Her loyalty had meant everything to her. She'd been determined to prove that she wouldn't betray her brothers the way her father had betrayed them all.

It seemed she had been the only one.

Richard heaved a great sigh. "And now, after what he's done, I'm beholden to that impossible ass. For the rest of my life. It doesn't sit well with me."

Her own brother had just told Margaret that he'd tried to barter her place in society for his dukedom, and his primary concern was that because he'd failed to do so, he found himself in Ash's debt?

And then there was Ash. Margaret swallowed hard. He'd given it up. He'd given it all up—for her. And she knew, more than anyone else, what the dukedom had meant to him. It meant his brothers. His security. His certainty.

From behind him, her father stirred. Richard shook his head. "Well," he said. "I should let you get back to…get back to looking after him. Margaret, for what it is worth…I am sorry. The lords will be discussing the matter at Saxton House all the rest of the afternoon, and it makes me ill to think matters could have gone as I'd intended. To be honest, I think if Turner hadn't acted as he had, they would all have spoken against me, and I'd have lost it all for nothing. It was that close." He shook his head. "They're still deliberating, but they'll come round to me." He spoke more as if he were still trying to convince himself than to convey information to Margaret.

"And if you had it to do over again, what would you tell them?" Margaret asked.

He looked at her and then shook his head ruefully. "Precisely what I did before," he said. "Some things cannot be changed."

Margaret shut her eyes. Richard was gentle. Richard had been quite kind to her in the past. But every time he'd had to choose between his own skin and Margaret's well-being—it had been Margaret he had sacrificed. He hadn't given his loyalty to Margaret, the way Margaret had delivered hers to him.

Behind them, her father stirred. In the months since his apoplectic fit, he'd improved. Which was to say, that tiny hint of vulnerability that she'd seen in him that long-ago night had disappeared, replaced by this irascibility.

"There you are," her father said, meeting Richard's eyes. "And how did the meeting go? Do I have a man for a son?"

Richard's gaze slid to Margaret and then back to his father. "You do," he said quietly. "I'll inherit everything."

Margaret waited for her father to come up with some cutting rejoinder, some harsh remark. But instead, her father's gaze rested on Richard. "That's good," he said. And then, more softly: "That's my boy."

Margaret's vision swam in front of her. Her brother stood, paused before her, his hand raised in benediction. He wiped at his eyes suspiciously and then he shook his head and turned away. "Yes," he said quietly, standing at the door. "I suppose I am."

The door closed behind him.

"What, Anna? You're not sulking, are you?"

Loyalty was a curious thing, Margaret realized.

She'd placed it in the care of someone who did not return the favor. She stood up and set her towel in front of her. As she did, her gaze fell on her father's signet. The heavy, carved sapphire twinkled up at her.

She reached for it. The gold was warm in her hands, heavy. Not so heavy as it had once been; the band had been resized for an invalid's hand.

Or perhaps a woman's.

It slid neatly over her knuckle, clasping her finger. The sword in the sapphire winked up at her.

I think if they could find a way to disinherit me, after the trick I played... Somewhere out there, Lord Lacy-Follett and his companions were still discussing the matter. With no intervention, they would settle on supporting Richard.

Perhaps they could still find a way not to do so.

"What are you doing?" her father asked.

"Putting on your ring." It felt well there. Right. *Warm.*

"Richard's ring," her father corrected. "We'll have to get it adjusted to fit him."

She had never wanted to be like her father, betraying her family. But from here on out, she was going to have faith in someone who deserved it. The man who had stood by her, who had never hurt her. Who had told her, from the very first, that she mattered, and demonstrated it by his choices.

"Richard is my son now," her father was saying.

Margaret leaned over him. "No," she said, her voice harsh. "No, he is not."

"He will be, when—"

"By your definition, *I* am the only son you will ever have."

He blinked at her. "I beg your pardon?"

She hadn't known she was going to say it, but the words seemed *right* coming out of her mouth. "I am going to Saxton House to present my case. I am going to marry Ash Turner. If what Richard said is correct, the lords there are looking for any reason to abandon him. A continuation through the female line is not traditional, but the excuse will suffice. So understand this: *I* will choose the next Duke of Parford. *I* will inherit the estate. *I* will have the entailed property." Margaret's hand clenched into a fist.

"I can't believe I am hearing this." Her father stared up at her in dim incomprehension. "What would your mother say, if she could see you now?"

What would her mother say?

Her mother had carefully tended the estate, training servants, choosing decorations, caring for the gardens. She'd built a home to pass on to her children. It had killed her to believe that Parford Manor would go to a stranger. But then, with Margaret married to Ash…it wouldn't.

Margaret's hands balled into fists. "I believe," she said softly, "that if she could speak at this moment—if she knew that *I* would inherit her house—I believe that she would be cheering."

Her father stared at her in stupefaction. She had waited all this time for some sign that the man she remembered was still inside her father. But maybe that part of him had vanished, along with his strength and ability to stand. Maybe he'd lost the piece of himself that cared for her. Maybe she would never see it again—at least not now.

Margaret leaned forwards to kiss him on the forehead. "Someday," she said quietly, "when you truly understand everything that's happened, you'll be cheering, too."

And then, still wearing the ring, she turned and walked from the room.

HOME. IT SEEMED A STRANGE place for Ash to return to, after everything that had transpired that afternoon. After he'd left Saxton House earlier, he'd not wanted to return here. But when he stepped inside, Mark was waiting for him in the entry. Ash had felt so bruised, he'd not wanted to believe that time would continue to pass.

But Mark smiled at him, all light and innocence. Ash felt a last bitter tinge. Seeing his brother only drove home how much he had really lost.

"You would be proud," he finally said. "I realized that I didn't have to do any of this. I didn't."

"The news has traveled even to me," Mark said. A cryptic description, but Mark seemed unfazed by the loss of the dukedom.

Ash looked at him. "I'm sorry," he finally said. "I know you didn't care about any of this for yourself. But—I just had this notion, see. I knew, somehow, that if I were the Duke of Parford, someday I'd have made things different for you. I didn't want to give up on that. But then…"

"I've always managed to take care of myself," Mark said dryly. "Today should prove no exception. You know I would never be angry at you for doing the right thing."

"I've abandoned you enough."

"Abandoned me?" Mark's hand was curled about itself, and he turned to Ash with a quizzical expression on his face. "When have you ever abandoned me?"

"There was the time I went to India."

"Which you did in order to make enough funds for the family to survive. I can hardly begrudge you that."

"And there was that time at Eton. You'd told me that Edmund Dalrymple had begun to single you out. That he was pushing you around. And you begged me to take you home."

"I recall. You read me quite the lecture—told me, in fact, that I had to stay there."

"Two weeks later, I returned to find you battered and bruised, your face bloodied, your eyes blacked and your fingers broken. And all I could think was that I had done that to you. I'd abandoned you, for no reason other than my personal pique and vanity, and you paid the price."

"Vanity?" Mark shook his head. "I thought that was one of your ridiculous instincts, Ash. Horrible to hear about. Impossible to argue with. And as usual, entirely right."

Ash felt his throat go dry. "That wasn't instinct."

Mark raised one eyebrow. "Really? Nonetheless, it was still the right thing for you to tell me."

Ash had to say it. He had to tell him, before his nerve gave out and he let another decade slip by. "That," Ash said quietly, "was fear. You had to go to school. I didn't want you to turn out like me."

"Oh," Mark said with a roll of his eyes, "I see. Because you're so unimpressive a specimen."

Ash took a deep breath. "No. Because I'm illiterate."

"Well, you don't even appreciate Shakespeare, and that does rather speak against you." Mark shook his head and reached for Ash's hand. "Here. I have something—"

Ash pulled his fingers away. "I meant that in the most literal of senses. I can't read. Words don't make sense to me. They never have."

Mark fell silent. He looked at Ash as if his world had been turned on his head. He frowned. "I don't understand."

"I can't read. I can't write. Margaret read your book aloud to me."

"But your letters." Mark leaned heavily against the wall. "You—you sent me letters. You wrote on them. I know you did." He paused, and then said in a smaller voice, "Didn't you?"

"There are a few phrases I've committed to memory. I wrote them over and over, hour after hour, until the words came out in the right order. Until they said what I intended, without my having to look at what I wrote. There were some things I needed to be able to tell you, when you were away."

"Your postscripts always said the same thing," Mark said. "'With much—'" he broke off.

"'With much love,'" Ash finished hoarsely. "With more than I could possibly write."

Mark passed his hand briefly over his face. When he looked up at Ash, he lifted his chin.

"Nobody knows," Ash warned him. "If anyone were to find out, it would—it would—"

"You protected me." Mark's voice was uneven. "All these years, you protected me. From Mother. From the Dalrymples. From my own wish to go build a cocoon and stay there. Do you think I don't know that?"

"I— Well—"

"Do you truly think that after all this time, after

everything you have done for me, that I would not protect *you?*"

He'd been the elder brother for so long, had been carrying that burden for all these years. It wasn't just recent events that had fatigued him. But with that light shining in Mark's eyes, suddenly the future seemed manageable. Ash had been exhausted before; now, he felt refreshed.

"And next time you need someone to read to you, if— But, oh. You distracted me. Here. I'm supposed to give you this."

"Give me what?"

In answer, Mark held out his fist and unfurled his fingers. Cradled in the palm of his hand was a black key—its bow a curlicue of iron, crossed by a sword. A master key. *The* master key to Parford Manor.

Mark smiled knowingly at him. "Margaret brought this by."

Ash felt a dizzying flush. She'd been by? His heart rose. But then—she hadn't stayed to see him. His stomach sank. And she was returning his gift—not good.

But what use would she imagine he would have for the master key to Parford Manor, with her brother lord there? His emotions warred between elation and despair. "What do I do?" he asked Mark. "No—never mind. I already know. I have to see her." He was halfway to the door before Mark's voice arrested him.

"Ash, you *cannot* call on a lady looking like that."

Ash looked down. His trousers were spattered with mud he'd collected over the course of his perambulations. He'd discarded his cravat hours ago. "I can't?"

"Even you cannot." Mark's eyes glinted with humor. "I *am* protecting you, recall."

A few minutes' delay. Ash juggled that with the

prospect of looking civilized for her. He supposed the time wouldn't matter anywhere except in his own racing heart.

"Damn," he swore, and he raced up to his room.

"Don't do anything I wouldn't do," he heard Mark calling from behind him. He ignored that.

He didn't bother ringing for his valet—the man was too fastidious, and the toilette he would insist on putting Ash through too time-consuming. Instead, Ash shrugged off his sodden coat and tugged at the sleeves of his linen shirt, eager to remove it.

And that was when he heard a gentle, feminine clearing of a throat. He froze, his hands at the buttons of his neck.

"You know," a voice said behind him, "if you rush the disrobing, I don't get nearly so much enjoyment from it."

He was almost afraid to look about, lest her voice prove to be a product of his fevered imagination. Slowly, he turned around anyway.

If this was his imagination, he realized, his imagination had produced a gray silk dress and hung it over the back of his dressing chair, not six inches from him. He reached out and touched the silk gingerly. It felt real. It *smelt* of roses.

And then he lifted his eyes from the chair to his bed. If this was his imagination, his imagination was glorious. Margaret lay on his coverlet, stretched out full length. She still wore a corset and petticoats, but they'd been hiked up so that he could see where her garters tied at the knees. She crooked one finger at him and smiled.

"Margaret. What are you doing here?"

"I," she said, "have been procuring my future."

His mind went blank. He didn't know how to take it. She'd decided to have him, after all. She'd realized she didn't need him, not one bit. His head pounded. His heart swelled in a mix of hope and despair.

"I want you."

Hope. Hope. It was all hope. He took a careful step towards her.

"Wait. There's a condition."

"You know," Ash said, his throat closing, "that if you are half-naked on my bed, all conditions will be met. Instantly."

"Ah, but this is one of the conditions I did not deliver to Lord Lacy-Follett earlier today."

If he'd been overwhelmed by her appearance before, he was stunned now. "You talked to Lacy-Follett? You cannot be serious."

"Oh, but I am. I had to renegotiate, after I'd heard what you had done. I had been so blinded by my loyalty to my brothers that I could not see that I owed loyalty to you, as well. I was wrong. I love you, Ash."

He swallowed.

She smiled up at him. "I love that you make me feel as if I'm the only woman in the world. I love that you'll always be there for me." She sat up on the bed, and her petticoats fell, so that only her toes peeked out at him from underneath those layers of fabric. "I want to paint my own canvas, Ash. And I want *you* on it with me."

Delicately, she stretched out one leg. Her foot flexed, and then her toes found the floor. He was helpless. Just seeing her push to her feet got him hard. And seeing her in his room—on his *bed*—made every part of him reverberate with the rightness of it.

She shook her head at him. "Still nothing to say? Lord Lacy-Follett and his group will vote down the bill in Parliament. I told them to do it. They agreed—every one of them—but to get them all on board, they wanted to ensure the duke's line would continue. They insisted that we marry."

"Have you any plans tomorrow?"

She held up one hand. "I'd like to ask for a wedding gift. Not—not an *allowance* for my brother. But an independence. I know it's possible to obtain titles, if you make a donation to the Crown. If you know the right people. Could you do that for him?"

"After what he did to you?"

"Yes. After what he did to me." She tilted her head, and her unbound hair spilled over her shoulders. "Because we've had enough of vengeance between us. Because I don't want to be so caught up in what has been done that I forget what we could have in the future instead."

"And what of you?" Ash asked hoarsely. "When we talk of what could be, what of *you?*"

"Yes, indeed." Her smile broadened. She minced towards him, stopping mere inches from him. He could have reached out and drawn her against him. He might have leaned down and taken her lips in a kiss. "What of me, Ash?" she asked.

Instead, he laid one finger on the gold chain of her necklace. He hooked his little finger underneath it and then undid the clasp. "Here," he said, dropping the master key back onto the necklace. "That's yours, my love." He let it drop, and the key slid down the chain. It hit her locket with a clank.

Ash fumbled in his waistcoat pocket, until he found what he was looking for. "And this—" he pulled a second key from his waistcoat "—this will unlock my rooms in town." He let it fall down the chain, as well, and it slid to clank against the other key.

She opened her hand, and he let the tangled mass of chain and keys and locket fall into her waiting palm.

"It's yours," he said. "As am I, Margaret. Always. Now what are you going to do with me?"

Her mouth curled up. But she turned from him and glided to the door. For a second, he thought she might actually walk through it—but instead of turning the handle, she jiggled the key he'd just given her into her hand. And she locked the door.

"You mean, before I marry you?" She gave him a saucy smile, freed of sadness. "Until you can get that license, what are you doing for the next few hours?"

He walked forwards, his steps finally sure.

"Margaret." He meant to say her name softly, but it came out on a growl. She watched him come close, and she smiled as he did so. He didn't stop, not until he'd placed his hands on each side of the door, until he'd pressed his chest against hers, until she was flattened against him, her heart beating in concert with his.

He breathed in the scent of her hair, as intoxicating as a sweet white wine. His lips found her neck; his hands slid down her body to rest on her waist. He drew back just enough to look into her eyes.

"For the next few hours," he said quietly, "I believe I shall be occupied with you. Only you."

EPILOGUE

Parford Manor, June, 1840

THE SUN WAS HIGH IN a blue sky, untroubled by clouds, but Margaret could not relax. The servants had set the al fresco luncheon off to the side of the house. A pile of old rugs and a low table, brought out for this occasion, graced the north lawn, just beyond the waving heads of the rosebushes.

They'd lunched outside often enough in the nearly three years since Margaret's marriage—when the weather was fine, when Ash's brothers visited. There was nothing unusual about the sight of that old, dented wood, graced with uneaten crusts and the green tops of strawberries. What made this day different was the sight just beyond the table.

Ash had stripped off his coat and his cravat, and had rolled his cuffs to his forearms. And he was circling Richard, who was garbed similarly.

"Keep your fists up," Ash advised. "No, *up*—what part of *up* makes you think you should let them hang by your belt?"

"The part that wants to protect the bits just below my waist," Richard shot back.

Margaret held her breath. For years, she'd been inviting her brother to visit. For years, he'd refused. He'd been angry with her and ashamed of himself, all at the same time, which hadn't made for fond conversations. But after a year, they'd begun to exchange letters. At first, they had been tentative, awkward missives.

This year, he'd finally accepted her invitation to visit. And on this, his last full day at Parford Manor, somehow Ash had inveigled him into a sparring match. A *friendly* sparring match.

Or so she hoped. Her heart stood still.

"Don't mind me," Richard said as he circled her husband. "I'm just trying to determine how to bring you to your knees without causing permanent damage. I shouldn't wish to upset my sister."

"That's for damned certain." Ash's remark stirred the unspoken tension that had hung in the air since Richard's visit—the too-polite conversations, the glances her brother cast her way. There was still a great deal left unresolved. If this went badly, it might take years before he visited again.

Margaret had a great deal of hope for the coming years—that Edmund might come around; that her own family, a mere two strong at this moment, might take root and grow.

Beside her, Mark stirred. "Don't worry about that," he called out. "This is how Ash makes friends—by beating you into a pulp, or getting beaten in turn."

Ash didn't take his eyes from Richard. "True," he said shortly.

Circling opposite Ash, Richard seemed pale and thin. He lacked Ash's sense of vitality, his sense of *grace*. Margaret wondered briefly how terrible a mistake she'd made. She didn't want this visit to end with a hasty ride to the physician. She reached for Mark's hand and gripped it tightly.

"So simple?" Richard asked. "Fight with you, and we're friends? Never seemed to work before."

Ash smiled faintly. "That's because it will only work when you win."

Richard's jaw set, and he brought his fists up. Not high enough—Margaret could see that—but at least a little higher.

Ash gave him a light tap on the shoulder with his fist. "If you're going to be my brother," he said, "you'll have to learn how *not* to embarrass yourself in a fight."

Be gentle, love. Margaret's hands gripped the table. They had no way of changing what had been done. All she could hope was that there was room for forgiveness in the future, room for both her families to find some semblance of peace. But if this went badly…

Richard just laughed at Ash's pronouncement. "If you're going to be my brother, you'll have to learn how to handle the shame of defeat."

"Fine words." Ash punched him on the shoulder again, this time slightly harder. "They'd mean so much more if you could block my blows."

"Blocking's not my strategy," Richard admitted, ducking another one of Ash's fists.

Richard swiveled around to avoid another blow.

Ash turned to him once more. "Apparently, neither is hitting. You'd best conjure something up, and quickly."

Richard feinted to his left, and seemed to contemplate this for a moment. And then he shrugged—shrugged, in the middle of a fight!—and said, "Very well."

Before Ash could do more than narrow his eyes—before he could properly turn—Richard stepped in close and swept his foot out from underneath him. Neatly. Properly. *Cleanly.* And Ash went down.

She and Mark let out a joint exhale of relief.

Thank God. Their strategy had worked. Richard blinked, even more surprised than Ash must be at this turn of events. He stared at Ash on the ground before him, as if he didn't quite understand what he'd done.

Ash sat up gingerly. "Damn," he said. And then he looked over at Mark and Margaret, sitting next to one another. Margaret tried to school her expression into some semblance of angelic innocence. Mark did it so well—but she could not keep that naughty smile from creeping over her face.

Ash stood and then held out his arm to Richard. Slowly, her brother took that outstretched arm, clasped it tightly. And in that moment, a dark shadow in Margaret's life flooded with light.

After they released each other's hands, Ash looked over at her once more. But instead of shaking his head—she *had* set him up for this, after all—he walked towards her, smiling. And he didn't stop until he'd folded his arms around her and pulled her to his chest—in front of both his brother and hers.

His mouth found her ear, and he gave her a gentle nibble that sent pleasure sparking through her. "Next time," he whispered, "tell me ahead of time what you've taught him to do, so I know how to bait him into doing it."

Margaret froze in his arms. "You knew?" she whispered back. "But—"

"Of course I knew."

"But you let him—"

"I made you happy, didn't I?" he responded smoothly.

"Surely, by now, you must realize I'd do anything to make you smile."

His arms were around her, powerful and strong. He loved her. He cared for her. And no matter what happened, he was dedicated to her. Margaret swallowed. She was the luckiest woman in the world.

"If you meet me upstairs in fifteen minutes," she murmured, "we'll see who makes who smile."

His hold on her tightened, fierce and needful. "Well, my dearest love," he finally answered, "that sounds like a challenge. I'll have to take you up on it."

* * * * *

Look for Mark to be tempted in
UNCLAIMED
Coming soon from
Courtney Milan
and HQN Books!

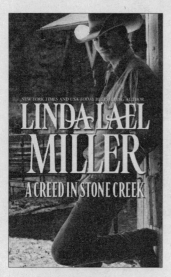

PRESENTING...THE SEVENTH ANNUAL
MORE THAN WORDS™ ANTHOLOGY

Five bestselling authors
Five real-life heroines

This year's Harlequin
More Than Words award
recipients have changed lives,
one good deed at a time. To
celebrate these real-life heroines,
some of Harlequin's most
acclaimed authors have honored
the winners by writing stories
inspired by these dedicated
women. Within the pages
of *More Than Words Volume 7*,
you will find novellas written
by Carly Phillips, Donna Hill
and Jill Shalvis—and online at
www.HarlequinMoreThanWords.com
you can also access stories by
Pamela Morsi and Meryl Sawyer.

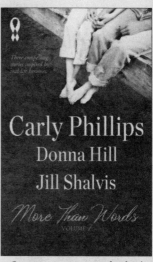

Coming soon in print and online!

Visit
www.HarlequinMoreThanWords.com
to access your FREE ebooks and to nominate
a real-life heroine in your community.

Proceeds from the sale of this book will be
reinvested in Harlequin's charitable initiatives.

REQUEST YOUR
FREE BOOKS!

2 FREE NOVELS
FROM THE ROMANCE COLLECTION
PLUS 2 FREE GIFTS!

YES! Please send me 2 FREE novels from the Romance Collection and my 2 FREE gifts (gifts are worth about $10). After receiving them, if I don't wish to receive any more books, I can return the shipping statement marked "cancel." If I don't cancel, I will receive 4 brand-new novels every month and be billed just $5.74 per book in the U.S. or $6.24 per book in Canada. That's a saving of at least 28% off the cover price. It's quite a bargain! Shipping and handling is just 50¢ per book in the U.S. and 75¢ per book in Canada.* I understand that accepting the 2 free books and gifts places me under no obligation to buy anything. I can always return a shipment and cancel at any time. Even if I never buy another book, the two free books and gifts are mine to keep forever.

194/394 MDN FDC5

Name	(PLEASE PRINT)

Address	Apt. #

City	State/Prov.	Zip/Postal Code

Signature (if under 18, a parent or guardian must sign)

Mail to the **Reader Service:**
IN U.S.A.: P.O. Box 1867, Buffalo, NY 14240-1867
IN CANADA: P.O. Box 609, Fort Erie, Ontario L2A 5X3

Not valid for current subscribers to the Romance Collection
or the Romance/Suspense Collection.

Want to try two free books from another line?
Call 1-800-873-8635 or visit www.ReaderService.com.

* Terms and prices subject to change without notice. Prices do not include applicable taxes. Sales tax applicable in N.Y. Canadian residents will be charged applicable taxes. Offer not valid in Quebec. This offer is limited to one order per household. All orders subject to credit approval. Credit or debit balances in a customer's account(s) may be offset by any other outstanding balance owed by or to the customer. Please allow 4 to 6 weeks for delivery. Offer available while quantities last.

Your Privacy—The Reader Service is committed to protecting your privacy. Our Privacy Policy is available online at www.ReaderService.com or upon request from the Reader Service.

We make a portion of our mailing list available to reputable third parties that offer products we believe may interest you. If you prefer that we not exchange your name with third parties, or if you wish to clarify or modify your communication preferences, please visit us at www.ReaderService.com/consumerschoice or write to us at Reader Service Preference Service, P.O. Box 9062, Buffalo, NY 14269. Include your complete name and address.

COURTNEY MILAN

77485 TRIAL BY DESIRE   ___ $7.99 U.S. ___ $9.99 CAN.

(limited quantities available)

TOTAL AMOUNT $ _____
POSTAGE & HANDLING $ _____
($1.00 FOR 1 BOOK, 50¢ for each additional)
APPLICABLE TAXES* $ _____
TOTAL PAYABLE $ _____

(check or money order—please do not send cash)

To order, complete this form and send it, along with a check or money order for the total above, payable to HQN Books, to: **In the U.S.:** 3010 Walden Avenue, P.O. Box 9077, Buffalo, NY 14269-9077; **In Canada:** P.O. Box 636, Fort Erie, Ontario, L2A 5X3.

Name: _____
Address: _____ City: _____
State/Prov.: _____ Zip/Postal Code: _____
Account Number (if applicable): _____

075 CSAS

*New York residents remit applicable sales taxes.
*Canadian residents remit applicable GST and provincial taxes.

HQN™

We *are* romance™

www.HQNBooks.com